# Feathers of Trials and Truths

## The Acquisitionist
E. Anders

Fantastic Frog

Feathers of Trials and Truths / E. Anders — 1st ed.

ISBN: eBook: 979-8-9891807-7-6

ISBN: Paperback: 979-8-9891807-8-3

www.eandersauthor.com

# Dedication

*To Ethan:*

*My little treasure hunter*

# The Earthen Calamities

In **2016**, Earth was forever altered by **The Aperien Event**.

In an inexplicable moment, everything humanity anywhere in the world had ever imagined became *real*. No one understood *why* or *how*, but the *who, what,* and *when* were cataclysmic.

Every myth, every monster. Every story and every dream. All the things that went bump in the night and the virtues descended from various heavens. Gods, demons, vampires, dragons. Magic powers, dangerous alchemy, and a dozen recipes for the elixir of life. Wishes, witches and wendigos. Undead, rebirth, immortality. Apocalypses. Lots and lots of apocalypses.

If there'd been a story about it at some point in human history, it suddenly *existed*. All of it. All in the same instant.

And as one might imagine, it was a mess.

# Feathers of Trials and Truths

In **2244**, the world has largely settled after two centuries of apocalyptic events and heroic interventions.

The Baker's Hills is a long standing Independent, one of the few regions not under direct oversight of the Icelandic Citadel of Knowledge and Accorded Law. Brites de Almeida, Aperien and immortal human Legend, protects Portugal through her generosity, bravery and alchemical baking recipes coveted worldwide.

The rest of Western Europe is comprised of small outskirt communities and the Accorded Territory known as the Velvet Emporium, centered around what was once Paris, France. From there, the European continent is impassable, scarred by a never-ending veil of violent weather known as the Storm Belt, the remnants of an early Calamity where gods of thunder and the sky from all over the world clashed, killing themselves and billions of people overnight.

# Content Warning

This novel contains explicit sex scenes, violence, off screen torture, and mentions of childhood neglect.

# Chapter 1

T he *Colinas do Padeira*—the Baker's Hills—was gorgeous this time of year. Lusa took some time to study up before they arrived in the region and forced Res to do the same. Her business partner and closest friend would perform tonight at Brites de Almeida's yearly festival canonizing the Battle of Aljubarrota.

She breathed in the fresh air as she perched on a segment of stone fencing, appreciating a rare place so vibrant and lush and, most importantly, peaceful. Lusa unfolded a worn map from her shoulder satchel, the page torn from an atlas printed in the late 1990s, and reviewed her handwritten annotations regarding Portugal.

She couldn't help a grin as she basked under the cloudless summer sky, reading the faded tourist recommendations from a time where people could just pack up and take a vacation wherever they wanted. Back when airplanes were a thing and humans weren't nearly extinct. Tourists, she mused, placed a really high importance on rating their food.

What was it, going on two and a half centuries now? Two hundred years since the Aperien Event, when everything humanity had ever imagined became real. As far as Lusa knew, even all those important beings in the Icelandic Citadel of Knowledge hadn't cracked the why or how of it all.

And then there were the Calamities. The inevitable apocalypses following, say, ten different incarnations of the god of something specific all cropping up and needing to establish dominance.

If Lusa squinted east, she could make out the purple hue of the Storm Belt on the horizon. In one of the earliest Calamities, that clash of gods resulted in an impenetrable wall of thunderstorms spanning from the Mediterranean Sea to northern reaches of Scandinavia and reduced a third of populated Europe into a wasteland overnight.

A sea bird trilled overhead, shaking Lusa from her mental wandering. She focused on the border she'd drawn in green, the territory currently under the control of Brites de Almeida. Like any Aperien considered a legend, Brites de Aledia drew power from her area of origin. She'd manifested right up the hill from where Lusa sat now, where she'd either beaten Castilian soldiers to death with her shovel or baked them alive when she caught the deserters hiding in her oven, depending on the tale.

Everyone was talking about her this week. Tomorrow marked the 826th anniversary of the Battle of Aljubarrota, an event inseparable from her personal story. The Citadel archivists speculated celebrating reinforced her existence, though Lusa got the impression Brites was a humble woman. She cared more about watching over her people, Aperien or mortal, and running her extremely successful alchemy business based around baked goods. Brites de Almeida was a major exporter around the globe, she wasn't aggressive, and she was well-liked. She deserved to be celebrated for more reason than one.

All of which made Lusa feel awful that she'd be stealing from her tomorrow.

But hey, she had to get by same as anyone else. She had those who depended on her, she reminded herself when the guilt crept up, and fulfilling this acquisition would help build her reputation. And when she had a real reputation, then she could afford to be picky with her contracts. She could do good and important things, instead of swiping a memory altering alchemical recipe from a beloved baker so the local aristocrat could drug his wife into forgetting his infidelity.

Lusa groaned, crumpling the page against her forehead.

It wasn't that she liked to steal; she just happened to be incredibly good at it. And it was hard not to enjoy being good at something. Silly, really.

Lusa paused to take a deep inhale of salt-air; they'd stayed near the coast all this month, moving easily north through a series of seaside villages before they reached the Baker's Hills yesterday. A peaceful jaunt and she'd always liked the ocean.

Well, at least in theory. Surface level ocean. Water so deep and wide, it became harder for anything to really put a stake down and say "mine, my rules," but it was also wet, cold, terrifying, and probably filled with more nightmares than the continents at this point.

For a brief moment, which tended to happen when Lusa found herself in a new place, she wondered what the human world had been like before the Aperien Event, which happened almost as often as she wondered what being a normal human might be like.

Maybe she'd have been a tourist.

Hah.

Generally speaking, the new world order was barely controlled chaos, and humans had long become part of the endangered species list. That made dusters like Lusa—half-humans or less—better off in the numbers game. It helped that being a duster could source from so many encounters and have so many results, most avoided being identified and cataloged.

But a lot of Aperiens got really nosey about it, especially the Icelandic Citadel of Knowledge. New beings only showed up in one of two ways and the archivists really, really enjoyed keeping good notes.

They served gods of knowledge, after all.

She puffed out a sigh; pondering the enormity of the magical global politics was very much not in her wheelhouse.

Disappearing from sight and mind? Being slippery like a little eel on the edge of the senses? Yeah, that was the only thing Lusa was any good at.

She smirked at the analogy as she headed toward the town proper, which was a riot of color on the emerald hillside. And like a slippery eel in the reef, Lusa moved through the crowd without so much as a ripple.

As long as she didn't draw attention to herself, Lusa wouldn't register as more than a passing shadow or maybe a trick of the light. And if she caught someone's full attention, as soon as they looked directly at her, she'd vanish.

Not really—at least not like her father—but she'd vanish from the perception of whoever or whatever was looking at her and slip right back into the crowded stream.

*Mixing metaphors now*, Lusa thought with a quiet hum.

Wait, were there any freshwater eels?

She'd had a few tattered nature encyclopedias growing up—all Earth animals, before the Aperiens—but that brought her thoughts far too close to her actual childhood memories to tolerate, so she waved it all away, water, eels, the past, and focused on the uneven cobblestone.

Lusa bumped arms with a tall, broad man dressed in handsewn linens, wearing a colorful scarf of red and green—Portuguese colors, Lusa knew from her atlas page. He might have been a satyr? A faun? His hooves clicked when he stepped. He smelled faintly of fur and feed, but his bulky straw hat covered his face. When he looked for whom he'd nudged, set to apologize maybe, his gaze swept all around where Lusa stood.

Lusa felt the cold, familiar sensations of deep shadows at her back, the world around her shifting into a murky, muted hue of reality.

A frown ghosted over the man's features before he shrugged and moved on.

That was her. Slippery even when she didn't want to be.

The bump had been her fault. She'd have apologized given the chance.

Lusa rubbed her nose and walked faster toward the far side of town, where Res, her partner in crime both literally and figuratively, parked Wags for the week. Her mind rattled; what was it about new places that made her all . . . *thinky*?

But here her mind went again, unbidden.

She was short, so would that stranger have overlooked her, regardless?

She was plain, head to toe. Black hair and dark brown eyes. Brown as in unremarkable, and not even wet dirt. Just dirt. Not chestnut or chocolate, just brown. Would she have faded into the crowd, anyway?

It never mattered what she wore. She'd gone through what she mockingly called her "neon phase," but it had only confused people more and the colors gave her a headache and were horrible to clean, so now she stuck to sandy beiges and browns to help her blend easier instead of fighting the inevitable. Certainly, the plain leather slacks and taupe poet's blouse wouldn't stand out anywhere, least of all in a town rioting with celebration.

No one would ever see what she looked like.

What she really wondered, though, more often than she cared to admit, was what the hell had her father actually looked like?

She'd never seen him. And how could she? He was tariaksuq, an Inuit shadow person. Unlike Lusa, who was only a half-bred, looking directly at her father actually *did* make him disappear into the tariaksuq parallel, a shadowed reality that existed beside the real world—well, the Aperien world, at least. Stories she'd chased over the years claimed when a tariaksuq died, they'd leave a body behind, something about being half-man-half-caribou.

At least she'd never seen her dad's corpse?

Maybe she was better off not knowing. Maybe she should just be happy being plain instead of half cervid. Maybe she should definitely not think about the logistics of how she came to exist in the first place.

Well, they say love is blind after all. Lusa snorted, loudly, but then felt queasy.

Her mother had been blind.

Lusa shivered as she scratched at her neck, and the leather strap that hung around her throat. Clipped on the end was a piece of bone carved in the shape of a seal, so worn down now it barely had any detail left. It was the only thing left from her childhood, hanging beside her silver dog whistle. It was the only thing she had of her father, that he'd left for her, and her mother kept it from her until she died.

And that was enough of that, because thinking of mother never, never ended well.

With the stranger's attention off her now, the cold press of the shadowlands waned, and the color bled back into her surroundings. For now, she'd be a passing figure in the periphery until anyone looked right at her again.

She rolled her eyes. Melancholy was so annoying.

So Lusa ran, satchel strap tight in one fist, her necklace in the other, unwilling to risk losing this contract, which meant money and food for the tiny family she'd found after losing her own. Even if Wags didn't have eyes and Tick, like all cats, could only sense magic and not see it, she could still pet him and he didn't freak out.

And of course, she had Res, the one person who always saw her. Lusa grinned, wondering what kind of trouble her handsome friend found himself in today.

# Chapter 2

It was nearing sunset when Lusa crossed the outer villa rows and into the field reserved for visiting troupes, travelers, and their beasts or transports. Her own transport was a bizarre combination of the two, tucked near the field's furthest edge. She tromped along the flattened grass and mud, smells of all kinds chasing her: grilled meats, wet fur, campfires, and oiled wood.

Lusa walked easily through the gathering. The day performers were done, and it wasn't quite time for the night sets to start, so most of the performers were taking a well-earned break or eating a meal before they hit their stage.

None of them noticed her passing by, so she stared like she always did. It wasn't rude, not really, not if no one could see her do it.

The largest group here for the celebration was the well-established *Circul Celor Uitate*—their entire sketch revolving around memories of lost things. Dead Aperiens, relics of Earth before, or anything else you didn't see anymore. They had an impressive court of musicians, most who played instruments she'd never seen, and they sang in dead languages. They performed traditional dances from all over history and myth. More than two dozen wagons, all gilded and gorgeous and exploding with color, neatly formed a wide triangle.

Lusa stopped near the outer edge of their ring, excited to glimpse their leader again. And there she was, Ileana Cosânzeana, chatting with a few of her performers, the iridescent singing flower of the Aperien's myth tucked within the golden plaits of her long braid. The flower wasn't singing tonight, but three centaurs played a lazy suite while a few other performers danced in the firelight. The dancers may have been dusters, Lusa wasn't sure, but their skin shimmered like diamonds.

She observed for a few more minutes but moved on when Ileana stopped them to make corrections. It felt too much like intruding then, even though no one would know she was there and she didn't speak Romanian.

And she didn't want to miss Res on his break. Maybe she still had time to convince him to turn down the extra slot he'd taken for tonight and watch the shows with her for once, so she could feel like a person instead of a shadow.

Lusa skirted Aperiens, dusters and the like, careful to avoid bumping anyone because she felt bad when people searched around trying to figure out what knocked them, and getting jostled constantly because no one could see you left bruises since they couldn't try to sidestep. And the shadowlands weren't exactly welcoming on any day.

She might be half-tariaksuq, but that was only enough to put her at the border. She'd never been able to actually step into that world. Maybe hunt down her long missing father. Lusa had tried enough times over the years to know better than to bother anymore.

Nothing new, she reminded herself, chasing the thoughts away as she arrived at their meager camp. She didn't want to worry Wags with a sour mood, so she strode up with her head high and a big smile.

Compared to the other wagons parked on the field, Wags was rather tame, but that didn't make Wags any less spectacular to Lusa. Wags was a goshoguma, which meant back in her heyday, she'd served the truly fancy. She may have even carried an imperial line at some point when she lived in Japan.

"Hey Wags!" Lusa rubbed a palm along the finely lacquered wood as she ducked under the poles used to attach oxen. The four-wheeled cart was a simple design, box-shaped, aside from the flared roof.

Under her petting, the wood warmed. The red silk flaps covering the doorway parted and tied themselves, leaving space for Lusa to slip inside.

"Not yet, madam," Lusa scolded. She threw her satchel through the opening before grabbing the rags and polish she kept stowed in the undercarriage compartment. "You've gotten muddy again from everyone milling around."

Wags couldn't speak. Tsukumogami were all over the world now, and their abilities varied, but when they'd found Wags beaten and broken in a junkyard six years ago, it had been obvious she had a spirit and was sentient. Wags, if she was a truly authentic piece from the right era of old Earth, more than met the hundred-year criteria to become alive and self-aware. According to Japanese mythos, which Lusa had spent months hunting down answers about when they met their new friend, a lot of objects were discarded or destroyed before they reached that birthday to avoid them becoming tsukumogami. And sometimes they'd get pissed and become yōkai or demons instead.

Lusa wondered if there'd been a whole Calamity of household objects revolting after the Aperien Event. She snickered as she wiped away the mud splatters, imagining an army of angry forks and spoons.

Wags was likely a museum piece, which were hot spots when the Aperiens first showed, looted, and later abandoned or used as hoards or fortresses. Someone must have discovered Wags was alive, then tossed her out into the cold when they didn't want to deal with her.

Jerks.

The patterns of inlaid stones along the cheery tree carvings were probably all pink at one time, but Wags had never protested each time Lusa found some semi-precious stone to replace the missing ones. There was a spot on her back end that still needed some work, but soon Wags would be as fancy as she deserved.

"Okay, much better." Lusa tucked her supplies away and gave the wheel a pat as she climbed up and in. The curtains swished shut, and the Portugal air vanished behind her.

They might have found Wags because they'd needed transport, but the lost goshoguma had taken care of them right back. Lusa suspected that, like many Aperien manifestations, magic items, creatures, and even gods had grown and evolved beyond their sometimes-humble beginnings. For a tsukumogami, being cared for and loved seemed to be more than enough to inspire.

From the outside, the wagon was maybe six feet wide and ten long. Inside, Wags gave them an entryway, two bedrooms, a small kitchen complete with a wood-burning stove and sitting area, a bathroom with inexplicable plumbing for both a modern shower and toilet, and enough storage space for the absurd amount of clothing, hats, and shoes Res hauled around.

And the best part was if they had an unexpected and likely unwanted guest, Wags always knew it, and they'd find a bland interior with two sleeping mats and a few battered trunks, Wags's inside shrunk to match her exterior.

How did it all work?

Lusa had no clue, but she'd never, ever take it for granted. And because Wags didn't have eyes, at least in the traditional sense, she knew Lusa.

"Thanks, Wags," Lusa sighed.

Her friend simply understood. The entryway warmed, smelling of oranges and cloves, Lusa's favorite type of tea. Sure enough, a tea kettle whistled from the stove. Lusa grabbed her satchel before she stepped out of the narrow hall.

Tick jumped from the wooden table with a light thump before winding between her ankles affectionately. Lusa bent and scratched behind his ears; one simply didn't *not* pet a cat—even if in this case, all superstitions and Aperiens aside, Tick truly was just a cat.

Granted, cats had inherited several mythos traits from the pre-Aperien era, including nine literal lives, the ability to cause bad luck under the right circumstances, and a knack for sensing ghosts and other creatures that often went unnoticed.

Like Lusa.

"Yes, yes, you're the best boy," Lusa cooed as she smoothed his gray tabby fur, and he purred sweetly in reply.

"Really, Lusa, we all know that's not true."

Lusa smirked as she straightened, crossing her arms. "Do we though?"

Res sat at their modest table, which was all but covered in his somehow elegant, rainbow-feathered tricorne. As was normal after one of his performances, the hat overflowed with baubles, trinkets, and coins from at least a dozen different old Earth countries. Res didn't look up from sorting his haul into a series of mismatched glass jars, his mop of emerald green hair hiding his expression. Today, his hair was dusted in silver glitter and pinstriped in burnished gold.

She turned to fetch cups and the tea. "I know Tick was here with Wags all day long, except for maybe a little mousing nearby. Sounds like the best boy to me."

By the time she turned around, the table had extended out another half foot, giving her space to set the drinks, along with a cork pad for the kettle so it wouldn't mar the surface. She plopped down in the empty chair, and Tick was in her lap before her feet settled.

"And I'm also pretty sure he didn't flirt with any married people, offer his body for money, subtly insult and likely confuse the local aristocracy," Lusa counted off on a finger for each item and couldn't keep the hurt from her voice when she added the last: "Or booked an extra evening performance when his very, very best friend in the whole entire world asked him to go watch the shows with her tonight."

Res stalled his sorting, setting down a sixpence on the little tower he'd been building, and sighed. He raked a hand through his hair with his perfectly manicured nails, hesitating before he answered. So he did feel bad. At least a little, but then he ruined it when he looked up at her with one of his theatrical pouts he used on his conquests.

"Don't." She pointed a finger at his face, her nails still caked with dirt from polishing Wags. "I'm not some skirt chasing after you, Res."

The expression dropped off cold, and Res seemed genuinely unhappy now.

Good. But also unfortunate, because it only made him more handsome when he didn't hide behind his cultivated veneers.

He was an undeniably beautiful man, with sharp and almost delicate features that somehow complimented a powerful jawline. Flawless skin, almost gilded even without his cosmetics. He'd cleaned most of them away, as he liked to change his appearance between his performances to keep things fresh, but traces of peacock shimmer accented his cheekbones and eyelids. He also had unfairly long eyelashes for a man. And a mouth, Lusa could only guess, that was made to kiss.

Despite his disarmingly good looks, he passed for a human with relative ease. Flashy colors didn't mean magic or power. Hair dye and makeup came from hundreds of sources, magical and mundane, with varying levels of dramatic effect. Playing the pretty man on a stage suited him well.

But he wasn't on stage, not here with her. And sure, she always got lost in his striking, unusual eyes. They were emerald bright for most of the iris, with a strange sort of heterochromia that left a feathered effect in ruby red around his pupils, with streaks of golden starlight throughout. But as much as her breath caught when he looked at her and saw her every time, Lusa would not put up with his nonsense.

Res rubbed his face. "We've talked about this. Whenever there's a big event, the night before is always the most lucrative. As you might recall, I've been at this since long before you were born."

"As you love to remind me."

"It's a proven pattern. Celebrants get really drunk and generous day before and the day of the main day, then pinch pennies and nurse hangovers and regrets on the following."

"And every performer knows that, which means all the performances on the following days are half-assed."

Res tsked. "I never half-ass anything, sweetling."

Lusa rolled her eyes as she added honey to her tea and stirred. She pointed the spoon at him. "You sure? Because this afternoon looked a little flat. Uninspired?" She grinned when he narrowed his eyes. "Maybe you need to spend some time watching instead of always being on stage. It might spruce up your acts a bit."

"Flat," Res repeated as he smoothed his brilliant cerulean silk shirt. "Uninspired, hmm? Were you actually watching me while you pickpocketed my entirely enthralled and captivate audience members?"

She lifted the hand petting Tick, made a so-so motion. "Nothing I haven't seen a hundred times."

Res leaned forward on both elbows, but now he was grinning back at her. "Insulting my delicate and very easily bruised ego is no way to lure me away from a chance to prove you wrong."

Annoyed, she set down her teacup hard enough it sloshed hot onto her fingers. "Come on, Res. I asked you about this like a week ago."

"Mmm, you mentioned it," he agreed. "Same as I asked you not to chase your little scheme tomorrow night, of all nights, when you could make us a killing working the crowds."

Lusa's hand's tightened into fists. "You know if I'm going to fulfill this request, I need to do it when everyone is distracted. I have to go into the Baker's house to get this recipe, not pocket it from some fruit stand." Her voice hitched when she added, "And it's not just some little scheme."

She saw the moment he realized he'd overstepped, and Res's expression softened. "Your dream is not a little scheme, but what this man is asking for is beneath you, and we both know that. So why are you insisting on this request? You've passed over others before when they didn't sit right."

She'd passed over one request because it involved a type of poison that's only use was murder. Lusa tucked her fists against Tick's fur. His tail swished hard against her thigh. "This guy isn't some backwater nobody. He has connections. If he gets what he wants, he might spread the word, which might lead to more requests. Maybe even the kind I want. The kind that can do some good."

"And you think this man, seeking to alter his wife's memory to hide his numerous affairs, is a man with connections who want to do good. Truly? Come, Lusa. You know better."

"Weren't you the one who told me I can't be picky starting out? Take the gigs as they come, you said, just like you had to when you were stuck doing card tricks on street corners for tips?"

Res frowned, leaning away from her. "I don't like when we argue."

"You think I do?" she huffed. When her fingers tightened in Tick's fur, he wiggled off her lap with a yowl. He padded off down toward the two bedrooms, vanishing behind the curtains into hers.

Well, at least he wasn't a complete traitor.

After a bloated pause, Res stood. "I'm sorry I took the slot. I didn't realize how important tonight was to you, Lusa. But it's too late for me to back out for this evening. Reputation is—"

"Everything. I know." She ignored the sting in her eyes.

"Not everything," Res murmured, so low she almost didn't catch it, and then he shook his head, glitter dusting the air between them. "Reputation is very important, especially at a celebration this well known." He dipped his head in a final apology of sorts, then moved toward his room to prepare for his performance. "I'll make it up to you next stop, I promise."

Lusa didn't watch him go, hoping he didn't notice the way her heart lurched when he was so close like that. When he treated her like he treasured her. Then again, she did have six years practice hiding she was in love with him.

Nothing else do to tonight then, she headed out early to work the crowds.

# Chapter 3

Late the next evening, the 826th anniversary celebration of Battle of Aljubarrota was deep underway, with the legend of the hour, Brites de Almeida, in attendance. Meanwhile, Lusa crouched outside the stone fencing surrounding the Baker's personal holdings, a modest estate with a handful of tasteful villas surrounding one larger building.

She'd scoped out everything the first day they'd arrived in the Baker's Hills nearly a week ago. Brites focused on baking until the festivities began three days prior. The first two days, the legend seemed to hide in her own home, but today friends and family had ushered her from her work to be properly celebrated.

Maybe Lusa could've swung her theft during the daylight hours, but ever since Res saw her for the first time, she realized how lucky she'd been before him. Those with Quetzalcoatl blood likely weren't the only creatures in the entire world who might possess the means to see through Lusa's natural gift. Wags and Tick were proof enough. And Res had no idea how many cousins he might have. Or half-brothers, for that matter, being as those with Ques blood only produced male offspring. She knew not having family since his mother died made him sad, although he hid it well under all his pomp.

She wrinkled her nose. How was he so distracting when he wasn't here? Rolling her eyes at herself, she brushed thoughts of Res away and focused on her task.

The Baker's Hills had an alchemy academy and culinary school, along with a nice library. In town, one could buy books about cooking and alchemy, many of those volumes penned by Brites de Almeida herself, or shop for various food stocks and rare ingredients. One could even study under her, and several proteges had come and gone over the years.

What one couldn't find in any store, book, or lesson was a single recipe combining all the baking and alchemy.

Those were in Brites de Almeida's personal kitchen, attached to her living quarters. Rumor was once she created a recipe, she'd also memorized it, but luckily for Lusa and the man who hired her, she also kept detailed, private records.

A recipe for disaster, Lusa mused with a grin, before hurdling the waist-high fence. She tried to ignore the way her stomach twisted at the lack of security around such a treasure, but then again, this was the immortal baker who cooked for anyone who needed it and barely charged above market for her goods. She was basically a saint, if not by the strictest definition.

What did that make Lusa, then?

"Someone who wants to do better," she murmured as she cut a path through lavender bushes in full, tall bloom. Careful not to disturb any of the plants, she made her way around the back of the baker's home.

She only felt worse when she found the door unlocked.

Shouldn't this at least be difficult? Res wasn't wrong; she hated this request, but not all nobles were bad guys. Not everyone in the world was a self-serving jerk. This guy was, but he had to know people who weren't.

Right?

Lusa pursed her lips and toed into the mudroom, the bakery warm and welcoming, and it smelled like fresh bread. It was clean, the ovens so old school it made her pause and stare. Magic didn't need things like electricity, after all. Lusa moved on toward the connecting hall, which lead to the stairs.

Her palms were sweat slicked, which was weird, because Lusa rarely got nervous. If things went sideways, she vanished from sight and saw herself out of trouble. Sometimes, she was the trouble, sure, but this felt . . .

She gritted her teeth and went up to the second floor, the first door on the left open halfway. Lusa peeked inside, and there it was: The Baker's famed recipe book, sitting on a nondescript desk, open to a random page. An ink pot and quill rested nearby. The room was otherwise empty, save for a simple bed with a handmade quilt and a standing wardrobe. A single candle lit the room, the wax never-melt and the flame larger than normal.

Lusa licked her lips, pulling out paper and pencil from her pocket and clenching them in one fist. She approached the desk slowly, but nothing suggested traps or wards or anything else.

What would it feel like to have such trust in the world around you?

Lusa shook her head once to clear it, then touched the very corner of the book.

Nothing. The paper felt warm, but that was it. She scanned the open page—a recipe for bagels, enchanted to help with joint pain.

Gods, Lusa was the jerk, wasn't she?

Grimacing, she flipped the pages fast as she could skim and eliminate what she didn't need. She wasn't here to steal anything else, just get the job done and move on to better things.

Lots of things for aliments, sickness, and making the bread fill a belly with one bite. Helping pregnancies, conception, birth control. Fire resistance, warming, and three pages for helping with digestive issues. An entire chapter of animal feeds. Lusa kept flipping, scanning, then stilled when she felt the air shift with some sort of presence.

For a heartbeat, the shadowlands touched her back, but then the cold waned and colors popped.

That was definitely her cue to get the hells out of here, and fast.

Ah, there.

The next section was marked hazards.

The list of different poisons was startling, and Lusa swallowed hard when she read about a recipe to ease one comfortably into death.

Then she found it, the memory altering recipe. She scanned over it as she uncrumpled the paper, pencil in hand. She tapped the paper a few times, gaze darting back and forth between the blank page and the recipe that would—maybe—give her what she'd been chasing.

And what was she chasing, Lusa wondered. The thoughts went on when she had no time to waste, about wanting to do good things, to take care of people, to help instead of stand by and be invisible while horrible things happened right in front of her.

Lusa squeezed her eyes shut.

She had to write this down and get out of here. She'd felt the shadowlands, which meant someone or something had looked her way. If they didn't see her, they saw the pages of important recipes flipping on their own. There had to be someone on their way to check in by now.

But did she really want to be the person who stole from a saint to help some worthless jerk cheat on his wife?

Mind made up, Lusa wrote quickly, because now she heard voices coming up the path, and they didn't sound happy. She shoved the paper between the pages on the memory altering recipe and shut the book.

A door slammed open downstairs, and she threw back the shutters and scuttled her way down the drainage pipe. Lusa couldn't help a little giggle as she hit the dirt. People ran up the stairs, and she didn't look back, racing through alleys of rosemary and thyme and oregano, her giggles giving way to a laugh.

She'd done good, Lusa decided, like she wanted, even if no one would know it was her. But was just her life.

It could be enough, right? At least until a better chance came along.

She wondered what Brites De Almeida would think when she found her note:

*I just thought you should know Harold Gessipe is a big jerk. He wanted to steal this recipe to use on his wife. Oh, and awesome party!*

# Chapter 4

Lusa didn't stop running until she'd lapped the fields and made her back to town from the opposite side of the Baker's home. From there, she waded into the crowd, saturated in music, magic, and a bit of mayhem. Her head swam from the influx of sensation and the flagging adrenaline rush.

Leaning against an adobe building helped Lusa catch her breath, and also kept her from getting jostled, which let her absorb everything in full bloom. No colors dampened by the shadowland's edge, no white noise from being pushed half out of reality, no cold sweats from the general feeling of unwelcome she always felt when she toed that line. Instead, she tasted spices on the air: hops and a burst of citrus from a nearby stall. Perfume and colognes, both floral and sweet, and dark and musky. Laughter came from everywhere, cheers down the street from the stages, performances in full swing.

Lusa grinned. If she hurried, she'd catch the end of Res's set.

For all the hard time she gave him earlier, he was magnificent on stage. He knew it, too, so no sense inflating his already oversized ego.

She moved quick and quiet, doing her best to avoid attention, but it was an impossible task in a crowd this large. Seconds later, her back pressed against the border between reality and the shadowlands, and she focused on getting to Res's stage as fast as possible. She'd find a perch outside of eye contact.

By the time she reached the midway, everyone was so absorbed with the spectacle that the world came briefly back into focus for Lusa. The town center opened wide, green and red Portuguese colors flapped in the night breeze, with flowers and herbs decorating everywhere and everything. Dancers filled the streets. A firebreather stood on a tall platform, his magical flames shifting between pink, green, and orange, his skin covered in copper scales. Music came from all over, yet somehow made beautiful melodies. Every other step waited another food stall, all of them overflowing with baked goods of every kind imaginable.

The colors and sounds muted again when an old woman stumbled against her. Lusa planted a hand on her shoulder to keep her from tumbling, then quickly stepped back. The woman laughed as she turned, speaking fast in what might have been Spanish and waving to someone behind Lusa. Lusa smiled anyway and shuffled toward the main stage, using the distraction to pocket a sweet roll.

It was no surprise Res had wiggled his way into another main stage set, given he had an enormous crowd already. Lusa grappled her way up an empty balcony and leaned on the rail as she enjoyed her snack.

Res was deep into it, laughing as he twirled. His shirt was open to his navel, his pants flared and layered with blue, green, and turquoise tassels to match his hair. He had a knack for pulling off any kind of look, and today he'd lavished himself in golden trinkets, chains, and makeup, down to his gilded lipstick and fingernails.

But that was the least impressive part of the show. She couldn't hear him this far away, but he engaged the closest people in the crowd, winking as he stepped and held up a finger. Then he called out, hand to his ear, and the crowd went wild.

Lusa smirked; she couldn't help it. He was such a showboat, and nothing about his performances was ever flat despite her earlier teasing.

With a flourish and spin, colors saturated the air around him before bursting into a sea of illusions. Res, after all, wasn't just a pretty face.

The sky swarmed with a story.

While Res might be a duster and his magic largely superficial, it was breathtaking.

Brave warriors in Portuguese colors clashed against Castilian dragons and hydras. Fire rained in purples and silvers, waves surged in brilliant yellows, and the entire mess crashed and exploded in a sea of butterflies over the crowd before bursting again, this time showering the gathering in glittering pigment.

Res grinned when people started to clap and then snapped his fingers.

Everyone who was touched in pigment shimmered and glowed, before the color lifted from their skin in a kaleidoscope of rainbow fireflies. More cheers, more joy, more laughter from the crowd, and Lusa grinned along like the idiot she was.

And then Res saw her.

She knew the moment he did, when one eyebrow—colored to match his hair—lifted in question. She shrugged back. When he smirked, she rolled her eyes and mouthed: *You were right.*

When he bowed with a flourish, as much for her as the crowd, Lusa laughed. He met her eyes one last time with wink, then a quick glance backstage, a silent question if she'd meet him after his set.

Her heart fluttered. He spent most nights after his shows in someone's bed, and she was grateful he never brought his many lovers home to Wags. She wasn't sure if Wags didn't let him or if he preferred to keep his causal affairs away from his home, but he almost never missed a chance to "play," as he liked to call it, after his performances.

Res wasn't asking Lusa for that. He'd been blatantly clear in his disinterest on that front, and their friendship was far too important for all that nonsense, anyway.

This was an offering, his attempt at an apology. A demonstration that he valued their friendship. He wanted to make it up to her for being booked tomorrow night too.

She nodded at him, then wiggled her eyes at the crowd of drunk excited people who certainly wouldn't miss a few coins.

Lusa's pockets were absolutely stuffed by the time Res's show ended, and she palmed a bit more as she made her way through a rowdy crowd that showed no interest in dispersing between sets. Why would they? *Circul Celor Uitate* hit the stage next, and she was pretty sure people had killed to see them perform.

She darted under a few flailing arms, dodged a dancing couple, and sidestepped a particularly drunk centaur who could barely stand on four legs. All the while, the shadowlands hedged her back, the festival's beauty muted by half-existence.

Lusa plucked a peacock feather from an obnoxious hat and tucked it behind her ear—a gift for Res, not that he didn't have enough of them already. She still grabbed him feathers whenever she could. They were cheap, usually cast-offs people wouldn't miss, so she didn't feel guilty about stealing such frivolous things. Mostly she pinched coin, because they needed to eat, buy clothes, and keep Wags in good repair. Otherwise, she stole food. If she did grab the occasional bauble, it was never anything too important or fancy, never too much from any one person, and never anything from the poor.

She knew what being poor and starving was like. She wasn't going to push anyone deeper in. It wasn't like Res was a starving artist, but opportunities like the Baker's celebration were few and far between, at least in easy travel range. The Velvet Emporium was a frequent stopover for them, but Res never talked about a permanent gig, and Lusa was along for the ride.

Not like she had anywhere else to go, or anything else to do with herself, especially now that she'd blown off the job from that sleazy noble.

Lusa sighed as she kicked at the cobblestone and shifted away from the crowd, moving toward the backstage area before the wagon yard camp. If she was going to wallow, she needed to do it all the way in reality, not with the shadows and the cold creeping at her back.

And she'd made the right choice, even though it cost them a lot of money. And cost her potential connections, because she didn't want those kinds of connections. Res would never let her live it down, but he'd been absolutely right in that she didn't want to build a reputation working with men who cheated on their wives and abused them so they could keep on doing it.

She just . . . well, she wasn't immortal like Res. Lusa was only twenty-four, but she didn't have forever to figure her life out. It felt like she'd spent so much time already doing nothing, being nothing, that sometimes she just felt itchy about this whole life thing.

Lusa blew out a breath as the shadowlands retreated, the summer night air warming her skin now that she was between people's gazes. She paused for a minute, looking up at the cloudless sky and all those bright stars, and smiled.

She really needed to stop being so thinky this week. Lusa had a home, she had friends who knew she existed and enough in her pockets to take care of them. Maybe they'd travel up the coast and relax for a bit. Res would get bored after a few days and need more attention than just hers, but Lusa could use a break from being constantly shoved between two worlds, neither of which wanted her.

She shook her head and kept on, peeking around backstage as the *Circul Celor Uitate* trope adjusted their costumes, this set all bright oranges, bronzes, and reds, like fire and sunset. She hugged the normal shadows to keep from being observed so she could see all those gorgeous colors in all their glory. Maybe she and Res could find a spot to watch them perform, although she'd have to listen to his endless critiquing, she thought with a fond eyeroll. He was such a diva.

She circled the backstage area twice but didn't find Res. There was no way he'd forgotten. He'd just signaled for her to meet him back here ten minutes ago. If he'd gotten himself distracted, she was going to punch him in the nose. Or maybe get Wags to run him over a few times.

A shimmer caught her eye at the very edge of the backstage area. The color combination was distinct, a specific mix of red, green, and gold she'd know anywhere. A single feather, the iridescent shimmer almost metallic, sitting on grass worn away from so many performers coming and going this week. She frowned as she knelt to grab it, because he was never careless with his things, and then she stilled.

This wasn't a costume feather.

Her throat tightened. A splash of liquid the same color at the feather's tip, liquid emerald, plucked free from flesh.

"What the hells . . ." Lusa whispered.

Res was a duster, but his Quetzalcoatl blood meant his true form was a huge feathered serpent. She'd seen him once, after a night of heavy drinking when she'd beat him so badly in cards it was the only way she'd let him out of his debts. He'd been the most beautiful creature she'd ever seen. And considering the world they lived in, that said a lot.

He'd never explained why his blood was a secret, why he never wore his true skin, and she'd never pushed him. She, of all people, understood having complicated feelings about one's nature. That he'd told her the truth at all, that he'd trusted her with what he was when it was his most guarded secret? It meant the world to her, especially when he'd revealed she was one of five people who knew, and that included his parents. His father wasn't in the picture, and his mother, whom he adored, had been human and died years earlier.

She knew he wouldn't flaunt his true form here, in the middle of a festival of all places, or let someone pull a literal bloody feather out of him.

Lusa pulled her necklace from her shirt, the only item of true value she owned. With a wince, she pinned the feather's tip through the clip holding the whistle and her father's bone seal carving, hating that she pierced it, but there was no way she'd risk losing it. Her skin hummed when she touched it, first her fingers, then over her breastbone when she tucked it back away under her shirt for safekeeping. She scrubbed the mud with her boot until the bit of blood disappeared. She didn't know why, but it felt important. As important as finding Res, because she was scared as hells he was in trouble. Big trouble.

The footprints where she found the feather changed quickly from a boot size she knew into taloned claws, then a massive form being dragged by at least two people, given the other prints, moving toward the outskirts of the tent park.

# Chapter 5

Lusa could barely breathe by time she rounded the bend, the tall tents at the gathering's edge hiding exactly what she'd feared: Res, in his Ques form.

She skidded to a stop, her heart in her throat.

The beautiful winged, feathered serpent she'd only seen once was a tangled mess, twenty feet long from his wolf-like snout to his fanned tail. Res was drenched in mud, his pearly feathers—a normally brilliant mix of crimson, emerald, and gold—mucked in dirty brown. His head hung limp in the mud, eyes shut, his wings awkwardly bent. Two men milled around him, brandishing knives.

Bloody knives.

Liquid emerald blood.

One knelt by Res's upper arm, a rucksack at his feet, and Lusa blinked a few times as her mind tried to catch up with what she saw. His hands were covered in wet green, a bit darker than the feathers, a handful of which were stuffed in the bag. Res's shoulder was almost entirely bare, and as she stared, he sliced another feather from Res's skin.

Both men wore nondescript black clothing. The first waved at the second, from where they'd been cutting the feathers from Res's shoulder and upper arm and filling the bag—*Why?* her brain asked uselessly, *why, why, why?*—and pointed at Res's face.

"We don't have much time," the first hissed, a roll to his voice that suggested duster blood. "No telling how long the dart will keep him down, and organs are worth more. Get an eye, be quick."

The second man nodded, moving down Res's long neck toward his face.

To cut out his *eye*.

*No*, Lusa thought, her head spinning. No, no, that was not happening.

Someone had discarded a mallet after they'd finished hammering in the last tent post. She'd never been so happy over another's laziness in her life.

Lusa didn't hesitate.

She hefted the mallet and swung at the man still kneeling over Res's shoulder and connected with his head with a dull thunk.

He didn't see her coming, because of course he didn't.

He jerked sideways and fell hard, his knife and a handful of Res's feathers scattering. His head hit the tent post on his way down, colliding with a louder, sickening crack.

Lusa's chest heaved. He didn't move, at all, like, not even a bit. New blood swelled onto the muddy ground, red and bright.

She tasted bile.

Was he dead? She circled the man she'd just beaten in the head—gods, he really did look dead—as the shadowlands sucked at her, making her suddenly numb hands colder.

"What the fuck? Hey! Get up, man!" The second man searched for what the hells just happened, passing Lusa over again and again as she stood there like a complete idiot, clutching the mallet to her chest, the fallen man's blood creeping from his cracked skull toward her muddy boots.

"Who's there!" he yelled, keep his knife up in front of him, but he didn't get up, not yet.

There was a cut below Res's eye, a thin line bleeding bright green, but he hadn't gotten far, thank the gods, every last one of them.

How fast did Ques heal?

Lusa had no idea.

Her gaze flicked to the man lying in the mud.

*The* jerk *lying in the mud*, she though with a snarl, the hope that he wouldn't heal so sharp it shook her from her haze.

Shuffling drew her attention back to the other man, and Lusa balked. He hadn't made any effort to help his friend, nothing at all. All he did was flinch at the shadows as he stuffed all the cut feathers into the rucksack.

Lusa seethed.

"Not a chance, you evil piece of garbage!"

The man jerked his knife up, but Lusa already swung, and she didn't flinch this time when the mallet connected with his hand, or when the man screamed in pain, or when he went silent when she smashed him in his horrible, awful face and he collapsed backwards into the bloody muck.

Lusa dropped the mallet with a gasp, and she crashed to her knees next to Res's head. "Oh, gods, Res? Res, can you hear me?" Her voice cracked, the cold of the shadowlands receding with the second attacker unconscious or dead too.

Didn't matter, couldn't think about that now. More important things.

Lusa held out a shaking hand in front of his snout and nearly fell over with relief. He was breathing. Right, they'd mentioned a dart. It must have been magic or alchemy, some sort of tranquilizer or sleeping concoction.

The cut under his eye was thin, but deep, and his blood crept out in a sluggish stream. Those bastards, gods. Organs are worth more? What the hells did that even mean? And who cared? You can't just cut out someone's eye!

"Res, please, you need to wake up for me, okay? You're hurt, and I don't know how to help you like this."

She bit her lip, because she'd never touched him aside from the day he'd caught her wrist when she tried to pickpocket him. She didn't touch anyone except Tick and Wags, at least not for more than pinching coins or a nudge for distractions. Lusa certainly hadn't touched him when he'd showed her his brilliant, beautiful Ques form the first time; doing so now felt almost like a betrayal of some sort, but there was no way she could move him. He needed to wake up.

Lusa rubbed her sweaty, dirty palm on her pants, trying to clean it. Warm it maybe? She didn't know. Then she exhaled and pressed her palm against his cheek.

"Res?"

His feathers were so, so soft. Strange, how he was a mix of a wolf and dragon in the shape of his head, and instead of scales he had feathers, but they were silky like fine fur.

Gods, what was she doing? Why was she petting him like an idiot?

She let out a little sob; she couldn't help it.

"What do I do?" Lusa leaned down, pressing her forehead against his, breathing in the scent of him—which wasn't much different than the way he smelled normally. Spicy, magical, and almost like smoke and fire, cloves and cinnamon.

Like home. Her home.

"Res . . ."

Lusa froze, the shadowlands creeping along her skin.

Someone was here.

She spun, fumbling for the mallet as she glared at the stranger, sizing him up as he stumbled to a halt with a gasp.

"Oh, bloody hells. Res? Is that you?"

Lusa blinked. He knew Res? And he knew what he was?

The newcomer was tall, but not alarmingly so, and at first glance he looked like he could be human. He had really nice clothes though, a fancy robe made from expensive material in white and different blues. His skin was dark, like the night sky, and smooth—no beard or hair. His gaze made her doubt human, though, as he surveyed the chaos with apprehension, his irises like starlight. When he glanced back the way he'd come, she caught the faint sheen of scales on the back of his neck under the moonlight.

What was he?

Then Lusa didn't care because he was moving closer. She hefted the mallet over her head, gritting her teeth and ignoring the cold tears on her cheeks as she swung.

The man caught the mallet an inch from his shorn skull, and for a second he locked eyes with her and Lusa stared back, mouth hanging open . . .

But just like that, the moment was over, his gaze flicking up, down, left right, trying to see her and not. He'd instinctually sensed the attack, but he couldn't see her, and she didn't know what to think, but then he jerked the mallet from her grip and retreated a few steps, his expression dangerous.

Of course he'd disarmed her easily. It wasn't like she was a fighter, but Res was still unconscious, so she said, "That's not my only weapon, you know."

His gaze focused in the general direction of her voice because she hadn't made any effort to throw it, a neat trick she'd learned years ago, useful since the shadowlands didn't swallow her voice, just everything else.

And suddenly, everything about the man in front of her softened, and she swore he looked relieved, which didn't make any sense at all until he said, "You're Lusa."

All she managed back was an inelegant, "Uhm . . ."

"I know him," the man offered. "My name is Theodore. We're friends. He told me about you three years ago when I spent time with him in the Velvet Emporium after one of his performances."

"Oh."

He gestured at Res. "May I?"

Oh, right. "Can you help him? They said something about darts."

Any doubts Lusa had about Theodore evaporated when he knelt right down in the mud, not caring that he was getting his robes filthy, which were worth more than anything she'd ever owned in her life, to help their friend.

"Did they say anything else?" Theodore spoke quietly as he checked the wound near Res's eye, then winced when he saw his shoulder and the bag of feathers.

"Something about organs being . . ." Her breathing hitched. Gods, her heart felt like it was going to crumble to dust as she whispered, "He's going to wake up, right?"

"Yes, the effects are temporary, though he'll likely be lethargic for a few days. The wounds will heal, but—" Theodore stalled, glancing her direction even though he couldn't see her, almost thoughtful. She knew that look. He didn't know if he was saying too much.

She crossed her arms, for her own benefit. "I know what he is."

Lusa couldn't parse his expression, but he dipped his head in a shallow nod.

"When one with Quetzalcoatl blood is wounded in their true form, that which is lost does not recover."

She sucked in a breath. "Gods, so they were just going to poke out his eye and leave him blind?" Lusa laughed, and it sounded hysterical. "Maybe I should stop feeling bad I killed them."

"You should," Theodore muttered. "Though only one is dead, and it seems the fall killed him, not your blow. The second is merely unconscious. For now." That last part sounded ominous, and not like it had to do anything with her mallet. "Is the wagon still with you?"

"She's not just some wagon. Her name is Wags," Lusa snapped before she could stop herself.

She couldn't help the anger she felt over how objects like Wags—with souls—had been treated in the Enlightened Sun. Any objects over 100 years old in Japan after the Aperien Event were tossed into the ocean and magically sealed under the surface, so no one had to deal with everyday items acquiring sentience. As far as she knew, they still threw them out like trash.

Wags was a person, not a thing, and they were lucky to have her.

"My apologies, sincerely. I didn't know her name."

"Yeah, well, when Res wakes up, I'm going to kick his butt for not telling you."

"Please do. Once he's had enough time to properly recover. Can you summon Wags here? Or do you need to go get her?"

Lusa worried her bottom lip. Much like Res, they didn't like revealing too much about Wags's capabilities, because who wouldn't want a living home who made things awesome for whomever she let live inside her?

"I can force him back into his human form," Theodore went on, "but I can't do much about the magic keeping him docile. And I need to clean up this mess so you won't be followed."

Her heart skipped. "Are there more of them?"

Theodore's lips pressed in a thin line, and once again Lusa got the sense she was missing part of a bigger picture. "It is possible, yes. Or new dangers might catch the scent of his blood. I can eliminate any trace of tonight and dispose of the bodies. Brites is a friend, and she wouldn't condone these hunters on her land." He gestured at the feathers. "Take those with you. He'll want them."

Lusa felt colder by the second; she never liked being touched by the shadowlands longer than necessary. And then she felt like a right bastard. Here was Res, bleeding and drugged, and his feathers would never grow back, and she was put out for being a little cold.

Scoffing at herself, she pulled out her necklace, fumbled between Res's feather she'd recovered earlier and her father's bone carving for the silver dog whistle.

It was for emergencies only, but this qualified, and she brought it to her lips and blew out the silent note. Wags would hear and come rolling, probably drawing unwanted attention. She'd paint Wags different colors after, maybe give her an entire new set of polished stones for her inlays too.

Theodore's hands glowed as they hovered over Res, and the feathered serpent slowly shrunk back to her friend. She was crying again, tears pouring down her face as she stared at the scar slashed across his cheekbone and the terrible, bleeding mess of his shoulder and upper arm.

She covered her mouth at the pained little noise she let out. He was so vain. He was going to hate this, if what Theodore said about his feathers being gone for good translated to his human form. He'd have scars. Her beautiful, brilliant, fancy showboat was going to be scarred inside and out. "Oh, Res."

The rickety sound of wooden wagon wheels in mud came from the clearing, and Lusa had never been more relieved to see Wags rolling up the hillside.

"Keep him warm and well rested, especially until these wounds close," Theodore said as he rose, not bothering to clean off his now filthy robes. Instead, he pulled out a golden hexagonal box about the size of his fist. "Take this with you," he added as he tucked the strange object into the rucksack of bloody feathers. "I have a feeling it belongs with you now, given this turn of events."

Res groaned then. Lusa threw herself down next to him, the golden gift forgotten. "Res? Res, can you hear me?"

His eyes remained pinched shut in pain. "Lu . . . Lusa?"

"Yes," she sobbed. "I'm here. I'm right here, okay?"

She felt the shadowlands creep away as the air against her skin warmed. Lusa glanced over her shoulder and found Theodore's back.

"Hurry now," he said without turning. "Travel far as you can and lie low until he's healed. I'll see to the rest."

Gods, she was a mess, about to burst into tears all over again because Res cared enough about her to tell this Theodore guy if he wasn't looking at her, she could really be here with Res.

"Thank you," she whispered.

"Take care of him, please. He'll need you."

"I will."

She slung the rucksack over her shoulder, making sure she didn't leave a single feather behind. Lusa hauled Res to his feet despite his groans of pain and half dragged him to Wags. The curtain doors swung open, the front entryway converted to a triage area, and Tick yowled as they stumbled inside, thrashing his gray tail in panic. The fabric door swished shut, and Wags rolled them down the hills, into the night, and away, far away to safety.

# Chapter 6

## Eight Months Later

Northern France was beautiful this time of year. They'd selected a nice hilltop overlooking a serene little village, overlooking the blue-gray sea. Lusa adored all the flowers filling the meadows to bursting, smiling as she knelt beside the clear, spring-melt stream.

It was as a good a place as any to burn more time.

Lusa squinted uphill at Wags, her well-varnished wood reddish in the late afternoon sun. Her new stones gleamed in a rainbow of tree leaves all around the windows, the curtains inside drawn tight. She sighed, trying and failing to quell the disappointment that Res shut them again as soon as she let him for the day.

It had been eight months since they'd fled the Baker's Hills with Res drugged, bleeding, and delirious while Wags tore through the countryside, Tick yowling like the world was ending, and Lusa thinking it might. They'd pulled through, the sorry lot of them, and Res's wounds had slowly healed.

The ones on the outside, at least.

Lusa worried her bottom lip, pushing the thoughts aside as she fished out a shiny rock, this one a quartz, remarkable in that it was flawless and milky white. Perfect. She could finally fill the last missing piece on Wags's left flank. Lusa pocketed the stone and dried her hands, glancing downhill at the village.

It wasn't a busy place, and not very large being this far out from the Velvet Emporium, but the residents were simple, honest folk and didn't mind campers on their outskirts. The children were especially fond of Wags and came to look at her almost every day, but the adults visited for a different reason.

She wondered if anyone stopped by while she wandered today. Unlike this new, reclusive version of Res, she couldn't stand spending the entire day in her room. She'd go nuts. Instead, Lusa explored the village, the woods, the meadows, all the way down to the sea, all while waiting patiently for any sign that her friend might be ready to come back to himself.

When she got back to Wags, she couldn't help a grin. Tick lay out in the grass, the big gray tomcat snoozing in the sun, probably high on catnip again. She really needed to hide that window box, or maybe ask Wags to put it higher up.

"Hey, Wags. Hey, bum," she greeted, nudging him with her boot. Tick purred up at her and stretched, but didn't move otherwise. "Lazy," she scolded, but he didn't even bother to open his eyes. She knelt next to him and scratched behind his ears, then turned her attention to the new member of their little crew.

Beside Wags rested a wooden box with an envelope slot on the top. Carved on the side, in Lusa's careful woodworking, read:

*Mundane Wishes, Requests and Acquisitions!*

*Drop yours in the Box and see what might come true!*

Above the box, attached to Wags's side, was a golden face. It looked a bit like a Greenleaf man but made from twined metal instead of plants.

"Did we get anything today, Kiki?" Lusa asked as she plopped down on the grass.

The face whirled, a clockwork noise, before the eyelids snapped open, glowing an eerie red. The metal twirled and twisted the mouth into a smile as the face spoke. "Yes, yes, three!"

Lusa couldn't help but grin at the excitement in Kiki's voice, an almost childlike wonder overlaying the otherwise mechanical sound. With more chirps and whirs, the face shifted before her eyes, the only constant the red glowing stone anchored in the strange being's middle as the clockwork creature changed into a cat with a set of tiny wings.

Kiki chirped, "Open, open!" as it pawed at the box, mimicking Tick's motions whenever he wanted into something.

"Alright, alright, just a second." Lusa grabbed Kiki like she would the real cat, scooping it under the armpits and setting it on her lap. It headbutted her chin, which hurt a little considering Kiki was all metal and no soft fur, before it plopped down and started grooming its paw—another mimic of Tick.

Kiki—or Kikikaloria, it told them—was the golden box Theodore slipped in the rucksack of feathers the night Res was attacked. He'd said nothing about it aside from that it might be helpful. Three days into their panicked flight from the Baker's Hills, Lusa had been sobbing next to Res, certain he was going to die. Kiki had unfolded from the box and shaped itself like Tick. It watched Res for a good ten minutes, then touched a paw to his chest. An hour later, Res shook off the effects of his attackers and finally started to recover.

Kiki didn't know much about itself. All it knew was that a bad man made it and used it for bad things until a good man stopped the bad man and took it away. It had been told to stay in the box, but Kiki wanted to help, so it broke the rule and was very sorry and very much hoped Lusa wouldn't be mad.

Lusa's best guess? This little clockwork creature had a philosopher's stone inside its chest. That must be what gave it life, but she had no idea what else Kiki was capable of and was kind of afraid to ask. She really didn't want to know what bad things a bad man could have done with something like Kiki, especially when Kiki had been able to cure Res without so much as a blink and seemed able to reshape itself into anything it wanted without limits.

Kiki's favorite shapes, however, were a cat so it could irritate the hells out of Tick, and the magical face on the wagon so it could talk to anyone who came by to make wishes.

"Open, open!" Kiki chirped again.

Lusa did, and laughed when Kiki shrunk enough to climb inside and hand her the letters one at a time.

The first was about a livestock field. The farmer didn't know what the issue was, but the sheep kept escaping no matter how many times he mended the fences. Maybe the wish face could figure out the problem. She read it to Kiki, who made a little hiss.

"Naughty sheeps."

"We'll check it tonight," Lusa said, moving on to the next. "This next one is all you, Kiki."

"Kiki?" Kiki flapped its ears. Gods, it was so adorable. She was really glad Theodore got it away from whoever that bad man was, and she hoped she never had to find out.

"The blacksmith heard someone helped the mason turn his brittle bricks into hard stone. He's wondering if copper can be turned to steel."

"Yes!" Kiki jumped from the box, wings flapping a few times as it floundered around and stepped on Tick's tail in the process. The tomcat hissed and swatted at Kiki, and then they were chasing each other around Wags.

Lusa grinned. A little transfiguration never hurt anyone, and she wouldn't let Kiki get too carried away. It wasn't an unheard-of skill, and as long as they weren't suddenly turning a mountain into five thousand tons of gold, they shouldn't draw too much attention. A little help to a poor village? No one should really notice.

While the cat and the "cat" went from chasing to wrestling, Lusa opened the last letter and her breath caught. A child's writing.

*Dear Magic Wagon Face,*

*My birthday is in three days. I will be six. Can I have a magic show?*

*Love, Lils*

"Oh, this is just what we need," Lusa whispered as she looked up to the window with the drawn curtains. Letter in a tight fist, and determined not to take no for an answer, Lusa climbed into Wags and stalked to Res's room.

# Chapter 7

"N o."

"Res, you didn't even let me finish talking."

"Magic show was enough. Not interested."

Res, short for Resplendent, the egotistical, vain, showboating performer who'd probably worn more makeup in his time than most women, scowled at her from his bed. She stared back at him, trying to think of what to say next, but she found herself a little lost taking him all in.

She'd tried to give him privacy over the last few months and avoided coming in his bedroom, since the once social man had all but become a recluse holed up in his fortress of solitude. She still wasn't sure if Wags physically forced him out of his room every night for dinner, but at least she got to spend time with him once a day.

Wags was spacious inside, and Lusa had her own room, and the kitchen and dining area were plenty big. She preferred outside anyway, so she'd never felt like it was struggle to give Res space during this recovery, and since he'd taken to hiding himself away, she'd let him have it.

But clearly, she should have been coming in here more often.

Wags was magic; she cleaned herself within a blink. Yet somehow Res's room looked like a tornado came through on an hourly basis. Dirty clothes piled up in the corners, and she was pretty sure he hadn't changed his sheets since the last time she did when he'd still been bleeding. The room reeked of sweat, and while Res normally smelled stupidly good when he was sweaty, this was too much. He'd left most of the lights off, a wax-less candle high in one corner, and a sheet tossed over the vanity mirror where he'd spent hours primping himself before his performances. His connecting closest, previously bursting with shimmering outfits and glittering accessories, was closed off, making the entire space feel a hundred times smaller.

Res himself lounged on the unmade bed, one hand behind his head, his hair unwashed. She blinked a few times, realizing he'd tied it up every time he emerged for their quiet dinners, so she'd missed the fact he hadn't bothered to bathe in . . . well, she had no idea how long. She'd just assumed he did when she wandered around the countryside keeping herself busy.

The dim light cast sharp shadows on his stubbled jaw, dark circles stark against his pale skin. He wore a gray poet's blouse, open to mid-chest, but it was wrinkled and stained. His pants were a plain tan, his feet bare. Res waved the book he'd been reading at her. "Anything else?"

Lusa huffed through her nose, reminding herself he'd been through a hells of a trauma, even if they'd never talked about it. Even if it had been trauma for her too—she'd killed someone, for gods' sake, and she'd never even told him—but they'd never talked about that, either. Because he'd needed time. Because he was scared and scarred and . . .

Res didn't look at her, instead picking at his fingers.

For whatever reason, *that* bothered Lusa.

Not the stench, or the dirty hair and clothes, or hiding his room.

The way he dismissed her and acted like he wasn't a big, sulking mess.

Through gritted teeth, she said, "Res, this is a child's wish."

"Yes, well, good a time as any to learn that wishes are a riot act, don't you agree, sweetling?" He flicked his gaze to hers, his eyes bloodshot, and her anger deflated at bit at how dull and lifeless they looked. The halfmoon scar under his left eye was bold as the night it happened and would probably never fade.

Lusa didn't doubt he'd covered the mirror so he didn't have to see it.

She sighed as she tiptoed around his mess and plopped down on the bed beside him. He raised a brow at her.

"You smell terrible."

He snorted.

"Wags gives us a working shower with hot water, and this is how you thank her? By stinking up the place? By marinating inside her?"

Res grimaced. "Gods, only you could make it worse."

She plucked the book from him, not bothering to look at the title, and tossed it in the discarded clothes. "Take a shower, ask Wags nicely to clean your room, and then meet me for dinner so we can have an actual conversation."

"I'm not in the mood."

"I'm not asking."

When he tried to pout at her, of all things, so she stood and ripped the curtains open, letting in the late afternoon sunlight.

Res howled and buried his face in the pillows.

"Come on, you big baby. You can't stay in here forever."

She thought she heard a "can too" from the pillows.

"Wags likes me more. If I tell her to kick you outside, you know she will. So why don't you get clean and fed before we have that fight."

She left before he could argue more, pacing around the kitchen for a few minutes, trying to decide what she'd do if he refused to come out.

Lusa slumped with relief against the counter when she heard the shower turn on.

It took Res almost an hour to emerge and join Lusa at the dinner table, which was set by then, along with two very troublesome cats. Tick slept on his cat bed on the far side of the table, but Kiki liked having its own chair, which Wags had manifested for it in a shape which kind of reminded Lusa of a baby's highchair.

"Gods, that smells heavenly," Res muttered as he strolled in, looking a bit more like himself. His hair was wet, but brushed, and hung loose around his shoulders in slick waves, the color a muted green. He looked exhausted still, but he wore a pale purple shirt and black leather pants, a step up from the bedroom, but still nothing like his normal self.

Of course, he was adornment free—no makeup, no jewels, and no illusions—but Lusa had always found him most attractive this way, simply as himself.

He narrowed his eyes at her when he sat. "What are you smiling about?"

She shifted to a smirk and shrugged, helping herself to a dinner roll. Thank the gods Wags could cook, because neither of them could. She'd outdone herself with a full homecooked meal tonight.

"You need to trim your eyebrows," Lusa offered, trying to distract him.

Res let out an offended grunt and ripped an entire leg off the roast chicken, biting into it like the uncouth savage she knew he was underneath all the glitter. "And I suppose you believe I should take tips from those caterpillars crawling on your face?" She threw the roll, and it hit him right between the eyes, and Res didn't even blink. "Though, I must say, I can see the appeal. Less work. *Au naturel*, it is?"

When the second roll hit him on the nose, Res laughed, the first time she'd heard the sound in eight months.

Lusa's eyes stung.

She was going to start crying. She missed him so much; he really had no idea.

Sure, she had Wags and Tick and Kiki, but he was her best friend, and he'd been *gone* for months and she . . . Gods, she'd been so lonely.

"Lusa girl?" he asked, his voice soft, his expression softer, and she cleared her throat.

"Sorry, caterpillar in my eye, you know how it is now."

"Ah, do I now." He didn't buy it, but he wasn't going to push.

Besides, tonight wasn't about her. It was about helping him get out of this funk. Lusa pulled the letter out of her pocket. "Kiki is really excited about this one."

Kiki perked up with a whirl. It had been pretending to eat from the empty plate, and blinked a few times at Res. They didn't really know each other yet. Lusa had told Res how Kiki helped him heal, but again, they didn't talk about what happened that night, so they'd never even spoken about *who* gave Lusa Kiki to begin with.

Lusa really hoped that would change, because Kiki was kind of the best.

"Yes, yes," Kiki chirped, and Lusa laughed, because she knew it wanted to burst out of its highchair but was trying to use *manners*, like she'd explained when Kiki wanted to eat at the table like a person but also didn't want to be person shaped because "persons are big and awkward." "Wish for magic birthday! Wish for pretties! Spoke with Kiki for all the colors and shinies she wishes!"

Res didn't say anything, just kept eating, albeit more civilized now. She did catch him glancing back at his bedroom door.

Lusa swallowed a few times, her tone gentle. "Res, you can't hide in here forever, you know that right? It's been eight months."

He wiped his mouth, the motion angry. "And you've decided that's enough?"

The bitterness in his tone shocked her, and Lusa leaned back in her seat. Kiki clicked softly and shrank down, ears flattened.

"I don't know what's enough or not, but I know that this," she waved the note, "is a nice place to work on finding your feet."

"I'm not interested in performing, Lusa. That life is over for me."

She would have been less surprised if he told her . . . anything else. "Res, you don't mean that."

"You've known me a few years, and think you have me figured out, is it? Well, sweetling, I can tell you I'm more than a pretty face."

Lusa shoved back from the table, the chair squealing against the wood floor so hard she winced. "Sorry, Wags." Then she glared at Res. "You really think I'd still be here if it was just for your pretty face?"

"Well, probably not," he said, his tone dry as he leaned both hands on the table and propped up his chin on his folded hands. "I've never put out for you after all. I would have lost patience waiting a long time ago."

For a heartbeat, Lusa was sure he saw right through her.

That he'd known all along she was a fool in love with him, the man who'd made it clear he viewed her as nothing more a friend. At least, she'd thought she was his friend. Maybe she was an even bigger fool than she realized. Was she a little puppy, then, or some desperate sidekick clinging for scraps of attention from the first person who ever noticed her?

Would anyone have the filled the void in her life?

Her human mother had been born blind, which meant she was able to live happily with her tariaksuq father. Until Lusa was born, and as soon as she opened her eyes as a baby, she pushed her father into the shadowlands and he never came back. Her mother withered away, miserable without him, until she died and Lusa was truly alone, wandering, always wandering and never belonging, never seen.

Until Res.

Gods, what he must think of her. The idiot girl who fell in love with the first person who could see her?

Maybe if she wasn't so afraid of losing him, she could tell him the truth. Sure, she'd been infatuated with the handsome man who saw her for the first time, but she fell in love with the man who became her friend.

The silly, vain, arrogant showboat who got just as angry as Lusa if anyone mistreated Wags. The man who saved Tick from freezing on a street corner. The man who had always been there when she needed him.

Even though, right now, he was pushing her away when he needed her, because he was hurting.

That had to be what was happening, right?

That idea was easier to take than the alternative, so she chose to believe it.

"I know you're hurting," Lusa whispered, fighting against the tightness in her throat. "But that doesn't give you the right to treat me like this."

She stalked by him, throwing the letter in his lap and heading out into the night because there was one thing she knew for sure: it was better to wander than be trapped.

# Chapter 8

Three days later, and Lusa hadn't seen Res. He hadn't left his room at all, not even for dinner, at least not when she was around. Fine, whatever. Let him be an immature jerk. He'd get himself out of his funk. Or something.

Right?

Right.

The letters kept pouring in for menial wishes. Kiki was having a blast, and Lusa had to admit, she was enjoying herself as well, despite the crater Res left in her heart over that dinner. It was only the second place she'd set up the acquisitions box, and the first with Kiki's face, which was turning out much better results.

After the mason and blacksmith's requests, more and more came in, and Lusa found a way to meet most of the asks. If she couldn't, she left little notes explaining the wishes were outside the acquisitionist's wheelhouse and they could try asking for something else. Of course, transmutation was the biggest winner.

She, Kiki, and Wags had cooked meals, mended a fence, fixed a dozen different broken objects, tracked down a missing dog, and trapped a dozen pheasants, all in the last seventy-two hours. They worked during the day, then delivered the requests under the cover of night, because who didn't like a little mystery with their magic?

But Lusa had yet to drop off the last decline notice, however, and she was running out of time. Little Lils's birthday party was set to start in the town square in less than two hours. She still hadn't seen, heard, or spoken to Res.

Now, she sat on top of a straw-roofed home, watching the villagers gather around the well. Lils was a thin-blooded duster, nothing to show for her magic blood besides pointy ears and pink-blond hair. Her parents were the same; most of the village were similar, although a gremlin ran the market, a pair of druids kept the orchard, and the local fishmonger was a naiad. About a dozen kids attended Lils's party, ranging in age from three to ten.

It really was a serene little place, Lusa mused. This wasn't technically inside the Velvet Emporium's purview, but they were the closest Accorded Territory and weren't aggressive expansionists, so lots of little towns and villages and homesteads populated this half of Europe, between the Storm Belt all the way to the Baker's Hills.

Lusa shivered. She had a feeling they'd never go back there again. Probably for the best, given Res got attacked there and she'd broken into the home of the most well-respected Independent in the world.

The villagers hung flower wreaths around the well, and she grinned as the druid pair made them burst with blooms. Lils squealed about magic and the talking face, and the heavy golden necklace around Lusa's throat warmed.

Lusa patted Kiki. She didn't dare let it out in its animated form where it might be seen, not with the bad man out there somewhere, and because even in a world of filled magic things, some were that much more precious than others. "Sorry, Kiks, I know she was excited, but we did our best. Maybe he'll be ready next time."

She was about to slide off the roof and sneak the apology note over to the feast table when a shimmer caught her eye. Lusa stilled, a grin spreading as she watched Res walk down the hillside, hands in his pockets, his stride lazy.

He wasn't dolled up in all his finery, his pants dark gray and his shirt an icy blue, but he'd slapped on one of his less fancy hats, with a few purple and yellow feathers clipped to the brim. He'd covered his wrists in golden bangles, but he wore no makeup, no glitter or shine, and he'd glamoured his hair pale blond.

He was hiding himself, Lusa realized. Instead of leaning into his natural beauty as a Ques duster, he was using those powers to fade into little more than a two-bit magician. And that was perfect for a child's birthday.

Lusa was still upset for how he'd treated her over dinner, but right now, she was so proud of him, her heart hurt. That pride filled her as he strode into town, preening as he called for the birthday girl before conjuring up a herd of unicorns ridden by fairies, of every color of the rainbow, and sent them galivanting around Lils. The little girl screamed and clapped her hands before running over to Res and throwing herself into his arms.

Lusa saw the quiet surprise on his face before he melted into the child's joyful embrace, a softness overriding the terror that had been riding him since that night in the Baker's Hills. He let her go with a winning smile, and Lils darted after one of the unicorns. Res scanned around until he spotted Lusa on the rooftop.

He offered a half-smile, one filled with regret and hope, then gave her a nod before returning to his duties as birthday magician. Lusa wiped her eyes, hoping he couldn't see her crying like a dolt this far away.

Lusa had lasted for about an hour before watching the wonderful party became too much of a reminder of how she could never join all the fun, so she headed back up the hill to hang out with Wags and the cats instead.

She wasn't sure how long had passed, but she'd fit the last stone in Wags's pretty tree design and waxed most of the goshoguma's wood paneling before she heard footsteps coming up the meadow. Cold didn't seep into her bones, so she knew it was Res. Also because Kiki and Tick couldn't be bothered to get up from their sleeping pile on Wags's front steps.

Lusa considered ignoring him. She was still hurt over how he'd acted toward her, but he'd given that little girl a wish of a lifetime and she cared about the big idiot, so she glanced over her shoulder at him as she wiped the buffing wax from her fingers.

He had his hat tucked under one arm, his sleeves rolled up to his elbows, and his hands in his pockets. And his hair was still that horrible blond, which made her grin as she went back to cleaning her hands because Res still looked good. He always did, even when he'd been wallowing in despair and lost like drift wood in a hurricane for months.

She wasn't going to make this easy on him, she decided. She'd spent weeks being his live-in nurse, then his very patient—maybe too patient—and supportive friend, and he'd never even said thank you.

She knew why he avoided talking about that night, and thanking her would be acknowledging the attack that left the unflappable Resplendent, the extraordinary illusionist Casanova, little more than a shell of himself who was afraid to leave his room. Lusa accepted that, even understood it.

But that didn't mean he got to treat her like crap. And he never had, not before she'd pushed him to grant this wish.

"That hair color is terrible," Lusa offered when Res didn't speak and the silence became a little too much for her to shoulder any longer.

He huffed, which might have been a laugh. "Well, yes, that's kind of the point. Anyone who met me before would never *believe* they were looking at the same man."

He tutted and Lusa couldn't help a smirk at the dramatic shake of his head, the blond falling away in a shower of sparkles, replaced by the muted green of his normal hair color. Well, almost normal. It still lacked the emerald shine from before.

"There, all better," Res said with a bow, the gesture lacking his signature flair. He turned the hat over, picking at the feathers with a frown.

Lusa sighed and went back to cleaning up. She hated being mad at him. She hated being petty, with this sort of almost silent treatment, but did he realize how awful he'd been to her? She rubbed her temples. This was stupid. She should just tell him she was mad, and they could talk about it, and surely, he'd apologize and—

He grabbed her elbow, tugging her up to her feet so fast, she almost stumbled. "Res, what the—"

But then she was surrounded by warmth as Res pulled her tight against him, against his chest, and she felt his heart drumming under her ear as his arms folded across her body, one hand pressed between her shoulder blades, the other on her lower back, and he was squeezing her.

What in all the gods was he *doing*?

She kind of flapped her arms, smacking at his ribs, but then stilled when his chin rested on the top of her head. "Hush, you ninny, I'm just giving you a hug."

"Oh."

*Oh.*

That's what this was.

Lusa blinked a few times, arms falling slack as she stared at his shirt. His heart stayed a low, steady drum, but hers felt like it was going to explode out of her chest and run panicking down the hillside. She swallowed a few times, her mouth dry, her palms sweaty as she opened and closed them, fidgeting on her toes.

She'd seen lots of hugs.

People did them all the time, and she was a chronic people watcher.

She'd probably been hugged as a baby. Maybe?

Maybe before her mother realized her father was never coming back. Her father would have never tried to hold her; if she opened her eyes, he'd drop a baby on the head, not a great look. She didn't remember any hugs before her mother died. She didn't remember any kind of touches, really.

The only touches she knew were bumps in crowds followed by confused expressions. Brushes in passing. When Res caught her picking his pocket all those years ago, he'd held her wrist for a long time, and she'd been so startled by being *seen*, she'd barely registered being *touched*.

Why was she having trouble breathing?

And why was she so stinking hot?

"Lusa?" Res's voice was quiet, hesitant. "Should I not have—"

"No!" Gods, it was so weird, but good, and . . . She grabbed fistfuls of his shirt on both his sides. "Sorry," she said with a laugh, which kind of came out in a choked squeak. "Just not sure where to put my hands or whatever."

Res leaned back, frowning down at her, and for a second, she was terrified he was going to let her go and she'd never be this close to another person for the rest of her life.

"Have you . . . No, that can't . . ." He trailed off, his brow furrowed.

Lusa laughed, this time a real laugh, because he looked so, so confused. "Yeah, far as I know, you're my first hug. Lucky you."

"Lusa." Res watched her for way too long, making her cheeks too warm, making this hug thing suddenly awkward in a new kind of way, but then he hugged her again, this time even tighter, and one hand cupped the nape of her neck and she couldn't help closing her eyes. "I didn't know."

"It's not a big deal," she mumbled against his shirt. Even his not nice shirts were nice. Silky and soft and smelled so good. She rubbed her cheek on him like Tick enjoyed doing, soaking in the moment, experiencing what it felt to be held by someone.

This was . . . Wow. This was really nice.

*Nice.* What a lame word.

"It is a big deal. If I'd known, I'd have hugged you every day, sweetling." He sighed then, a long-drawn-out exhale that ruffled her hair. "I owe you an apology. I was horrible to you the other night, and I'm sorry. There's no excuse I can give you, nothing I can say besides beg your forgiveness and promise I'll never speak to you like that again."

"Forgiven," she whispered, and she meant it, all her anger evaporating. "I know you didn't mean it. You were just scared."

"Me, scared?" Res scoffed, holding her close. "Why don't you go ahead and shout for the entire world to hear how I've become a terrible, utter coward?"

Lusa didn't want to lean away from him, but this was too important. This was the closest they'd come to any kind of conversation about his attack. She let him go, patting his chest so he loosened the hug, and she stepped from the circle of his arms.

"You're not a coward," Lusa said, her chin lifted. "Those horrible men drugged you and cut pieces off of you." Her voice hitched, and she didn't miss the way Res's jaw flexed and his gaze went unfocused.

"But you're still here, you're still you, and you're still beautiful, Res. You just need time to get back to yourself, and you will. You can. You did. And I saw it today, with those illusions." She grinned, remembering Lils's absolute joy. "I mean, it might have been the best show you've ever done."

His attention was back on her now, and he all but sauntered closer. He leaned forward until their noses touched. "I'm sorry, I stopped listening after you told me you think I'm pretty."

"Ugh," Lusa groaned and rolled her eyes. "See, still you!" She side-stepped him as he flashed her a devilish grin, one she'd seen him use too many times on his conquests, and she couldn't look at him anymore. "Seriously, though. You really made her happy. She'll remember it for her entire life."

"Yes, well, you're the one she should be thanking, but she did blather on about the magical box and the talking face, so that will have to do for now. And for the rest, I let them know any other requests won't be met after today."

Lusa turned with a frown. "Why? Kiki said there were four more letters this morning."

Res rubbed his jaw as he walked toward Wags, shrugging a lithe shoulder. Sunset was an hour or so off, the air still warm, the breeze cool. "I'd like to leave, now that people have seen me. Just in case. Just to be safe."

Right. Lusa noticed the slight shake in his hand as he ran it through his hair and forced a smile, before his fingertips idly played at the scar on his cheek. He'd been brave today, for her, for himself, and for Lils. A big step up from hiding in his room.

Lusa hesitated, but then touched his arm, squeezing his bicep—because they touched now, right? He'd hugged her, so they were friends that touched?

"Whatever you need, Res. I'm here for you." She chewed her lip, wondering why she'd never told him this before but, "You're my best friend. You know that, right? We'll get through this, you and me. Okay?"

Res hung his head, hair flopping into his eyes, and he almost looked like a boy instead of the confident man she knew, before he nodded once and whispered, "Thank you, Lusa. For everything. And for every time I've been remiss about saying it since the day we met."

He ducked into Wags, and Lusa lingered outside for a little longer before she asked Wags to pack up and move them along, her cheeks warm against the cool spring night.

Hugs, she decided, were pretty great.

# Chapter 9

The next month went by in a weird sort of haze, but in the best way.

They stayed mobile, bouncing from town to town around the Emporium borders, never staying in one place more than three or four days at a time. Res, for all his fussing, fully embraced Lusa's wish granting scheme, but not without twisting it around with his own ideas.

"Lusa girl," he'd said, "helping others doesn't need to be entirely charitable by nature. Besides, if you're busy helping, it means you aren't stealing, so they really should be paying you anyway, don't you think?"

It frustrated her at first, but he wasn't wrong. If she spent nighttime fulfilling requests, she slept more during the day, and in turn, spent less time picking pockets. And while Wags was an endless source of magic, she couldn't make them dinner if her larders weren't stocked, so at the very least they needed food.

And so Res took it upon himself to resume performing, but not in the way Lusa expected. Every morning, he sat outside Wags draped in a new costume, each day making himself odder and uglier than the last. He camped next to Kiki's golden face and the request box, chatting up anyone who wandered by, spinning tales about the mysterious Acquisitionist.

And gods help her, it was working.

The letters poured in, and despite his ridiculous embellishments, Res made sure people's wishes were possible for them to complete. Between Kiki's skills, Wags's talents, her stealth, and Res's magic, they rarely turned anyone away, and the ones they did, Res encouraged to try again.

The second week, he started asking for down payments in exchange for their services. She told him not to, but he ignored her, and it wasn't like she could argue with him in front of their customers when she was backed against the shadowlands. But he'd been right again, and asking people to pay ahead of time increased their business.

When asked who or what the Acquisitionist was, Res came up with a fresh, fantastical story about what he did and didn't know about the strange benefactor who was probably invisible and enjoyed doing good deeds for good folks. He always insisted he'd never actually met the Acquisitionist himself, and that he was merely a "vessel of good fortune" and very grateful to have his job.

He was insufferable now that he'd left his room.

Res threw himself into this new form of acting, thriving in pretending to be anyone but himself, and while Lusa knew it alluded to a bigger, underlying trouble, it was better than him wallowing alone in his room.

She was better without him wallowing too.

He helped her clean Wags, which he'd never really done before the attack. They shared all meals now, and Res spent time teaching Kiki new creative swear words every day. The two got along well, and Kiki was delighted to have his attention instead of tiptoeing nervously around him.

And then there were the hugs.

Those had taken some getting used to, but once Res discovered he'd given her the first hug she'd ever experienced, he'd insisted on making up for her so-called drought.

She got a good morning hug when he joined her at breakfast and a goodnight hug before they retired or parted ways if she was running requests under the cover of darkness. Whenever she returned, if he was awake, he greeted her with open arms. She rolled her eyes and accepted the embrace, hiding her smile against his shoulder.

He touched her more often, too, she noticed. Little ways she'd seen other people do in her years of observations. A hand on her shoulder, a pat on the head. He'd even flicked her nose the other day when she'd told him he looked like an eighty-year-old grandmother in his newest getup. Two nights ago, after they shared a bottle of wine paid for in exchange for a necklace shifted from copper to gold as a wedding gift, Res taught her to waltz while he badly hummed accompanying music.

Lusa found herself returning the causal touches—offering to brush out his knotty hair, or patting his arm when she wanted to show him something, or elbowing him in the gut when he was snide.

She almost couldn't recall what it was like to *not* touch someone; it felt so natural between them.

They were on the coast now, the waves crashing near the docks of a fishing village of about thirty people. They arrived two nights ago, and yesterday Res wandered into town to give his little spiel about the Acquisitionist's wishing box. Lusa yawned and patted Kiki, whom she wore as a leather armband today. They'd spent all night mending fishing nets in trade for enough fresh caught seafood to last weeks in Wags's enchanted larder. Kiki was a demon with its little claws; Lusa only had to show it how to braid and tie the netting once before it could mimic the motions perfectly. Good thing, too, because there was no way Lusa could have done it all by herself, and Res was far too delicate for this type of work. His words, not hers.

"I need a nap," she mumbled. The armband whirred in agreement, although Lusa wasn't sure if Kiki ever slept. She knew it rested, or maybe went into a quite sort of stasis, but she didn't think Kiki was ever truly unaware of its surroundings.

She kept a palm resting affectionately on the warm metal against her bicep. Lusa had so many reasons to be thankful for meeting Theodore that night in the Baker's Hills. This wasn't the first time she wondered if she'd ever see him again. She'd been so scared and worried, she'd run off without thanking him for helping them, and the guilt of that gnawed at her every now and then.

Her boots sank into the loose sand, but the terrain shifted into sharp, dense grass, and she hummed as she found the trail through the dunes. Seabirds scolded her, and her arms itched from the sand, robe fiber, and the damn bugs.

Wags's red top appeared as she crested the hill, but Lusa frowned. The curtains to Wags's front entrance hung open, which sent a prickle of unease along her scalp. Wags never left those curtains open. It was one way she protected her nature. As long as the makeshift doors stayed closed, no one could peek in and see the space inside didn't match the outside footprint.

If it was open, then a stranger was already inside.

"Kiki," Lusa whispered. "Someone is here."

"Who?" Kiki whispered back as it slithered from her arm to form a snake head, eyes glittering eerie red.

"No idea, so you need to stay sneaky for now."

Kiki chirped and resituated, eyes closed as it became little more than a decorative armband again. Lusa moved on silent feet in the grass, padding around to behind Wags. She knelt by her wheel well and patted the back panel.

"Wags, let me in my room," Lusa whispered. The wood shifted

under her palm, molding into a square sliding door large enough for her to shimmy through. This side connected directly to her bedroom, and her curtain doors would be closed, as she always left them drawn when she wasn't inside sleeping. "Thanks."

She popped in on the floor next to her single mattress, the access panel melting away behind her feet. Muffled voices came from the kitchen as Lusa crawled to the other side of her small room, pressing a finger against the wall as she whispered, "Peeky hole."

The wood swirled, a hole opening just wide enough for her to press an eye against. And she swore the wall thinned, because suddenly the voices were clearer and she nearly choked.

"Yes, well, as you said," Res said, his tone the sickly sweet he liked to use when he was being extra sarcastic. "It's been nearly a lifetime since the festival."

"Don't be trite, my friend. It was an observation, not a barb."

Theodore, the very same person she'd been thinking about not five minutes ago, sat with Res at Wags's table, along with a poorly prepared tea set. Res hadn't dressed himself for his daily charade yet, his hair tied back and its normal color. Across from him, Thoedore looked much the same he had the first and only time Lusa encountered him, except he seemed less intimidating in the early dawn light. His skin was less an impenetrable black, more a deep, rich umber. His wore those exquisite, expensive robes again, this time decorated with koi fish and snowflakes.

"Good man," Kiki whispered, the sound such a quiet peep Lusa almost missed it.

The two men sat in silence for a few uncomfortable seconds, but Res looked away first with a heavy sigh and fiddled with his teacup. Given the mess on the table, he'd prepared the tea himself, not Wags, which meant she didn't know what to think of Theodore yet. Granted, she hadn't reverted her insides to a bare bones floor with hay mats. She must have picked up Res knew him and didn't feel threated by him, but Res wasn't exactly happy to see Theodore, either.

"Well, you found me," Res offered. "Very good, you're as clever and resourceful as you've always been, good show. And I made tea, proving I've yet to become a complete barbarian, so if that's all?"

"It's not."

"Of course it's not," Res muttered. "Whyever would it be?"

Theodore sipped his tea, then grimaced and set down his cup. "How is Lusa?"

Res went oddly still, his gaze flicking around Wags, and Lusa realized he was looking for her. She bit her bottom lip; she shouldn't be spying like this, but she was curious and she had no idea how to step in now without it being weird.

"That was pillow talk," Res said, his tone entirely put out, and Lusa's cheeks flushed as she realized exactly what kind of *friends* they were. "I didn't realize it would come up outside the bedroom." He waved a hand, flippant, and Lusa couldn't help a wince. "Why would you even ask?"

Theodore canted his head. "I'm starting think this conversation should wait until she is here."

Res narrowed his eyes. "What conversation?"

He ignored the question. "You left the Baker's Hills earlier than I expected."

Lusa was sweating now. And she wasn't curious anymore. All she felt was dirty guilt, because she'd never told Res his friend, the friend who had sought him out to check on his well-being, had been instrumental in saving his life.

She hoped Wags wouldn't be too pissed if she puked on her floor.

"It didn't live up to the hype," Res drawled, but Lusa recognized the growing tension in his voice. It was subtle, coming out in a sneer.

She needed to say something, because this crossed over into, well, she didn't know what. Bad. Worse?

"Res," Theodore started, his tone the kind for lecturing a child, but before he could say anything else, Lusa all but shouted through the wall: "He doesn't know you were there!"

Both men snapped to her direction, as it were, and Lusa kind of wished the shadowlands could swallow her despite the wall blocking her from view.

Theodore seemed confused and perhaps, she dared to believe, hurt by the confession yelled at him from behind a wooden wall by a voice he'd only heard once before.

Yeah, that made her feel great.

Res, on the other hand. He'd gone pale. No, more like an ashen sort of green, before he abruptly shoved to his feet and his face flushed an angry red up to the tips of his ears.

That was worse. Way worse.

"Don't be mad, please!" Lusa flattened her palms against the wall, too chicken to come out and not wanting him to barge into the room and see her cowering on the floor. "We never talked about that night. We tried, a few times, and you, well, I mean, us. It was hard. For both of us."

"And you just decided I didn't need to know someone else saw me in that state? Someone who knew me? Who *told* you they knew who and what I was?" Res all but snarled at her. Oh, he was really, really mad.

"No! Yes? I didn't really decide anything! We just never talked about it more than 'Some guys jumped you and tried to cut you up, but I got all your feathers, and we should keep running for now right and please don't die.'" She swallowed a few times. "And then you didn't want to talk about, well, anything. At all. For a long time."

Res didn't look her direction, staring instead down the hall toward the room he hid in for months, his fists opening and closing. "We've been speaking for weeks now. About many things."

Yeah, and it had been great.

So how was she supposed to bring up the memories that might have him running away from her again? The very topic that could send him spiraling back into himself, leaving her all alone? Again.

Was it selfish? Sure. But how could she explain that to him without sounding like a total jerk?

"Nothing to say now, Lusa?" Res sneered her direction, his hurt clear as day under the edge in his voice.

"She killed to stop the Ques hunters," Theodore said quietly, the timbre of his voice a gentle rumble in the storm filling Wags's warm kitchen.

Res blinked a few times as Lusa's stomach swooped and rolled, that particular point one she tried very hard to avoid thinking about unless her nightmares forced her hand.

"What?" was all Res managed; his voice was hoarse now, all the venom gone.

"In defending you, she killed one of the hunters." Theodore gestured to Res's scarred arm, which he covered with his other hand even though it was concealed by his long sleeve. "The one cutting the feathers out of your arm and shoulder. When she struck him, he fell and hit his head, and the impact killed him. Despite being shocked by what she'd done, when the second man tried to take your eye," Theodore went on, tapping his cheekbone, "she stopped him before he did any serious damage." His gaze flicked to the wall she hid behind, and he smirked. He *smirked* at her. "And then she came after me when I found you."

Lusa wiped her cheeks, not sure why she was crying. Kiki unrolled itself from her arm and curled in her lap, frantically patting at her thigh. Was it trying to make cat biscuits, maybe? To comfort her? She rested a hand on its warm metal head between the cat-shaped ears and Kiki relaxed.

Theodore turned his attention back to Res. "Before you let your wounded pride get the better of you, perhaps you should consider speaking of that night is not easy for your Lusa, either."

Res sank back into the chair, all but deflating. Lusa said nothing, unsure what she could or should do, as Res buried his face in his hands.

"You're right," he mumbled, scrubbing his hands through his hair. "We're overdue to talk about it, that's for sure." He sighed again. "Ques hunters, though. You're certain?"

"Lusa, you gave him the feathers?"

She clutched her necklace, which still had his single feather clipped to it, the one that helped her find him. Otherwise, "Yeah, I gave him the whole bag."

"And you couldn't deduce as much?" Theodore mused.

Res grunted. "She's right when she said we haven't talked about it. I've done my best not to think about it either. I haven't even looked at that fucking bag, let alone opened it."

"Why do people hunt Ques?" Lusa asked. "Is Res still in danger?"

Res flashed her smirk, but there was a kind of melancholy to the expression she didn't like. "Have I ever not been, Theodore?"

Theodore shook his head, a bit of amusement there, but it died away when he spoke. "Anyone with Quetzalcoatl blood, no matter how thin, bears the true form of a feathered serpent as the god Quetzalcoatl did. And all can take a human shape."

"Yes, yes, *archivist*. We don't need the whole history lesson, do we? Perhaps just the juicy bits?"

Archivist? Lusa sucked in a breath. Theodore was from the Icelandic Citadel of Knowledge?

Before she could even process he was part of the organization that bound the Accords, the magic that held the world order together, he went on, as Res put it, for the juicy bits.

"Yes, well, anyone from the Quetzalcoatl line is highly sought after, due to the unique alchemical properties of their feathers and organs," Theodore said. "As long as they are removed while in their true form, those items will never decay. When ground into powder by the proper means and measured correctly as a replacement, they function as a true universal ingredient in any alchemy recipe."

# Chapter 10

"Holy hells," Lusa whispered.

Her mind reeled, and she hated her first thought was about the number of feathers she'd stuffed in the bag and the absurd value they represented, especially if they'd never go bad. The second hunter was still a jerk for leaving his friend and trying to escape with the loot, but . . .

Tons of alchemy recipes did amazing things. Ungodly things. Crazy things, not least of all granting immortality. She could think of at least a dozen deadly, horrible concoctions of the top of her head. Plagues in a bottle with enough kick to wipe out an entire city. Poisons tailored to a specific blood composition. The kind of mythical stuff that made fields permanently fallow or oceans barren. She'd once heard whispers about mimic genies with unlimited wishes, and an entire Calamity stemmed from two alchemists having a disagreement.

Thankfully, the more powerful and dangerous the recipe, the rarer the ingredient list. Just because everything imagined became real with the Aperien Event didn't equate to an unlimited supply. Myths had come and gone, creatures had been hunted into extinction, and some plants would never bloom again.

But if an alchemist got their hands on someone with Quetzalcoatl blood . . .

Gods on high, they'd gotten an entire bag of feathers from Res from stripping one arm, and they'd planned to take his eye next, and if she hadn't gotten there, would they have ever stopped? And his scars . . .

"They don't grow back," Lusa said. "When you're hurt or your feathers are cut off in your true form, you don't heal."

"She's always been a clever girl, this one," Res said, clicking his tongue.

At first, she wanted to throw something at his head, but she recognized the anguish in his voice.

And then Lusa's heart stuttered because he'd *told* her what he was years ago. He had no idea if she knew about Ques and their unique value. She could have sold him out for a new life. She'd had nothing when she first met him, and they'd known each other less than a year when he told her the truth about his nature.

But he'd trusted her.

His fear wasn't just about the scars and his vanity. Res might have lived his whole life in inherit danger, but that night in the Baker's Hills was the first time the threat found him. No wonder he'd hidden himself away, dressed up like anyone but himself, and wanted to avoid going near crowded places like the Velvet Emporium.

"I'm so sorry, Res."

"Pity is droll, sweetling. I won't have it now, not after you've been doing so well keeping it to yourself."

And then he'd gone and made her angry, just like that. "Good thing you're so rude," she snapped. "Kind of makes pity difficult."

"Good thing," he agreed, kicking his feet up on the table and staring at the ceiling. "Now that all that is out and awkward, why in the hells are you really here, Theodore?"

"I meant it when I said I came to see how you were doing. Granted, I didn't know you were missing information as to why I might be curious." Theodore smoothed his robe. "But it's not the only reason, you're right. I would have left you alone otherwise, knowing you'd want to lick your wounds in private, on your own terms."

"Seeing as everyone is keen to fuck that up, did you have some great words of wisdom about reclaiming my inner fire?"

"Don't be rude?" Lusa asked from behind the wall, and when Theodore laughed, she grinned. Res glared her direction, but there wasn't much heat behind it.

"Wise words," Theodore agreed. "And it seems you're in capable hands on that front, so I'll keep my great wisdom to myself for today."

"Lucky me," Res said.

Theodore wave him off, which only made Res pout again and Lusa uncomfortable, because it felt a bit like flirting, and she should be happy if he was but really didn't feel very happy about it.

"Lusa, do you still have the box I gave you?"

Box? She had no idea what he was talking about until Kiki jumped off her lap and bolted out of her bedroom. She watched through the peep hole as Kiki scurried through the hall and up onto the kitchen table, using Res's thigh as a vault.

"Ah, menace!" Res swore, barely catching the teapot before it crashed to the floor.

Tick, who had been watching all this from the shelf above the stove, turned on the gathering, flicked his tail once, and promptly went back to sleep. Kiki preened and pranced over to Theodore in its cat form, fluttering its pretty, filigree wings.

"Good man!" Kiki chirp-purred and headbutted Thoedore's chin. He laughed and did his best to pet Kiki like a real cat.

"Amazing," he crooned at Kiki, who whirled and chittered under the attention, all excited sounds and no words. "Last time we met, the best you could manage for a construct was a small beetle."

"Kiki practices with Tick!"

"Tick?" Thoedore quirked a brow, and Res pointed at the sleeping gray cat. "Ah, of course. Mimicry then, through extended observation?"

"Kiki started being a cat almost right away," Lusa offered. "It came out of the box a few days after we left the Baker's Hills." She bit her lip; this might be her only chance to learn more about Kiki. "Kiki said you saved it from a bad man?"

"I did," Theodore said fondly. "Right before I came to the Baker's Hills. I wasn't sure what to do with it yet, but I was in town visiting a friend and saw Res performing. My plan was to stop by and say hello, then return with Kiki to the Citadel and determine a safe home for it. However, given its nature . . ."

"A philosopher's stone," Lusa said, which got another little curse, this time of realization, from Res.

"Yes, which is why I knew there was a chance it might be able help Res recover from the drugging. And I knew Res already had more than enough reason to steer clear of alchemists who might want to get their hands on our little friend for nefarious purposes."

"Good friends, good friends!" Kiki cheered, hopping and flapping and knocked around the cups and tea set.

"Mutal preservation," Theodore said.

"Kiki's a good friend," Lusa insisted. "That's reason enough to keep it safe, and besides, it's pretty much the whole schtick behind the mysterious Acquisitionist deal Res made up to keep us fed."

"Lusa, sweetling, you made that ugly box, and Kiki made the ugly, talking face. All I did was fabricate a palatable story to go along with the mess you two were making so we could at least be profitable along the way." Res huffed, glaring at Kiki as he mopped up the spilled tea.

"Ah, yes." Theodore picked up Kiki to set it on the floor. "The other reason I sought you both out." His gaze moved to Lusa's hiding place, as if asking her directly when he said, "I'd like to place an acquisition request."

# Chapter 11

Lusa said, "Of course!" at the same time Res said, "Absolutely not."

Oh, hells no. She was not doing this behind a wall. She'd have to squat at the edge of the shadowlands because of Theodore, but Res was going to have to look her in the face if he was going tell her a request from an archivist from the Icelandic Citadel of Knowledge, the good guys of good guys in the world, wasn't worth their time.

This was exactly the thing she'd been chasing.

By the time she ran from her room to the kitchen, Theodore sat politely with his back to the hallway. Man, she liked him more and more every time she met him, and the first meeting was pretty hard to beat considering he saved Res's life and gave her Kiki.

"Res, why the hells would you say no?"

"Why the hells would you say yes without hearing the request first?"

Lusa put her hands on her hips. "Okay, I guess that's fair, but why the hells would you say no without hearing the request first?"

Res scowled. "Because I know *him*, and I know he's always neck deep in trouble in at least eighteen different parts of the damn world at any given time."

Lusa studied the back of Theodore's head and neck, where the faint shimmer of scales danced in morning light. They wrapped higher up on his head than she noticed before, silverly-blue but very hard to make out unless one was really paying attention. Theodore calmly waited, his shoulders relaxed, his robes clean and without a wrinkle to be found.

He didn't look like trouble to Lusa.

"What's the request?"

"Lusa . . ." Res warned, but she shook her head.

"He came all the way here to find *us*. He's an archivist, Res. Don't you think there might be a good reason he wants our help?"

Res crossed his arms. He was all sorts of disheveled at this point.

She ignored him and faced Theodore, or at least the back of his head. "So do you want to just tell us, or do you want the box and for Kiki to make the very cool—and not ugly, by the way—face for you?"

Theodore chuckled. "No, I can just tell you. And you're right, Lusa, I sought the pair of you for your specific skills, in addition to your interest in fulfilling requests and helping people."

"By granting mundane wishes," Res interjected, "in backwater towns. Not solving high-profile Citadel affairs."

"The Res I know doesn't shy away from a bit of challenge and adventure."

Theodore didn't see Res's flinch, but Lusa had a feeling he knew exactly how the verbal blow landed. Res shrank a bit, irritation flashing, but it was mirrored with a discomfort she didn't like seeing on him.

Theodore took full advantage of silencing Res. "There is a cuélebre residing in Northern Spain, not so far from where we are now. This type of dragon does not move from their claimed space, and they hoard treasure and riches beyond belief. He lords over Mount Pindo, calling himself Bartholomew. The area around him is an unofficial Independent of sorts, and they pay tribute for his protection.

"Every year, on Saint Bartholomew's day in August, the dragon calls for a festival, but it is really a ceremony of offerings. Those who wish his protection and his blessing bring treasures of all kinds. This includes entertainment and company. He selects a group of performers to come inside the mountain to witness his wealth and entertain him for the following month. Otherwise, Mount Pindo is inaccessible the rest of the year."

"Alright," Lusa said, "so you want Res to earn entry to perform, but why?"

"This Bartholomew has held his ground since the Aperien Event. His hoard is well fortified, and the mouros—the Gallaecian giants—serve him and protect his wealth in a vast maze of caves within the mountain's belly. The belief is any treasure brought in never sees daylight again. And there is something within his collection I require."

And there it was, exactly how Lusa could help.

"You need to me go, since no one can see me, and pinch this something you need." She licked her lips, remembering that horrible noble from the Baker's Hills. "I won't agree to anything until you tell me what I'd be stealing and why you want it."

"A reasonable request," Theodore said. "I need a bird of truth, and the only known pair were taken to Mount Pindo shortly after the Aperien Event. They've never been documented elsewhere. There are friends of mine, good people, who may soon face an Archival Tribunal. The only thing that can save them is the truth, and there are many heavily invested against that truth being revealed."

"Why the birds?" Res asked, leaning against the wall now with his arms crossed. "There's a hundred different ways to pull the truth from a person."

"And nearly all of which involve a personal touch for the delivery, which leaves room for tampering. Say, improper mixing for a potion.

A lie from the person appointed to determine the truth of the matter. The simple fact that some measures, such as that of the soul or the heart, require the death of an individual to acquire said truth. As you might imagine, I do not wish my friends to find exoneration in death.

"The birds are simple creatures, with no political alliances or motivations. They cannot be swayed. And, given they are currently locked away in an impenetrable vault, my friends' enemies will not expect the birds, and therefor will not prepare a countermeasure. That is my hope, at least."

"What happened to your friends?" Lusa asked. It wasn't like she was going to say no; Theodore already said they were good people, and he'd proven to be a good person to her, but she was curious. And the more information, the more ammunition to help sway Res.

"Two people who weren't supposed to love each other, loved each other anyway. Someone hated them for that love, and he used his position of significant power for revenge. They fought for their love, and he died for his hatred. All we have is their word and the death of an Accorded official in an Independent Territory. If I cannot help the truth come to light . . ." He sighed, the sound bone deep, and for a moment, Thoedore seemed very old and very tired. "It cannot mean nothing."

He stood abruptly, clearing his throat but not turning around as he smoothed his robes and headed toward the door. "I have some matters in town to attend."

Lusa snorted at the obviousness of the lie; they were at a nowhere fishing village, too far outside the Emporium's reach to be considered Accorded territory. There was no Citadel business here of all places, except inside Wags right now, and Lusa had a feeling this conversation wasn't official.

"I will leave you two to discuss my request and, of course, what you would desire from me as compensation. I'll return this evening."

Wags snapped the curtains shut once he stepped outside, leaving them in silence. When Lusa turned on Res and opened her mouth, he pointed a finger in her face and said, again, "Absolutely not."

Then he stormed down the hall and disappeared in his room, his bedroom curtains swinging shut in his wake.

At her feet, Kiki chirp-chirped in the saddest little voice, "No help good man?"

# Chapter 12

"Give us a minute, Kiks, okay?" Lusa said, patting its head when the clockwork cat jumped on the table and fretted in little circles. "I'll get this sorted."

"Yes, good," Kiki whirred, plopping down on its haunches and watching her head down the hall with those strange red eyes.

Lusa never stopped to wonder about the technicalities of magic that allowed for Kiki, fueled by the height of alchemy, to see her, but it was only one of many reasons she was grateful Theodore entrusted Kiki to her care. She'd never take it for granted, same as she'd never take any of the other connections in her life for granted, few and far between as they were.

Connections were tenuous and fragile, rare to form and easy to fray and break, and sometimes, they couldn't be fixed.

Whatever friendship Theodore and Res had was beyond some fling, because Res didn't just tell people about his nature. Now, of course, she fully understood *why* that was so important, but he'd trusted Theodore. And Theodore had trusted Res enough to come ask him for help with this problem.

And Lusa too. And Lusa trusted Theodore. It was a feeling deep her gut. He was a good man, he had to be, because bad men didn't walk away from bags of fortune. He could have taken Res's feathers that night, and Lusa wouldn't have known it mattered. He also didn't need to cover their tracks, smooth things over in the Baker's Hills, give Lusa Kiki to help heal Res, or sit here in this kitchen with his back to her so she didn't have to disappear.

"Res," Lusa said, her voice firm and all the warning he got. "I'm coming in."

He didn't answer—of course he didn't—and Lusa pushed inside. If Wags had any strong opinion on all this, she would have turned the curtains into a locked wooden door, so Lusa took that as a good sign that Wags was on her side. Not like they could go to Mount Pindo without her.

Res lounged on his bed, tossing a coin in the air, his ankles crossed. Wags had cleaned up for him, and it almost looked normal inside, aside from lacking his normal flares of colored fabric and accessories from before he was attacked. His vanity remained covered.

Lusa crossed her arms. "Can we skip the sulking and talk like adults?"

"If we must."

Gods, he could be annoying. Childish, really, when he was at least four times her age. Now didn't seem like the best time to call him old, though, because when she'd used that jab in the past, he'd almost seemed worried about it, like he could wrinkle or something.

"Why don't you want to do this?"

He flicked the coin in the air, and it burst into a dozen more which spun in a lazy circle above his head. "*This* being bamboozling a dangerous Aperien by sneaking into his lair and stealing one of his prized possessions?" He snorted. "Why, sweetling, whatever could possibly go wrong?"

"Please, he has a hoard so big there's an entire maze built into a whole mountain to hold it all. If you have that much stuff, it can't all be important."

"You miss the point, Lusa girl. Big, powerful beings don't like having one pulled over on them." Res poked one of the coins and turned it silver. "It's not even a matter of if the birds are important at all, or if he even remembers they exist. But they certainly will matter if a lesser creature dares to take them from him. Dares to trick him and swipe them from right from under his nose." Res arched a brow. "This isn't picking pockets. This is dangerous."

"I know that," Lusa said, uncrossing her arms, crossing them again. "But it's important."

He flicked the coins, one at a time, and they burst into sparks until he was left with only the real one between his fingers as he stared right into her and asked, "Important to whom?"

She frowned at him. "To Theodore, obviously, and to his friends. Who are in danger."

"And not us." Res's expression remained detached as he swung himself up to sit, so much so it made her stomach roll, and not in a good way.

Her gaze ticked across his features—the hard line of his jaw, the set of his shoulders under his blouse, the cant of his head, the lazy way his eyes hooded.

He was lying, she realized. He was acting, putting on a show and playing the part of blasé, heartless cad.

"You care," she said. He raised a brow, the mask still in place, and Lusa shook her head. "He's your friend. And I care about this because I want to help them. And because this is the chance I've been after for years—to do something that matters—and since you care about me, you care about that too."

"Caring doesn't override practically, sweetling," he crooned at her. "And you can't do this without me, so I'm not sure why we're still talking about it."

"Because you're afraid and you won't admit it, that's why," she bit out. Res rolled his eyes and smirked at her, but he stood as he did, and she didn't miss how he turned his scarred side away from her, so she went on fast before he paraded out more excuses. "Ever since that night, you've been a shadow of yourself. And I haven't pushed, because I care about you, too, and you needed time to heal, and I get that.

"But after you did that girl's wish . . ." She smiled, she couldn't help it, recalling the joy she'd seen on Res while back in his element, performing at the center of attention, using his magic to bring wonder to the people around him. "I thought you'd come back to me. But you didn't, not really. You're still hiding behind your disguises, pretending to be something you're not."

Res scoffed, his expression flaring with anger, but she'd take that fire in his gaze over the apathy any day. "And what, pray tell, does the ever-observant Lusa think she sees, hmm? Since you're so wise from your shadows?"

Lusa lifted her chin, ignoring the barb. "You're being anyone but yourself, because if you're *you*, you have to face that you're afraid to live like you did before."

"And you don't suppose there's a good enough reason for that? No?" He all but snarled at her as he tore at his shirt, and for a second, she didn't understand what he was doing—*why was he getting naked*—but he only pulled it off his left side, revealing his arm, the top of his shoulder, the scars wrapping all the way around to the bottom of his shoulder blade on his back. "They pulled pieces off me, Lusa, and it will never come back. They took from me. *Diminished* me."

"Gods, Res, it's just scars," Lusa said, her voice pitching higher. How could he not see? "You're still beautiful with them and you're still amazing, why don't you see that?"

"It's not just the scars," he ground out, turning his back to her as he wrestled his shirt back in place and buttoned it. "It's my magic. What they took from me, it's my magic too. I *am* less. Each feather they cut off me makes me . . . less."

*Oh.*

She clutched the feather she kept tucked under her shirt, wishing now more than ever there was some way to give it back to him. All the way, to fix whatever scar it came from and return the piece of him they'd stolen that night.

Lusa's eyes burned, and she didn't think, she just threw her arms around him, pressing her forehead between his shoulder blades.

"Res, I'm so sorry. I didn't know. I . . . I'm sorry I didn't . . . I didn't get to you sooner."

"Don't do that, please." Res turned, and she was consumed in one of his bruising hugs as she sniffled, his chin on the top of her head. "I won't have you taking this mess on your shoulders, sweetling. The Ques hunters are an awful bunch of fuckers, and nothing they've done is your fault."

"Your magic is still amazing, Res," she whispered. "I know that bag had lots of feathers in it, but I've watched you for years, and when you performed for Lils and her village, it might have been the most lovely moment I've ever seen you make with your illusions. You're magnificent, you know? You're still *you*. And you are, and always will be, great."

He sighed, hugging her even tighter and resting his cheek against her hair. "I don't deserve to have you around, you know? I'm insufferable on my best days, and my best days have been few and far between. For a bit there, after my wounds healed, I wasn't sure what came next, if anything at all. But then I thought, well, at least there's dinner with Lusa." He chuckled. "Because if I didn't join you, you'd ask Wags for nothing but dessert for every meal."

Lusa laughed, pulling back at bit to wipe her cheeks and mock glare at him. "That was just for like a week. I really liked that candied walnut chocolate cookie recipe, okay?"

"I know." He shuddered dramatically. "I'm not sure I can ever eat walnuts again." Then Res grinned down at her, a flash of white teeth and charm, and Lusa blushed a little despite herself. She cleared her throat and pushed back from him, rubbing her nose on her sleeve. His face fell slightly, his voice barely a whisper. "I'm terrified, Lusa. I'm terrified of what would happen if they find me again and I'm not so lucky next time."

When Res traced the scar under his eye, Lusa grabbed his wrist to stop him.

"Being scared is okay," she said, and she meant it. She'd been scared a lot over the years for a lot of reasons. Some of them never went away, fears that curled deep in her belly and bones and liked to crawl to the surface at the worst times. "Don't let it stop you from living. Besides, I'm not asking you to do this alone. We'll do it together, just like we've talked about."

Res hummed. "We've talked about stealing from dragons before, have we?"

"No, but we've talked about using our skills to figure out how to do something important."

He lifted a finger. "To be clear, *you've* talked about using *your* skills for doing something important. I'm just here for the show. And the company."

Lusa rolled her eyes. "So that's a yes, then?" When Res grimaced, Lusa beamed at him. "Sounds like a yes to me." Res groaned, flopping back on the bed, all very, very dramatic, but it definitely wasn't a no.

# Chapter 13

## Four Months Later

Getting to northern Spain proved pretty simple, and as they began a pilgrimage of sorts on the winding pathway leading to the summit of Mount Pindo, Lusa poked her head out from the window curtains as Wags rolled along.

"Did they really make a cobblestone path the entire way up the mountain?"

"Appearances suggest as much. When one demands yearly offerings, one must make sure they can be delivered," Res mumbled from up front.

Lusa hummed and went back to taking in the sights as they kept on at a really slow pace in the very long line of locals bringing offerings for the festivities. So far, she'd mostly kept herself from the shadowlands, given the single file line, and it was nice to let Wags's windows down and curtains back for the coastal breeze and fresh mountain. They'd decided to play the part of meager travelers hoping to win a coveted spot as one of Bartholomew's entertainers, and as such, Wags kept her insides modest once they'd joined the caravan line.

They never bothered with maintaining oxen to pull the wagon, even though it suggested bigger magic at work. Enchanted wagons and other vehicles weren't that uncommon, and beasts of burden were expensive to upkeep. Wags still had the seats up front for a teamster who would drive the theoretical animals, which was where Res sat now, arms and ankles crossed, his feet propped up as he feigned disinterest.

Lusa knew he was nervous, and it got worse once they reached the base of Mount Pindo. How would he be by the time they reached the summit fairground and he had to perform? She bit her lip; she could try to distract him more, but idle conversation seemed to annoy him more than help since they'd joined the caravan. Not that she blamed him; if anyone happened to look over, they'd see him talking to himself. She'd stayed inside Wags for that reason, but then he'd started complaining she was giving him a neck crick when he turned to listen to her chatter, so she'd given him a break.

Kiki had plenty of questions anyway. As they slowly, monotonously, made their way along the paved trails, Kiki whirred about all the flowers and trees, and nearly burst from the window when it saw a peregrine falcon swoop overhead. But Kiki got bored eventually, too, and went to practice cat things by pretending to nap with Tick on the kitchen shelf.

So Lusa peered out the front window again, to where Res reclined with a straw hat, of all things, pulled down over his face, pretending to nap too. He'd dressed himself like a farmer, probably to avoid attention, but that had backfired on him spectacularly.

She wondered if the family in front of them tried to talk to him again, and couldn't help a wide grin. They were pig wranglers from the south edge of Bartholomew's influence, and the cart lumbering up the cobblestone path in front of them was laden with adolescent swine. A pair of boars pulled the cart, and if Lusa had to guess, they carried magic in their breeding because they were absolutely huge. The family had been friendly to Res, and chatty, especially the first day they fell in line, especially the two kids, who were fascinated by Wags's pretty woodwork. The family had satyr blood, or something similar, as they all had goat legs and cloven hooves.

"No company this morning?" Lusa asked. About a dozen pig faces poked out of the cart, snuffling and biting at any branches in reach.

"Mercifully, they've been quiet for most of the morning," Res mumbled from under his hat. "Everything smells like pig shit, though." He canted his head her direction, glaring at her while keeping his face hidden. "If you'd told me we'd spend two days winding up a damn mountain behind a cart filled with pig shit, I'd have told you no. Wags would have told you no. Her wheels must be drowning in feces by now, gods." Res let out a little whine, like he was in physical pain, and Lusa laughed.

"You're such a baby," she said, still giggling. "I'll clean the wheels for her when we make camp. And they're nice people; don't be mean."

"Lusa, dearest girl, nothing, and I mean no amount of magic or otherwise, can expunge this aroma."

"You're also a snob."

He waved a hand. "And the sky is blue and the grass is green. Can I sleep now? Or try, at least." He grumbled something about being afraid to fall asleep with his mouth open.

"Could be worse?" Lusa offered, and the look he gave her set her off laughing again, but his lips twitched before he turned away with a huff.

Sunset neared as they finally crept toward the summit. Lusa nudged Kiki, who came bounding over to the window, wagging its tail in a decidedly *not* cat manner, and Tick ignored her completely. After watching the landscape shift with open sprawling approach, Lusa moved to the front of Wags and slapped Res on the back of the head.

"Ah, menace!" He caught his straw hat before it tumbled away, glaring back inside the curtains. "What was that for?"

"We're almost there. Less pouting, more looking," Lusa said and pulled the curtains shut in his face, abandoning the small front window in favor of the picture window Wags opened up for them as their travels progressed.

Lusa had seen a few different places in her short life, starting with the flat, icy expanse of the subarctic. Her parents lived in far north of the Coalition of Creatures, on a parcel reserved for indigenous human tribes and various native animals from before the Aperien Event. She'd never gotten the chance to learn much about her Inuit roots, being as her blind mother moved off to live alone with her tariaksuq father so he wasn't constantly being shoved into the shadowlands when people saw him. After her mother died, years after her father vanished and never came back, Lusa tried staying around her mother's village. She talked through walls and windows to her aunts and uncles and cousins, but none of them wanted to make space for her. She was a reminder of her mother; first, her abandoning her family unit, and secondly her death. Or a reminder of Aperien elements the Inuit tribe wanted to live without.

It was one thing to be invisible. It was another thing to be invisible when people knew you were there and didn't like having you around.

Lusa wandered through different regions in the CoC for a few years, but nothing really appealed to her. Lots of stuff was pretty—she saw mountains and forests, lots of forests, and green for days, but it was all empty, at least when it came to the connection Lusa didn't even know she searched for at the time. She'd passed through the Eastern Seaboard Conjunct, which was crowded and way too bright and loud when she wasn't edged to the shadowlands, so she snuck onto a rare boat making an ocean crossing and eventually ended up in the Velvet Emporium.

Sensation seekers tended to be a little more open minded. She ended up having some pretty interesting conversations with people high out of their minds. And most permanent residents of the Emporium who weren't workers were reasonably affluent, so she didn't feel as bad stealing. And then she met Res and things changed, and she started traveling based on his whims.

So Lusa had seen some places, experienced a few different landscapes, and all that stuff.

The summit of Mount Pindo at sunset though, overlooking the Death Coast, a sharp crescent of beach hugging brilliant blue waters, with the World Serpent's bleached spine curving up into the clouds and back to the sea in a huge arch? With the dimming sun turning from sharp gold to shimmering bronzes and flaming oranges?

What a view.

And that didn't account for the crazy rock formations. Giants, they'd been called before the Aperien Event. She'd read about them in her worn-out 21st century travel guide and map. All the rocks were smooth granite from the rain and sea winds, unlike the jagged snowy peaks in the cold north of the Coalition. Every now and then, they rolled passed one that looked particularly person shaped, with a square body and round head, and Lusa swore there were arms carved into the sides, but they were all natural formations.

It was weird, too, how this natural place, once considered mystical when magic was just myth, now served a powerful Aperien's needs and wants. A cobblestone path paving what was probably once a difficult hiking trail, wide enough abreast for wagons and huge beasts, was just the start.

Lusa tore herself away from the sunset side to take in the summit

itself, including the rebuilt castle and all the extraordinary mechanisms awaiting them. A pagan queen kept a castle here once, later a
fortress, and much later grounds for warfare and looting until a once
prominent palace had been reduced to rubble.

No longer.

This Bartholomew had transformed the ruins at the peak into a
new world wonder, and Lusa couldn't tear her eyes from the spectacle.
Tomorrow was Saint Bartholomew's Day, but Lusa wondered how
much this place shone all year round.

The castle glittered, gold from towers to foundation stones, almost
blinding in how it caught the setting sun and the shifting sky. At this
altitude, it also captured the Storm Belt to the far east, dappling the
faceted, metallic surfaces in a kaleidoscope of deep purples and shivering slivers as the lightning continuously flashed miles and miles away.
Archways made of the same gilded stone flanked the cobblestone road
as they rolled closer to the courtyard, which was already crowded with
visitors of all stripes and colors. They unpacked their goods, bartering
between one another and taking turns depositing their offerings on an
enormous golden dish in the middle of the flattened pinnacle.

"Shiny, shiny, shiny!" Kiki chittered beside Lusa, jumping up and
down like a maniac.

"Yeah, it sure is," Lusa said, her mouth sour.

How could this dragon possibly need *more* when he had a home
like this already?

Wags jolted slightly as she turned, rolling them out of the line and,
Lusa noted with a laugh, away from the pig cart. She almost teased Res
about it, but there was a separate section of the courtyard marked off
for entertainers vying for the month-long entry.

Lusa wrinkled her nose; she really didn't like this Bartholomew. All
she saw so far was a greedy bully who used his power to take from

others who had less than he did, when he already had more than enough.

Well, taking one bird from him wasn't something she'd let herself feel guilty about, she decided. Especially not when it was helping people in trouble.

Cold crept up against her back, and Lusa sighed, tugging shut the curtains as Wags parked. A young woman from the neighboring stall peered curiously in their direction. A few seconds passed, and the colors bloomed again as the shadowlands faded away. Kiki whirred in disappointment, but didn't argue, as it already knew the importance of remaining unseen. Lusa could disappear, but Kiki could not unless she was wearing it, and they were about to risk the attention of a very greedy Aperien. A philosopher stone-fueled sentient clockwork creature with magical alchemical powers seemed just like the kind of thing this Bartholomew guy would want to take for his hoard.

Muffled voices sounded from outside; Res, she recognized, making small talk with their new neighbors, but he excused himself after a moment and stepped inside, closing Wags's curtains behind him. It wasn't the first time Lusa was thankful that despite being made of fabric, once Wags shut her doors, they locked to outsiders without magical means to break her natural warding. They didn't have to worry about any sort of casual break-in.

Lusa put her hands on her hips and couldn't help but grin at him. This was the first step, but they were here. And it was all a little exciting, wasn't it?

"Well?" she asked him.

Res tossed his straw hat on Wags's kitchen table and tussled his hair, currently an unremarkable brown. His handsome features pinched, and he sniffed the air once, before he said: "Pig. Shit."

# Chapter 14

Early the next morning, before dawn, Lusa set off to explore a bit, always more comfortable sneaking around during those in-between hours, with less people up and about. Silly, maybe, but when the air was cooler, and dimness left the world muted, she felt less like an outsider when her back was up against the shadowlands. She left Kiki with Res, Wags, and Tick, not entirely sure yet what they'd be dealing with in terms of the gathering.

The cuélebre everyone came to entertain and worship, as far as Lusa understood, wasn't fancier than any other dragon. In fact, it seemed to her as if his monumental greed was really the only thing exceptional about him, and that was saying something considering most dragons were hoarders by nature.

Lusa skirted the entertainer's plaza, not interested in watching the tributes pile up. Instead, she set to scope out Res's competition, but she was a bit taken aback by how little there was of note.

She felt terrible thinking it, but this was nothing like the Baker's Hills festival, or even the Velvet Emporium performers, and really, why would it be? They were competing to give a month of their lives to serve the whims of a spoiled Aperien. The celebration for the Baker only lasted a week, and there was no contest about the performances, only a general adoration for the woman who protected Portugal and its people since the Aperien Event. As for the Emporium, every day was a party of some sort, be it theater or music, or the saucy displays of the historic Red-Light District. Everyone was welcome, no matter blood or territory, be it to peddle their meager talents to escape from their daily lives, or just a chance to see something incredible beyond mundane struggles of survival.

Lusa sighed; she hated the elitist mindset, that the Accorded Territories were somehow better than everything else, but disliking the truth didn't make it less true. The Baker's Hills was a rare success as an Independent, largely thanks to the isolation of the Iberian Peninsula and both the Annwn Queensland of the pre-Aperien United Kingdom and the Emporium's distinct lack of interest in aggressive expansion.

Power got more power, and more power led to more control, and for better or worse, in their world, that control kept magic from running wild and, in turn, kept Calamites, deadly creatures, and chaos generally in check. Outside of this unique stretch of old Europe, most areas outside the Accorded were untamed, dangerous wildlands that few ventured into and fewer returned from alive.

And then came Aperiens like Bartholomew, who took advantage on the fringes.

Lusa wrinkled her nose, shivering as she circled the campfires, tents, and various temporary setups, wondering if she should cool her thinking. Really, she didn't know anything about this Aperien, and even if she thought he was a jerk who took advantage of others, assumptions wouldn't get her anywhere. Tomorrow, she'd meet him—because Res would win a slot without blinking, she was sure—and they'd spend their month underground in his company. No sense deciding she was going to hate every second of this more than she needed to; besides, wandering around a huge treasure hoard was bound to be filled with all sorts of adventure, right?

Lusa grinned as she watched a young man, no older than herself, practicing his juggling. He was pretty good and had a flare for making the balls shine and jingle in a melody. Whatever small village he'd come from would miss him if he got selected, no doubt appreciating him far more than this dragon ever would.

She bit her lip; there she went again. Lusa might as well get back, she decided, because there was no competition to warn Res about she could determine, although he could probably use the threat to stir up his puffy ego. And maybe replace the fear that Res performing again would end with daggers slicing off his feathers.

She cut through the plaza's center this time, firelight muted and smells distant, watching the families huddled around their meals, smiling and laughing and drinking, already celebrating. Other pilgrims had already come and gone, and despite the general wastefulness of the offerings, in Lusa's opinion, everyone seemed happy.

Maybe the cuélebre really did protect this region, despite his heavy-handed tributes. Lusa hummed. She wasn't sure how, if he never left his gold pile. He must have minions; he could certainly afford to make his entire castle on the Mount Pindo summit, which stood empty year-round aside from these few days, totally golden.

She smirked as she sidestepped a woman carrying tankards to her fellows, laughing as she slipped. Lusa caught her elbow and steadied her before she fell, but she was too drunk to notice the touch. She only laughed and went on her way.

Lusa ignored the little pang in her chest. She'd gotten spoiled by all the casual touches with Res, not that she'd go back to how things were before.

Well, she would, but only if it meant Res never got hurt, of course.

A voice caught her attention, whispered and harsh, as Lusa headed toward Wags.

"—make it in this year, I'm sure of it. This has to be the place, we've tracked 'em. No way it's a mistake."

Curious, Lusa did what she did best. Keeping herself in the line of sight of a few nearby visitors chatting over their meal, the shadowlands held her back as she leaned closer to the tent.

Another voice. "We're going to be rich. Richer than this dragon. All you gotta do is look the part, eh boyo?"

A snort sounded further in the tent. "Yeah, all they ever want, right? Quick flighty fucks, all of 'em."

"Ques are always fancy fuckin' boys, them pretty dandies." One of the men laughed. "Never sure why all the ladies like those girly men so much."

Lusa forced herself to exhale when she realized she'd been holding her breath.

"Well, we get this score, and we'll be set up for life, you get me?"

She backed away a few steps, torn between listening more, getting more information, and running back to Wags as fast as she could.

Because these were Ques hunters, right here, within close reach of Res, after she'd talked him into coming here and promised him this would all work out.

A gong sounded, followed by the shrill sound of underused gears grinding to life, and Lusa stepped out of the tent's shadow as the gilded castle on the summit split it half, opening the belly of the mountain to the sky, signaling the festivities to begin.

She had to warn Res.

# Chapter 15

I t took all Lusa's willpower not to run from the spot. She needed to see these men so she knew exactly who was after Res. A few seconds wouldn't make or break things, right? The men inside the tent, the Ques hunters, already moved, cursing and stumbling over each other at the gong.

Music followed, muted with the shadowlands against Lusa's back, as people ran from every direction to the plaza center, where the gilded castle opened to reveal the entrance of Mount Pindo and all the glory within. They cheered and screamed, the neatly organized campsite descending into complete chaos within seconds.

Apparently, Bartholomew liked to keep people on their toes, because she was pretty sure he wasn't supposed to emerge for another hour. Lusa hoped Kiki was safe inside Wags and Res was already on his way toward the center of this mess. For now, the best she could do was get her look at the hunters, then bully her way through the crowd and count on her nature to get her to Res far faster than the hunters could.

What if they were dusters? What if they were Aperiens? Who knew what kind of powers these hunters might have.

She hugged the tent, reaching the entrance as the four men burst out. None of them were armed—no one was supposed to bring weapons into the festival proper, so she was certain they had their evil knives in the tent—and all but the fourth wore dark leather armor and were tall and thickly built. Two had red eyes, one had curled horns coming from his forehead, and the third had a twisted, forked tail. Demon blood maybe? Lusa didn't know. Nothing really stood out, but she'd seen enough she'd recognize their faces.

The fourth man, however, left her confused because he was dressed to the nines as a performer, and if she didn't know better, she would have pegged him as trying, and doing a poor job, to impersonate Res. Peacock feathers, tight-fitting pants, heavy makeup. His hair was obviously dyed, a passable green similar to Res's natural color.

His eyes, however, gave him up. Res's eyes had always struck Lusa as unique, with their color banding of emerald green and crimson, dusted with gold sparks. This man's eyes were green, but entirely unremarkable. Nothing like a Ques, if all Ques had eyes like Res did.

Why, though? Why would a hunter dress like a Ques?

"Let's go," one of the bigger men said, all but shoving the dressed-up guy forward. "We get lucky and this will be quick."

Right, it didn't matter why. Get to Res, *that* was all that mattered. Steeling herself for a lot of bruises, Lusa took a deep breath and sprinted toward the central plaza and the mass of bodies.

Being short let her duck elbows and dart under arms, but she had to shove by people and shimmy through gaps in very impolite maneuvers, over and over. Her skin chilled, and Lusa winced each time she shouldered by someone and they yelled at the innocent person behind them or beside them, ignoring how she had to step on feet or elbow people in the ribs to get by faster.

She nearly fell a few times, especially when people tried to keep others from pushing ahead, and the crowd got tighter and tighter the deeper she went. The music was still loud despite the shadowlands at her back, which meant it must have been deafening, but everyone cheered and thrashed, and for a few seconds, Lusa got lost in spectacle when she chanced to look up.

The castle was entirely open now, spread like a vast golden flower opening to the sunrise, the morning light gleaming and refracting in prismatic rainbows. Even with her dulled senses from the shadow-lands' hold, it was a wonderous sight, and it just got better as the first of Bartholomew's entourage emerged. They were entertainers; that was clear from first blush. The crowd erupted when fireworks flashed and banged, and a dozen people draped in golden sashes and bells and feathers burst into dance as a huge platform crested from within the parted mountain.

And behind them, the dragon. The cuélebre, Bartholomew, in all his glory, lounging on enormous pile of silken cushions, a makeshift throne, and he was easily ten times the size of Res in his Ques form. Instead of feathers, though, he was all hard gold scales, and a pair of wings unfolded like sails, fluttering in the mountain breeze as their own sunrise. He lifted his serpentine head, opened his maw, and breathed a plume of fire two miles long across the blue sky.

The crowd went nuts.

Lusa nearly lost her footing as she tore her attention from the drag-on and scanned for Res, catching brief sight of a shock of emerald hair near the platform. She almost laughed; she would have if she wasn't out of breath from struggling through this mess of people, because of course he would have put himself in the best seat and shown up early. It was so very him.

And it was going to make it that much harder to get to him.

Luckily, Res was off to one side of the open castle, probably because he could stand up on a ledge to make himself look taller. Give himself head and shoulders above the crowd. She smirked; she knew him a little too well, maybe, but he was her best friend.

*Only friend*, tugged at her mind, but she shook the thought away because it was silly, not true, and really not important right now.

At least if she was having this much trouble digging through the massive mob, those hunters would be worse off. And they couldn't just grab Res in broad daylight, right? Or maybe they could. Who would notice one person hauled off in a crowd like this? And who would care, with everything going on? While everyone was distracted?

She shivered, wishing she could feel the heat from the dragon's fire as he bellowed again, his deep, thrumming voice speaking Spanish, no doubt welcoming everyone to his not-so-humble show.

Lusa darted through a gap, trying her best not to shove anyone off balance, and finally got a good look at Res, who was fine. He was really fine, actually, and to her surprise, he was talking with one of the dragon's performers. That was odd, because the rest were all the still dancing, most throwing flowers and ribbons and treats into the crowd.

Both men were up a few steps now, Res in all his finery he'd laid out the night before, the first time she'd seen him since the Baker's Hills in all his bells and whistles. His hair was brightened and streaked with silver, matching his feathered hat, silver skintight trousers, and bright green blouse which, of course, hung half open to show off his bare chest, splashed with glitter. Res threw back his head and laughed, really laughed, as he clapped the man's shoulder, and they both looked out at the crowd with huge grins.

Lusa almost tripped over her own feet.

Res's new friend had the same color eyes. Bright, beautiful and unique, that emerald splashed with crimson she'd never seen anywhere else, complete with gold specks catching the sunlight. The dragon's performer was just a few inches taller than Res but with the same long and lithe build, and completely bare aside from a loincloth and a lot of gold and red body paint.

Lusa's cheeks warmed. Gods, they were both gorgeous, and it was only worse with them standing right next to each other. The man laughed again, then leaned in close to whisper in Res's ear, and his cheeks flushed.

She blinked a few times, cold in the pit of her stomach, realization setting in with ugly, insistent fingers. Res was coming back to himself, which meant these last weeks, where they'd shared all their time together, just them, were coming to end. As soon as he was confident enough to perform, he'd be back to his other ways too. Dancing between beds and lovers, living life to the fullest.

Lusa couldn't take her eyes off the pair, how easy they talked to each other, how they leaned against each other. How they touched without any hesitation or awkwardness. The interactions effortless even though they'd met seconds before. It was just who Res was, without his trauma, a beautiful bird who was always meant to soar.

Definitely not hang out in backwater towns with an invisible girl.

She shook her head, once, so hard it hurt.

What the hells was wrong with her? It wasn't like he was going to throw her out just because he was himself again. Gods, they'd been friends for years, and he'd gallivanted around entire towns, and it had been great. Maybe no goodnight hugs now, but whatever, she'd be fine, and he'd be great and . . .

But . . .

Why did it feel so bad?

Because she was being a selfish jerk, Lusa thought with a huff, taking both hands and smacking herself hard on the cheeks twice.

Bigger problems. Ques hunters.

Her eyes widened.

Ques hunters.

*Ques* hunters.

And if that was a Ques standing next to Res, maybe they weren't hunting him after all.

But that only meant both of them were in danger, right now.

It also created another problem, but she'd have to deal with how the hells she was supposed to steal from Bartholomew when one of his cronies could *see* her, but first she had to make sure said dragon crony didn't get skinned alive for parts.

There, she realized, right behind Res, was a section of the castle which wasn't connected to the moving pieces. It wasn't much more than a few pillars which dropped off near the granite stone face, but she was small enough to tuck herself behind there, and hopefully that would be enough. And she could get Res's attention, and they'd figure something out.

She hoped.

If he wasn't too distracted by his new boyfriend.

"Get a grip," Lusa scolded herself, then grunted when a big duster almost knocked her off her feet, drunk as hells, and his elbow hit her ribs so hard the air whooshed from her lungs. She ping-ponged between a few people, another elbow catching her in the face, and she hit the ground *hard* on her knees.

For a second, she couldn't see anything but the ground, legs, and dust. Her head swam, and she grabbed at anything she could—boots, ankles, legs—but confused glances before people shuffled on was all she got. She even called out, but it didn't matter. Lusa was cold, invisible and alone, underfoot. Something hit her face, the world wobbling. She squeezed her eyes shut, wheezing. Gods, was she going to get trampled? A girl shrieked, tripping over her, hard, and crashing down next to her with a cry. Lusa reached out, try to help her when she cursed and looked down at her scraped hands.

Feet hit Lusa again, then more shins banged against her legs and her bruised ribs, two more people tripping over her body and hitting the ground before enough people noticed and starting helping each other up. No one helped Lusa, of course, but it gave her the opening to scrabble to her feet, holding her side as she swung wide, limping, back to where the masses thinned and the golden plaza tiles faded to normal cobblestone.

By the time she made it around, scaling boulders on the outskirts of the plaza, she was wheezing and her vision was spotting, but she just had to *get away* and the shadowlands finally let her loose, so now the sounds and smells were a deafening cacophony that made her nauseous. Her nose was bleeding, and so were her knees and her hands and elbows, and her entire body ached from head to toes.

She could almost hear Res reminding her this was all her idea in his teasing tone, and she managed a choked laugh as she struggled over to the plaza's far edge and hauled herself up over a few more rocks with a grunt. There seemed to be unspoken rules that everyone stuck to the cobblestone or else. Lusa had no idea what "or else" might include, but Ques hunters and what they might do seemed worse than any or else, so she kept going. Her palms stung, her nails shredded between falling and climbing, but she finally hauled herself up to the first of the pillars and ducked behind it.

Lusa peeked around to confirm that Res and his friend were still there, not being cut into pieces with their feathers ripped out, so she hid again and rested her head, which throbbed incessantly as she tried to catch her breath. She closed her eyes, needing just a few seconds, but that was a bad idea.

The night in the Baker's Hills choose right then to come flooding back in full sensation.

The vivid fear at seeing Res hurt.

That emerald sheen of his blood.

The way it mixed with the blood of the man she'd killed, rushing out into the muck.

The horrible sounds Res made as he came back to awareness.

That crack when the man's head hit the tent spike.

Lusa's eyes flew open, finding the blue sky instead of that moment she'd lived over and over in her nightmares. Her hands were numb and cold and shaking, but the shadowlands were nowhere near her.

But she'd face all that again and more if hunters tried to hurt Res. She could be strong. She could deal with nightmares. She could deal with bruised ribs and a few scrapes right now.

She could *not* deal with losing her best friend.

Grunting and trembling, Lusa pushed to her feet and stumbled between the pillars, keeping her gaze locked on Res's back. And the other Ques. They kept talking, watching Bartholomew, the show, the crowd, and thankfully didn't turn around as Lusa collapsed, tucked safely out of view, behind a pillar two back from the plaza's edge.

"Res! Hunters!" Lusa shouted, throwing her voice so it mixed with the crowd's direction, hoping he'd be able to guess her general direction. Then she peeked around the pillar's edge.

She couldn't look long, couldn't risk getting caught, but she managed a glimpse of Res's tight expression: A mix of fear, fury, and determination, but instead of running, he grabbed the other Ques by the shoulder and ducked them both behind the closest pillar, one in front of Lusa's hiding place. He spoke hushed and quickly, the other Ques blinking in surprise, then his expression growing hot with anger before he said something sharp to Res, and then he was rushing off toward the dragon's platform.

After a few seconds, Res called out quietly without turning. "Lusa?"

"I'm here," she mumbled, closing her eyes with a huff. He was safe, so she could relax, at least for the moment. Then she grinned; she couldn't help it. "And look at you, after being so worried you were scared."

"Jokes later, sweetling. Now, what do they look like? Guatemoc said he's going to get some muscle."

"First name basis already?" Lusa tried to keep her voice even, not sure what she was feeling exactly, but it wasn't pleasant and her head really, really hurt now that she was sitting still. Curiosity still got the better of her after she rattled off a description of the hunters. "Is he really a Ques too?"

"Seems as such, yes." Res hummed. "To think I've gone eighty-seven years and never met a hunter or another of my bloodline, and now here we are, with the proverbial flood."

"I thought they followed us here, but maybe they're after him?"

"Hard to say, though Guatemoc didn't seem shocked by the threat, but rather angry, so perhaps he's dealt with them before. We'll know soon enough. There now, he's headed back over with more friends."

Lusa managed a peek, and sure enough, loincloth-clad Guatemoc strode in Res's direction, flanked by two intimidating men covered in dark scales. They both looked like some sort of dragonkin, but nothing like Bartholomew's golden visage.

"Res," Lusa whispered before they got too close, "this is going to be a problem. He'll be able to *see* me. What the hells are we going to do?"

"Well, you wanted a challenge, didn't you? Too easy wandering the backwater hills, was it?" Res said, and she could hear the grin in his voice.

"That is not what I said!" she hiss-whispered as she heard him shuffle to his feet.

"Show must go on, and all that? Unless you're quitting on me now?"

"Of course not."

"Then for now, stay hidden. From here, we improvise."

# Chapter 16

Lusa stayed out of sight easily enough—at least Guatemoc's, as he led the two henchmen tearing through the crowd to round up the Ques hunters. She'd made her way halfway back to Wags, leaning against a cart now, buried behind a few barrels, when the celebration came to an abrupt halt.

Bartholomew roared, and Lusa felt the reverberations under her heels. People gasped in a mix of wonder and horror, the performers ceasing and the music cutting off. In front of the gilded litter, where the cuélebre rested on his massive pile of silken cushions, Guatemoc and the dragon dusters dragged the hunter group roughly to center stage. By this point, the morning sun heated the mountaintop granite, the entire plaza a giant cooker.

Lusa winced, rubbing her forehead, her vision swimming under the harsh light. She wondered if she had a concussion, but as Res said, the show must go on, right? She sunk down on her butt, thankful for once to have the shadowlands cooling her heated skin.

She couldn't make out the conversation at the dragon's feet, but the Ques hunters were shoved to their knees, protesting as Bartholomew uncoiled himself, two dozen feet tall, his maw a snarling tangle of razorblade teeth as he spoke.

"These hunters come, threatening those who would seek celebration, to steal and maim those of blood much more worthy than their own. None," the cuélebre bellowed, "threaten those on and under my mountain, and those who dare shall pay in the old ways."

It happened so fast, Lusa might have blinked and missed those massive jaws coming down on the first man—the one who dressed fancy like a Ques performer—and biting off the entire top half of his body in a bloody burst. The cuélebre's taloned claws came down next, pinning and shredding two more hunters, as the last struggled to stand, and with a bursting billow of white-hot fire, they were all reduced to little more than ash swirling on the morning breeze.

Silence followed, weighted and thick, the crowd captivated, horrified, mesmerized? Lusa had no idea; she couldn't parse her own feelings. Bartholomew let out another jet of fire, clearing off the rest of their remains, and the executions were over with any evidence gone.

"We are most fortunate to have bravery among those in attendance this day," Bartholomew went on, as if his teeth weren't flecked in blood, as if five deaths didn't stain his hands, and he gestured with those red-touched claws to his left. Guatemoc stepped forward, and at his side, was Res. "Resplendent, a magician come from the French countryside to perform for a coveted seat under the mountain this year, put aside worries for himself to protect all of those attending today."

Res was hesitant; Lusa read it all over his posture. He hadn't expected being pulled up on center stage as a reward for his troubles, but he covered his hesitation quickly, offering the great golden dragon a deep bow.

"He has more than earned his place in my halls for the coming month. He, and he alone." The dragon canted its giant head to Res, then glared over the murmured disappointment rippling through the gathering. "But this day is not done until the sun sets, my many friends. Dance, drink, and celebrate. To another prosperous year."

The music strummed to life, the dancers burst into a new routine, and within seconds the crowd had forgotten that the Aperien they celebrated had just killed five people—no trial, no verification, no questions asked.

Lusa's stomach reeled, a nasty taste on the back of her tongue.

What if she'd been wrong?

No, they'd been clear. They were hunting Ques, even if it wasn't Res, and she'd seen the horrors of Ques hunter work firsthand. No way she'd stand by and let them hurt anyone.

And holy hells.

They did it. They were in. They'd gotten inside Mount Pindo, a step closer to finding the birds of truth and helping Theodore's friends.

Granted, they had to deal Guatemoc being able to see her, which would making stealing from the dragon's hoard a whole lot harder, but they were in.

And there, up on stage, Res laughed and danced with Guatemoc before casting an absolutely beautiful trio of dragon-shaped illusions through the crowd, which exploded into thousands of sparkling petals.

Lusa grinned. She hadn't seen Res so happy since the stage in the Baker's Hills, before that terrible night crashed down around them. Maybe this whole thing would be just what he needed after all.

She winced as she stood. For now, she needed to get back to Wags and get some ice.

Wags was the most magical thing to ever exist, *ever*.

By the time Lusa dragged herself back and ducked inside the door curtains, she was two seconds away from falling over. Between exhaustion, her aching body, and being so overstimulated from the day's events and the massive crowd, she was about to explode or collapse, or both. As soon as the curtains swished shut, the noise outside faded to nothing and Lusa sighed. Wags had a knack for only letting in and out the sounds she wanted but making sure they never missed anything important.

"You're the best," Lusa mumbled as she patted the wall and toed off her dusty boots with a groan. Both Kiki and Tick jumped down from the kitchen shelf and raced to meet her, the actual cat yowling for dinner while Kiki chattered and whirred like crazy.

"Shiny dragon! And dancing! And music!" Kiki chirped like a manic, jumping up and down when Lusa bent to pet Tick, unable to hide her wince. Kiki immediately stilled, miming sniffing as it inspected her knees. "Lusa hurt?"

"I'm okay, just a few scrapes. I have good news though!" She laughed when Kiki stood up on its hind legs, ears, wings and tail all twitching. "Res got us into the mountain."

Kiki trilled, bounding around the room, bouncing off the table and chairs, shelves and counters, and Lusa could swore she felt Wags groan as its claws chittered across all the fine wooden surfaces. Tick huffed and wandered off, far too dignified for all this nonsense, clearly. Lusa laughed, then winced again at the ache in her ribs, her head, her everything.

"Res will be a bit, probably until all the celebrating calms down. I'm going to clean up."

Kiki crashed to the floor by her feet, shadowing her down the narrow hall as she tossed her dirty coat on a kitchen chair and made her way to the bathroom, limping a little. It whirred, observing her with narrowed red eyes. "But bleeding."

"I'm okay, Kiks, really. I'll patch up after my shower, no biggie." She waved Kiki away, not wanting company in the shower. They had a few early conversations about modesty, but the little clockwork creature still didn't fully get it, especially when Tick wasn't always held to the same standards.

Lusa stalled as she looked in the bathroom.

"*Oh my gods*, Wags, I love you."

Their modest shower stall was nowhere to be found, replaced with a copper tub filled to the brim with steaming water and bubbles that smelled like lavender.

Lusa hadn't intended to fall asleep in a perfectly sized bathtub with bubbles that never ran out and water that never cooled lower than perfectly hot, seeped with some sort of Epsom salts that made her muscles all gooey, but by the time she came to, it was almost sunset.

She listened for a few minutes, but Wags was utterly silent inside, still muffling the party outside, evidenced by the flashing fireworks lighting up the partially opened window curtain. She had no idea if this affair lasted deep into the night, but at some point, they'd make a big show of the dragon going back underground, with Res in tow as a reward for outing the hunters.

"Thanks for the bath," Lusa mumbled over a yawn, pulling herself up and toweling off. "I feel a lot better." Her head still ached, along with all the scrapes and bruises, but her muscles were much less sore. Hopefully, come morning, she wouldn't feel like she got run over by a mob. She smirked as she left the bathroom, and dug up an old shirt from her clean clothes. It was baggy, big enough she wore it as a nightgown, and she tossed it over it her head. She needed to clean and bandage her knees at least before she got dressed the rest of the way.

She stopped at their storage room, rummaging around through their medical supplies, which had been greatly diminished after Res's attack. Lusa hadn't replenished everything yet, so they mostly had local remedies and the like, aside from a single bottle of healing tonic with a few doses left. Lusa left it on the shelf; this was nothing a few bandages and a poultice couldn't fix.

Supplies gathered, she settled at the kitchen table, where Tick slept on a hot pad designed for keeping tea warm. Wags had a second one set up, a cup of medicinal tea awaiting Lusa, along with apple slices and a hard-boiled egg. Kiki was back at the window over the kitchen sink, watching the festival with a swishing tail.

"Thanks again, Wags," Lusa said, plopping down on her butt and propping up her feet. Her legs were bruised already, up and down with ugly mottled red and purple, but the cuts had mostly stopped bleeding. She had just popped an apple slice in her mouth and took up a clean cloth when Wags's door curtains swung dramatically open and Res burst inside.

He turned back almost as fast, laughing as he hung half out, half in Wags's doorway. "Yes, just a bit. I need to make sure my cat didn't get out before we move the wagon, and change clothes. Half an hour?" Lusa couldn't hear the response, since Wags was muffling outside sound. Res gave a bow and another laugh. "Thrilled, certainly!" Then he dropped the curtain and spun around with his arms out wide.

Kiki raced down to greet him, running around his feet in a circle. Res danced a little jig as Kiki whirred its giggle-noise.

"Kiki did you see the show?"

"Yes, yes! So shiny! So pretty!"

"Yes, isn't it? Amazing!" Res threw back his head and laughed again, tossing his hat and his jacket across the room, completely missing any sort of target and sending a burst of multi-colored confetti and glitter everywhere. His smile was ten miles wide, his brilliant eyes so bright they shone like multifaceted gems. And his hair was a right mess, smeared with paint and gods only knew what else.

Lusa could only grin around her mouthful of apple as she took him in. He was a marvelous, beautiful, happy mess.

He looked like Res. The Res who had been lost and hiding for months.

She had no idea what the hells was all over his shirt—smears of gold, red, silver, and pink—and gods, she wasn't sure if she should wish for paint or some sort of food or wine for Wags's sake. He pulled scents from outside with him in a hurricane. Firework powder, smoked meats, and more flowered scents that Lusa could parse, and so many spices, yet it all came together in some sort of wonderous, melodious mess that was just *him*.

And Res was so sweaty. Lusa snorted; he'd probably been performing and dancing for hours now, and he looked ridiculous and out of sorts in the best kind of way.

She tapped under her eye, speaking with a full mouth. "Your mascara is running, party animal."

Res snorted, then gave her a flourishing bow, flipping back his messy hair when he stood. "Can you believe this? Only us, Lusa, the only invite inside the mountain for this . . ." He trailed off with a blink, and all the mirth and joy drained from his expression.

What replaced it made her blink in return several times as he took her in, head to toes, before scowling, a hot, primal fury she'd never seen darkening his features as he strode over to her chair and knelt in front of her as she scrambled to sit up straight.

"What are you—"

"Who the fuck did this to you?" His warm palm caught her chin, tilting her head to examine her face: the black eye, the bruised and cut forehead, the split lip. "Did those hunters put their gods' damned hands on you?" His gaze flicked down her body. "High holy hells, your legs. Your hands." He snatched both her wrists, examining her palms. "Lusa, answer me. What the fuck happened?"

She blinked again, taken aback by the growl lancing his words, the absolutely fury in his gaze when it snapped back to her face.

"No, nothing like that." She tried to pull her hands back, but he didn't let go. He was staring into her in a way she wasn't used to. Sure, he could always see her, but this was different. This was . . . she didn't know what this was. Lusa cleared her throat. "It happened when the crowd got rowdy. I tripped and so did a few other people, and it took a second to get my bearings."

Res closed his eyes and huffed. "You mean you got trampled because no one could see you to help you up."

"It wasn't that bad."

It was kind of terrible honestly, but it was over, and she was fine, so it didn't really matter.

The look he gave her told her he saw right through her, but then his expression softened. "Why didn't you say something, sweetling? I've been out there for hours." Res scoffed then, shaking his head. "Sit back." He surveyed the table, her supplies, then *growled* again. "Where in the hells is the tonic?"

Lusa rolled her eyes. "I don't need a healing tonic for scraped knees, Res. That's for emergencies." He ignored her and strode down the hall, returning with said tonic a few seconds later. When he reached for a cloth, she snatched it from him. "I'm serious."

"So am I," he snapped, jerking the cloth back from her, which made her hiss, her hands still raw. "Shit, I'm sorry."

He set the cloth and the tonic on the kitchen table, and Lusa made a strangled little noise when he grabbed her face in both hands, his nose almost touching hers.

"Now, you listen to me, Lusa girl. That tonic is good for bruising as well, and I refuse to have you running around sore and looking like this," he looked up and down her body, then pointedly at her face, "when I have the means to fix these hurts, especially when I know you likely bullied right through the middle of that mob to get to me as fast as possible when you saw those hunters, because you were concerned about my safety more than your own. Now, please go ahead and tell me all about how wrong I am—*lie to my face*—and I'll go put this tonic right back."

Lusa considered doing it, because this was all ridiculous, but she'd never seen him quite so serious. His cheeks were flushed, and now that he was so close, she realized he didn't smell the least bit like any sort of booze.

He was upset she was hurt, that she'd gotten hurt on his behalf, and he wanted to make it better. Still, she blinked dumbly at him for a few seconds, because she'd gotten used to his hugs and casual touches, but *this* touching was something else entirely. This felt . . . intimate, and now she was blushing, too, and couldn't find her words.

"Please, sweetling," Res added, his voice barely above a whisper now, all the harshness gone. "You nursed me back from the brink of death, and then insanity, for months. This is barest shadow of what I might do to attempt to return the favor." He closed his eyes and rested his forehead so gently against hers, his skin soft, warm, and flushed. "I can't stand the idea of seeing you hurt."

Oh. Her cheeks were even warmer now. And she was feeling fluttery. Everywhere, especially in her tummy. And awkward. And it was hard to swallow, her mouth was so dry, but she cleared her throat and managed, "Well, since it's all about you, sure."

Res laughed, a bit of mischief back in his expression. "As long as we're on the same page."

He let her go and rocked back on his heels, and it felt like the sun felt out of the sky.

Res tossed her a wink, his cheeks still pink, but his smirk was back in full force as he waved a hand at her in a very imperious manner. "Now sit back, not like we have all night for this nonsense. And no whining, mind you. Or bleeding. I have a weak constitution, as you know."

Kiki jumped on the kitchen table, almost knocking over the tonic, and the moment's tension snapped.

"Menace!" Res hissed out, but Kiki only stamped its little golden paw.

"Fix Lusa!"

Res softened a bit, but still flicked Kiki on the nose, which set it into a flurry of mock cat hisses right back at him. "Yes, that's the plan, now shoo."

"And then what?" Lusa asked, eager to move away from whatever all of *that* was. She wasn't sure she could handle thinking about it.

Res grinned up at her as he gently applied the tonic on her shins, the cool drift of low-level healing magic sinking into her skin, making her sigh. His eyelashes sparkled, she noticed, and she hadn't been lying when she told him his makeup was smeared, but he wasn't a bit less handsome right now, seated at her feet, taking care of her.

Her throat was tight again, but Res distracted her when he drawled, "Oh, well, nothing much, besides riding the big golden lift down into the giant mountain of treasure with the enormous golden dragon in, say, twenty minutes or so."

# Chapter 17

Lusa almost forgot all the complications that came with the cuélebre, the mountain, and the fact they were planning to steal from said dragon's mountain, because she got a little lost in Res rubbing all her hurts better. She ended up half-slumped in the chair, eyes closed, tea empty, with Tick purring in her lap while Kiki rested its head on her shoulder.

Especially because Res held her face now, gently petting the tonic-infused cloth on her bruised forehead. Looking at him felt weird, so she'd closed her eyes.

"Are we going to be late?" she mumbled. "You're taking forever."

Res hummed. "Almost done, don't fret."

Then her eyes shot open, because they had very real things to fret about.

"Res."

He arched a brow. "Lusa."

"*Res.*" She grabbed his wrist and sat up, dumping Tick on the floor. He landed on all four feet, gray tail thrashing before he sat down to clean his paw like nothing happened. "If Guatemoc is a Ques like you, he can *see* me."

He let out a little puff. "Did you hit your head harder than you realized, sweetling? We already established this."

Right, they'd talked about it for like two seconds when she told him about the hunters, right after she'd been trampled, and then all hells broke loose, the dragon ate said hunters, and then everyone partied while she took a nap.

Lusa wrinkled her nose; what the hells even was her life right now?

"You don't think that requires a bit more conversation than 'we'll improvise?'"

Res hummed. "Probably."

"Probably," she deadpanned back.

"Probably after we don't keep the esteemed Bartholomew waiting by delaying his celebratory descent back into the mountainside for the coming year?" Res practically crooned at her as he dabbed the cloth on her split lip.

She winced, then grabbed the cloth from him and slapped him away, everything about the moment way too confusing to have him touching her *mouth* while he cupped the back of her head and sat so close, all but kneeling at her feet with that worried expression for her, while they talked about another person being able to *see her* when they were supposed to be stealing from a very powerful Aperien.

Res held up his hands in surrender as he rolled back on his heels, then stood.

Lusa kept the cloth over her mouth, even after the tonic sealed the cut, because it also covered most of her cheeks, which were burning hot right now. "Can you not be a smart mouth for thirty seconds?"

"Ironically, I'm not," Res muttered as he glanced at the old-fashioned cuckoo clock above Wags's stove. "I'm expected soon, and I need to change."

"You don't think—"

"We're in over our heads and possibly careening toward disaster?" He tapped his chin. "As a matter a fact, I do and we are, but I can't very well trot back outside and say, 'Well, no thank you, I don't think I'll accept your wildly exceptional offer to be the exclusive entertainer for a month-long engagement under Mount Pindo for the famed cuélebre Bartholomew because my invisible friend and I are were planning to raid his coffers, but we can't now that we have a pretty good chance of getting caught?'"

Res canted his head at her, lips pursed, and when she grimaced, he said, "I thought not," and headed for the bathroom.

He returned in less than five minutes, cleaned and changed, his hair damp and slightly curled around his shoulders, buttoning up his shirt as he stalked back into the kitchen. Res's expression was cool now, calm and collected, without a trace of his earlier sarcasm. A few wrist flicks, and he was adorned with an illusion in place of his usual makeup.

He'd said half an hour when he'd ducked into Wags, Lusa realized, and he'd used all that time to carefully treat her bumps and bruises instead of getting ready to perform. No wonder he seemed out of sorts now; he didn't get nervous before he took the stage, at least not before the attack, but he'd told her before he liked the quiet time to prepare before he slipped into his role of performer. Part of that process included donning his costumes.

"Sorry," Lusa muttered.

Res dusted off his hat. "For what?" He examined the feathers, fluffing them as he glanced at Wags's doorway curtains. When she didn't reply, he glanced over at her, and she shrugged. He lifted his chin. "For partaking in this whole mad idea to begin with?" He tucked the hat on his head, the peacock feathers glittering as he offered her a roguish smile. "Just promise me you'll make Theodore write a very flattering article about my untimely demise for the Archival dossiers."

"Res, that's not funny."

His grin was extra toothy. "I know." He paused, his sigh very dramatic, even for him. "One thing at a time, Lusa. Get in, then we'll figure out how you'll avoid Guatemoc for a month."

They shared a look; easier said than done, and they both knew it, but Res was right. They couldn't back out now.

"But you're well now?" Res asked as he pulled on a different coat, this one a dark navy with thread the color of starlight.

Lusa rolled her eyes. "I was fine before you started babying me."

"Then get dressed. No telling what we're in for, and better not to be caught flatfoot or barefoot." His gaze darted pointedly at her feet, but then took a rather slow drag up her bare legs, which was when Lusa realized she'd been wearing nothing—literally nothing—but her baggy T-shirt nightgown this whole time.

Her cheeks flamed and she jumped to her feet, pulling down the hem even though it nearly hit her knees. "Yup, got it," she mumbled and fled to her room.

It didn't take long from there, Wags moving with a lurch as Lusa stumbled from her bedroom in appropriate attire. Not like she paraded around Wags half-dressed or anything on a normal day—that shirt was for sleeping, private, in her room alone—or that she dressed up to impress Res—why would she even begin to bother when he was his own walking fashion show?—but something about being caught, then tended to, half naked and not even wearing underwear, and not noticing, left her dizzy and out sorts long after Res stepped outside.

Maybe she did hit her head harder than she realized.

*Focus, Lusa.*

This plan was about to get very dangerous, because any minute, they'd descend. Kiki scaled her shoulder, careful with its claws, and perched when Lusa settled by the window overseeing Wags's empty oxen tethers. They rolled through the crowd, Res leading the way as he walked with Guatemoc, their backs to the window. Even so, Lusa felt the shadowlands at her back as people watched their passage, curious more than anything. Enchanted transportation wasn't so rare that Wags moving on her own would draw suspicion to her greater gifts.

Ahead, the golden dragon lounged on his litter, tail slapping like Tick when he was bored, the gilded plaza cobblestones alight with sunset colors.

"Pretty, pretty," Tick chirped in her ear, and Lusa patted its head in agreement.

They rolled and bumped along, taking a left that put them off to the side of Bartholomew's throne and where the dancers performed, which Lusa knew put them square on the moving platform, soon to sink into the mountain. What she could make out of the open castle glimmered in reds, coppers, and brilliant orange, twinkling like fiery starlight. When Wags parked, Lusa was careful not to move the curtains, and the shadowlands receded so she could really take in all the colors.

Wags let the sound in now, too, and there was a lot of grandstanding about how important Bartholomew was, how prosperous the region was under his protection, and how satisfied he was with this year's offerings, *blah blah blah*. He droned on a in deep, echoing voice, but the crowd seemed entranced by him, and Lusa wondered if he pumped magic into the air to make people like him so much when all she saw was a greedy, powerful Aperien who had no scruples when it came to doing whatever he wanted, including murdering people in broad daylight.

And they were about to live with him for a month.

Peachy.

If Res could hear her thoughts right now, he'd remind her this was her idea.

Res stood among the dragon's entourage, once again called forward and thanked, touted as a valiant hero worthy of reward. Then they rolled the big cornucopia of more stuff the rich dragon didn't actually need onto the platform, and the entire mountain shuddered.

Lusa felt more than heard the gears grinding, being they were directly on top of whatever kind of massive mechanism opened and closed the entire mountain top, and within seconds, they were sinking, faster and faster, enough that her stomach swooped with the acceleration. Wags's top opened with a moon roof, and Lusa gawked as the massive castle folded itself closed in an origami masterpiece of stone and metal before shutting out the sky and casting them into total darkness.

It only lasted a few seconds before the stone walls started glowing, some kind of bioluminescence or enchantment? Lusa heard voices outside Wags, a handful of conversations happening at once, and she couldn't really pick much out, beside the occasional deep, resonant rumble of Bartholomew speaking. The platform didn't speed up more, just fast enough to scare Lusa, and by the looks of it, Tick, too, who arched up and fluffed out up on his shelf.

Kiki, on the other hand, was having a blast, all chirps and whirls and wiggles, so much so Lusa had to kick it off her shoulder before it maimed her with its claws.

The lights got brighter the deeper they went, and after about five minutes, they slowed. Lusa swallowed a few times, wondering exactly what the hells they were walking into, and peeked out the windows until she found Res. He stood on the side facing the dragon, arms crossed with his back to Wags as he spoke with Guatemoc, their heads leaning in close. She kept the curtain drawn, peeking through a tiny gap.

Bartholomew, for all his fanfare earlier, looked bored out of his mind.

They came to a gentle stop, mechanisms hissing and gears clattering, echoing through what sounded like huge chasm. Lusa shivered. Outside, all the cuélebre's people were already in motion, heading off in different directions, gathering up items strewn about. The two large fellows who'd captured the hunters wheeled the giant offering bowl out of Lusa's view to gods only knew where. Res and Guatemoc shook hands before he patted Res roughly on the shoulder, all smiles and genuinely welcoming. Res grinned back, his cheeks flushed, but Lusa read the tension in his posture. Then Guatemoc motioned toward Bartholomew before saying he'd see Res at dinner and heading off.

The noise died back after a few minutes, Wags dropping her muffling magic completely now that they weren't being assaulted from all sides by noise. Lusa pulled the curtain back a little further, but as far as she could see, no one else was left on the platform but Res, Wags, and Bartholomew.

Res cleared his throat and took a few steps forward, then stalled when the dragon shifted form.

All dragons, as far as Lusa understood it, could assume a humanoid shape. It seemed like a universal trait, even if the mythos of a particular dragon didn't allude to shapeshifting. Enough of them did to make it a thing.

The vast serpent body faded into a fine, swirling mist, the entire thing a bit anticlimactic for how big the cuélebre had been, and without so much as a pop or a fizz, a man a good head taller than Res stepped down from the pillow throne and toward her friend. Lusa tensed, peeling back the curtain to see him better since they were only ones here now and his attention was fully fixed on Res.

Bartholomew spread his arms in welcome. "Resplendent, Resplendent, I've been looking forward to meeting you properly."

Res gave him a bow, a clean one without all the fancy flourishing. "The feeling is more than mutual. And please, Res is just fine."

Lusa studied Bartholomew like she always did when people couldn't see her—unabashed staring, taking in all the little details. Aside from being tall, he was broad, and every inch of his exposed dark tan skin was covered in golden tattoos. Tribal, almost, but the edges were squared instead of sharp, and she didn't immediately recognize any of the designs, except for angry faces in the mix. He wore a tunic that fell to his knees, and sandals, but those words did a poor job describing the regalness of his attire. The weave was impeccable, the patterns intricate, and the colors a bold mix of metallics and deep crimson. His hair was dark as a starless night, swept back in a tight knot, and his eyes were the color of sunlight, a deep molten gold.

Bartholomew stopped close to Res, not shying away from his personal space but not touching, drinking Res in. "You saved a man's life up there."

Res chuckled. "Who, me?"

"No need for false modesty. You could have run and spared yourself any trouble. Guatemoc said you told him the second you saw them in the crowd."

Almost the truth. Lusa was the one who found them out and told Res, but who was keeping track, really? She smiled a bit as she studied this dragon in human skin.

He was an original Aperien based on the mythos surrounded Mount Pindo, and it showed. There was power in the way he moved, the deep tenor of his voice, how he didn't cast himself as a dewy youth. He wore a face of maturity, with laugh lines and wrinkles, and confidence squared broad his shoulders.

Lusa really hoped they got out of here without royally pissing him off.

"I had a run-in with them some months back," Res offered, "and I wouldn't wish that on my worst enemy, let alone a fine gentleman who even might be my kin."

"Oh, he is your kin," Bartholomew answered. "Quetzalcoatl only had two sons." He crossed his arms over his barrel chest, his expression amused now. "That would make anyone one with Ques blood a brother, a cousin, or a nephew."

"Gods." Res laughed. "That's a strange thought."

Bartholomew inclined his head. "I'm sure you'll have more questions at dinner. A private affair, to begin in a few moments. I'd like you to meet my inner circle."

"Yes, of course. Did you have anything specific in mind for tonight's performance?"

"You misunderstand me, Resplendent, although I did put on a show for the masses. It's what they come for, after all. You're not here to dance for me. I want to thank you, properly, for seeing to Guatemoc's safety. He's been with me for near a century now, and acts as my right hand."

"I . . . see."

Lusa could tell by his tone, Res did not see. She squinted, leaning further forward, wishing she was just a little closer so she could make a better guess at if Bartholomew was being entirely genuine.

The dragon's gaze flicked to Wags.

No, not to Wags.

To the window. She must have moved the curtain.

Then Bartholomew smirked. "First, though, I need to know who the Eskimo girl is."

Lusa froze, stock still, because the air remained warm. The shadowlands were nowhere to be found.

# Chapter 18

A heartbeat passed, then two, before Res glanced over his shoulder at Lusa, his eyes widening in a way that would have been funny if the situation wasn't *the dragon can see the invisible girl* before turning back and saying, "Oh, her."

Another beat passed and Res huffed. "Sorry, in all the flurry, proper introductions completely slipped my mind." Improvise, he'd said. Lusa's heart was in her throat, and she couldn't move, couldn't breathe, as Res waved a dismissive hand in her direction. "That's Lusa. She's the help. My help. My, well, travelling companion."

Lusa cringed, because the warmth was leeching from Bartholomew's expression as he stared *into* her, and as Res was the only other person who'd ever seen her, really seen her, Lusa *didn't know what to do.*

"I'm a terrible mess," Res added. "She cooks, she cleans, does the laundry, runs my books. Keeps house and the like. Gods know I'd never remember to feed the cat." He cleared his throat, tossing another glance over his shoulder as he leaned closer to Bartholomew in a too-loud stage whisper to add, "And of course, nocturnal entrainment."

Lusa blinked once. Twice. Three times.

She was going to kill him.

Wags would help, she was sure of it.

Somehow, she kept the murder off her face, mostly because *that* was the statement which took the Aperien's expression from suspicious to smirking, then laughing. A loud laugh, the rude kind, really, given he followed it up by mumbling, "To each their own," before patting Res on the back like he deserved some kind of award for having sex with her.

Her cheeks were so hot, they hurt.

She was going to extra kill Res and feed him to Tick.

Never mind, Tick didn't deserve that.

When Bartholomew added, "Bring her along then, we need to lay the ground rules for your stay. I assume she knows your nature since you didn't take issue with her eavesdropping on a private conversation?"

Lusa blushed further, because she hadn't even tried to be subtle. Gods, she'd been starting at Bartholomew like, well, like he couldn't see her.

"She's a trusted confidante," Res said, his tone serious now. "She saved my life when the Ques hunters found me." He eyes found hers and held, giving her a small nod of encouragement. "But if you'd give us just a moment, she isn't used to being in the spotlight. Lusa is quite shy."

"Five minutes, no more," the dragon said, and it wasn't a suggestion; it was an order. Whatever dinner plans Bartholomew had, Res was expected to attend, and now, so was Lusa. And Guatemoc, she assumed, who suddenly wasn't their biggest problem.

Imagine that.

Bartholomew gestured forward, where the solid mountain stone cut out into a massive hallway behind the big fancy pile of cushions he'd lounged on all day as a dragon.

"Center hall leads to the receiving area; first left is the dining hall.

Don't keep me waiting." And with that, he strode away, his heavy footfalls echoing through the antechamber of the mountain's hollow center.

Res didn't hesitate, inside Wags's doorway in seconds, the curtains swishing shut behind him. Lusa tugged the window curtains shut, too, though Wags would shelter them. And then she just stared at Res while he paced the kitchen, glancing at the clock as he ran a hand over his face.

Her mind was a hurricane, battering her thoughts in impossible circles inside her skull.

"We'll have to tell him," Res mumbled. "About your nature. Who knows who he'll have at the dinner. We can't play it off if half the table can't see you."

"You . . ." Lusa started, clenching and unclenching her fists.

Res stopped, eyebrows high. "Me?"

"Did you really just tell him I'm your . . . your . . . *wagon slut*?" she blurted, her voice ending in a shriek.

Res opened and shut his mouth once, and then a slow, smoldering grin spread across his lips as he leaned against the wall and crossed his arms. "Wagon slut? I'm pretty sure I said no such thing, but it *does* have a fancy sort of ring it, doesn't it?"

"You!" Lusa sputtered, kind of squeaked, and Res grinned wider.

"Yes, sweetling, me, indeed."

She let out a shriek and grabbed the closest thing—an empty teacup—and threw it at his head.

He ducked, barely, and it shattered behind him against Wags. The entire wagon shuddered, both of them stumbling and catching themselves on the kitchen table. Tick yowled and hissed, racing down the hall and disappearing. Kiki, who'd been silent since they'd arrived at the bottom of the mountain, abruptly changed into its box shape.

Lusa sucked in a breath, her eyes stinging, and she flattened her palms on the table. "Sorry, Wags. I'm sorry."

"Lusa," Res started, and when she glared up at him, his expression was much less assumed. "I was as shocked as I'm sure you were that he saw you. I—"

"Improvised. By calling me your *nocturnal entertainment*." When he flinched, Lusa pressed both palms to her face and groaned. "You seriously couldn't think of anything else? Anything?"

He caught both her wrists and tugged her hands off her face. "If you recall, I also said you wash my clothes."

When she snarled, he laughed and pulled her into a tight hug. She punched him in the ribs, kind of, then just sort of slumped against him and mumbled, "Gods, I hate you sometimes."

"I did say you're my trusted confidant, so surely I didn't muck things up entirely."

"The dragon king things I'm your wagon slut, Res," she muttered against his shirt, and he laughed again.

"Oh, come now, surely there are worse things. In case you aren't aware, I'm quite the catch."

She shoved away from him, and he let her go without a fight, his expression still mischievous. Lusa decided it was better to ignore the fact that they were lucky Bartholomew actually believed Res was lowering himself to sleep with someone like her, given his comment about taste, and hadn't asked more questions. She turned away so Res didn't see her grimace.

This was entirely outside her wheelhouse. She never had to deal with people judging her from a look. Finding her lacking at a glance.

It felt better being invisible.

"Shame you weren't in that frumpy T-shirt," Res chortled as he cleaned up the broken cup. "Granted, I'd never wear something like that, but it could have passed very nicely as the perfect casual garb thrown on after a quick wagon romp."

Lusa closed her eyes.

If they didn't die trying to steal from the dragon's hoard first, she was definitely going to kill him.

"Remember," Res said, his arm slung over Lusa's shoulder as they walked down the stone hall, through the receiving room—which wasn't much more than a hollowed-out rock chamber with a natural spring and some nice chairs—and toward the dining room, as instructed. He was leaning down, closer, his warm breath tickling her ear. "I'll do the talking. We don't know what we're dealing with, so honesty is the best move here, as much as we can. Given he has the birds of truth, and if he hasn't forgotten they're buried in the basement, let's avoid outright lies as much as we can."

"Got it," she mumbled. "So we tell the truth about what I am, what you are, and we came here because you're trying to get over your stage fright after being attacked by Ques hunters."

"There's a good wagon slut," he murmured.

Lusa elbowed him hard and stopped walking.

"Don't do that, Res, it's not funny." She couldn't look at him, and her stomach was a wreck. "I'm nervous enough thinking about people seeing me, let alone thinking that on top of seeing me, alright? Just . . . don't."

Genuine concern flashed across his handsome face, his brows furrowed as he studied her. Then he gave a sharp nod. "Apologies, I won't joke about it again."

They resumed walking, which didn't leave much time, and she was fidgeting. A lot. She never had a fidget problem, or really hadn't cared if she did, because no one would see anyway.

"Anything I need to know?" Lusa asked.

"About what? You know as much about this place as I do. More, as I'm certain you paid more attention to Thedore's prattling on than I ever do."

"No, not that. I mean being at a dinner with other people besides you."

"Ah." Res glanced down at her, frowning again, and she didn't like that it felt suspiciously like pity.

"Never mind, I'm just being stupid."

His hand came to rest on her lower back, gentle and warm. "You're not. But do chew with your mouth shut."

"Gods, Res, you—"

"Don't stare like you tend to do, even at those who can't see you."

Okay, that was a good reminder.

"Otherwise, let me be my boorish self, and it should help keep most of the attention off you." Res canted his head, something flitting across his expression, something dark, then it was gone as he added, "And don't take any drinks you didn't see poured at the table."

She wanted to ask why, but they'd arrived. Res took off his hat, swept it in front of him for her to go first—good manners, she knew, something a gentleman would do, and Lusa could barely contain her relief when his hand found her lower back again as they walked into the dining room.

The ceiling was tall, a split of quartz and granite with burning braziers hammered into the mountain at styled increments. The table was also stone, black slate polished to a reflective shine, and it was covered to bursting with food and drink. The scents were rich, decadent, and Lusa couldn't help licking her lips. Another natural spring ran in the room's far corner, a twisted moss-covered tree growing toward an enchanted orb of sunlight.

Bartholomew sat at the table's head, comfortable in a finely carved seat, but it wasn't nearly as ostentatious as the throne he'd brought up to the mountaintop. While the room was fancy, regal almost, it smelled stuffy, like they didn't use it often.

*They* included Guatemoc, at the dragon's literal right hand, who was deep in conversation with another duster next to him. He was similar in stature and looks to Guatemoc but dressed modestly in plain slacks and a loose-fitting tunic, his head shaved. Guatemoc had lost all his fancy paint, and he'd chosen an ivory shirt with golden thread and matching pants, his bare feet resting on the table's corner.

Three other men sat at the table as well, backs toward her and Res, and there were two empty seats by Bartholomew's left side. The chairs didn't quite match the set, so she assumed they'd been brought in for her and Res, and that these five made up the cuélebre's inner circle.

Guatemoc saw them first and surged to his feet. "Ah, the man of the hour," he canted his head, and Lusa was struck at how the motion and his curious smile reminded her of Res. "And a friend?"

Guatemoc moved around the table to greet them properly. Everyone turned, the entire room focused on their entrance.

She sucked in a breath when she realized the man at the furthest end of the table was hideously scarred, but that wasn't what drew her attention the most. He wore a cloth blindfold as he half smiled in their direction.

Lusa stole quick glances down the rest of the table, remembering not stare so she wouldn't look like a weirdo to the people who could see her, waiting for the awkward conversation about *what friend* and then *what's a tariaksuq* to be done and over with.

That was when she realized she was sweating.

Because the shadowlands weren't at her back, chilling her skin and her bones, because everyone in this room except the blind man could see her.

# Chapter 19

Lusa wondered how bad it would be if she fainted right now. She must have projected how she felt enough, because Res's hand shifted from her back to hold her elbow.

"Yes, this is my traveling companion, Lusa." Res said, his tone imperious as he gestured toward the empty seats. "Might we sit before we continue introductions?"

Guatemoc flashed his brilliant smile, and if he thought anything of the request, or Lusa, he didn't show it. "Of course. Have a seat, and I'll get the wine while you all get acquainted."

Lusa arms and legs were numb as Res tugged out the chair as she'd watched men do for ladies a thousand times, and plopped down so he could push her in, blinking down at the fine dishes and silver cutlery, and a napkin folded like a crane.

Res sat heavily beside her, making her startle, and said, "Bartholomew, again, thank you for hosting us. This place is a wonder." He spoke as he leaned back, taking in the sparkling wall and ceilings, the faerie lights, all the little bits of magic making this underground cave nothing short of fantastic.

Lusa felt like the walls were closing in to crush her to bits.

"You're welcome, again," the dragon said, chuckling as he reclined as well, glancing between them as Lusa concentrated on blinking and breathing. "I took the liberty of filling in the rest of our company on your actions at the summit today."

"We're grateful," the man directly across from Lusa said, the one who'd been chatting with Guatemoc when they'd entered. "I'm Coz-catl, but everyone just calls me Oz." He was more serious, Lusa gathered, than Guatemoc, and when he looked to Bartholomew, he nodded. "I'm also a Ques, so you did me a solid as well in getting rid of those bastards."

Lusa blinked a few times, wondering if she was just blind or foolish, but now that she really looked, she noted Oz's eyes were darker than Res's and Guatemoc's, but they had the same swirled coloring of emerald, crimson and gold. The colors were a touch more subtle, making it less obvious from a distance but undeniable up close.

Guatemoc trotted back over and popped the cork on a wine bottle and started to fill her and Res's glasses with a grin.

"No shit," Res mumbled, then laughed. "All my life, and now two in one day. What are the odds."

"Low," the man besides Lusa rumbled. When she turned on him, he shrugged. Like both Oz and Guatemoc, and Res, in fact, he had darkly tanned skin and was unnaturally handsome. Lusa squinted.

Same eyes.

"Is everyone here a Ques?" she blurted out. "Well, except me, obviously." She was a woman, so of course she couldn't be Ques. "And Bartholomew."

The man beside her inclined his head. Unlike the others, he wore a simple set of robes, and the sleeves were stained in paint. His hair was long, braided, each cord a different shade of brown. "No, not exactly. I'm Pollock, and behind me is my brother, Matthais."

The brother leaned forward, and he was a carbon copy of Pollock, but she knew at a glance he was far less serious. His hair was cut short, spikey all over the place, and colored a bright purple. "Mommy wanted us both to be painters, but alas, only Pollock here got the gift. Even my stick figures are ghastly."

Matthais shuddered dramatically, and Lusa grinned; out of all of them so far, he reminded her the most of Res. Especially when he leaned across Pollock, who grunted in protest about being shoved out of the way. He took her hand and kissed the back of her knuckles. "But you, pretty little thing, you can call me Matty."

Lusa couldn't help blushing a little bit, even if she recognized the over-the-top flirting routine from Res. "Are you all like this then?"

Pollock shoved Matty back into his chair as he laughed and asked, "Like what?"

"Hopeless dramatics?" Guatemoc suggested as he filled Lusa's glass, then Res's. "No. As you can see, Poe is a stick in the mud. And Oz is grumpy at least half the time."

That got a laugh around the table, but Lusa only nodded, leaning around so she could see the last person at the table, who sat quietly, head canted to the side as he listened. Despite the extensive scarring, Lusa could tell he'd been just as handsome as the rest of the Ques around the table.

Then she frowned, because she'd assumed he was a Ques, but if he was, and had those scars, then . . .

"Ah, the inevitable, uncomfortable quiet," the blind man said, dabbing his mouth with a napkin, his voice a gentle roll compared to the rest of the room. Easy on the ears, and obviously not one for competing with the rest of the noisy gathering. "My name is Erandi. And yes, I am also, or rather was, Ques as well."

"You still are," Oz grumbled.

Erandi inclined his head that direction. "Debatable, as what makes a duster a duster is the magic in their blood, and with all my feathers gone, I have none."

Silence crashed over the table, almost sticky, and Lusa couldn't help leaning toward Res. Their shoulders touched, and he was trembling. She didn't even think, resting her hand on his knee under the table and squeezing. Res's hand found hers a second later, lacing their fingers together and squeezing back; his palm was clammy with cold sweat.

"I'm sorry that happened to you," she said softly. "That's awful."

"It was," Erandi agreed, although his posture read unmoved given the topic of his personal torture. "But it was a long time ago. No sense darkening this fine dinner when we haven't even gotten to the fun part yet."

"Fun part," Res huffed. "I've just met five other Ques, and I've never had the pleasure." He cleared his throat and untangled their fingers so he could take up his glass in a toast. Lusa almost spilled her wine, and everyone followed suit but Erandi. "To new friends, then, and kin."

Erandi laughed, but took up his glass, too, when he realized it was a toast. The other Ques around the table were all grinning like mad, stealing glances at Bartholomew, who had let the exchange play out without any comment. Lusa glanced at the dragon in his human form, wondering how a Spanish cuélebre managed to collect so many with Quetzalcoatl blood.

Her throat went dry as the rest drank and Bartholomew watched her over the lip of his glass, his expression amused. He raised a dark eyebrow as he set down his cup, his smirk conspiratorial as she took in his eyes, much, much closer now than the first time he'd taken human form out on the descended plaza.

And they were an entirely different color.

Gone were the solid golden irises, a perfect match to the beautiful cuélebre at the top of Mount Pindo. Now, his eyes were shockingly bright in the dimly lit room, stark against his tanned skin and black hair. They nearly glowed, the green outer ring a shimmering emerald, the center spokes closest to the pupil red as fresh-spilled blood. Motes of gold peppered his irises like a night sky.

"I think the little Eskimo has figured it out."

"Inuit," Lusa said as she stared into that eerily familiar yet entirely different gaze. There wasn't a trace of the warmth, kindness and joy she saw every time she looked at Res. What looked back at her now was cold, sharp and she knew without a doubt, far more dangerous than they'd expected.

Bartholomew only hummed, then waved a hand, as if permitting her to speak.

Should she? Was this a test? A trap?

"You said Quetzalcoatl only had two sons," Lusa managed. She glanced around the table. Guatemoc grinned, and Oz covered his mouth. Pollock looked like he could care less, but Matty wiggled his eyebrows, encouraging her. Erandi, down at the end of the table, had gone back to eating. She looked back Bartholomew, because when she asked next didn't really make sense, because he was supposed to be a Spanish Aperien dragon who'd manifested from his own mythos. "Are you one of them?"

"Close," Bartholomew—but not, Lusa knew now—said. "Both of Quetzalcoatl's sons have been dead for some years now."

"Well, fuck," Res muttered.

Matty laughed, jumping over from his seat to smack Res hard on the shoulder, so hard he lurched forward with a grunt. "Yup, half-brother or cousin or nephew, whatever the case might be, say hello to your dear old grandfather, Quetzalcoatl."

The rest of dinner passed in blur for Lusa. It wasn't every day one met a true Aperien god, let alone one in hiding, living under the guise of an entirely different mythos.

This whole day, Lusa decided, couldn't get any more bizarre.

But the story of how Quetzalcoatl came to be Bartholomew wasn't really that farfetched. He didn't speak much about what he'd done or not done before, but once he realized the nature of his feathers and organs in relationship to alchemy, Quetzalcoatl's outlook shifted from "casual Aperien god doing whatever the hells he wanted" to being a little more careful with himself, and by extension, his progeny. Or, in his case, not having any more sons.

One of Quetzalcoatl's two sons, who were both born after the Aperien Event, however, had no such qualms, and despite his desire to protect his kin, more and more Ques dusters came into the world, and by extension, more and more people learned about the universal nature of their parts in dangerous and powerful recipes.

"There were many more like Erandi, locked away to be farmed for greed," Quetzalcoatl said, his tone grim. "I determined to find a solution. A sanctuary, of sorts, where I could keep my grandchildren safe if my sons refused to take responsibility."

What better place than Mount Pindo, home to a reclusive dragon who only left his mountain once per year, never let anyone inside, and had a system in place already to keep precious treasures safe? He'd killed Bartholomew, taken up the mantle, and created a place to protect the Ques.

"I take the tithes to keep up the ruse and do my best to keep the region stable without tipping my hand," Quetzalcoatl continued. "A fearsome Aperien angered by any potential threat to his treasure hoard does work wonders."

"And you're well positioned," Res said. He leaned back in his chair now, his cheeks flushed from drink, the awe having worn down a few notches after a bit more wine and time to digest he sat in the presence of his grandfather. "The Baker holds Portugal peacefully, and the Emporium supports healthy trade lines between. The Queensland hasn't shown any interest in expanding since before the Accords were founded, as far as I understand it."

"Yes, they're very insular," Oz agreed. Lusa got the impression he might be the cleverest of the bunch, aside from maybe Erandi, but it was hard to tell because the blind Ques hadn't spoken again.

He might not be able to see, but Lusa recognized someone who took everything in while he wasn't being closely observed. Which was just another reminder that, as interesting and awkward and fun—at least for Res—as this family dinner had been, they were here to steal from not just a greedy dragon, but a god.

Goodie.

And saying Oz was clever and Erandi might be smarter wasn't to take away anything from the rest of them. If they were anything like Res, the exterior was just that, a surface level illusion, for better or worse, which people easily got lost in.

Good thing for Lusa, she knew Res's nature inside and out.

"Enough about the Ques, though," Quetzalcoatl murmured, as if making his voice soft so he didn't scare away a little mouse. "What about you, Lusa. You're the only one at this table who is an unknown."

He probably did see her as a mouse, didn't he? If he was a god, could he sense things about her? Would he sense the shadowlands if someone else living down here walked in to get the dishes and pushed her back up against that cold darkness? No, probably not. The Ques mythos stemmed from Aztec culture, an ancient Mesoamerican people largely extinct long before the Aperien Event. The Inuit people were few and far between, but from a lot further north.

"Uh . . ." She shifted in her chair, sweating again with everyone looking at her. Even Erandi had his ear cocked in her direction, as if he was suddenly paying much more attention to the conversation. "What do you want to know?"

"What are you?" Quetzalcoatl asked, bold as brass.

And rude, but guess you could do whatever you wanted when you were a god. She glanced at Res, who gave her a weak smile. They'd intended to give as much truth as possible before they walked in this room. Just because everyone could see her right now didn't mean they weren't still in a bind. Dozens of performers had ridden back down on the lift with them. She got the impression Quetzalcoatl kept a miniature city down here, for all he didn't leave.

Lusa scratched her cheek, then dropped her hand to her lap. "I'm a duster, half-human, half-tariaksuq." When no one spoke, clear they didn't know the first thing about her people's mythology, she shrugged. "Shadow people, from Inuit mythos. From the shadowlands."

Quetzalcoatl nodded, the invitation clear for her to expand, but she didn't. She just looked down in her lap, because aside from Res, she'd never talked about herself. She never really talked to anyone besides Res about anything. Just Tick and Wags for years, and they didn't talk back, and now Kiki, and that had only been for a few months and not about *her*.

The rest of the table seemed fascinated, though, so she didn't have to wait long for questions to start.

"Shadowlands," Oz said, rubbing his chiseled chin. "This is a place you can go?"

"Full tariaksuq can, yeah, but not me. I can just kind of," she wiggled her fingers, "brush by it."

"What's it look like?" Matty asked, leaning around the table on his elbows. He seemed younger than Res, but anyone with Ques blood was immortal. And if Quetzalcoatl's sons had been dead a long time, it meant Matty was likely a lot older than her even if he acted young.

"I don't really know?" She glanced at Res, then tugged at her collar. Sweaty. Warm. She wasn't used to this, all eyes on her. He frowned at her, questioning, but she shrugged and looked back to Matty. "I can't really see it, but it just sort of creeps up on me. Makes things feel cold and muted. And dim."

"Sounds awful," Matty drawled, leaning away from the conversation. Pollock shot him an annoyed glance and he said, "What?"

"How do you do it?" Guatemoc asked, studying her closely now, and she felt like some sort of bug. "This morning, I swore I heard someone yell right before Res pulled me aside, but I didn't see anyone."

"Yeah, uh, I was behind those pillar things."

Res's hand came up to rest on the nape of her neck, making her jump. She glanced up at him, surprised to see his expression grim. "She was the one who saw the hunters, because she recognized them from when I was attacked. She came to warn me, even though she'd been trampled by the crowd."

Guatemoc whistled. "You were in the middle of that mess? Tough girl, then. About a dozen people were pulled out for healing."

"Yes, and she had to get herself up and out since no one could see her." Res looked at her rather pointedly, his thumb tracing along her throat in a way that made her feel warm and funny in an entirely different way than the rest of the room's attention.

She swallowed a few times. "Yeah, when people see me, it pushes me up to the shadowlands. Normally, at least. For a full tariaksuq, it sends them home, all the way. Me, I just turn invisible and get cold."

Oz huffed. "Illusion then, isn't it? And we can see you, because

Ques can see through illusions."

Matty chuckled, his voice a throaty purr when he said, "Well, lucky us then, isn't it?" He grinned at Lusa around Pollock's wide shoulder, who didn't look amused at all. Erandi hummed from his far end of the dinner table.

"I am, yes," Res said quietly, his tone carrying something Lusa couldn't quite discern.

Quetzalcoatl didn't say anything, his expression unreadable.

# Chapter 20

"I don't like family dinners," Lusa announced when they finally stepped into Wags after what felt like three lifetimes later. "I need a shower. I've never been so sweaty in my entire life."

Res stumbled into Wags after her, the door curtains swinging shut behind them with a snap. Lusa had never been so happy to be home, even if home was now trapped in the belly of one big fat mess that was getting worse by the minute. A quick survey showed Tick safely asleep on his shelf and Kiki bounding over to greet them.

"Hey guys," Lusa mumbled, sighing as she kicked off her sweaty boots and gave Kiki a head pat. Kiki seemed to sense her unease, sitting on its haunches quietly.

What the hells were they going to do?

No. Nope. Shower first.

Lusa needed to scrub the feeling of so many eyes on her off her skin before she could do anything resembling thinking. When she turned on Res, not sure what she wanted from him, she found him sagged against the door frame.

She frowned and poked him in the forehead. She had to stretch all the way up on her socked tiptoes to reach, and he opened bleary, bloodshot eyes halfway to peer down at her.

Lusa scrunched her nose. "Are you drunk?"

Res blinked once, too slow for a normal person, which was answer enough, before he shrugged. "Possibly. A bit." He squinted down at her, seeming to reconsider. "Yes?"

No help, this one. Not that she could really blame him, considering the day he'd had. All things being fair, it was definitely weirder than hers.

Lusa still rolled her eyes. "I'm taking a shower." She didn't realize he was following her until she reached the bathroom curtain. When she turned, she bumped into his chest. "Um, you aren't invited."

"Hmm?"

Was he broken?

"To my shower, Res." Lusa spoke slow, like she was talking to a small child. Or a drunk Res, she supposed. For all he partied and danced and stayed out all night, Res never came home drunk or high or anything like that, especially when it came to his performances. He'd once told her only fools relied on liquid courage.

Which meant Res wasn't doing well at all, despite being on point during the dinner of a thousand revelations.

"Why don't you sit down or something? We can talk while I shower, just don't come in or anything weird like that." She wasn't sure why she added the last part, ducking inside the bathroom as she spoke to hide her flushed cheeks.

But she swore she heard Res mutter, "Perish the thought."

Lusa waited until she stripped and got under the warm spray—*bless you, Wags*—before she asked him, "Are you okay?"

He took so long to say anything, Lusa wondered if he'd passed out, before he gave her a mumbled, "No."

Lusa washed and rinsed, half-smiling because this was better than him crawling off to his room and never coming out again. "I mean, it was a lot, but you seemed excited to meet some of your family. I know you miss your mom sometimes."

They didn't talk much about family. Res knew the bare basics of her sad story, and he'd never pressed her to talk about it after she'd made it clear she didn't want to dwell in her past. And while Res didn't seem overly bothered his father had never been in the picture, his mother had been a loving human woman who supported his love of performing until she'd passed naturally in her eighties. Her death was the reason Lusa had met Res at all, because he'd been content in his mother's orbit until she was gone, and then he'd taken up travelling. He'd mused more than a few times about if he had any half-brothers out there.

Now, he had at least five possibilities, and if they weren't half-brothers, they were cousins of some kind. Maybe nephews or great-nephews? Regardless, they'd all welcomed him.

Lusa wasn't really ready to think more about his *grandfather*, but there was that, too.

Res went silent again, long enough for Lusa to finish her shower and dry off, then wrap herself up in a towel. She didn't normally do all this naked stuff with Res half-passed out, half-camped at the door; she wasn't nearly as free about her body as him, which was kind of odd, considering normally no one could see her.

Hah.

What even was normal?

She hadn't thought to grab any clothes though, because her brain was mush, she was exhausted, and she was worried about a million things, including the drunk man outside the bathroom. She sighed and wrapped herself in the towel, then pulled the curtain back.

Lusa almost laughed, but she wasn't sure how Res would take it, so she kept it in. He was sprawled on his back, with Tick loafed in the middle of his chest, happy as a clam. Kiki hung back, because it clearly didn't know what to make of the fancy man lying on the hallway floor.

Res stared blankly at the ceiling.

"Wow, do I have to carry you to bed?"

His attention flicked to her, his expression confused, then curious, before a salacious grin parted his pretty mouth. "Well, now, what do we have here?"

She rolled her eyes. There he was. "Never mind, I take it back. Not helping you. Good night."

"Wait, I . . . ouch, *shit*!"

Tick yowled and scuttled off, dipping into Lusa's room and under her bed. She crossed her arms as she watched Res labor to his feet with a dramatic groan.

"I thought we weren't supposed to drink."

"I only advised you not to drink if you didn't know the source of the drink."

"Did you know the source?" When he gave her a sour look, a little green around the edges, she grinned at him. "Oh, come on, I'm not allowed a little fun at your sloshed expense?" She held her fingers out with a tiny bit of space between them.

"Only if it makes you feel better, because I know that little mind of yours," he leaned down and flicked her in the forehead.

"Hey!"

"And it is undoubtedly spinning itself out of control in a merry little panic."

"Is not."

"Lusa, sweetling, I'm drunk, not stupid."

"That's a whole lot of debatable."

"Gods, can we not argue?" Res winced as he set both on hands on her naked shoulders, swaying slightly. His lips pursed, and for a second she thought he might have something important to add, but he instead, he said, "I think I might already be hung over."

Lusa looked down at her bare, damp feet, chewing on her lip.

Because he was right. She *was* freaking out. Pretending she wasn't? The furthest that got them was tomorrow morning, which sounded *fine* until Res needed to corner her about it.

"What are we going to do?" she whispered. "And if you say improvise, I'm going to knee you in the nuts."

Res huffed. His hands stayed on her shoulders, his very warm hands, and he slumped so his forehead rested on her wet hair. "Honestly, not a clue. Guatemoc said he would give us a tour in the morning. A lunch, then another dinner in the early evening, and . . ." He cleared his throat. "Quetzalcoatl asked to speak with me privately tomorrow."

She swallowed. "Do you think he'd just give you the bird? Since you're his grandkid? I mean, he's not Bartholomew, so maybe he doesn't care about all the stuff down here."

Res hummed, stepping back a pace and rubbing his face. "I think it's too soon—and I'm too drunk—to make any decisions tonight. Nothing so far suggests we aren't here for the month, as expected, so we have time."

Lusa nodded. "Yeah, just, I almost wonder if coming clean might be the best idea. They told you the truth."

Res watched her for a few seconds, and she shivered at the cold calculation. She realized she'd seen that same look at the table head tonight. "Seemed a bit easy, don't you think? To trust complete strangers so readily? When we were walking back here to Wags, Guatemoc mentioned only those in that room tonight know the truth."

"At least two dozen performers came back down here with us," Lusa said.

"Yes, and I got the impression a lot more people live down here, almost a small town of sorts, which makes sense attending both Bartholomew and now Quetzalcoatl's whims." Res shrugged then, still watching Lusa a little too closely for her liking, as if he was trying to puzzle something out. Or maybe it was just the alcohol, but then he said, "I understand why he told me. What I don't get is why he told *you*. And until we know, we keep our cards close—including why we came here in the first place, Lusa girl. Agreed?"

Lusa nodded, chilled, even though the shadowlands where nowhere to be found. "Yeah, agreed."

# Chapter 21

Lusa was surprised how put together Res was the next morning, no sign of a hangover to be found. He greeted her with coffee instead of tea, sitting cross-legged at the table next to Kiki, who was alert but still as stone. She took a drink; it was good coffee, because Wags made it, but it was black and bitter and made her grimace.

"Okay, what's the deal?"

"The deal?" Res asked, sipping from his own mug then setting it down. Empty, she noted, which meant he'd been up a bit.

"You're drinking death coffee, you have no makeup on, you're not even dressed fancy—I mean, for you—and Kiki looks so serious I'm not sure if its awake." She poked Kiki on the nose. It blinked once but otherwise didn't move. "What's the deal?"

Res checked his shirt; it was lavender today, which somehow didn't look awful with his hair and eyes, and his pants were gray with nothing for embellishments, and he wore plain, comfortable black boots. He blinked up at her.

"Should I change?"

"Res."

His grin was a flash, and gone as quick. "We need to be careful, so I think its best if Kiki stays with you."

When she crossed her arms, Kiki sat up taller, puffing out its chest. "Kiki keeps Lusa safe."

And that deflated her annoyance. She patted Kiki's head. "I appreciate it, Kiks, but I don't need a babysitter."

"No," Res argued, "but my assumption is you still intend to look for the birds."

"Once we get the lay of the land a little and figure out how I'm going to wiggle around being seen, yeah." Lusa swallowed, knowing the risk was higher now, but, "I don't want to leave Theodore hanging, especially when we have no way to get him any kind of message."

"Before you get too caught up on his well-being," Res said with a sniff, "I can assure you that man has at least fifteen balls in the air at any given time. I find it very hard to believe we're the only option he's perusing to help his friends."

Did he sound jealous? Lusa almost snorted at the thought. "I'm not worried about him, but I am worried about his friends. And I got the impression he doesn't like asking people to put themselves at risk without a good reason. Given what he said, I agree we might not be the only option, but we might be the best one."

"Then given the new complications, take Kiki. Wear it around with you and then at least we have the added benefit of a second set of eyes at all times."

Kiki chirped. "Kiki keeps Lusa safe *and* hunts for shinies!"

Lusa laughed and leaned down close, whispering to Kiki, "I see the truth. You're bored being stuck in Wags." Kiki blinked a few times, making a curious noise, and she couldn't help a grin. It didn't quite get sarcasm, and she'd keep working on it, but this was also serious. "You need to stay put though unless we're sure no one else is around to see you. You," she added, poking the golden kitty nose again, "are exactly the kind of treasure a greedy dragon would want for his hoard."

Kiki let out a little growl, very fierce, but then a knock sounded on Wags's frame.

"That would be Guatemoc for the morning tour," Res muttered. "Shall we then, if you're done with your death coffee?"

Lusa handed him the full cup, minus one disgusting sip. "Yup, all done."

He narrowed his eyes but took the mug and placed it in the sink as Kiki scaled up her body before shifting around in hiss of metal and settling into a warm, rather plain belt around her hips. She really had no idea how the magic of Kiki's stone worked, but the belt had an ornate buckle in tarnished brass, with a few chipped red stones for embellishments. The rest was worn leather looped between metal rings, an antique styling but not expensive, and totally what she might pick for herself she ever bothered with accessories. She patted the belt, gave Res a nod, and they stepped outside.

Guatemoc waited for them, far less dramatic than he'd been yesterday as ringleader performer and subdued compared to his role as their dinner co-host. Lusa got the impression that for all Quetzalcoatl was the boss, Guatemoc ran the day-to-day affairs under Mount Pindo, whatever those might be.

Guess they were about to find out.

He greeted them with a warm, genuine smile, carrying his own steaming mug of black coffee, and Lusa wondered if it was a thing for hungover Ques.

"Gods, my head is killing me," Guatemoc said after they'd gotten good mornings out of the way, pulling a face that made Lusa laugh. "Always a big day, always an after party, though normally not quite so eventful." He shook out his hair, which still held streaks of gold without all the paint. "I was thinking a tour first, so you can get your bearings, unless you're hungry now?"

They declined food, so off they went.

The plaza platform, where Wags was parked, was darker this morning, most of the magical lights dimmed or off. Darkness loomed, nothing above them except the rail leading up to the surface, to which the platform attached. Everything else was cleared away from the day before, and Lusa noted the huge winch and gear contraption tucked against the stone, the heavy chains used to operate the mechanism absolutely massive.

"Crazy, isn't it?" Guatemoc said when he noticed both Res and Lusa staring. "I'm certainly glad all this was already a thing before I came around. I can't imagine the work that went into crafting a place like this."

"You don't know who built it?" Lusa asked.

"No one does, or no one remembers. And the mouros aren't talking," Guatemoc said with chuckle. "Well, at least not to me, and if they've ever chatted up granddad about it, he hasn't mentioned it."

Lusa licked her lips, reminding herself he could see her so she couldn't look at Res and wiggle her eyebrows like *did you hear that, he mentioned the giants that guard the treasure!*

"Did they make the caves?" Lusa asked, aiming for casual conversation, unsure if she came anywhere close. Given the side-eye Res shot her, maybe fifty-fifty. "I mean, didn't lots of stuff just kind of show up with the Aperien Event?"

"That's a good point," Guatemoc said. "What I do know is the deep halls are older than the platform and the city."

"City?" Res asked.

"Such as it is, yes." Guatemoc gestured the opposite direction from where they went last night, toward a wide very well-lit hall carved out of the stone face. "Most residences are that way, along with pastures, fields, water reserves, and the general matters required to keep an underground society fed, functional and happy. Most workers and staff live that direction with their families. Many of them moonlight as performers, as you saw yesterday during the festival. Come on, you've already seen receiving."

Lusa felt an itch she couldn't quite place as they turned away from the nondescript hallway and made their way to where they'd had dinner the night before. The hallway wasn't much different—wide and tall enough to be comfortable and not give the feeling one was being crushed under a billion tons of rock—and the receiving area was, as she remembered, rather plain with a few places to sit. Today, the firepit in the center held a smokeless purple fire, which smelled like lilacs and pleasantly warmed the room. They chatted about idle things as they moved through the space—how did they sleep, how Res and Guatemoc both drank too much, how excited Guatemoc was to show Res the rest of their home.

Lusa faded into the background, walking behind Res and Guatemoc as they spoke, and to be honest, it was a relief to not be the center of attention. Was that what Res felt like on stage? Hot and sweaty and all riled up all the time? She knew he loved performing, but at the end of the day, he was also happy to come home to Wags, put his feet up, and be himself.

This was going to be a long day.

Hells, it was going to be a long *month*.

The end of the receiving room was marked by a fancy set of double doors. They weren't locked, and swung open easily when Guatemoc nudged them with a hip

To say the shift across the threshold was dramatic was a dire understatement. So far, the entire underground seemed almost casually chiseled out of the rockface, but nothing about it spoke to the excess she'd expected when Theodore spoke about Mount Pindo and the dragon's underground hoard.

Well, that all changed right now.

Guatemoc said workers and staff so casually, Lusa hadn't really thought much of it. Every city needed workers to function, even in a world with magic. *Magic* needed workers to do the magic, and a lot of it wasn't as glamourous as humans might have imagined back in the day, especially when it came heating water, running lights, or dealing with sewage now that most of the world didn't have stuff like electricity anymore.

But Lusa and Res spent a lot of their time around simple people living simple lives. Even within the Velvet Emporium, for all its pomp and art and sensation magic, everyone was just kind of there, doing their thing, getting by on their skills, mundane or otherwise.

This was different.

This was a kingdom, serving a god, and they'd just stepped into the nobles' castle, while the commoners kept to their business separately across the hall.

Lusa pursed her lips, doing her best to keep the revelation off her face. For one, she felt a little stupid, because she should have known this coming in. And second, Guatemoc didn't seem like a bad guy, and he was absolutely delighted show them his home—especially Res, his long-lost family. So Lusa plastered on a smile, keeping in the annoyance that spiked when she realized Res was entirely, utterly smitten.

And there was no denying, it was breathtaking.

A literal castle, carved into veins of marble and granite, and, *hells*, the open gateway a huge, shimmering amethyst geode. The art style reminded her of the Spanish sculptures and reliefs on their climb up the mountain, a cobblestone courtyard laid out in welcome, with what she guessed was a mosaic of the once great dragon Bartholomew, before Quetzalcoatl came along and took over his parade.

Right, because no one else besides six people knew the cuélebre wasn't really a Spanish dragon anymore, but instead a winged serpent

Aztec god who probably ate his successor. Changing the décor would be a dead giveaway.

But man, was it shiny and pretty, and within a few minutes Lusa was lost in all the landscaping—under a mountain, so points for how impressive that was—and the giant fountain—with koi fish, like, two hundred of them—and that was before they even got to the glittering castle front doorway, and the castle proper itself, which once again, Lusa could barely wrap her mind around was *thousands of feet underground*.

"You might meet Bastina later tonight," Guatemoc mentioned when he caught Lusa starting at the golden orb hovering in the vaulted ceiling. "A daughter of Bast, but I think her father was some sort of sky creature? Keeping the gardens lit up is no skin off her nose." He shrugged. "She ended up here after the Second Ten Calamity and never left. Come on, let's go inside and I'll show you the main rooms."

So many rooms.

Dancing rooms, smoking rooms, card rooms. Two theater rooms, at least five different dining rooms, and a half dozen libraries. Sitting rooms, a drawing room—whatever that was for, because it wasn't for drawing—and quite a few bars and parlors. They just kept going, and Guatemoc had stories for each room, often involving one or more of the other Ques, and at times Quetzalcoatl himself, though Lusa was starting to get the impression that the big guy didn't spend much time at all with his grandchildren.

When they came to an open space with floor-to-ceiling picture windows, they found Matty and Pollock, the former dozing on a couch while the latter painted. The easel was massive, at least ten feet tall, and Pollock perched up on a stepladder, palette in hand, brush hard at work. The painting was of a woman, clearly a piece he'd been working on for quite some time. The subject was stunning, nude, and surrounded by Asiatic lilies of all colors.

"We each have our own sleeping quarters, bathroom and personal space in this wing, and a shared common room we tend to muddle around in most evenings. This one is Pollock's studio," Guatemoc said as they strode in without an invite. Matty perked up from the couch, giving them a lazy salute, but Pollock didn't cease working.

Maybe they should have knocked or something?

"Welcome," Pollock said without turning. "Tea service just arrived."

"Or hair of the dog, if you need," Matty said with a sniff, an open bottle on the end table beside him, no glass, no label. Lusa assumed they made their own alcohol down here with everything else.

Well, their servants did.

Guatemoc wandered over to Matty and sniffed the bottle. "Bourbon?"

"Mhm."

He splashed a bit in his coffee, leaning against the arm of the couch. Matty peered over at them, and Lusa realized then both she and Res lingered in the doorway. Matty waved a hand. "Don't worry, none of us bite unless provoked or asked politely."

It reminded Lusa so much of Res, she couldn't help a grin. She shoved him into the room. Res sighed, dramatic, as if warming up to the part—really, as if he hadn't been at it the entire time with Guatemoc so far this morning, so she wasn't sure why he hesitated now.

Lusa walked a little closer to Pollock and his painting, leaving Res to the others. "It's really pretty," she offered, quietly in hopes she wouldn't disturb his work.

"Thank you," Pollock said, his tone steady and a little stern, same as it'd been every time she'd heard him speak. She got the impression he was a bit more serious than his relatives.

"Does it have a name?"

"Pretention and Lilies," Matty called from the couch, which got a laugh from Guatemoc. When Lusa shot them both a look, Matty held up his hands in apology, though he didn't seem even a little sorry, but Guatemoc cleared his throat.

"Leave him be, Matthias. Come along," Guatemoc said, tugging Matty up by a sleeve, who whined in protest but followed. To Pollock, he said, "See you at dinner," before heading to the door with Matty in tow like a spoiled child. Res followed with hands in his pockets, his expression a bit serene and melancholy at the same time.

When she turned to say goodbye, Pollock watched her, the first time he'd stalled his work. A heavy stare, really seeing her, and the hairs on the back of her neck prickled, and now she was sweating again. She'd have to ask Res later if it was normal to sweat when people looked at you.

"You've an eye for detail," he noted.

Lusa shrugged. He knew what she was, so she didn't really see a point in denying anything. "Most of the time all I can do is watch the world go by, so yeah."

He nodded once, then went back to painting. Lusa figured that was a dismissal, and she needed to catch up before she got lost in this weird, shiny, underground castle.

When she reached the door, Pollock said, "If you're interested in painting, feel free to stop by." She glanced back, unable to hide her surprise at the offer. And if she wasn't mistaken, Pollock seemed embarrassed when he added, "I have a suspicion you know how to be quiet company."

Lusa grinned. "I do. I might take you up on that, thanks. A month is a long time."

He stopped painting again, his expression one she couldn't decipher, but she slipped from the room to catch up to the others.

# Chapter 22

Lusa's big takeaway from the tour was that Ques, aside from Pollock, loved to hear themselves talk. It made the day a little easier for her, because they were too busy entertaining themselves and each other to notice when she went quiet and settled into her default mode of observing, although Res constantly checked she was still there.

They spent a lot of time in the personal rooms. Oz joined them when they found him in his space, which was a very modern gym, complete with a hot tub, sauna, wrestling ring, and lots of complaining about how the other Ques commandeered his space on the regular instead of making the same kind of amenities in their own areas. It also seemed like Oz enjoyed making them all exercise, so it worked out for everyone.

Matty's space was a very fancy bar with an extremely comfortable sitting area for playing card games, overlooking the back gardens of the castle, which were more extravagant than the front. Half of his room was a balcony, and the entire set tasteful and surprisingly peaceful given Matty's seeming constant role of jester within the group. And she was pretty sure if she asked him, half the art at decorating the space was done by his brother.

Guatemoc's space was an office of sorts, which started up a fifteen-minute argument about why Guatemoc was the most boring of the group from Matty, then Guatemoc defending the fact that if he didn't keep things running the way they were down here Matty wouldn't have the half the fun he did.

Pollock joined them for lunch, which was awkward because the dusters who brought out the food service didn't put down any plates or silverware at Lusa's seat, but the familiarity of the shadowlands on her skin was such a relief, she didn't really care. Most of the meal was ostentatious finger food anyway. Res passed her some of his extra silverware and his bread plate, along with his glass of water. The others didn't notice.

They were leaving lunch when Lusa realized they'd never seen the last Ques, Erandi, or his rooms. When she asked, the group quieted for a moment, and it was Matty who shrugged and said, in earnest, "He's more private than the rest of us."

Lusa considered for a moment, because she knew very well that soul-deep feeling of being left out of everything, and asked, "Have you thought about maybe knocking?"

That comment even got a laugh out of Pollock, and then everyone else had excuse to leave besides Guatemoc, since he was the tour guide. He sighed, then pointed at Lusa. "If he's angry, you're to blame."

"Okay," she'd answered with a shrug.

They'd knocked on Erandi's wing, Guatemoc having her do the honors, and he'd told them to come in after pause long enough to be awkward. Guatemoc pushed open the door and darkness greeted them.

"Hells, Erandi, don't you have any lights in here?" Guatemoc muttered.

"And why would I?" Erandi's voice floated from deep in the dark chamber, and he didn't sound very happy with the interruption. It carried a low cadence, raspy and annoyed, but there was more to the tone. Petulant, almost, but also tired, and if Lusa dared, a bit raw and almost pained.

He sounded like Res on those long days, weeks and then months he'd hidden himself away in Wags. She touched Guatemoc's arm when he moved to cast what she guessed would be a light-based illusion into Erandi's space.

"We can go if it's not a good time."

"You didn't say you brought better company than yourself, Guatemoc." Erandi's voice was less snide now, and it did a bit better hiding the underlying stress, but Lusa still heard it. "A few moments, if you please, and I'll join."

They shut the door and waited in the hall. Lusa occupied herself looking out the window while Guatemoc and Res made awkward small talk. She tapped her finger on the windowsill, wondering if she'd ruined the mood of the entire day by asking after Erandi.

She might know what it felt like to not be a part of things, but on the other hand, she knew nothing about being part of a group of people, and all the nuances that came with navigating a social circle. After all, she only moonlighted on the edges of one for the first time last night.

Lusa rubbed her eyes. Maybe she should have just stayed in Wags until it was time to sneak around. At least then, she couldn't make things worse.

The door opened a few seconds later, Erandi dressed the same as the night before, in clean, crisp clothing, plainly colored and impeccably kept, his eyes covered. He shut and locked his door—odd, as she hadn't seen anyone else do so. Erandi moved with a sort of grace that might have been surprising considering his blindness, but for Lusa, it had a very different effect.

Suddenly she was five years old again, living in a rundown, drafty pop-up wooden home two miles outside her mother's village. Lusa barely left the house because her mother kept a key ring on her belt, and the front door had three deadbolts that locked from the inside. The rest of the keys were for the cabinets and dressers, the ice chest, the cellar, her mother's hope chest, and a jewelry box.

Her mother barely acknowledged her by that point, already wasting away in depression and grief for her vanished husband, but since she ate like a bird, Lusa only ever went hungry if her mother forgot to eat entirely. At night, Mother locked herself in her bedroom alone, and Lusa slept on the fur rug and snuck peeks at the cold outside world, which she'd always dreamed of being warmer than her home.

She wasn't wrong in the end, but that wasn't what drew her into the memories.

It was watching the precise movements of a blind person navigating the space they'd memorized with their other senses and claimed as their own. Erandi hadn't been blind his whole life like Lusa's mother, but he'd acclimated to his condition. He didn't fumble for the doorknob and he didn't guess which key he needed; she watched the quick flicks counting on the ring, a deft brush with his thumb over the selected key's teeth, and the key slotted without any sort of slip. She never would have guessed from watching his back that Erandi couldn't see.

And yet Guatemoc, who had lived with him for probably decades, reached out to take his elbow as he turned from locking his door. Lusa winced when Erandi caught Guatemoc by the wrist before he touched him, hearing or guessing his intentions, maybe both. Erandi disguised the entire exchange as a polite decline of assistance, but Lusa didn't miss how Erandi's finely manicured nails dug into Guatemoc's wrist. Or how Guatemoc's features stuttered with frustration, then annoyance, before he schooled his expression into his winning smile when he looked back to her and Res. Or the razor edge to Erandi's own smile when he greeted them.

Lusa hadn't needed many reminders from her mother that she was blind, but not an invalid, and she didn't need help in the space she knew. A few sharp cracks across the jaw had taught her fast enough. But it had only been the two of them most of the time. Lusa was a child, and her mother hadn't had her eyes cut out for alchemical ingredients. In the rare times anyone else from their extended family unit came up to check on Lusa and her mother, maybe once or twice a year, her mother seethed at any attempts to coddle her, so much so it eventually drove away visitors entirely.

And here was a quiet and obviously private man, who'd been through hells and back, trapped under the mountain with a family who clearly loved him but probably had no idea they were smothering him with their good intentions. Or reminding him of exactly what he'd suffered when they left him in his room to wallow like Res had. She wondered if he'd even wanted to come to dinner last night, or if he'd been forced.

Gods, Lusa's head hurt again. She was sweaty and nauseous, too, this time unrelated to people staring at her at least, so she supposed that was something.

The four of them toured through more rooms, an endless parade of excess. Guatemoc was a good host, and smart about reading his audience. He was much more subdued around only the three of them, but no less charming and witty. Erandi lacked charm but radiated a sort of calm Lusa wished she could bottle up and keep in her pocket. Res remained at ease, his shoulders and stride relaxed as they continued on. She wondered if Kiki was enjoying itself at her waist or was getting as bored as Lusa. Her feet were starting to hurt when Matty reappeared to tell them Quetzalcoatl wished to speak to Res in the solar. Must be another kind of fancy room, Lusa guessed. That got Res twitchy again, but that was probably a good thing so he didn't stroll in and forget he was talking to a god.

They were headed that way, apparently, when Lusa noticed they bypassed what looked like an entire wing of the castle. "What's down that way? More dining halls? Or sitting rooms? Extra closets?"

Guatemoc laughed, sensing her gentle barb and taking it in stride. "No, actually." He leaned closer, as if sharing a secret despite not bothering to whisper, and she tensed at the proximity she wasn't used to beyond Res. "That's the way to those mysterious mouros." He laughed again at her wide-eyed expression because, well, that was good to know. "Don't worry, they don't come up here, but that leads to the deeper levels and the mazes with all of Bartholomew's hoard."

Really good to know.

And there wasn't even a door, just a stone hallway, curving around the corner, and she assumed, down into the rock. "Wow, so you can just go down there?" Lusa asked. "It's not dangerous?"

"Debatable," Erandi said. "Rumors are the mouros and their various kind not only made the maze of tunnels but also created much of the treasure below. Some of them are altruistic in nature, at least according to mythos, but there isn't exactly a catalog of what's down there. And as far as we know, they're still digging. If Quetzalcoatl gets anything of note from his offerings he doesn't want or need, he'll send someone to drop it off at the end of the hallway. By the next day, it's gone, no doubt added to the mess."

"Amazing," Res drawled. "To be so rich you don't even need to keep track of what makes you so. Aren't you even a bit curious?"

"We've been down a few times over the years, but never very deep," Guatemoc said with a shrug. "Found a few fun relics, but it really is a hedge maze of rock down there. Without a map, only the mouros can find their way around, and getting lost down there for eternity is not on my bucket list, curious or not."

Lusa tapped her belt—Kiki—who she knew listened to every bit and piece of their conversation.

"You shouldn't keep him waiting," Erandi reminded them all, his head canted in the direction they'd been headed before Lusa distracted them.

"Alright, well," Guatemoc hesitated, because they all knew Lusa wasn't invited. "Can you find your way back to your wagon then?"

Erandi cleared his throat. "I'm more than capable of acting as an escort."

Guatemoc hesitated again, then said a quick, "Of course," and him and Res went off, with Res giving her a shrug that looked casual, but to Lusa, spoke to how terrified he was. She waved him off, giving him two thumbs up, which got an eyeroll, but at least he seemed a little less nervous.

Lusa turned back to Erandi, who was still, hands folded behind his back as if waiting on her. She wondered if the silver bracers he wore had any kind of magic that helped him maintain his bearings, which gave her an idea. Probably a bad one, but what the hells.

"Since you're stuck escorting me, I assume that means Res and I aren't allowed to run all over the place without a babysitter?"

Erandi chuckled, the tightness in his posture loosening up a bit. "Not yet, no." He almost sounded apologetic, but she also had a niggling suspicion he didn't mean it.

"Cool, I get it." She paused then, long enough for him to incline his head. "Wanna go try and find some mouros?"

# Chapter 23

Erandi didn't respond right away, sort of frozen in place at Lusa's suggestion. There was no way he didn't hear her; they were only a few feet apart.

"You want to find the mouros," Erandi said after a bloated pause, his words slow as if she was dim-witted, or maybe how he was used to talking with the other Ques when they were hungover and bothering him. "The mythical giants living under the mountain who don't like people bothering them or their treasure?"

"Yup, them. They worked directly with Bartholomew before the hostile takeover, right? Maybe they've been down there this whole time waiting for someone to visit."

When he finally cracked a smile, albeit a tiny one, Lusa relaxed a little. The few interactions she'd witnessed between him and the others gave her the impression they treated him like he was delicate. Maybe they didn't joke around with him as much, worried he couldn't take it. She was assuming a lot, but the way he'd sat at the dinner, far enough away he could have been alone, spoke louder than any words.

"I doubt it," Erandi offered, but he faced down the mysterious hall now, and as much as Lusa hated the fact she was manipulating him a bit to find access to search for the birds of truth, she didn't want to let him go back to his dark room alone, either.

"I could guide you, if you've never been that way," Lusa offered, then quickly added, "Just by voice."

"Plan to tell me everything I can't see myself as well?" He wasn't quite snide, or self-deprecating, but if he was going for humor, it wasn't working for him.

"I can, if you want. I have a pretty good eye for detail, being most of the time I don't get to do anything but watch from the sidelines." Lusa shrugged, exaggerating the motion so her shirt rustled. "I just thought it might be more fun than doing nothing alone for the rest of the day."

The more honest, the better, she knew. Erandi couldn't see, but he cataloged every sound she made, same as her mother had. She didn't know how long he'd been blind, but she was pretty sure he could guess a lot from tone of voice most people missed. He was probably as good at reading between the lines of people's words as Lusa was with body language.

She rocked on her heels, and added, "But I wouldn't want you to trip or anything," because she had a feeling Erandi's ego hadn't been completely stripped away with his feathers.

Sure enough, he stiffened.

Lusa knew it was a risk; he probably knew she was baiting him.

But when he said, "Alright, let's go on then," she grinned like the cat that got the canary.

"Cool! It's about thirty feet ahead to the bend, which goes right. Smooth stone, but a slight downward slope. Good?" When he nodded, she kept ahead of him a few paces, deliberately making her steps heavier than normal. "Do you ever use a white cane in new places?"

For not knowing the way, Erandi moved at a steady pace. A glance back showed he stepped almost exactly where she did. "A white cane?"

"Oh, maybe that's only a human term? It's an aid for walking. Checking for obstacles, that kind of thing. The shape isn't really that much different than a normal cane, but you don't lean on it for support, and it's a bit longer."

"You've spent much time with blind humans then?"

"My mother human and blind, so yeah."

Erandi hummed. "That explains a few things."

"We're headed right. There's a little lip, only a few inches high, but you can brace your hand on the wall if you need to feel for it." Lusa waited, watching as Erandi followed her directions, toing the bump with his leather shoes before stepping over it and moving away from the wall. "We're a bit steeper now, but so far, it looks like this just heads down without much going on. And what does what explain?"

Their footsteps echoed off the stone tunnel, dry, well-kept and dimly lit by scones cut into the rockface. Lusa peeked in one. The glow seemed to come from inside crystal packed into the recesses.

"Your awareness. I assumed you were observant, given your blood. Or simply empathetic to others' discomfort. But your handling of me is a bit too specific."

"Handling, huh? Am I that obvious I didn't want you to go back to your dark room alone?" She aimed for lighthearted, but her heart ached a bit nonetheless.

"I'm not entirely sure why you care, aside from entertaining your-self."

"Ouch. What happened to my empathy?"

"What I lack in empathy, I make up for in observation with the senses I do have left." Erandi said. "How hard did Res blanche when he saw me and figured out what I was?"

"You mean another Ques?"

Erandi stopped walking. "I want to like you, Lusa, despite the fact that you're a stowaway on an invitation that wasn't yours to take."

Lusa turned, frowning. "I was always going where Res goes. We've travelled together for years."

He held up his hand. "I don't care. What I care about is being dismissed as a fool."

Lusa crossed her arms. "I don't think you're a fool."

"Then don't play coy with answers that do nothing but avoid my question."

Well, at least arrogance stayed in place when feathers didn't.

"Did you ever stop to think that maybe how I answered has nothing to do with you at all? Maybe I want to like you, too, but I don't know anything about you aside from that you're all a bunch of Ques living under a mountain, which was a big shock to my best friend. Maybe I don't know what you guys want from Res, and maybe I care about him more than making a good impression on you or all your brother-nephew-cousin people. Maybe it's not my place to talk to you about Res's feelings about his experience with the Ques hunters or how he felt seeing another person who was hurt by those jerks."

Lusa huffed, her cheeks warm after her little rant and her eyes stinging, but she swallowed a few times and finished, "And maybe I also don't want to talk about how it made him feel because of how it made me feel, too, alright?"

Erandi turned his face away from her, would have been looking down at his feet if he could see. "I didn't fully consider the ramifications of my question." He cleared his throat and actually sounded embarrassed. "I'm not the best of company on a good day, and last night's dinner was . . ."

"A lot?" Lusa offered. "Because it was a lot for me, and I'm not even related to any of you."

Erandi chuckled, but then his expression was serious again. "It's unfortunate that Res was attacked, and very lucky they didn't do more damage. But it is a good reminder of how precious the home our grandfather provides for us truly is." He dipped his head. "I believe you're leading a blind man to see some mythical giants?"

"It sounds really stupid when you say it like that." Lusa winced. "Do you want to go back?"

"No, not right now. I was wallowing, you're right, and no good will come of it. At least this way I can stretch my legs and see our guest entertained for a few hours."

It took them about twenty minutes before the sloped hall flattened out and the lights grew brighter. They were coming up on something, but Lusa had no idea what. She'd kept a slow pace, and her and Erandi had chatted about safer topics, mostly surrounding what life was like under Mount Pindo the other 364 days of the year. To Lusa, it sounded decadent, peaceful, and really boring, but given what Erandi had suffered, she figured if anyone deserved a quiet, boring life with good food and comfortable living, it was him.

Despite enjoying Erandi's company and finding access to the treasure halls, when they reached the end of the descending hallway, the entire idea seemed like a monumentally terrible one.

"Oh, gods, wait wait wait!" Lusa lashed out, grabbing Erandi by the elbow and switching sides with him, despite knowing it would piss him off.

Because the only thing on the left side was a drop off, with little more between them and careening off into an abyss than a rock edge about two feet high.

"Holy hells, sorry," Lusa muttered once she had Erandi backed safely against the wall. She let go of his sleeve and smoothed down the fabric. "The side there falls off into nothing and there's no handrails or anything. I figured I'd rather have you mad at me for grabbing you than falling over a cliff to your death." Lusa edged away from him, peering over as she sucked in a breath. "Oh, wow."

"Don't keep us in suspense."

"Huh?" She glanced back at Erandi, at his blindfolded face—because he was blind—and was glad he couldn't see her blush in utter mortification. "Yeah, of course, sorry. I was . . ." She grimaced. "A jerk, sorry."

"Still a joy, comparatively," Erandi said, smirking.

Lusa laughed. "Oh, come on, they can't be that bad."

He shrugged, then motioned around them at nothing specific. "Tell me what you see."

"A really big cavern, and I can't tell how far it goes down, but it almost looks natural. We're standing on a bridge, but it doesn't go far before it divides into three spirals leading downward in different directions." Lusa toed over to the edge and the way-too-short barricade, peering over again as she sucked in a breath. "They fan out, the paths, once they get down about a hundred feet or so, but . . ." She swallowed a few times. "But it looks like a honeycomb or a lattice or something down here, all carved into the bedrock. Halls and rooms. It just keeps going. Down, up, all directions. More spiral stairs, more paths, more chambers . . ."

How in the hells was she supposed to find anything in this place? Someone could get lost down here for years.

"You sound disappointed. No giants?"

Lusa would have laughed if her head wasn't spinning. She didn't know why an underground maze of treasure hoarding hadn't prepared her for the pure scope of this place. There was just so *much*. "Hah, hah," she mumbled. "No, I just . . . Are all these rooms really filled with treasure?"

"I'd imagine so, yes," Erandi said, his tone almost curious. "The mouros are guards, but their nature—some mythos at least—also is to weave and create golden wealth. If they've been down here from almost two hundred and fifty years, largely unbothered, they've probably turned this entire mountain into an anthill of sorts."

"Wow," Lusa replied, and even she heard the blandness in her tone this time.

"You must have truly enjoyed the morning tour, then."

Lusa tore her eyes away from the winding maze of treasure, lights, mysteries, and waste below her, and shrugged knowing Erandi wouldn't see, but maybe he'd heard the motion. "I grew up really poor. It's a bit much, honestly."

Erandi inclined his head, a level of understanding in the way the humor left his voice. "It's an adjustment to come from less, lose more, and then be handed everything one might imagine you desire."

The moment felt weighted with things left unsaid, and not just from Lusa.

"Anyway, good talk. We should probably head back now though. I mean, I took care of my mom." When her mother let her, occasionally, or had no choice, like in those last few months of her life. "But we rarely left the house. And when we did, we only walked down the same flat road on the rare occasions she wanted to go outside. I'm not really comfortable guiding you around spiraling paths over a yawning abyss with no handrails. No offense."

Erandi chuckled at that. "None taken. I imagine dinner will be soon. I'll escort you back to the wagon."

Lusa resisted the urge to correct him about Wags, since they hadn't shared her nature. "Right, sounds good."

Because the other message was clear. Lusa wasn't invited to dinner this time around.

# Chapter 24

"Kiki, what in the world are we going to do?" Lusa asked as she slumped down at Wags's kitchen table. Erandi had dropped her off a few minutes ago, warning her that Res would probably be late. And since Wags was the best, there was a sandwich waiting for her. She stuffed a few bites in her mouth, trying to reconcile the true scope of the mountain maze.

Kiki slithered from around her waist, shifting from belt to winged kitty. It plopped down next to her early dinner. "All shinies and pretties?"

"Down in that hole?" Lusa wiped her mouth with the back of her hand. "Yeah, and more we can't even see. It looked like those rooms and halls go down forever."

"Oooooooo." Kiki blinked a few times, red eyes shimmering like rubies as it dreamed about treasure.

Lusa couldn't help a giggle. "Kiks, this is not a good thing."
"Why?"

"Because that place is unmapped. And we're only here a month, and we need to find one thing. That's like trying to find a needle in a haystack." She rubbed her forehead with a sigh. It wouldn't matter who could see her or not. There was no way she could search that place from top to bottom, let alone not get lost doing it. "We don't have anything to point us in the right direction or keep track of where we've been and haven't."

She groaned and thumped her head on the tabletop. A few seconds later, Kiki tapped her head with a metal paw.

"Lusa needs map?"

"There isn't one."

"Lusa wants map?"

She propped her chin on her hands. Kiki flattened itself on its tummy so they were eye to eye. "Well, yeah, if there was one, I would want it."

"Kiki make map?"

Lusa sat up and Kiki mirrored her. "What do you mean?"

"Kiki make map for Lusa."

"But, how, Kiks? You've seen it."

"Just seen."

Lusa pursed her lips, reminding herself Kiki was just trying to help. "I know, but I mean you haven't been in all those rooms. You don't know where they go, what's inside them, so how could you make a map?"

"Kiki see, Kiki know." Kiki stood, patting its feet like it did when it got excited. "Papers," it chirped. "Papers!"

"You want paper?"

"Maps are paper."

Gods, Lusa was getting a headache. "Okay, sure, Kiks."

Not like they had anything else to do but wait for Res. She fumbled around in her room until she found a sketchbook she hadn't used in a while, most of the pages empty. When she got back to the kitchen, Kiki had found an inkwell from somewhere, or maybe Wags produced it.

"Here you go."

Kiki chirped and nosed the book open to a blank page while Lusa sat back down, and dipped it's claws in the ink. Impressively, with no spills. And more impressive, it only took about a minute for Kiki's drawing to come to life.

"A map," Lusa whispered.

Kiki was sketching out the entire castle grounds Lusa had walked on the tour today, starting with where Wags sat on the platform, in clear crisp lines and intricate detail. It paused once, crimson gaze flicking to Lusa for approval when it chirped, "Map?"

"Yes, Kiks, map. Yes, please."

Lusa could have watched Kiki work for hours, the careful way it used little cat claws to capture things in perfect proportions, adding labels when it got to the personal rooms, and adding other little notes, like how the magic sun in the front garden was powered by sky and god magic, by a daughter of Bast.

"Kiki, this is amazing."

"Kiki see, Kiki know!" The little clockwork creature preened, a whirling impression of purr, before it went back to work. It seemed to enjoy the work, and Lusa grinned at all the little unnecessary flourishes, like spending extra time drawing flowers in the gardens, and a rough sketch of Pollock's painting.

Lusa helped pull a page out, setting it aside to dry so Kiki could keep working. There was no denying this would help; if Kiki could track where they'd been and the rooms they'd checked, and with such precision, it would save them so much time. And it would keep them from getting lost.

But unease gnawed at Lusa's belly; the uncomfortable feeling that this type of memory in a crafted creature probably wasn't an accident. Kiki seemed to be enjoying making the maps and recalling everything it had seen, but she shuddered at the thought of what the "bad man" might have used this gift for.

"Kiks, you can draw anytime time you want, okay? It doesn't just have to be if someone asks you for help."

Kiki chirped-chirped, its happy yes noise, and kept on working.

Lusa smiled, stroking Kiki's back while it worked like she'd pet Tick, who slept on his shelf as usual, hoping Kiki's joy in little things never, ever changed.

Res was home sooner than Lusa expected. She was pinning another picture of Kiki's, this one of Tick, over the stove when he slipped inside the door. "Can you do Lils from the village? The one who asked for the birthday party. Oh! Res! Look!"

She waved her hands around Wags's kitchen, which was papered in drawings from Kiki. The maps had been set aside hours ago, in a neat pile for Lusa to use later, and they'd moved on to other things, much to Kiki's delight. After about fifteen different renditions of Tick, Kiki did a portrait of Lusa, Wags, and a half dozen of Res, mostly since Lusa kept asking for of him.

There were also twenty different kinds of flowers pinned up over the ice chest. An entire pile of small squares Lusa cut up for Kiki to draw bugs in amazing detail, and there was even a picture of Theodore, the good man, taped to one of the cabinets. There were animals, random people from the various villages they'd travelled to over the months since Kiki joined them, as well as scenic vistas that felt like snapshots into her memories.

"Kiki is amazing!" Lusa cheered with a hoot, which made Kiki hop and down on the table and splat inky paw prints all over the wood. She'd have to scrub Wags later, but the kitchen felt warm and cozy and *happy*, so she didn't think Wags minded. "Kiks drew all this stuff from memory, look!"

Lusa spun, taking in Res as he surveyed the art, the mess, and them, but his expression was dull and his eyes unfocused. He didn't really seem to take anything in at all. She frowned, stepping down from the chair and patting his cheek.

He startled, blinking down at her with a frown. "What?"

"Did they get you drunk again?"

He scoffed, turning away. "No."

"Hey, sorry, it was just a joke." She caught his sleeve, and his shoulders slumped with a sigh that deflated him entirely. "What's going on?"

Res ran a hand through his messy hair, which was unlike him, his gaze still distant as gripped the back of the chair. "I met with Quetzalcoatl before dinner."

"Right." Lusa still held his sleeve, unable to let go. "Bad?"

Res scoffed again. "Gods, I don't know." He shook his head again. "The invite down here isn't to entertain for the month, Lusa. He's invited me to stay. To live down here, with my . . . family."

The way he hesitated on the word family made her heart ache for him, at the same time her lungs cinched up tight.

Quetzalcoatl asked him to stay? Here?

That wasn't . . .

"But . . . you . . ." Lusa blinked a few times. "Res?"

He leaned away from her, scrubbing his face with both hands, and she reluctantly released his sleeve. "I told him I'd consider it, being that I couldn't refuse, could I?" Her heart was beating so fast, Lusa felt like she was underwater. "When I asked about you, he seemed surprised you were even a consideration." He still wouldn't look at her, not really. "Then he shrugged and said he'd give you a job with the staff after the month was up, if I felt obligated."

Obligated.

Did . . . did . . . he want to stay here?

Lusa could only stare at Res, the way his hands grabbed the chair, white-knuckled, as he continued. "At dinner, when the topic came up, Erandi suggested putting you on the castle staff and in residence with me, since everyone else has already forgotten you'd be invisible to the rest of the people who live down here."

Lusa didn't know what to make of Res's tone or posture.

Did he really want to live here, underground, away from the rest of the world? And the sun and sky? Did he really to stay in a pampered castle, with fancy rooms and food, waited on hand and foot, the exact opposite of the years they'd spent travelling together? Living minimally, exploring the countryside, watching the stars, and sleeping with Wags in a new place every few nights?

Did he think *she* would want that?

Would it matter if she did?

And . . . should it?

Maybe that was the more important question. He'd found his family, for the first time since he'd lost his mother. Cousins and brothers and nephews. He'd met his grandfather, the sire of his bloodline, who was a god. Why wouldn't he want to be with them?

Lusa chest ached, her heart ratcheting up so fast she was pretty sure she might vomit, and she couldn't think of anything to say that wouldn't sound a lot like begging and *please don't do this.*

Instead, she blurted out: "I found the mouros caves."

Res blinked up at her, his brow furrowed.

Her heart still raced, but this conversation was safer. Familiar territory. Expected. "They're huge. Kiki drew the cavern entrance." She shuffled the papers around until she found the right one and held it up, her hand shaking.

Res took it, letting out a low whistle. "Gods, that's crazy. It just keeps going, doesn't it?"

"And Kiki can draw anything it sees," Lusa added, clutching her fingers together in an effort to keep them still. She smiled at Kiki, who chirped softly, almost a question, and she laid a gentle hand on its head. "That will help so much with the search."

"Search?" Res asked.

Lusa's heart thudded again, skipping around uncomfortably. "The birds of truth, for Theodore."

"Right, sorry." He tossed the drawing down on the table. "Gods, it's been a long two days. Do you might if I head off early? I really need to get some sleep."

"Yeah, uhm, sure. What about tomorrow?"

He sighed, rubbing his face; he really did look exhausted. "I'm not sure, aside from more getting to know this place, so I've been told. Erandi said to tell you no more babysitting, whatever than means."

"Sure," Lusa said. Res already wandered down the hall. She swallowed a few times before she managed a dry, "Good night."

"Night, Lusa girl," he mumbled as he ducked behind his door curtains.

Lusa slumped into a kitchen seat, her head spinning.

The Ques here might be his kind, but she knew deep down her bones, Res didn't belong locked inside a mountain, miles and miles under cold stone. He needed to fly. Lusa really, really hoped he remembered that on his own. He'd been through hells, and a month was a long time.

# Chapter 25

"Death coffee again?" Lusa asked the next morning as she slid into the seat beside Res. It was early, and she guessed by the look of him, he'd slept as well as she had, which was to say like garbage. He slid a mug across the kitchen table to her, but he'd left it half-filled this time. She added an obscene amount of cream and sugar, ignoring Res's raised brow as she turned the black liquid into a nice, sweet, caramel-colored mess.

"I see the sweet tooth is thriving," he mumbled, blowing on his coffee.

Lusa sipped hers and gave a happy sigh. "You can have your evil acid; I'll enjoy my normal people coffee."

He hummed. "The lies we tell ourselves."

She shrugged, and for a few minutes, they drank their drastically different coffee and ignored the day.

Res caved first, sort of. "So."

Lusa took another sip. "So." His side-eye was a bit of a glare. "Big plans today?"

He finally cracked, laughing, and she grinned at him when he slumped in the chair. "I don't know how you do that, Lusa girl."

"What? Be hilarious?"

He tried to flick her nose, but she smacked his hand away before he could. His grin made her blush a bit despite herself, and Lusa looked away first.

"Make me laugh when I'd very rather crawl into a hole and never come out."

"You mean when you're being overdramatic?"

Res sat up a little taller, taking one of her hands then. She watched him, not sure what he was after, as he turned it palm up and traced the lines of her skin. "How you keep your chin up when things are difficult."

Lusa sipped her coffee, trying to ignore the fluttery feeling she got all over from him touching her palm like this, an almost tickly sensation she felt all the way down to her toes. "All you have to do is hang out in the castle with the other fancy boys. How hard can it be, lounging around all day like little kings?" She tried for flippant, but her voice came out a little breathless.

"I'm trying to pay you a compliment, Lusa girl," Res said, looking up at her from under his unfairly long eyelashes, with those bright, beautiful eyes. The ones that could always see her and, sometimes, see right through her.

She shrugged. "I just do my best, Res, that's all."

He closed his eyes and gave her a nod. "Right then." When he opened them again, he seemed a bit more focused. "I'll play my part. They'll probably expect to see you about, and I suppose the less important you act . . ." Res rubbed his chin, obviously uncomfortable, and she patted his hand as she stood.

"I get it. Act more like a servant and they'll pay less attention to me, and then that makes my job easier."

"Right," Res mumbled, frowning.

"I'm sorry this is getting weird for you, you know, with the family stuff."

He waved a hand. "It's strange, I'll give you that, but as you've pointed out, I'm certainly not suffering. Just keep Kiki close. Who knows what you'll find down there."

"Kiki keeps Lusa safe!" Kiki chirped, diving bombing them from the shelf, spilling both their coffees and, thankfully, breaking the awkward tension.

Lusa didn't head right for the treasure maze. She made a show of grabbing a croissant from the breakfast spread, then leaving Res with his family, and she was happy enough not to keep "court" with Quetzalcoatl. Res might be right about her fading into the background, but this morning there wasn't a chair for her at the table, and she wasn't about to literally act like a server or linger around like she needed scraps of attention. She excused herself politely, and wandered into the front gardens, staying within line of sight of the windows.

Once they were done with breakfast, she waited to see how they divided off, and when Pollock ended up alone in his art room, she joined him. She asked about painting with him, and what times he preferred company. He was open to most days, enjoying the morning light—even thought it was all artificial and magically produced—and suggested they start off with free form the next day. He'd set up an easel for her, and she could decide if she wished for lessons, or art for the joy of it.

Lusa spent a few hours perusing one of the many libraries, setting aside a stack of books she wouldn't mind reading once she made sure she had permission to borrow them. Before she left, she placed an old atlas from before the Aperien Event on top of her pile. She'd always loved maps, and maybe Kiki would like it too. Grinning, she poked her belt; she loved Kiki's maps best now, and would make sure to tell it later.

Lusa peered out into the hallway, doing her best not to look like a person sneaking about. After all, she didn't need a babysitter anymore; Lusa rolled her eyes at that one, but more importantly, Erandi hadn't seemed bothered by her curiosity about the maze, the mouros, and whatever else she might find below the castle grounds. He certainly did seem worried she might be a thief, Lusa thought with a grimace.

But then she lifted her head high and walked down the hall without shame. She wasn't a petty thief. At least not this time. She was helping people in need by taking one thing from a gigantic hoard, an item they probably didn't even know was down there.

It didn't matter *they* were unexpectedly Res's family, or they'd been nice so far, or one of them was a god.

Or they wanted him to stay here . . .

Whatever, one issue at a time.

She couldn't take something she hadn't found yet.

Lusa strode down the ornate halls, passed all the fancy rooms, trying not to enjoy the plush carpet under her worn boot heels too much, then took a left down the hall leading to the spiral, carved stone paths, and the endless hive of rooms. No one noticed her walking by, or if they did, they didn't care enough to say something. She never felt the shadowlands, so she didn't cross paths with anyone from the staff.

And just like that, she descended, much faster without Erandi, and then she looked out over the vast, crazy place she'd be exploring for the next four weeks. The air was cool, crisp, and slightly damp. It didn't smell at all dusty and tasted a little bit like salt.

"Here goes," Lusa mumbled, half to herself and half to Kiki, who was warm around her waist.

She picked the closest of the three downward paths, trusting Kiki to keep track of everywhere they went this afternoon. She figured if things got weird, or any of the Ques got suspicious, she'd lean into her natural curiosity and their conversations about the mouros. If things got weirder, she could sneak down here at night.

Future problems, she decided, because all of those things were true too.

It would be pretty cool to see mouros, and nothing suggested they'd see her back, so she could stare all she wanted. *Thanks for the complex, Res, even if it was and still is good advice not to stare at people who can see you*. And Kiki's excitement for shinies was contagious. Who knew what the hells they were going to find down here?

One last glance up showed she hadn't been followed or anything, so Lusa descended, trying not to shiver. It was colder already, down in the deep caves, but not any colder than the shadowlands' edge. What really got her was the drop into dark nothingness and no handrails. She did shiver this time, and hurried across a stone walk that seemed to hover over nothing to the other side of the chasm.

It still reminded her of a honeycomb, though it was a bit of an illusion, she realized. Once she reached the threshold, it became clear inside was much more well-lit than the center—Hub? Void? Chasm of Doom?—and the rooms were endless, but some walls were thin, almost gossamer, probably polished quartz or a similar mineral.

And they really did shine.

The walls that shouldered up to the drop-off were thicker, so Lusa hadn't been able to make out the contents from across the chasm. Now, she just kind of stared for a minute into the first chamber, a simple room no larger than Wags's kitchen. The granite floor smoothed downward in a bowl shape, but she couldn't tell how deep it went because it was overfilled with coins.

"Shiney," Kiki chirped in the quietest little peep.

Lusa barely held back a giggle as she reached a hand across the archway.

No door, no barrier. No fence or anything, magic or otherwise.

She waved her hand a few times, and nothing happened. Lusa wasn't particularly sensitive to magic, but a lot of wards carried warning sensations to deter unwanted guests. She didn't feel anything except the room was a bit warmer due to the enchanted torches. She assumed they were, because she couldn't imagine anyone coming through to relight them every time they burnt out.

Lusa stepped inside; nothing happened.

She edged closer, then squatted next to the concaved floor and the mountain of coins. American pennies from the United States before the Aperien Event. She recognized them because Res liked to use coins for a few of his illusions. He enjoyed rattling off where they all came from, and a bit of the information stuck over the years.

They were copper coins, which held little value even when they were in circulation. And there were so many she could swim in the pile. She picked one up, figuring if she was going to trigger some sort of alarm, she might as well get caught with a penny between her fingertips instead of a one-of-kind, mysterious truth-telling bird. The metal was cool. The date read 1955.

"Wow, that's like almost 300 years old." Lusa made sure it sounded like she was talking to herself, but the words were also for Kiki, who stayed quiet despite the earlier chirp. They didn't know if or what they'd meet down here. As long as Kiki stayed attached to her as a piece of her attire, Kiki would disappear when Lusa did at the shadowlands' touch. If Kiki paraded around as a cat, Lusa couldn't hide it.

Lusa slipped the penny in her pocket. Res hadn't gotten any new coins in a while, so she knew he'd like it, beyond the little litmus test for their doom.

"That's one room," Lusa said, dusting off her hands and retreating to the hall. It seemed to extend forever, an endless row of square doors carved into the mountain in front of her. "Only like fifty-five billion or so to go?"

Lusa stayed down in the maze for about three hours. Turned out another one of Kiki's many talents was timekeeping. By then, Lusa was more than ready to head up, because maze was an understatement. That first hall had been deceptive.

The next hallway split nine directions at the first divide.

No big deal. Kiki could handle that.

The next split was five. The next, eight more hallways.

By then, Lusa was more than lost.

The rooms also stopped being nice, orderly and all the same size.

She'd also had to give up the hope that after seeing twenty-seven rooms in a row filled with different kinds of coinage, there would be an organizational scheme to this place, even if it wasn't documented.

Just . . . nope. Not even a little.

The room of armor scared her half to death. Lusa thought they'd walked into an actual army, because the suits were all posed, with half of them set up on horse skeletons (also with armor). There were even two sets of griffon armor, three unicorn helmets, and a wyvern chainmail getup, all set up on a matching skeleton like something out of a pre-Aperien Event human museum.

The room of cups—no, goblets—had been interesting, until she realized half of them had stuff in them. One of them was the shape of a bull skull, with what looked very much like blood inside. She'd left that room quick.

An entire room, twice the size of Wags's interior, stuffed so full of spun wool and thread, she couldn't even step inside.

One had a fountain that whispered about the coin her pocket in English and sung about *ranas* in Spanish, and Lusa kept right on walking.

Carpets. Rolled up, stacked, piled on the floor, spread out, in every single color and more. Not a speck of dirt or dust anywhere, and Lusa moved on when some of them started wiggling in her direction.

She'd probably stayed too long in the icy room, because it was so neat. It was the least crowded room they'd come across, and it felt like stepping back into old northern Canada where she'd lived as a child, all brisk winter air, fresh snow, and frost. Lusa had no idea what the source of the winter magic was, and didn't poke around. She just sat in the snow for a little bit and took a break, enjoying the feeling of real weather for the first time since they'd arrived under the mountain, because the magic sun orbs didn't fool her senses. In here, it smelled, tasted, and *felt* like she was standing in winter, not miles underground. Maybe she'd come back, or bring Res down to see it, since it wasn't too far into the maze.

On it went. More coins. A room of what she guessed were rubies, with one of them as big as her head, all the way down to a basin filled with ruby dust. A ship that looked a little sad to Lusa, because it was propped up on wooden silts rather than out on the ocean having a grand adventure.

They come across at least five rooms just for swords. So many swords.

One thing was certain. Lusa didn't feel any active magic, but something kept the maze spotless. As still and undisturbed as everything seemed, a place like this should have been caked in decades worth of dust and dirt from the shifting stone, and she'd seen more than her share of spiders skittering around, but no webs.

The mouros kept a clean house was Lusa's guess. Which begged the question of where were they, how many were they, and how they felt about fingerprints on their very tidy treasures?

Lusa tried not to touch too much; gods only knew how dangerous half this stuff was, but now and then she couldn't help it, like with the snow. She'd left footprints. And there was no hiding her snow angel.

Well, too late now, and until there was a problem, she and Res were sticking to honesty whenever possible. Lying, she knew well from years of observation, tended to get tangled and messy and cause more trouble than it ever solved. She never bothered, although until now she'd had the luxury of never needing to lie.

Wags didn't need lies. Res seemed to thrive on her being frank with him, given the time he spent putting on a show. Tick was a cat, so no lying there. And Kiki was so pure, Lusa couldn't imagine any reason she'd ever need or want to lie to Kiki.

But it was easy to never be pressed into a lie when you never had to interact with more than four people, and only two of them could talk back.

Lusa's feet were killing her by the time Kiki guided her back to the central spire by warming the belt left or right. She yawned as she padded up the main spiral, then up the sloped hall she'd walked with Erandi. Still no mouros, she mused. Maybe she'd tell him next time she saw him what she'd found. He might find it interesting. Or maybe she'd wait until she encountered one of the giants, if she ever did.

Maybe he didn't care at all and had only been being polite.

Lusa frowned at the errant thought. Did it really matter? If he didn't care, he'd tell her and she wouldn't bother him again. Right? But would she be able to tell if he told one of those white lies, the ones people used to be polite?

Gods, as interesting as all this was, and as excited as she was for Res and his new family, she was struck suddenly by how much she missed it being just them, with Wags and Tick and Kiki, and fresh air and real sunshine.

She heard laughter as she came back into the castle proper, a mess of voices she recognized and some she didn't. They must be having dinner still? No, it was probably too late for that, so on to card games and drinking most likely. Lusa shrugged and followed the sounds, enjoying the upbeat music as she got closer to one of the larger main rooms on the first floor. An entertaining hall, she believed Guatemoc called it. The double doors were cracked, warm light filtering through, and she figured she might as well stop by and say goodnight to everyone.

Voices got louder, laughter loud and rowdy, but when Lusa pushed the cracked door opened and peered inside she froze.

She didn't know what she expected to find, but this was not it.

The Ques were all here, Res among them, and Quetzalcoatl reclined on a large chaise settled above the gathering. There were dozens of others in the room and they were . . . Well, they were all beyond gorgeous, to say the least. And not wearing very many clothes.

She blinked a few times as incense and perfume tickled her nose, along with sweat, drink, and after a few belated seconds, she realized, what must have been the heavy scent of sex.

A dais of sorts decorated the room's middle, two women and a man tangled on the reflective surface, their skin painted and shimmering, without a stitch of clothing between them. Contortionists, because normal bodies didn't bend so much or those directions, but contortionists didn't normally rub all over each other naked like that either. Matty picked that moment to join them on the little stage, stepping up as he called over his shoulder, but Lusa's heartbeat thrummed so loud in her ears she couldn't hear anything he said.

Matty was bare-chested, his pants half open, and he grinned as he poured brightly colored liquor on one of the women's chests, who arched her back closer when he did. She held the top of a twisted body triangle, one arm out and one leg back as she balanced herself on the other two dusters. Her tail curled in the air, a perfect, sleek punctuation to the show. Her skin was sunset and starlight at the same time.

Matty leaned down and licked the liquor from her throat, then her breast, before sucking her nipple between his lips.

Lusa tore her gaze away, landing on Pollock, who leaned back, lazy and relaxed, as he observed the scene in front of him. He below out a plume of smoke, his hair half loose around his shoulders, his shirt unbuttoned. A female duster with pupilless blue eyes and folded butterfly wings brushed out his braids. She was naked too.

Beside him sat Erandi. Lusa don't know why it shocked her so much, as if he never left his room except with her yesterday. He was dressed the same as last time she'd seen him, with one hand running idly through the hair of young man sitting between his legs, with his cheek resting on Erandi's thigh. The man was nude and tied, bound head to toe in a complicated set of crimson ropes, on his knees in a position that seemed painful, but his expression was absolute bliss.

A shrill noise caught her attention, coming from the back of the room, from a bed shrouded in curtains that didn't do much for privacy. It must have been the woman Oz was having sex with, by the motions, because no other Ques was quite as broad as him, and she was pretty sure that was his back and naked butt on full display, with a pair of pale legs wrapped around his waist.

Lusa stared at her feet, her eyes burning from the smoke and blinking so fast the room almost spun.

She wasn't a voyeur. She never had been.

There'd been a thousand chances in her life to watch people have sex, and she never bothered. Sure, no one would ever know, but *she* would, and she didn't invade others' privacy like that. It just felt gross and wrong. Obviously, Oz didn't care about privacy right now—no one else in the room did either, whatever the hells this kind of orgy party-thing was, but she still couldn't bring herself to look any more than her unintended peek.

Now, she had watched people kiss a number of times. That had never seemed quite so private, especially when people readily shared such affection in public places all the time. And maybe she'd stared a little too long now and then, wondering what it might be like to have someone look at her adoringly, or what a kiss would feel like if she ever got to experience one. But of all the people she'd watched when she couldn't quite help herself, what drew and held her attention was how loving and tender those embraces seemed.

All this? The primal and messy, sloppy, needy side of things? Those were the times she looked away.

Yet it still made her feel flushed now, head to toe, and she couldn't help peeking up again, because Res was in here, because she caught a glance of him, and she shouldn't have looked again, but there he was, seated next to Guatemoc. Guatemoc was shirtless, which wasn't so unusual in what she'd seen of him so far. Res was fully clothed, which shouldn't have sent a weird sort of relief shuddering through her, but all that crashed away when her gaze settled on the woman seated between them.

She was half in Res's lap, speaking in his ear with her hand resting on his chest. Res grinned while he listened, nodding along, and when she leaned back, Lusa's breath caught.

She was stunning. Her skin was bronze and pale at the same time, her hair slick and black and shiny, unlike Lusa's, which just was kind of there. This woman's mane was a sleek river, with not a hair out of place, pinned back from her fine-boned features with golden clips crested in yellow sapphires. Her hands, Lusa noted, were delicate, flawless, and tipped in finely manicured black nails. Dark eye makeup and deep, dark red lips, but her eyes left Lusa breathless. True cat eyes, bright green with slit pupils, heavily dilated as she grinned at Res, her canines pointed and her tongue delicate and pink.

Lusa needed to look somewhere, anywhere else, and somehow, she picked the worst place. When her frantic gaze landed, it landed on Quetzalcoatl, and he stared right at her.

No, he stared into her.

He saw everything single thing Lusa felt and didn't fully understand herself.

The knife digging under her ribs and making it hard to breathe at all.

The shame heating her cheeks at the uncomfortable ache between her legs.

The way her heart felt like it was going to break into a million tiny pieces when it didn't have the right.

A hundred, thousand, million other things hammering through her mind so fast, she couldn't hope to process any of them at all, let alone form what she should or shouldn't feel about anything she was seeing right now.

The god in front of her saw all of this at a single, piercing glance, and offered her a single shouldered shrug, as if to say *what did you expect* without saying anything at all.

No one else noticed her.

The shadowlands never touched her, and not a single one of the other Ques realized she was in the doorway, not even Res.

Lusa didn't look back as she fled to the safety of Wags.

# Chapter 26

A harem, Lusa processed by the time she'd been back in Wags for a few hours. She'd done nothing but sit at the kitchen table while Kiki eagerly mapped out all the places they'd gone, too excited to notice her silence.

Of course Quetzalcoatl had a harem. He was a god. That was exactly the type of things gods did in like fifty percent of mythos. Of course, the other Ques would enjoy the benefits of the harem. They lived here, after all, and Quetzalcoatl seemed determined to see his grandsons well taken care of.

So, of course he would show Res said harem, because he was trying to convince Res this was where he should stay.

Lusa took a shuddering breath.

No big deal.

Res was a sexual creature; he always had been. He'd been that way long before she met him, and continued that way for years after she started travelling with him. He'd been polite enough to keep his encounters away from Wags, which was great. It also meant she'd never gotten such an up-close look at his conquests until tonight.

Was that really what he liked?

Sex that was a big show, with an audience? Another kind of performance?

Lusa shook her head, blowing out the air from her lungs so hard her hair ruffled.

None of her business.

He just hadn't indulged for so long, that was all, that had to be it. Since the attack, Res hadn't stayed out at night, taken any lovers, or so much as flirted, at least that Lusa witnessed, when before he used to charm people out of their pants with no effort. Like it was a sport, almost like he did it just because he could. She used to tease him about it. And back then . . .

Well, back then, she didn't care. Not really. She accepted it, and maybe deep down it stung just a tiny bit that she wasn't what he'd ever want, but whatever. She was an adult, and she put her love for him away from being "in love" into *loving* her best friend a long time ago because otherwise, she'd need to leave him. And it had worked, honestly. She didn't spend her life pining over him, and she wasn't bitter about him enjoying other company. It just was, and it was fine, and over the years, the initial sting faded away because he was worth more to her than her tiny wounded pride at his rejection. And he was an awesome best friend.

But then after the attack happened, things . . .

She rubbed her face.

No, after the attack, Res was vulnerable. Lacking any physical affection after so much time hiding and alone. And one platonic hug and turned into a change from them not touching at all to physical affection, but it was all *platonic*. Friend stuff. And she liked having that with him. She'd watched lots of friends who touched, and it was fine. It was good. It was a way people showed they cared about each other, and she'd never doubted Res cared for her even if he'd never viewed her in a sexual way.

Lusa almost laughed. Gods, it wasn't even about sex, not really. She didn't care that all she got was hugs and touches, and to punch him on occasion now. She just wanted him in her life. Maybe it was pathetic, but when he'd looked at her all those years ago and told her to "please not make moon eyes at him because they couldn't be friends and have sex" half-joking, she'd accepted it.

Right now, she wasn't upset because she wanted him to come back and have sex with *her* instead of the lady with cat eyes.

Lusa winced.

Okay well, maybe . . .

Maybe that wasn't entirely, one hundred percent true, but she was letting her imagination run away because she'd been caught off guard by a room full of very sexy people doing sexy things.

Lusa rolled her eyes.

No, the bigger problem was she didn't care that Res didn't do sexy things with her but suddenly didn't want him doing those sexy things with anyone else.

That little sting was a raging, gaping, burning wound and *that* was not okay.

Not okay in the least.

Because it wasn't fair. He'd set the boundary, she'd agreed, and she been fine all this time, and now?

Lusa was very much not fine at all. Not even a little bit.

"Crap," she muttered, her head dropping into her hands. Her eyes burned, this time not from smoke, and it only got worse by the flash of how Quetzalcoatl looked at her like she was pathetic. Like how dare she ever think she could be good enough to be his companion with all a god could offer him instead?

Maybe she was a fool, but that condescension, when he knew nothing about either of them? Nothing about Res?

Sure, Res liked sex. But Res lived to perform and make people happy. Res's illusions wouldn't mean much to a room full of people who could do some version of the same magic. And he wouldn't keep bringing joy to a harem of the same couple people after they'd seen his tricks a dozen times.

Res wouldn't light up with joy like he did when he made Lils's birthday party the best moment of her entire life.

Lusa let out a little growl and surged to her feet.

"Easy there, Lusa girl. You look like you're about to murder someone."

Res stood in the doorway as Wags's curtain dropped behind him, a lazy smirk on his pretty mouth, his body loose with his jacket slung over his shoulder, and he smelled like weird smoke and definitely like sex.

And suddenly she was mad at him instead of Quetzalcoatl now that he was standing right in front of her. Being logical and fair flew out the metaphorical window because that uncomfortable stab was back under her ribs again and her heart was thrumming so fast it felt like it might burst.

She could have handled these feelings, she would have figured it out, but not if he was going to come back to Wags every day for the next month, *smirking* at her like that, after he just got done doing gods knew what with that cat lady and everyone else in that sex room.

"Yeah? Maybe it's you," Lusa snapped.

Res's expression shifted; all the playfulness was replaced with a severe frown. "Did something happen today?"

It was so absurd, she laughed, then laughed again. Unhinged, ugly, bitter barks, which made her sound like a lunatic. She slapped a hand over her mouth, afraid of what might come out if she removed it.

Behind her, Kiki wasn't sketching maps anymore. Res remained stoic, hanging his coat without his attention leaving her, then holding his hands out as if calming a skittish animal. "Lusa, talk to me."

She shook her head, her hand still firmly over her mouth. Bad idea. Then Res's calm shifted, almost as fast as she'd shifted from frustrated to angry to maniac.

"I'm exhausted from spending the entire day performing for them and—" he waved a hand behind him as he spoke, but she didn't let him finish.

She couldn't. She made the mistake of dropping her hand, and then she snorted and let out one of those awful laughs again.

"Oh, wow, you must really be *suffering*."

Res looked as shocked as if she'd slapped him. She would have been less shocked if she had. Lusa had never spoken to him like that. She'd never spoken to *anyone* like that her life. Not that she'd spoken to many people, but still. Hateful and cruel and awful, same as the bitter laughs that kept coming out.

"I'm sorry," she gasped out, bumping the table as she retreated. Kiki hopped onto the stove, then the shelf, cowering in a pile with Tick. "Just forget it. Never mind, I'm—" She tried to run, to disappear, but she didn't make it an inch before Res caught her wrist and spun her around, her back thudding against Wags's wall.

"Not a fucking chance." Res's tone was as harsh as hers a second before, those beautiful eyes drilling into her, searching, so she squeezed hers shut. This would all be so much worse if she started crying now too. "What the hells is going on, Lusa?" When she shook her head, he caught her jaw, and her eyes flashed open. Furious was the only word to explain his expression, the same one after she'd been trampled by the crowd and he thought someone hurt her. "Someone obviously upset you. Who was it?"

Then she was mad all over again, because he was so ready to battle on her behalf but had no problem *being* the problem.

"You did!" She yelled right in his face, really leaning in, sounding completely nuts again, but she didn't really care anymore. She shoved at him, both hands on his chest, hard, and he backed away from her in surprise.

"What? What the hells did I do?"

She laughed again.

Gods she really needed to stop making this horrible sound.

"Seriously?" Lusa flapped her arms, and they slapped hard against her legs when he said nothing. He didn't seem a lick calmer than she felt, which just made her angrier. "You told them you were sleeping with me!"

His expression shifted from angry to cautious. "I said that to Quetzalcoatl, and only him, when we were caught off guard because he could see you. Which we discussed after, and as you may recall, I made a point of telling him you were more than that."

"Yeah, your 'trusted companion,' right?" Lusa used air quotes as she said it. "You really think he didn't tell everyone else I'm the cheap entertainment you haul around? The poor little invisible girl who keeps your bed warm when you're bored?"

His voice remained level, even as hers got more and more hysterical. "Where is this coming from?"

Lusa scrubbed a fist under her eye; great, now she was crying in front of him. "I was going to just, I don't know, say goodnight to everyone, but I saw all of you with his harem or whatever."

Res's jaw twitched. "The company I've kept has never bothered you before."

"That's before you told everyone that's what you use me for! Gods, Res! What the hells does that make me look like? We haven't even been here two whole days and you're already off with all his other girls—women, I mean, or men, whatever. It doesn't matter. That's not the point." It wasn't the point, but it mattered. All of it mattered, but she kept yelling now that she'd opened the door. "You're making me look like a pitiful, desperate, pathetic duster you've thrown away at the first chance for a free upgrade!"

Res had his hands on his hips now, eyes closed and head back, staring up at the ceiling but not. She realized he was calming himself, as she tried to do the same for herself and failed.

Her chest heaved and her hands shook and she couldn't say what she really wanted to say, what she probably should say—*I love you and I always have and I was okay with how things were and now I'm not and we really, really need to talk about this*—but how could those words do anything but make everything so much worse?

"Let me get this right, sweetling." He lowered his gaze to hers, his expression stony, a coldness there that made her take a step back. "Your sterling reputation is the only thing on your mind? When we came here because you wanted to this job for Theodore? Because you seemed ready to do whatever was necessary so you could do a good thing. Or was that simply if I was paying the price and not your perceived virtue?"

"What? No!"

"No *what*, Lusa? No, you only care about how a few strangers see you? Hmm? Or do you just not like that you're having to suffer some discomfort in this little gamble as well?"

"You're a jerk," she hissed, but it came out as more of a whimper. "Yeah, shame on me for worrying about how people *see* me, Res. It's only never happened before, except with you, and I guess you fooled me into thinking it was safe to be seen." She shoved by him, or at least tried to, but he grabbed at her again. "Let me go!"

"I didn't fuck anyone, Lusa."

She stilled at his words; she didn't want to, but she did.

"No one thinks those things about you," he added quietly.

"Pretty sure Quetzalcoatl does," she mumbled.

"He's a god, sweetling. He thinks everything is pathetic besides himself. I'm honestly not sure where even his grandchildren fall within the scope of his judgement."

He squeezed her elbow and tried to pull her closer, but she leaned away.

"Fine. Okay. I'm sorry I yelled."

"That's not enough."

She tried to jerk away from him, but he spun her around, and then he was picking her up by the waist and plopping her down on the table.

"What the hells!"

Her protesting sort of tapered off because he was standing between her thighs, his hands braced on the table so they were face to face, eye to eye, so close she could barely focus on his face.

Gods, he was always so handsome, but now it was somehow exacerbated by how serious he looked. Normally, his charm was increased by his smirks and grins and all of his jokes and sarcasm. Now, though, she was seeing a different edge to him, and being the focus of such intensity left her unmoored.

"Lusa," Res said, his voice calm and cool, devoid of any of the lighthearted jesting he lived by. "Talk to me, please." When she winced, he cupped her cheek in one hand, resting his forehead against hers. "I know I shut you out for months, but please." He gave a morose chuckle. "I'm not sure I'd survive the same treatment."

She pushed at him again—gods, she just needed some space to breathe, couldn't think at all with him so close—and he leaned away. "I'm not. I won't, okay? I'm just upset."

"Alright," Res offered. He hung his head for a moment, and she resisted the urge to reach out and run a hand through his silky hair; it was a little tangled right now, a bit messy, yet she knew it would still be softer than hers. Good thing she didn't, because he looked up after only a few seconds. "Tell me something, will you?"

"What?"

"Have things shifted, between you and I?" His gaze held hers, searching, almost desperate as he took in her face. As he watched her, studied her, his gaze flicked rapidly over her features before coming back to pin her again. "Since the night I was attacked. What we are, together, has it changed for you? How you feel?"

He didn't have to say *for him*. It burned unspoken in the air between them, the question a bonfire scalding the heavens. Its own little calamity in the middle of Wags's nice kitchen.

Res wouldn't ask her unless . . .

There wouldn't be reason to wonder, right? If things, feelings, hadn't shifted for him?

He was asking her how she felt about him. What she felt for him.

The truth was he'd never actually asked before. He'd made a joke that sealed off the conversation like a tomb, and neither one of them had ever touched the topic again. He'd closed that door before either one of them truly looked inside, and she'd accepted that.

But it felt wrong to lie to him now, if he really wanted to know.

She was already shaking her head.

Res scoffed and pushed back, his laugh a bit like her angry, bitter sounds from earlier. "Right, of course." He waved a hand. Lusa frowned, trying to find her voice, trying to find the right words for all this, but he was leaving? "Forget I said anything. Long two days, big changes, and not every day one deals with meeting your grandfather, who also happens to be a god."

"Res."

He was walking down the hall already, away from her, talking over his shoulder. "Do me a favor, sweetling, and don't bring it up? You know how fragile my ego is."

"Res, just shut up for two seconds."

He stopped, but he didn't turn.

Lusa swallowed a few times, then a few more, and her voice came out in a hoarse whisper. "You asked if things have changed for me, but the answer is no."

"Yes, Lusa, no need to hammer your point home."

"The answer," she said loudly and rudely and talking over him, but whatever, "is no because I've been in love with you since way before you got attacked. Pretty much the whole time I've known you, honestly," she added with a helpless little shrug when he finally looked her direction. When he canted his head in silent question, she looked down at her hands in her lap. "Maybe not the entire time, but it was like three days before you made it pretty clear you weren't interested in me, so at first, I convinced myself I was in the love the idea of someone seeing me.

"But then I really got to know you. The real you, not the fancy showboat." She grinned when he scoffed, still not looking up as she picked at her fingernails. "But yeah, it didn't take long for me to fall for you for real. But like you said, friendship was more important, so." She ended in another shrug. "I let it be, because I wouldn't do anything to risk losing you. Or making things weird forever when you didn't feel the same way."

Lusa felt him getting closer but still didn't look up. She couldn't, because her doubt was filling his silence and she wasn't sure if she had the strength to give her biggest fear a voice, then have it come true seconds later.

Res tucked a finger under her chin, coaxing her face up. He was close again, his expression soft. "I believe what I said was fucking and friendship rarely make for good bed fellows."

"Aren't you and Theodore friends?"

Res blanched. "Gods, it's going to be awkward, you privy to the places I've been. And Theodore and I are acquaintances who had one drunken fuck that has haunted me for decades, and continues do to so, as evidenced by where we are right now." When she laughed, he flashed her grin, but then he was serious again, and her breathing hitched as he cupped her cheeks in his hands, the gesture far more intimate than any of their hugs or other touches. "What I was trying to express, and likely failed to do so properly, was that after three days, I realized that I valued you more than any person I'd ever met, and I wasn't willing to risk that for a night of sex, which is how I handle most everyone else."

His thumb brushed her bottom lip. "I put you away in a box as well, sweetling. The only example for a relationship I had was my father, whom I never knew, who took a woman as lovely as mother to bed after convincing her she was his everything, only to leave her a few months later." The pad of his thumb was so soft, the motion lazy as he moved back and forth across her lip, watching it like he couldn't believe it was his hand touching her. "You're precious, like she was, not to be used as a conquest or a game, not to be won because I could, because, sweetling, you didn't hide as well as you thought, at least not at first."

Lusa's cheeks burned hot with embarrassment, but he shook his head.

"Hush. I'm not trying to embarrass you, but I want you to know I saw a beautiful girl looking at me like I'd hung the stars in the sky, and I knew damn well I wasn't what she needed. Ah, now, don't argue." He leaned forward, running his nose across hers. "You needed a friend as much as I needed one. I could get an ego stroke anywhere. What I couldn't get was someone who saw me as much as I saw you.

"And then you got good at hiding, and I don't pine. It doesn't suit,"

Res said with a sniff, then laughed when she rolled her eyes, but she was smiling now too. "But you kept your secret, so I assumed the shine wore off, and our friendship is my most treasured gift. And then you went and saved my life, love."

"Res," Lusa whispered; it was almost too much, all of this, after so long, but he kissed her forehead.

"And then you stayed, and then you became my stars. Or really, I realized you've been my whole damn sky for a very long time." Res sighed then, his lips on her forehead for another kiss, then resting there as he breathed. "Now I'm bound to flounder here, being a lover and not a fuck. And I will probably fuck things up in all the wrong sort of ways, hopefully along with the best sort to make up for it, but I can tell you with unfailing certainty you are not a person one grows tired of."

Lusa rested a hand on his chest, over his rapidly beating heart. "I know you aren't like your father, Res. I've never thought that."

"Excellent," he said, rearing back, his eyes trained on her lips. "Now unless you have an objection, I want your mouth."

Lusa blinked at him. "W-what?"

His smirk was sly and slow, and sexy enough that her stomach did a little flutter so intense it almost hurt. "I'm going to kiss you now."

"Oh. Uhm. Okay."

# Chapter 27

Lusa had agreed to kissing him—*kissing!*—but Res didn't just dive right in like she thought he would. He waited, nuzzling his nose against hers again, which was very nice, and her head spun a little because he'd said *she was his whole sky.*

"Breathe, sweetling," he whispered, his breath a warm puff over her lips, and she inhaled sharply because she had been holding her breath.

"Sorry," she whispered.

"None of that now," he replied, and then lips found hers.

Lusa shivered—she couldn't help it—both hands flying up to grab his forearms. He held her face with gentle palms, his lips soft and warm pressed against her own. Her eyes fluttered closed, and she leaned forward into him without really meaning to. When he chuckled against her mouth, she jerked back.

"Oh, sorry, did—"

His thumb shifted from her cheek to her lips. "There isn't a single thing in this moment that wouldn't make me fall to my knees for you, love." When she wrinkled her nose, he rolled his eyes. "Lusa, if I wanted some sort of performance, I could find it down the hall. You're what I desire. Just you, as you are. Do you believe me?"

Lusa nodded. She did. He'd always given her his honesty.

And she loved him.

"Good," he said. "Though I am looking forward to most thoroughly proving it to you nonetheless."

This time when he kissed it her, it was different.

Very different.

Different enough, she was pretty sure she was about to melt into the floor, catch on fire, or maybe both. His mouth was hotter, then open, his tongue sliding along her bottom lip so he could suck it into his mouth, and then when she opened hers in a little squeak at the sensation, the very good sensation, it got even better.

Her first expectation wouldn't have been that having someone else's tongue in her mouth would feel so good.

She was wrong.

His exploration of her mouth was firm and sensual, wet and hot, and she tried to mimic him, squeezing his forearms so hard her knuckles hurt. He retreated after a few seconds, nibbling at her bottom lip, then whispering, "No hurry, love, I'm not going anywhere. You have me."

Then he dove right back in, his hands shifting to her hair, tugging gently so her head fell back a little, and she let out a whine.

Gods, what an embarrassing noise, and it kind of ruined the moment for her. Lusa pulled away, hiding her face against his neck while she tried to catch her breath. Res only hummed, a hand still buried in her hair as the other ran down her spine, making her arch into him like when she petted the cat. She squeezed her eyes shut tighter.

"What is it, sweetling?" Res asked against her hair.

"Embarrassed," she mumbled against his throat, but even as she said it, she was melting against him, relaxing into his soothing.

"Why's that?"

Lusa tried to burrow into him a little more. He was warm and cozy, he smelled so good, and she really didn't want him to change his mind because she sounded like an idiot, or threw herself all over him, or shoved her tongue down his throat because she didn't know what the hells she was doing. She loosened her grip on his arms, winding them around his lower back in a hug—she knew how to do those, lots of practice now—instead of clinging to him like she was drowning.

"Lusa girl." His tone was soft, but a touch scolding.

"I don't know. I feel like I'm being weird."

"Weird?"

She shook her head against him. "Do I have to make that noise again for you so you know what I mean?" Her cheeks were so hot they hurt at this point.

"Gods, I hope you make that sound all night," Res said, and when she pushed back, his grin was smirky and sexy and she kind of want to kick him. He must have read it in her expression. "I've never had the pleasure of being with someone as responsive as you are, love. Sex is a bore when it's a production," he said, rolling his eyes rather dramatically. "This," he added, tightening his fist in her hair and giving a little tug, as he leaned into her neck and kissed, right where her pulse was threatening to explode out of her neck, making her loose another little gasp, "is enough to drive a man mad."

"Stop teasing me," she whispered, but then his teeth found her skin, a bite just shy of really hurting, sending a delicious thrum through her blood. The needy throb started up between her legs again already. "Res . . ."

"Teasing is part of the fun, sweetling, but never at your expense." Res kept her close, her hands gripping the shirt on his back as he very aptly *teased* and nibbled her throat as he spoke. "And so you're aware, I have contraception protections in place, and god blood makes me immune to any human diseases."

Lusa giggled. She couldn't help it; her head was swimming. "That's sexy bedroom talk, huh?"

"In a sense, yes," Res replied, no trace of joking in his voice. "If I take you to bed, your protection is as important to me as your pleasure."

"Oh." That was actually really amazing.

And they were actually doing this.

Which was punctuated by Res's hands under her thighs, hoisting her up from the table. She fell forward into his chest with a little yelp, tightening her legs around his waist as he turned down the hall.

"Shall we then?" He peered down at her as he carried her, his grin boyish and his eyes sparkling. Delighted. The happiest she could recall seeing him since before that night in the Baker's Hills.

Maybe she should have felt hesitant or scared, but all she felt was excited and a little bit nervous, but it was a good nervous.

"Only if you kiss me more."

That got another laugh out of him, followed by a devilish grin. "Demanding already, is she?"

"Might as well see what all the fuss is about," she quipped back, but then he smacked her butt hard, and she screamed, "Res!" right before he tossed her on his bed. He followed after kicking the curtain shut, fastest she'd ever seen him move, and Lusa found herself pinned under his weight a flash later.

Instead of crushing, though, it was warm and delicious, and she bit her lip when he shuffled so he settled his narrow hips between her legs. His hair flopped forward, the flecks of gold in his eyes almost dangerous in the low light, and before she could summon any sort of response, his mouth descended on hers again.

This time, she couldn't help herself. She buried her hands in his hair like he'd done to hers, and it was just as soft and silky as she'd imagined. Lusa tried to match his pace instead of rushing, tried to keep her frantic mind and body from spinning out of control and focused on the moment, right here, instead of what came before or next or after. She felt his hum of approval in his chest, which deepened when she dug her short nails into his scalp, and when he returned the favor, she whined again, and this time, tried not to let herself get embarrassed.

Then Res rocked forward, pressing between her legs, and she jolted at the pressure, the hardness, because *oh.*

He slowed their kiss and pulled back the pressure between their bodies, leaning back to nip at her lips again. "Yes, that's me, love."

She snorted. Not sexy at all, but then he laughed, and then she did too.

"Stay there," he murmured against her lips, sucking the bottom one again and letting got with a little pop before he sat up and tugged his shirt over his head without unbuttoning it the rest of the way.

"Ugh," Lusa groaned, covering her face.

"Ugh? Truly?"

She peeked through her fingers at him, bare chested now. He was tall and lean, and of course, finely muscled in all the right places. "That looked like a move from someone who's done it like a million times."

"Lusa," Res laughed her name, then sort of tumbled forward before he lifted her shirt hallway and bit her stomach, a little too hard.

"Hey!"

"Think of it as years spent in preparation for your service."

Lusa snorted again. "I'm not sure that's better."

He kissed beside her belly button, then just under her ribs. It tickled a little, but also made her breath catch. "Immense sacrifices for the greater good." Another bite, right under her breasts.

Lusa gasped as she laughed out, "Oh gods, you're absurd!"

He was laughing, too, though she felt it where they touched, where his body pressed against hers as he pushed her shirt up to her throat. But then he stilled suddenly. When she peered up at him, he was staring down at her chest, his expression . . . well, it was startled.

Lusa had seen other breasts before. Hers were average, she figured, not too big or small, though her nipples were darker instead of light pink. She guessed that had to do with her human heritage. She'd never had a reason to doubt that her boobs were fine, adequate, or maybe even kind of nice. They had a pretty shape, and they weren't so large they got in her way.

Maybe Res wasn't looking at them, though. Maybe her stomach? Lusa frowned. He might have the perfect body, but she was a bit soft all over, with a little roundness in the tummy. Nothing that bothered her, but then again, she wasn't used to anyone besides herself seeing this much of her bare skin, let alone intimately.

"Res?" She lifted her hands to cover herself, but he shook his head as his finger crooked under the thin leather band of her necklace and lifted it high enough for her to see.

Oh. That.

The bone carving in the shape of a seal by her father. Beside it, the dog whistle Wags knew meant danger. And wedged in the little clip that held them together, the feather she'd found the night Res almost died.

"I . . ." Lusa trailed off as he stared at the feather, turning the necklace without touching it. While the iridescent gleam was nothing like when she'd seen him in his true form, and only twice, it was still a striking blend of crimson, emerald and gold, like his eyes, with a hundred thousand colors facets in each barb.

She couldn't read his expression. Seconds ago, he was open as she'd ever seen him, and now he'd disappeared for all he still touched her.

"I'm sorry," she whispered. His gaze flicked to hers, the necklace with his feather hanging between them. "I never put this one in the bag." She swallowed a few times as he stared at her, into her. She had no idea what he was thinking. "It was how I knew something was wrong. I found it, backstage, with some of your blood. It gave me a direction, and I clipped it to my necklace so I wouldn't lose it, and then everything was crazy, and . . ." Lusa closed her eyes. "This one helped me save you, and I just . . . I couldn't put it in that awful bag with all the other ones they cut off of you, so I kept it."

She fumbled for the clip. "Here, I can give it back; I know I shouldn't have kept it. I just didn't know when to give it back, or how, not without bringing up that night, and I—"

His hand closed over hers. She blinked up at him, worried she'd ruined this moment, ruined everything, but he shook his head.

"Keep it," he whispered, kissing her knuckles. "Knowing all that, maybe this is right where it should be." Then his serious expression melted back into a bit of a smirk, his gaze flitting back down to her bare breasts. "I think I like the idea of a piece of me always touching your skin."

Relief washed over her, but she didn't have time to dwell on it or the implications of his words. His mouth closed around her nipple and her mind whited out for a second. Her legs tried to jerk shut, because she felt a pulse between her legs with each suck of his mouth, but his body kept them open. She ended up squeezing his hips with her thighs, which made him groan, which was a whole other sensation, the sound wet and lewd against her breast.

Lusa threw her head back against the pillows, choking, because then he bit down on her nipple, just shy of real hurt, but the ache was so good her back arched off the bed almost violently. And the way he sucked and soothed after left her reeling.

She was pretty sure she was humping his stomach. She would have blushed more if she could, but her face was already so flushed, and rubbing against him felt so good, she couldn't seem to stop herself.

"Oh, you sweet, innocent thing," Res purred against her skin, licking a path to her neglected breast, and she turned herself toward his mouth. He chuckled at her eagerness, but she could feel the affection in the teasing. His delight. "And you thought hugs were good."

He was ridiculous, and that was only part of why she loved him.

"Is that so?" He nipped the underside of her breast, almost a reprimand as she realized she'd mumbled that aloud. "Lift your arms."

She did, and he stripped her top off almost as easily as his own and tossed it to the floor. Before she found the mind to tease him again, he was cradled back between her thighs, but this time, their bare chests rubbed together, and gods, he rocked against her clothed core as his mouth claimed her again, his kiss more aggressive. Those whines and whimpers kept slipping out, but he groaned in return, so Lusa stopped trying to hold them back. Then she let out a truly strangled sound when he caught one of her thighs and looped an elbow underneath her knee, and suddenly she felt all him, hot and hard and pressed exactly where she needed him to touch through his pants.

He hummed, rocking into her again. She scrabbled at his bare back, his skin touched with sweat now. "Just there, then," he whispered, repeated the motion, again, and again, his free hand planting on the bed, craning his upper body back so he could look down at her. He hummed again. "Look at you, beautiful, gorgeous little creature, finding her pleasure. I could get lost in you, love."

"Don't." She squeezed her eyes shut, distracted as he continued to rub, to grind against her, the friction driving her mad, but she didn't need any sort of lies from him. She couldn't stand it. He was the only one who really saw her. "You don't . . . *ah* . . . don't have to do that."

"Making you come is a requirement, sorry to say. Multiple times in fact."

She didn't know what he was talking about, but they were clearly having different conversations. Trying to have conversations. She grabbed both his hips, squeezing, and he stopped moving, concern flashing across his face.

"What's wrong?" He let her leg go, cupping her cheek again, the motion so tender it made her already racing heart stutter.

"You don't have to try to make me feel like I'm fancy or anything, Res." She was half-panting, but she needed to tell him this. "I know I'm not like all the others you've been with, and that's fine, it really is, but you don't have to pretend, or say things that . . ." She trailed off, frowning as his expression darkened.

"There's not a word I've said to you that isn't the truth." When she started to shake her head, he leaned a bit closer. "This may come as a shock to you, sweetling, but beauty is relative, and in many cases that aren't yours, superficial. This world of ours has magic and wonders wider than oceans, most of them with depths no deeper than a piss puddle." When she sputtered a surprised laugh, his expression softened. "You are a beautiful woman with a gorgeous, priceless heart. I would never belittle you with false praise when the truth about you is far superior."

Lusa lunged forward and kissed him. She didn't really know what else to do with him. Maybe she'd just kiss him forever and ever.

Res had other plans.

He broke the kiss, grinning lazily down at her while she tried to remember what breathing was, and almost purred the words at her when he said, "And you have a lovely mouth."

"Um, thanks. You do too?"

He arched brow. "Was that a question, sweetling?"

She laughed. "No, no, I'm just . . ." Lusa covered her face. "I'm not good at any of this stuff."

"And what stuff would that be?"

She dropped her hands to the mattress. He'd propped himself up on one elbow, though most of his warm weight still pressed against her body, and he twirled her hair in his pretty fingers. Everything about him was pretty, really.

"I don't know. Sexy stuff. Being sexy. Talking sexy."

Res hummed. "Well, you are sexy because you're you," he said as he held up a finger, then added a second one, "And I happen to be an expert in sexy stuff such as being sexy and talking sexy, so I'm fairly certain you have nothing to worry about."

Then he wiggled his eyebrows, and they both laughed, and then he was kissing her again and within a few seconds, Lusa didn't much care about anything besides touching him and being touched by him.

His skin was sleek and warm everywhere, and she loved the feeling of his back muscles moving under her hands. Sure, she'd felt them when they'd hugged, but this was so much better. She loved how he seemed to enjoy her hands on his skin at least as much as she enjoyed his against her own. Lusa almost forgot there was a destination in mind until he leaned back again and tugged at her leggings.

"Lift your hips, sweetling," he said, his voice husky, and she did without really thinking, and he took her underwear and pants down in one quick draw. She helped him, kicking them off and away, forgetting to be embarrassed about her own nudity as he undid his trousers while he took her in. It wasn't overly bright in his room, only a few smokeless candles tucked in the high corners, but they cast hard shadows across his gorgeous body. Lusa licked her lips a few times, which were a bit swollen from all the kissing, not that she was complaining. Somehow, he managed to get out of his pants without fumbling, his eyes never leaving her body as he did, and then they were both staring at each other naked.

Lusa swallowed a few times. She'd never seen a cock before, not erect like this, but his was as nice to look at like the rest of him, curved long and thickly up and out from his body from a thatch of hair between his thighs. He didn't have much body hair, but what he did have was dark and curled, and coarse comparatively. She didn't move, her hands folded under her chin, and her breath caught her throat when he reached a hand down to stroke himself, the motion subconscious need as his gaze roamed over her body below him. Lusa kept her legs closed tight, because she was so wet from kissing and touching and rubbing and seeing him like this, she wasn't sure what he'd think.

Some of her concern must have shown, because Res seemed to refocus, and then he was giving her that smirky smile of his again.

"See something you like, sweetling?"

Lusa bit the inside of her cheek, because while they teased each other all the time, this didn't seem like the right moment. If he teased her right now with the wrong words, she'd probably disappear into the floor and die. She nodded and waited, because she had no idea what to do next.

"Good," he whispered, holding out a hand. She took it, even though her eyes strayed back to his other fist, which still held his cock. He shifted a bit closer and reclined beside her, pressing her open palm to his chest. "I'm yours to touch however you like, love."

They lay sort of side by side now, her fingers trailing over his chest as he reached out to trace around her nipple, damp from his mouth. She touched his in return, and his smile was wolfish. "That's a girl."

She rolled her eyes and pinched, and he laughed, but then his hand took her wrist and skated it lower, and lower, until her fingers brushed his hot skin. His cock was warmer than the rest of him, and softer, almost silken despite being so very hard. And the tip was leaking, which made her feel less self-conscious about the growing slick between her legs. He let out a little hiss when she rubbed there, and she glanced up at him.

"Pretty, soft little hands," Res murmured, his own palm questing south on her stomach, and she pressed her thighs tighter when he caressed the curls nestled at their apex. "Open these legs for me, Lusa girl, and let me touch you."

"But I'm . . ." She trailed off, voice hitching as he brought his face to her throat, his tongue tasting her skin, her head falling back. She squeezed his length, which twitched against her palm.

"If you're not soaked for me yet, I haven't done my job very well."

Lusa whimpered, and when he shifted to try and look at her face, she tucked her head against his shoulder to hide a little but parted her legs like he asked. And Res wasted no time, diving his fingers down, his motions audible in the space between them.

"Res . . . ah . . ." She lost her focus, ceasing her exploring to cling to him instead, both her arms wrapping around his neck as his clever, clever fingers swirled her wet heat, spreading the slickness around, sending jolts through her entire body.

"Right here, love," Res whispered, kissing her temple. He wrapped an arm around her back, somehow managing to pin one of her legs to the bed and spread her further open to him. She let out a whine, then a sharp gasp when he settled on a particular spot that made her entire body light up. "Ah, there we are. How's that, sweetling? Less, more?"

"I don't know, it just feels good, really good," Lusa babbled as she pressed her face against his skin, delirious with the smell of him, the added taste of his light sweat on her lips.

"Have you come before, love?" He didn't stop moving his fingers as his spoke, firm circles that were making the edges of her vision tunnel and her body string tighter and tighter and tighter.

"Huh?" She managed, panting, trying to keep breathing while he asked her questions.

"Orgasms, sweetling. Have you brought yourself to a peak?"

She still wasn't sure what he was asking her, but now she was rolling her hips in time with his fingers, or her hips were rolling themselves? She didn't know, but she needed to chase down this feeling spinning up, racing where she trusted him to take her. Lusa let out a frantic little whimper, not really an answer, but she didn't care. And her words were getting more and more disjointed.

"That . . . *ah* . . . m-more . . . please, more . . ."

"Gods, you're unreal," Res groaned against her hair. "Let me have it, Lusa. I've got you, don't fight it. Let it take you, love, let it take you over."

Lusa gave in, and then suddenly his words made sense about a peak, because the pleasure crested, hard and sudden, and she let out a cry as it crashed through her. Wave after wave, rushing through her blood, heat and bliss, a flood that washed her mind clean and left her body trembling and tingling all the way to her toes. Res never faltered, his touch wringing every single possible second of this new, wild sensation from her body as she all but thrashed in his arms, but he held her tight as he kept whispering things like *good girl* and *perfect* and *gorgeous* against her ear.

She finally had to grab his wrist, and he stilled, but he didn't move away. He cupped her sex instead, drawing a shaky gasp from her lips, before his other hand tangled in her hair and tugged so she'd look at him. She couldn't, not really, her eyes a bit glazed and the entire world fuzzy.

"Look at you," he crooned, his nose running along hers, his lips ghosting over her own, his tone entirely different from any other she'd ever heard from him. "And you're going to look even prettier when you come on my cock."

All Lusa managed was a strangled whimper, and then he was kissing her again, and her eyes rolled back into her head when his fingers slid inside her body. She tensed—it didn't hurt exactly, but it was strange and new.

Res pulled back, shushing against her lips. "You'll tell me if it hurts, love," he said, not a request as he stared down at her, and Lusa nodded. Then he moved his fingers, and they both grunted. "No pain?"

"No, no, just . . ." Lusa panted; how was she coiling up again? Chasing a peak already when she'd only just discovered it existed? "It's good, just . . . gods, Res." She threw an arm over her face, then whined again when his fingers left her, but then his entire body was over hers as he shifted her how he wanted her, and she was helpless and pliable. She was his.

A thigh nudged hers wide open, a heavy palm on her hip, squeezing. "You're not going to watch? This is kind of a big deal."

Lusa laughed, dropping her arm down to look at him, kneeling up between her legs, and he caught her wrist so he could kiss her palm, his smile that devilish one she loved so much. Then he took himself in hand and pushed forward, and she tensed, and he tsked down at her.

"None of that, love," Res said, shifting a hand to her hip again, his thumb reaching to run soft circles right above where he pressed his cock into her, pleasure chasing up and down her spine again. "Ah, much better, take me all in, sweetling, and then the fun really begins."

She wanted to laugh, because he winked at her, and she thought that might have been his goal, because it chased away her last bit of her nerves, and then the breath pushed out of her lungs. Res filled her body in a long, smooth stroke, the sensation a bit sharp at first, pinching and almost too much, but it quickly became more like a stretch, a pleasurable stretch. She closed her eyes, losing herself to the sensation, strange and new and a lot, because she'd never really thought she'd get to be this close to anyone. Close enough, seen enough.

To exist enough in anyone else's world to be this incredibly connected.

Lusa sniffled, covering her face as Res's hips pressed against hers and he let out a sigh. He folded himself down, his body warm, wrapping his arms around her and pulling her close as he kissed the back of her hands. "Alright, love?"

"Yeah," she whispered from behind her hands. "It's just a lot."

"A good a lot?"

"Yeah." She sniffed again, and Res kept pressing gentle kiss on her fingers, one at a time, his body otherwise still. It felt nice, like this, the heavy heat and fullness of his body inside hers, even though they weren't really having sex right now. They had to move for that, she knew. She shifted, only a tiny bit, the muscles in her core tightening when she did, and they both let out little moans.

"Oh, Lusa girl, careful. My capacity to be a gentleman is limited at the best of times."

She managed to part her hands, staring up at him, and he pushed them the rest of the way off her face, smoothing back her hair and the tears that escaped. Her lip trembled when she smiled. "This is the pretty best time," she whispered.

Res chuckled, then kissed the tip of her nose. "Sweetling, you misunderstand me. This," he said as looked up and down their bodies, "is the best time. But I am *tormented* and if I have to be still much longer, there's a good chance I might actually perish." She laughed, which made her clench again, which made him groan and press his forehead against hers. "Can I fuck you properly, at least, before my end? I'd like to leave this world with my dignity intact, if at all possible."

As he spoke, he gave a gentle sort of grind against her body, and those sparks jumped through her veins again. Her arms were around his neck a second later, hiding her face against his throat again. She could barely keep breathing.

"How can you even t-talk when we're like this?"

He kissed her cheek. "Sheer, stubborn will that I don't make an ass out myself this first time I have you and put you off ever joining me in my bed again." Res ended in a grunt, rolling his hips again. Lusa whimpered into his skin; it felt good. Really good, and better the more he moved. "Gods, you've got a snug little cunt, love."

He was right about handling all the sexy talk. Gods, his words. They were a bit dirty, naughty even, but she loved it.

His pace kept steady, which was not very fast, but he did a sort of snap at the end of each stroke that was driving her mad. "Res . . ." Lusa panted, mouth open, her lips still pressed against his skin. She could feel his heartbeat in his neck, racing wildly for all he kept his composure. "Feels good," she whispered. Good, what a woefully lame word for all the sensations rocketing through her entire body. She'd never be eloquent like him, but she really needed know if he felt good too. "Does it for you?"

Res groaned, his hips stuttering as he tugged her face from hiding. His cheeks were flushed now, too, his eyes bright and wild. "You're mad, love, if you don't know."

Her brow furrowed. "I don't."

"You'll kill me, I'm certain." He hitched upwards, and she let out another undignified squeak as he tugged her thighs so they rested on top of his, and he patted one of her calves. "Tight around my waist, both legs, so I can fuck these questions right out of that pretty little head of yours." She did as he asked, locked her ankles together, and Res's grin was a little feral. "See, a natural."

Lusa rolled her eyes, but then they kept on going and rolled back in her head again when he flatted a hand on her stomach, and the other dove between her legs. Between them, where they joined, was a slick, hot mess. He hummed and teased around his cock as he gave a slow drag out and then shoved back into her, the approval in the growling rumbling that followed making her head spin.

"Taking me so well, and squeezing me so tight." He licked his lips, and then his thumb pressed in tight circles, and she was racing for her peak again, fast and almost violent, as his thrusts grew shorter and rougher. "Ah, there we are. Come on, love, and give me another, and I'll follow you right over that cliff."

She fumbled a bit, reaching, wanting to touch him. She found his thigh, and without meaning to, dug her nails in, which made him hiss and thrust harder. He was inching her up the bed, the sheets sticking to her skin, that tension coiling low in her belly again, and then he shifted his legs a bit, and the next stroke sent sparks through her.

Lusa gasped, gripping his leg tighter, and Res bit his lip as he watched her, as they watched each other, and then he pinched where his fingers played with her, at her most sensitive spot, and the pleasure exploded again.

"Gods, *fuck,*" Res mumbled, but he didn't falter, and Lusa could *feel* herself tightening around his body inside hers, almost like she was trying to pull him deeper inside her. She let out a panting moan with each wave of her climax, and right when it seemed like she might come down, her head thrown back in bliss, Res shifted and suddenly was pressing her bodily into the mattress.

His movement changed the angle, one hand slipped under her body, the other grabbing her rear, and then his mouth was at her ear, his voice strained. "Ah, that's my girl, *fuck*, gods you feel like . . . you're so . . . *shit,* Lusa," and his pace faltered. His thrusts became erratic, and she clung to him, because she felt him swell inside her, felt him pulse, and then his groan was long, and loud, and almost sounded pained against her throat, and him hitting his peak seemed to draw hers out even longer.

After a few seconds, a few more lazy pumps of his hips, Res slowed and stopped, his face still buried in her throat. She clung to him still, her arms wrapped around his neck and shoulders, her legs still around his hips. They both panted, with tiny whimpers on the end of each of Lusa's breathes as little quakes made her entire body twitch and tremble. Res rested on her, inside her, against her, but didn't crush her, his own breathing labored against her sweaty skin.

Then he kissed her neck, her shoulder, then her cheek before lifting himself partway to peer down at her. His hair was a mess from her hands and sweat, sticking up every direction. He was flushed, his cheeks bright, the color running down his throat and chest. And for a moment he just stared at her, his expression as dazed as she felt.

But then Res grinned, a lazy, slow smirk, and licked his lips, before he said, "Well, don't keep us in suspense now, love. Better than hugs?"

# Chapter 28

They'd laughed, then kissed, and then Lusa wasn't sure how they'd both ended up asleep so fast, still tangled up and sweaty. She wasn't sure how long they slept, either, only that when she woke her skin was cool, the sheets were wrapped around them, and Res was molded to her body like she'd never slept anywhere but his bed. He was curled with his front against her back, his arm snaked possessively around her stomach, the other arm cradling under her head as a pillow. Wags must have put out the candles, the only light a dim glow from the cavern outside the curtained window above the bed.

Lusa grinned because Res was snoring, oh-so-softly, against the back of her neck. She fought down a giggle, because as much as she wanted to tease him about it, she didn't want to wake him. She was exhausted; he must have been worse off, given the last few days. Letting him sleep seemed like the best idea, which probably meant she should go back to her own bed, despite how much she liked being right here, tucked in his arms, warm and snuggly and safe.

She'd had no idea what to except from sex. Lusa never imagined it would happen at all, so she certainly never wasted any time thinking about what happened after. She wiggled a little, seeing if she could sneak out of his arms and get out of the sheets without disturbing Res too much, but his arms only tightened. He was a bit like an octopus, she decided. Another wiggle, and she blinked.

Was that his cock, hard against her butt?

"I can't sleep with you thinking so loud, love," Res muttered, kissing her throat as he spoke, and then he rolled his hips against her backside and, yup, that was his cock, poking and prodding and getting bigger by the second. "But if you missed me so much, you only needed to wake me, or really, I'm not so picky. Could just start without me next time."

Lusa huffed. "I was trying not to wake you up."

"Too late," he rumbled, and she gasped when he shifted to grab her hip, pulling a thigh over his as his hand tickled down her belly and between her legs. But before she fully processed what he was after, his fingers were teasing, her body still slick and wet because they'd never moved after they'd finished the first time, but when he started to push two fingers inside her body, she flinched.

Res stilled, moving his hand away to the inside of her thigh. "Are you sore, love?"

"Yeah, I guess so. I didn't really notice until you touched me again." She was embarrassed and not sure why, so she started to shift away from him, but he tutted at her.

"Stay. I'll be right back." Res was out of the bed in a flash, sauntering out of the bedroom into the hall, and all Lusa could do was start at his very nice butt as he walked away.

A very fine butt, pretty just like all the rest of him, so she didn't really fault herself for being distracted, and it was worse when he came back, completely unashamed and glorious in his nudity. Res had a cloth in one hand, and he settled back on the bed and pulled off the sheet.

Lusa grabbed after it. "What are you doing?'

"Taking care of my lover. Now lie back." Res's expression was very serious, so she didn't argue, not even when he gently spread her legs and pressed the cool cloth against her center. "I should have done this right after, my apologies." He was tender about it, his brow furrowed, but it was all so intimate, Lusa found herself staring at the ceiling.

Then she felt the cool tingle of the healing tonic. Lusa jerked upright, snapping her legs closed on his forearm. "Res."

"Lusa," he answered, his brow raised.

"The tonic is for emergencies. I was just a little sore, you didn't hurt me or anything." She frowned at him when he sighed and tossed the cloth over his shoulder, which landed somewhere in the quasi-dark with a wet slap.

"You're mistaken," Res said. When she narrowed her eyes, he narrowed his right back. "I desperately need to fuck you again, sweetling. It's very much an emergency." He grinned, prowling over her as she tried to escape, but then she was against the headboard and his nose was touching hers and his grin was sexy-smirky again. "And clearly I didn't do a good enough job the first time if you don't feel the same way."

Lusa woke up in Res's bed the next morning, but he wasn't there. She rubbed her eyes as she sat up, smiling when she realized he'd tucked her in and threw a quilt over her. The bed was still warm, so she had a feeling he hadn't been up long. A yawn and a stretch, and she swung her legs over the edge, not too tired despite two more very energetic rounds before they'd both passed out again and stayed asleep. And she wasn't sore at all, or sticky, so she guessed she'd fallen asleep first and he'd cleaned her up again, probably wasting more tonic.

She rolled her eyes, but also smiled, so much her cheeks hurt. For all he'd been a ravenous, dirty talking monster, he'd also been sweet and tender and loving with her.

Lusa stared at her feet as she swung them back and forth, trying to keep her mind from racing in a million directions at once, because it wanted run run run. She didn't have a single regret. She'd loved every second of the night before, and she was pretty sure she loved him more now than ever after experiencing this side of him, but there was a particular thorn that was needling her thoughts as much as she tried to ignore it.

He'd called her his whole sky. He'd initiated this change in their relationship. She'd told him she loved him, that she was in love with him. And he'd called her love, many times, all night, during and outside of sex.

But Res hadn't told her he loved her back.

It was just words, she reminded herself as she slipped onto the floor, Wags's wooden panels always warm on her bare feet.

She darted across the hall without looking toward the kitchen, dressing fast and brushing her hair, putting it back in a quick braid. And this was all new, for both of them.

She didn't even know if he'd told his mother he loved her. Lusa was missing context, making jumps because her mind was busy and things were changing and there was still the matter of finding the birds of truth and getting out of here when a god had offered Res a life here.

Lots of stuff going on that was way more important than three little words, especially when his actions last night, all night, and even this morning when she'd been asleep, overflowed with what sure felt like love to Lusa.

They were just words, really, she told herself.

When she walked into the kitchen, Res sat with Kiki, looking over all the maps. He'd lined the papers together so they flowed into a continuous winding story of all the places they'd visited yesterday afternoon. Kiki sat on his shoulder, watching him study the maps with rapt attention. She didn't see Tick, but she knew Wags wouldn't let him wander outside her walls in this place.

"Um, morning?" Lusa said, then winced, not knowing why it came out a question.

Res turned, and his smile melted away her apprehensions. Almost all of them, at least. "Morning, love. Sleep well?"

She blushed. Of course he noticed, and there was the smirk. Lusa rolled her eyes, and he laughed. His hair was still damp, and he was otherwise unadorned, but his expression glowed. But that made her realize she hadn't showered; Lusa sniffed under her arm and frowned a little. She definitely could still smell his and her sweat, among other things.

Res watched her, his expression all smug amusement.

She squinted at him. "Are you going to make this weird?"

He became the picture of innocence. "I have no idea what you might mean. Coffee?" Res offered her a cup, and she was about to complain about his death brew, but the mug he held out was more cream than coffee, and she had a feeling it was overloaded with sugar too.

And now she blushed more as she took it, and mumbled, "Thanks," and he was kind enough not to point it out again.

They spent a few minutes going over the maps, with Kiki chirping details about the shiny stuff. Res was kind in his praise, which made Kiki preen. They agreed there wasn't much to do now except keep on as they were. Lusa would mill around some during the day, make appearances such as painting with Pollock as she'd planned, and then explore the maze more with Kiki. Res would see what he could find out today about how they passed the time down here, beyond what he assumed had been a few days of easy leisure after the mountain festival.

It all seemed normal, really, until they were about to leave.

Res pinned her against the doorframe and kissed her silly for about ten minutes before patting her on the rump and telling her not to stay out too late or he'd miss her.

Lusa needed another ten minutes to compose herself before she managed to leave Wags and start the day.

Things were a little weird, she decided, but a great weird.

It was probably silly to go looking for Res before she headed down to the maze, but Lusa justified it as part of her normal morning wanderings. She was really only kidding herself and not doing a very good job. Still, keeping up the whole appearance thing was important, so she headed by the room everyone ate breakfast in first, in case it gave her an excuse to say hi.

She grinned, blushing and arms swinging as she thought about last night, again, but how could she not? Lusa rubbed her cheeks a few times as she rounded the corner; they were very warm. A little much that she was blushing just thinking about seeing him again, wasn't it?

The door to the dining room was open, but she paused on the threshold when the shadowlands cooled her back, and Lusa looked up to see only Oz at the expansive table, a duster woman standing beside him. She must be staff, it was the only thing that made sense, as she was pointing to something on the breakfast spread with a bright smile, her pretty azure hair in a neat braid over her shoulder. Lusa was too far away to hear their discussion, but Oz leaned close as they spoke, grinning, but his gaze flicked to the doorway when she'd entered and the woman's followed long enough to press Lusa against the shadow-lands. She seemed confused at Oz's attention on an empty doorway, but shrugged it off, even though Oz watched Lusa with a raised brow.

Lusa wasn't sure what to do, but it seemed dumb to leave now? Oz pulled the woman close, kissed her check, and whatever he said was an obvious dismissal. She wasn't bothered a bit, and Lusa stepped inside the room, because she would have walked right into her otherwise. The woman grinned the whole way, a little skip in her step, and she blushed like Lusa had been blushing on her walk over here to search for Res.

Unwanted images flashed in Lusa's mind of the night before and walking in on Quetzalcoatl's harem, and she suddenly found herself wondering if the woman was the one Oz was having sex with in the back of the room.

She wrinkled her nose.

Then blushed herself, because it was none of her business, and not her place to judge anyone anyway. Not that she was, not really, it was just all very weird and not what she intended to be thinking about or wondering about right now, while Oz was sitting right over there after she'd accidently watched him have sex.

Lusa cleared her throat and glanced his direction, ready to make her excuses and leave, but Oz watched her in a way that reminded her a little too much of Quetzalcoatl. And then he smirked.

She must have been red to the tips of her ears now.

"Something on your mind?" Oz asked, lifting a brow as he buttered a piece of toast, an oddly plain selection given the fancy spread that seemed to be set up only for him.

"Um, no, not really." Lusa winced, then she rolled her eyes at herself. "Well, I was looking for Res."

"Hmm. Why's that?"

The knife scraped, and so did Lusa's nerves. It was still strange looking into a gaze so much like Res's and have it lack any warmth. Both Guatemoc and Matty were friendly, and Pollock seemed reserved and inverted, but not cold. Erandi, well, he didn't have eyes, so . . . but Oz, though, he was calculating. She'd noticed it at the first dinner, too. His questions had been more pointed. And right now, the look he gave her was downright smug.

And he didn't give her time to answer. "Worried he's run off to find more fun without you?" When Lusa frowned, Oz shrugged. "I wouldn't have brought out the sex party so soon, but Quetzalcoatl has a heavy hand at times." He took a bite, studying her as he chewed, then wiped his mouth. "Is the invisible girl a voyeur? I'll admit, I was expecting something a little less cliché."

"No, I'm not," Lusa managed through gritted teeth. Why was he goading her like this? "I was just trying to be polite and say goodnight, and when I saw what was happening, I left. It's not my thing." She stuck her chin up, too, not caring if it was trite.

He chuckled. "Seems like it's not Res's either. For a man clearly comfortable with his sexuality, he didn't play and was eager to get home to bed." Oz tossed the napkin on the table and stood. He was the tallest and broadest of all the Ques. Lusa wondered if he didn't have other magical blood in the mix as he strode around the long table between them. "Seems a bit convenient, isn't it, for a Ques to show up at a Ques sanctuary with no knowledge that it's here, the same day a group of Ques hunters arrive, only to be the very ones who sound the alarm?"

"Wait, what?" Lusa scoffed. "You think we had something to do with that?"

"You don't see a question worth asking?"

She snorted. "No, I don't. Why would I ever do something to put

Res at risk like that? I lo—"

She cut herself off, because everything between them was very, very new, at least this whole lover thing. Well, the love wasn't new, not for her, but the change between them and their relationship happened last night, for gods' sake, and she wasn't about to air all that to some duster she'd just met who was throwing around really rude accusations.

They did come here to steal, but still. Not the same at all.

"He's my best friend," Lusa said, firmly. Pointing an angry finger at Oz as she said it too. "And I would never, ever do anything to hurt him. We came here for the festival because he was scared after he got attacked and it seemed like a good way to get him back on his feet. To get him to stop . . ." Lusa winced, pleading a little bit when she added, "To get him to start performing again. Don't tell him I told you that, though. I'm not sure if he wants people to know. And believe me," she added with a huff, "I wouldn't have gotten trampled by a mob if this was all part of some master plan."

Oz considered her for a moment in silence, assessing, his expression cool, before he nodded toward the table. "If you're hungry, help yourself. I believe Res is with Guatemoc, touring the artist lane over in the town. There's a small stage there, so perhaps he'll get to perform this month after all."

And with that, he left Lusa standing in the dining room, wondering what the hells that conversation had meant, or would mean.

By midafternoon, Lusa and Kiki made their way back down to the mazes. With Kiki guiding her as the belt, they made it back to their previous night's exploration in about half an hour. After another hour of checking rooms—none with birds—they came upon yet another divide, but this one was different.

For one, Lusa heard running water to the left, where the stone floor angled deeper into the mountain caves, and this corridor wasn't flanked by endless rooms. Cool, as all the passages were this deep underground, but Lusa smelled moisture with a sharp, clean scent, like a spring.

She hesitated, wondering if they'd be better off down another hall, but they hadn't found anything alive yet. The birds needed water and food to live down here, so maybe there was some sort of organization to this mess after all.

Not for the first time, she wished Res was with her. Her cheeks warmed, not just because of last night, either. She rubbed her face. She was lonely, that was all. If she could, she'd enjoy Kiki's company just fine, but they needed to keep Kiki a secret. And she certainly wasn't thinking of Res's company only because it might involve kisses while they explored. Not at all. Not even a little bit.

Not making it weird, she reminded herself with a grin.

She made her way down the corridor on light feet, hugging the wall. The sound of water grew louder. A stream, Lusa guessed, and as she crept closer, she made out a single voice: Distinctly feminine and singing softly.

Lusa didn't understand the words, but the melody reminded her of a lullaby. She kept herself low and small, no longer entirely confident in the shadowlands to have her back, not after she'd met six new people who could all see her less than three days. They all had Ques blood, but still.

The air grew cooler, mist touching her skin as Lusa reached the entryway. This chamber wasn't overly large, but it seemed to serve as some sort of threshold. A stream, as she suspected, cut through the room's center, a steady flow of clean, clear water running down the rock face, pooling, then disappearing under the rock face on the opposite wall. A dark hall descended on the room's far side, no doubt leading to the next section of the mouros' maze.

More interesting, however, was the voice's source. The pool had a single stone in the center, just large enough for the woman seated there. Lusa might have thought her a normal woman. Maybe even human.

If she wasn't seated in the middle of a magical maze under a mountain owned by a god.

Her hair was firebrand red, falling down her back in tangled, knotted curls, and it looked painful as hells. She was pale, which made sense since there was no sun down here, and aside from her plain white dress, all she possessed was a golden comb she struggled to work through that mess of hair.

Lusa didn't step inside, studying the room for any signs of magic or traps, but nothing jumped out. There was a nice outcropping where the corridor joined the room, and the torches cast the right shadows. Lusa could tuck in there and probably avoid being seen without the shadowlands' aid.

Or she could stroll right in, make noise, and see what happened.

Although this place did belong to Quetzalcoatl now, and his children were masters of illusion magic. She had no idea how far Quetzalcoatl's abilities spanned; Lusa hadn't prodded Res about his heritage, as it hadn't really been her business. But being that Quetzalcoatl was a god, it stood to reason powerful and dangerous were part of the equation.

That said, none of the Ques or their grandfather had shown any interest in what was under the mountain below their castle. Which did nothing to erase danger from the math.

And it wasn't like she had a crowd to cover her tracks if things got messy, her normal backup. So Lusa moved quietly, sneaking her way into the naturally shadowed alcove, and picked up a rock. She tested the weight, and then very gently rolled it out into the open.

The woman stopped combing and singing and glanced over her shoulder. She was plain, but pretty, and her eyes were the same color as the stone room. She seemed hopeful, interested, and frowned when she didn't see anyone.

Lusa stuck a foot slowly into the light, and felt the shadowlands chill her skin. She exhaled in relief; she hadn't realized how much she'd been missing the ability to vanish, even if it didn't make crossing this room a given. She'd disturb the water, which would make noise, and movement in the water might be noticeable, especially if this woman was here all the time.

Lusa frowned.

Was she here all the time?

The woman's shoulders sagged, and she looked down at the comb in her lap. The golden comb was a treasure, as it was crested in, like, two dozen gems. It reflected the torchlight, glittering and shimmering, and Lusa didn't doubt for a second *that* was the trap.

Try and grab the fancy comb, what would possibly go wrong? It's only a helpless girl holding it.

Yeah, right.

But if that was the case, why did she look so sad that no one was there? If she was some sort of water devil waiting to eat anyone who might try and take her comb, shouldn't she be calling out? Luring people in for snack time?

Instead, she sighed and starting fighting her tangles again.

They could go back, Lusa figured, and explore another hall. It wasn't like they didn't have a million other places to look for the birds.

But this was the first sign of life they'd seen down here. What were the odds this woman—whatever she really was—might know something about this place? She wasn't a mouros, at least Lusa assumed as much, because she wasn't a giant; she wasn't much taller than Lusa.

And Lusa couldn't help the itching feeling that this woman was stuck down here by herself like all the other treasure shoved in the rooms they'd mapped, and that sounded like it really sucked.

Lusa licked her lips; what was the worst that could happen?

Probably a lot.

Still, Lusa mumbled to Kiki, "Get Res if this goes south," and then, before she changed her mind, she called out, "Are you some kind of evil guardian who looks all nice but then eats people?"

The woman spun, eyes wide, staring where Lusa stood, the shadowlands keeping her secret. Her red hair was a stark contrast to her pale skin, and she gripped the comb tightly, but she didn't seem scared, only surprised. After a brief hesitation, she shook her head. She still searched for Lusa, squinting as if she might tease out of the source of the voice.

"Sorry, my duster blood makes me invisible when people look at me," Lusa offered. "I'm staying here under the mountain with my friend for the month. I've been exploring."

Her posture relaxed a bit more, the comb teasing the tangled clump of hair pulled forward over her shoulder. The woman titled her head, considering. "Are you lost?"

Her voice was melodious, like her song, but Lusa didn't feel any sort of draw in her words. No lure or compulsion, nothing urging her to come closer to the water. She pinched her forearm; nothing changed except her skin stinging.

"Nope, not yet."

The woman chuckled, but it was mirthless. "This place is endless."

"Are *you* lost? Or, um, stuck?" Lusa asked. She couldn't imagine staying in this space by choice. "Or is this your bath time? I'm sorry if I'm interrupting."

She waved a hand, dismissive. "No, this is where I've been placed." The woman turned around, and Lusa's skinned warmed.

*Been placed* didn't sound great. "I'm sorry?" She framed it as a question. She didn't want to assume, but . . .

The woman shrugged. "You're nicer than the last person who came this way."

Lusa licked her lips. "Glad to hear it. I try not to be a jerk. Good way to live."

She titled her head, as if considering, then sighed. "You can pass, if you'd like to keep exploring. As long as you don't try to steal my comb, I won't hurt you."

"So you are a trap then. For greedy treasure hunters who would steal a poor lady's comb?" Lusa stepped from the shadows. Kiki was warm at her waist as normal but wasn't showing any type of worry for her safety. And maybe it was a bit of a risk, but Lusa added, "I mean, you clearly need it. Is your hair cursed or something? It's really pretty but it's so knotted up."

The way she went utterly still was uncanny. It made Lusa sink back to the hallway, because the air changed as well, not in a way she could put words behind, but it was tangible. Lusa frowned. The entire time she'd watched the woman, she'd picked at her hair with the pretty comb, but she hadn't made any progress.

She couldn't help a stab of frustration, like the idea of being invisible when you just wanted someone to see you, like having the perfect comb in your hand yet you couldn't untangle your hair.

Lusa huffed.

"Do you need help? I could comb it for you, if you want. You just can't look at me. Well, I guess you could, but then you'd just see a comb waving around in the air and that would be weird." The woman's hesitation couldn't have been clearer if she'd screamed, but Lusa didn't miss the longing in her profile, or the way she kept her gaze focused away from the sound of Lusa's voice. "I promise I won't try to steal it."

Her voice was hushed when she said, "It will take a long time."

Lusa was supposed to be searching for the birds of truth, but they'd only been here three days. There was also an endless sea of rooms down here, so there was a very real chance she'd fail Theodore and never find the birds, even if they were down here for years, which would be too late to help his friends anyway.

But Lusa remembered what it was like the first time Res saw her, and didn't miss the way the woman clutched her tangled hair and the comb now with trembling fingers. Lusa could give up a few hours and comb her hair before she walked away and left this woman alone in this room maybe forever.

"That's alright, really. I can explore more tomorrow." Chin up, Lusa strode out into the light, tiptoed across the stream, and sat down on the rock behind her, careful not to touch her except for picking up a clump of matted hair. She winced; this would take a long time, but whatever. "Can I take the comb now?"

She held up the comb—it really was a work of art, which was stupid for a comb—and Lusa took it, the metal chilly against her fingers. She started at the bottom, carefully working the teeth through silken strands. Lusa smiled; she'd be so happy once it was done, it'd be worth a little delay.

"My name's Lusa," she offered. The woman didn't share her name, which was fine, and Lusa got to work.

# Chapter 29

Lusa had been combing for *hours.*

Her head was nodding forward, half asleep, her fingers cramping from the repetitive motions. She actually dozed off once, waking up with a start when Kiki poked her belly. It didn't help that the woman remained still as a statue and didn't speak the entire time she combed out her brilliant red hair.

Her very long, very thick, incredibly knotted hair.

A few minutes in, Lusa had a moment a panic, wondering if this was some sort of never-ending tangling curse, but the strands she coaxed apart remained silky and perfect. There were just so damn many of them. She figured it would take her an hour or so, but at this point, she'd lost all sense of time.

But she was almost done. Finally.

Kiki had poked her awake a second time a few minutes ago, and she yawned, apologized, stretched and cracked her fingers and wrists, and pushed through. Now, she had the last bunch in her hand, teasing out the final tangles at the bottom on the length of fiery red, and Lusa really hoped the woman hadn't actually changed to stone.

"Almost," Lusa said, trying to sound chipper, but she was exhausted and hungry. She drank from the stream a few times, after getting permission and assurance it wouldn't kill her, and decided this experience was a good reminder that she was an idiot for not packing snacks and her own water before wandering down into a huge maze in case she really did get lost. Starving to death was not on her bucket list.

Her back and shoulders ached, but she wasn't a quitter, and when the golden comb pulled through that last pull, Lusa actually squealed. "Ah! Done! Wow, it looks so pretty, too. Like lava or fire." She ran her fingers through the gorgeous hair. "Did you want me to braid it or anything like that?"

The woman gave a minute shake of her head, not moving otherwise, and Lusa frowned. Her hands sat open in her lap, palms upturned, and she just stared down at them.

Not a single word. Not that Lusa needed to be showered with a praise, but a small thanks would have been nice. She stood with a grunt, her back cracking, and she grumbled when her foot splashed in the stream, soaking her shoe. Gods, she couldn't wait to get back to Wags and go to bed. Hopefully Res wasn't too worried. She felt like she'd been down here all night; she'd have to ask Kiki on the way up what time it was.

Yawning again, she reached over the woman's shoulder and carefully set the comb in her open hand. "Here you go. Hopefully it doesn't get all knotted again." More awkward silence; Lusa blinked a few times. Right then, guess it was time to go. "Alright, uh, bye."

Lusa stepped off the rock, across the stream and back toward the way she'd come, when the woman finally spoke.

"You truly did it."

Lua turned back with a frown as the shadowlands rushed over her, the chill chasing over her skin and the colors around her muting. The woman stood now, her hair shimmering around her shoulders, the comb clutched to her chest.

"Combed your hair?" Lusa asked. "Yes?"

"Honored your word. Fulfilled the task. And resisted temptation."

"That comb?" Lusa laughed. "It's a bit much, don't you think? I didn't want it at all."

The woman laughed, really laughed, the sound bells and chimes and music, and her smile was utterly serene. "You've freed me, Lusa."

"I . . . did?"

"The mouros bind us to guard their treasures. I'm not the only tied to service, but I never expected to find kindness in this place." She blinked a few times. "I wish I could see you."

"Oh, it's okay, not much to see," Lusa said, then she frowned again. "Wait, they really just made you sit here and watch that comb? Can't they do it themselves?"

She laughed again, and shrugged. "Such is the nature of mythos. I came into being as a moura. I was here and given my task. I've never resented it, save for the few moments hope crossed my path. And then to be so close, and to be certain you would decide the comb was yours to claim for your work, and I would be forced to drown you in return."

Lusa grinned; good thing she didn't like that comb, huh. Or better yet, she wasn't a complete selfish idiot. "You can be free now?"

"Yes, I am free now. I can return to the otherworld, far away from this place."

"That's great," Lusa said, meaning it, even though she said it around a yawn. "I really do need to get back though. My . . ." She hesitated, because it seemed weird to call Res her lover, so she settled on, "My friend will wonder where I've been. I'm glad I could help you, though."

The moura's smile didn't waver. "Do you not know of my kind?"

"I know the mouros make treasure and these caves and are giants. I didn't know they had women they turned into slaves, though." Lusa crossed her arms. Maybe she'd cross paths with more moura while she was down here. If they just needed stuff like getting their hair brushed, she might be able to free few more while she was searching for the birds. Hopefully it wouldn't take quite as long, but seeing this moura's happiness, it was hard to imagine she wouldn't end up combing hair for hours again. "Seems like the girls get the crappy end of the deal."

The moura chuckled. Although she couldn't see Lusa, she made a point of looking the direction of her voice. "We can impart boons. You can ask me a favor for your aid."

"Oh," Lusa said, her smile falling. "I didn't do it for that. I was just trying to help you."

The moura nodded. "Then let me help you in return, before I depart."

Lusa shifted on her feet a few times, because this really hadn't been her intent, but she'd be a fool to turn down help. She swallowed, then asked, "Do you know where the birds of truth are?"

She went still for a moment, before kneeling down and flatting her palm against the stone she'd been seated upon when Lusa walked in this room hours ago. She didn't move, not for a good five minutes, before the moura blinked once, and then said, "There are three spires in the first cavern, at the maze's beginning. You want the center, not this one." Then she smiled once more, beautiful and bright, and whispered, "Good luck, Lusa," before she sank into the stone and vanished.

By the time she dragged herself back to Wags, Lusa was dead on her feet. It was well past two in the morning, and even though she was starving, all she wanted to do was sleep. She didn't see anyone the entire way back, the castle and grounds quiet, and when she stepped up inside Wags, it was warm and home and cozy. Lusa kicked off her wet shoes with a groan, stuffing the sandwich Wags left out for her into her face in three bites. After giving Tick an ear scratch and leaving Kiki to make maps, she stumbled toward her bedroom, figuring Res was already asleep. She was a bit bummed she'd missed him, she thought with a yawn, because she was way too tired for more sex, but she would have loved a hug and a few kisses before bedtime.

Ah well, tomorrow, she thought with a sleepy smile, right before an arm slid around her waist when she reached her bedroom curtain.

"Where are you going?" Res hummed against her neck, his lips warm, tucked right under her ear.

"Oh, sorry, did I wake you up?" She kind of sagged into him. He didn't have a shirt on, she realized, which made him that much warmer and more snuggly. Lusa closed her eyes and sighed. "I was trying to be quiet. Wait, what are you doing?"

He tugged at her shirt as he steered her into his room. "Taking you where you belong."

"Res, I'm really tired, I don't think I'm up for it," she mumbled around another yawn, a little creep of anxiousness fluttering through her belly in a not sexy way.

What if she couldn't keep up with his sex drive? There were times he had a different lover every night of the week.

Despite her protests, she still let him pull her shirt over her head, and he was already undoing her pants as he kissed along her ribs. "Sweetling, we don't have to fuck, but you belong in my bed."

"I don't have to," she offered, sitting on the edge of said bed as he removed her socks next. He left on her underwear, and she crossed her arms over her bare chest.

Res leaned in, his nose brushing hers, his hair mussed, and his face bleary with sleep. "That's true. Do you not want to sleep in here with me?"

She bit her bottom lip. She really, really did, but she didn't want to be clingy or annoying, and this facet of them was all so new. They hadn't had a chance to talk today for more than five minutes over coffee and a kiss goodbye, and the promise things wouldn't be weird.

"If that's okay, yeah," she whispered, "I'd like to."

"Good, because this is where I want you." Res gave her bum a swat. "Up you go. You can tell me why the hells you're back so late tomorrow, unless I need to know right this second?"

Lusa laughed. "No, it can wait."

"Ugh, thanks the gods," he mumbled, pulling him against her and drawing up the covers before letting out a contented rumble, his face burying against her shoulder.

Lusa smiled, letting sleep claim her, in the warm arms of the man she loved.

# Chapter 30

Lusa woke warm and aching. She moaned, trying to shift, to wiggle, not sure if she wanted more or less, or if she was dreaming or awake, but it was a kind of heavy, delirious haze that she normally associated with waking from dreams.

Except normally, her dreams weren't so vivid. Or wet and hot between her legs.

Lusa tried to roll, but hands squeezed her thighs, moving them open, and that was enough to jerk her out of sleep.

"Ah, there she is, awake at last."

Lusa blinked a few times, staring down her very naked body at a very naked Res, who was sprawled out on his stomach, his lips pressing along her hip bone.

"Res . . ." A few more blinks, then a little whimper as he squeezed her thigh, high up, right near the center of her. Her cheeks burned. "What are you doing?"

"You," he said as he nipped at her skin, "left me all alone last night." Another little bite, this time on her tummy, right under her navel, followed by a kiss. "And thus, I went to bed without my favorite part of the day."

Lusa rolled her eyes. "You do know we have stuff to do, right? We're not just here on a vacation?"

He hummed, his hair a right mess as he rested his cheek on her hip and stared up at her, and she recognized the mischief as he feigned innocence. "While true, that doesn't mean one must deny themselves the little pleasures in life while working, yes?" Then he lifted his head again, his grin a bit dangerous—the kind he only gave when he thought he had a great idea and it was almost always trouble—but before she could ask, he mumbled, "Like having dessert before breakfast."

She frowned, confused, but he answered her unspoken question before she could string any words together, because he buried his mouth between her legs. Lusa twitched, almost violently because, gods, his *entire face* was right there, and then so was his tongue—*oh his tongue, oh holy hells*—but he didn't let her wiggle away from him. He was holding her tightly by both thighs, and the weight of his chest on her legs, and then she collapsed into the pillows because *his mouth.*

And she was making so many whiny noises, but gods, this was even better than his fingers touching her, and then he was sucking and she let out a shriek and covered her mouth with both hands.

Res laughed, a dirty little chuckle that kind of made her want to smack him, but only because he'd stopped. "That's my good Lusa girl. Now, let me enjoy this, sweetling, and I promise, you will too." He licked her again, a firm stroke with that devilish tongue, then sucked hard on her most singular spot of pleasure, making her vision spot and her legs jerk. He let off a bit then. "Sorry, sorry," he mumbled against her, giving her a gentle kiss. "I'll ease up."

Lusa couldn't form a single coherent thought, lost in the sea his attentions, his kisses, his tongue, licking, sucking, hot and warm and wet, and then she exploded over that peak so hard and fast, all she managed was a strangle cry of his name as her entire body trembled and shuddered.

Her body was still shivering and tingling, and Res was climbing over her as he wiped his mouth, kissed her cheek, and then gathered her tight to his body and sunk inside her with a drawn out, agonizing slide. The groan he let out right against her ear when he was fully seated took her breath away as much as him filling her body.

"Ah, fuck," Res mumbled, a growl lancing his words, and he nuzzled her neck as he started thrusting, his pace heavy and steady, and Lusa clung to him. "Alright, love?" He panted already, a hand wandering down to grab her butt and squeeze, hard. "This is alright?"

"Yes, yes," Lusa managed, her mouth hanging open as she panted with each stroke.

"Thank fuck," Res muttered with a laugh. "I think I'm addicted to your sweet little cunt, love. Never felt anything quite like it."

Lusa shook her head, which only made her dizzy. "I told you not to do that," she whispered, her arms tight around his neck, holding him as tight as she could.

"It is so hard to believe," he said, grinding into her body; she swore, his cock felt deeper than the first night. Lusa moaned as his free hand tangled in her hair, craning her head back, but she kept her eyes closed. "Hmm, love? Is it so hard for you to believe that caring about you adds a certain, ah gods. Fuck." He stilled for a moment, catching his breath as his forehead fell to hers, both of them sweaty already, his breathing hot against her lips.

When he started to move again, it was erratic, frantic almost. His words were much the same.

"I waited for you. Up all hours, wondering when my Lusa would be back." A grunt, a bite and suck on her lower lip. "*Pining,*" he added with a scoff, then another handful of hard thrusts that were wrecking her ability to think. "Me, of all people. Believe it, sweetling. You're like nothing else I've ever had, and you're going to have to . . . *Fuck.*"

His climax set Lusa into a bit of a tailspin, a second, smaller orgasm shivering through her as he spilled inside her. It wasn't as intense as with his mouth on her. Unlike the first night, this time, he'd been less focused on getting her to another peak before he finished himself off, and the way he groaned into her neck, she guessed it might have snuck up on him.

"Shit," he mumbled after a few seconds, pivoting up to glare down at her. "You're a menace."

Lusa perked a brow. "Me? You're the one who woke me up with your mouth between my legs!" Saying it made her flush, which made his glare turn into a leer. She rolled her eyes and covered his mouth. "I don't know what you're thinking, but just keep it to yourself for a second." She huffed, shivering, because he was still inside her and she was still quivering with little aftershocks and could barely feel her toes. "I need a second to catch my breath before you run your mouth."

His eyes danced with mirth, but he only kissed her palm, which she took as agreement, and they both groaned as he slipped from her body. She blushed when he cleaned her up; she tried to argue she could do herself, but he wouldn't hear about it, and then he had her cocooned back in the blankets and pulled against his chest.

"What time is it?"

"Who cares," Res muttered. "We have all damn day. Now tell me why you came back so late." He ran his fingers through her hair, twirling it and keeping his expression neutral, but she could tell he'd been worried about her.

Lusa wasn't sure what she supposed to do, besides enjoying snuggling up against him and how he touched her. She rested her hand on his chest, letting her fingers wander in a soft caress on his skin as she told him about the moura, her hair, and the comb, along with the boon of at least eliminating two thirds of the maze from her search.

"Impressive," Res said, his fingers still toying with her hair, in no hurry to get up it seemed.

"What about you?"

He shrugged. "Much of the same. The fellows seem to know how to keep themselves entertained. Matty wants to show me the vineyards today. Seems alcohol is his under purview." Res smirked, but then he frowned a bit. "Both Erandi and Quetzalcoatl are more exclusive with their time, it seems."

"I think they're all a lot for Erandi," Lusa offered. "I wonder if he doesn't hide himself a bit, like you did."

"Ever the kind soul, aren't you," Res said, kissing the top of her head.

"And the rest of them are kind of a lot. I mean one of you is a lot." She poked him in the ribs, and he chuckled. "Pollock is nice, though. He's quiet."

"Nice, is it?" Res frowned down at her. "He seems a bit dodgy to me."

"Because his choice of art isn't showing off?"

"Lusa girl, did you notice the number of paintings in this castle? He's showing off plenty, he just doesn't do it with his mouth." Res rolled his eyes. Then he sighed. "We should probably get up, though. Wouldn't want to miss breakfast."

"You go ahead. I'm going to shower and then look at Kiki's maps for a bit. I feel bad we won't need all that work."

Res leaned down, another kiss on her nose before he slipped from the sheets and to the floor. "Kind and sweet, see?" Lusa blushed when he stretched, entirely naked, but couldn't help but admire all of him as she leaned into the fluffy pillows and watched him dress. "And not so late tonight, yes?"

He didn't quite look at her when he asked, and she couldn't tell if it was out of worry, desire for her company, or maybe just wanting more sex, or some combination of three, but there was a soft pink on his cheeks, all the way to the tips of his ears.

"Okay."

"Good," was all he said, and then with a last quick kiss on the lips, he was gone.

Lusa took her time getting ready and decided to give Pollock a day to himself for his painting. She wandered the grounds for a bit, her usual game of putting in appearances, and found herself heading down the hall toward Erandi's chambers. She'd been thinking of him after Res and her talked about him that morning, and she wondered how he'd been doing. And besides, she hadn't found a mouros, but she did find a moura, so maybe he'd like to hear about it. At least then he'd know she wasn't just humoring him.

Or using him, she thought bitterly.

Lusa sighed. She kind of was, but she did like him and didn't really care for the idea that he seemed a bit ostracized, be it by the others or his own hand. She knew that feeling a little too well to ignore watching someone else in a similar situation. Besides, taking time out of her day to talk to Erandi for a few minutes wasn't exactly a hardship.

When she got to him rooms, she knocked and waited. And waited. She knocked again, because it was kind of early and maybe he wasn't up, or maybe he was at breakfast.

Maybe today he just wanted to be left alone.

She waited about ten minutes after the second knock, then shrugged to herself and left. Lusa would catch him another time. If she was lucky, she might have another cool story to tell him tomorrow.

She wrinkled her nose. Or unlucky? She wasn't sure. She didn't really fancy brushing hair all night again.

Not when she could get back to Res.

Lusa couldn't help a goofy little grin as she trotted down the castle hall, then stalled when she saw Quetzalcoatl waiting at the end. He leaned casually on the wall, but she knew the illusion for what it was; he was a god, he certainly didn't happen to be in a random hallway for no reason. And he stared at her like he always did: as if he could peer right into her heart, mind and soul.

Lusa gave a little wave. "Good morning." Was that good enough for greeting a god? She wasn't sure, but she wagered he'd let her know if she screwed up any unknown expectations. Curtsy? Bow? Grovel? When he didn't reply, she cleared her throat. "I was looking for Erandi. Do you know where he is?"

She didn't stop walking, but she edged to the opposite side of the hall and slowed her pace. He didn't overtly block her way, but he was a huge man with broad shoulders, and his very presence seemed to expand each time he inhaled. His existence took up a lot of space, although he didn't seem to be pushing any sort of magic or other Aperien gifts to influence her or affect the area around them. It was just a fact of what and who he was.

Quetzalcoatl considered her question for a longer than polite, normal conversation standards, making it super awkward, because of course he had all time in the world. It gave Lusa a few seconds to study him as she approached, and being that he knew her nature, she didn't hide her staring. Like before, he wore what she knew now was cultural garb from his Aztec mythos, and she wagered all his golden tattoos were the same. Now that she saw them again, all over his bare arms, and knew what he was, she could see how they were stylized renditions of his winged serpent form. His hair, inky black, was once again tied neatly back.

He never blinked. When he spoke, she felt the rumble of his voice in the stones around her. "Erandi retired early last night. He wasn't feeling well."

"Sorry to hear that," Lusa said, coming to a halt with maybe ten feet between them. She tried not to fidget. "Can you let him know I'd like to visit him when he's up for it?"

Quetzalcoatl chuckled. Unlike Res, the sound carried no humor or warmth. "Making requests of a deity after only four days in his grace?"

Lusa flushed. Right, that was dumb. But the cold calculation in how he studied her in return made her assume it was intentional. He'd welcomed them, had dinner as if they were guests, and given them the run of his castle, all illusions that she wasn't perched on the end of the very dangerous knife of his good graces, which could tip at any time for any reason. Res might be his kin, but Lusa certainly was not.

"I'm sorry, I spoke out of turn. I didn't mean it like that." Lusa shifted between her heels, trying to decide what to say next, or if she should just shut up, yet she kept talking for some reason. "Is it okay for me to ask you if Erandi will be okay?"

"He always finds his footing," Quetzalcoatl answered, and there was a finality to the statement Lusa knew better than to push.

"Thank you," she said, making sure not to mumble. She did glance down the hall beyond him, in case he didn't realize she wanted to walk by. Lusa scratched her cheek. Maybe she needed permission? "May I go now?"

This time, Quetzalcoatl smiled, and while he was handsome in a way that defied logic despite his crafted appearance of a middle-aged man, the expression lacked warmth. It lacked, well, humanity.

And he didn't answer her question. Instead, he asked, "What are you to Resplendent?"

Lusa had noticed he refused to call Res by the nickname he preferred, which seemed rude to her. She wondered if he was the same to Matty.

"He's my friend," Lusa answered honestly. He already knew they were sleeping together, even if he'd found out before they started. She shrugged under his unblinking assessment.

"I didn't ask what he is to you. I asked what you are to him."

Lusa frowned. She always assumed being a friend went both ways, but maybe not everyone did? "I'm his friend too. And I help out when we travel." Which wasn't a lie, only it left out that Wags's magic took care of most mundane tasks.

Quetzalcoatl pushed from the wall, his full height a bit dizzying, and Lusa retreated a step before she realized it. "A *friend*. In an invisible girl, a mortal duster who has tethered herself to his coattails, attached herself to the one place she can be seen."

Lusa's fists clenched, but she didn't move or speak. This felt more like a trap than the moura and her comb.

"I offer him a life of luxury and ease, among his own kind, protected and free to indulge any whim, and he hesitates." The god stared down his hawkish nose at her, the gaze lightening across her skin in the harshness of his judgement. "Is it because of you?" He hummed. "And if it is, and you are the friend you claim to be, would you allow him to deny himself this sanctuary, to throw away an immortal future, in order to selfishly tie him to your mortal coil?"

She swallowed a few times, her mouth so dry her tongue burned. Her ears were ringing, and the hall, the castle, the entire mountain felt suddenly very, very small and crushing.

Quetzalcoatl said nothing else, merely folded his hands behind his back, and left her standing in the empty hall, all things she might have argued tangled up somewhere between her head and her mouth.

Because Res wouldn't be happy here, even if it was safe, because he needed to soar. That had nothing to do with Lusa, their friendship, or the change in their relationship only days in the making.

It didn't matter what she was or wasn't to him.

It didn't matter if he loved her the same way she loved him.

But being stared down by a god and blamed for whatever Res felt about this place?

Yeah, well, it was hard not to wonder if Lusa's doubts did matter after all.

# Chapter 31

Lusa didn't talk to Res about her encounter with Quetzalcoatl.

She wasn't sure why not, or why *to* tell him for that matter, because it was clear he wanted Res here and Res already knew that. Telling him would just add more pressure, or worry, or even guilt, right? At least she'd tell herself that, then she'd be bothered when she wondered if she was lying by not telling him, and she'd be ready to tell him, and then they'd talk about something else, or he'd be smiling, or they'd be kissing, or going to bed, and she'd put it off again.

So, they kept on. Res spent time with the Ques, and Lusa and Kiki went down the correct spire according to the moura, which began more or less the same as the other spire. Lots of rooms, different treasures, but with nothing else like the moura, or any signs of the birds.

Things were fine for about five days, before all hells broke loose the morning Matty came and asked them to have breakfast with him.

"Pollock is boring, Erandi is still sulking for whatever is this week's flavor, and Guatemoc and Oz are out," he'd greeted them when he'd come to Wags first thing that morning. Res and Lusa agreed to join him in the dining room for breakfast.

"What do you mean, they're out?" Res asked once they'd settled into the meal of fresh fruit, omelets, and six kinds of pastries Lusa was happy stuffing herself with.

"Out," Matty said with a shrug. "Hells if I know what they do, but the big man apparently isn't as content as Bartholomew was with total isolation. It's not often, but business calls from time to time."

Res and Lusa exchanged a look, because this was interesting news, but then everything upended.

Guatemoc barreled into the dining room, covered in mud, and after a few seconds, Lusa recognized the other wet splatters.

Bright emerald green.

Ques blood.

A lot of it. A hells of a lot of it.

Matty and Res surged to their feet with Lusa, but Guatemoc held up a hand, and he spoke to Matty. "Oz and I aren't hurt. But we need Erandi, and the castle closed off and cleared of any staff. Now." And then he stalked out, leaving the doors wide open behind him.

"Shit," Matty mumbled, rubbing his face a few times. He was pale, hands shaking, and Res hadn't moved at all. Lusa followed his gaze and realized he stared at the bloody mess Guatemoc left in his wake.

"Matty?" Lusa asked into the silence, because neither of the men beside her seemed inclined to answer Guatemoc's requests, and they seemed pretty urgent. Matty blinked down at her a few times. "I can't help with the staff, but I can get Erandi?"

Matty swayed a bit, then straightened up, as if snapping from wherever his mind had slipped. "Right, good idea. Grab Pollock on the way, if you can."

"And what the hells do I tell them exactly?"

"Oh, right." Matty laughed, kind of. It was more of a choked exhale. "On occasion, Quetzalcoatl gets leads on other Ques. It doesn't happen often, and not in quite a few years now. When he does, he sends Oz and Guatemoc out to find them and bring them back. If they can."

"If they can," Res said, his voice hoarse.

Matty ran a hand through his short hair, then shrugged. "Yes, well, you know how the hunters are. They're not always keen on letting their catch slip away."

Lusa winced, unable to stop herself from shifting closer to Res and taking his hand. She wove their fingers together and squeezed. He didn't squeeze back, his palm cold and clammy, his entire arm twitching. He was terrified, but giving him a task would help. At least she hoped.

"Erandi is in his room, right?" Lusa asked, tugging Res after her as she headed that direction. He followed, his gaze drifting back to the bloody green footprints Guatemoc left on the floor.

"He should be. Yell at him, tell him Guatemoc and Oz are back and something's wrong. That should get his ass up." And then Matty was off as well, calling out as he raced toward the kitchens.

"Res, come on," Lusa urged, pulling him after her as fast as she could get him moving.

"Right, alright," he muttered, but he came, and soon they were jogging and then running upstairs to Pollock's room.

He was painting, as always, and frowned when he saw them out of breath. Lusa gave him a really quick summary—Guatemoc, Ques blood, clearing the castle—and Pollock was already down his ladder, paints set aside. "Erandi?"

"Matty asked us to get him," Lusa said. She'd offered really, and she didn't think Pollock needed to hear how Matty stood there in a near panic until she urged him to move.

Pollock gave her a nod, wiping off his hands on a cloth before he tied back his braids in a tight bundle. "Hurry then," he said, nodding down the hall, and then headed toward the dining room.

Lusa started off again, a few paces down the next hall when she realized she'd lost Res. She dashed back to the painting room and found him staring at Pollock's discarded paint pallet. Sure enough, there were streaks of emerald paint in the selection.

When she touched his elbow, he jerked away from her. She bit her lip, ignoring the sting.

"Res." He glanced down at her, staring at her but not really seeing her. Gods, she hated seeing him like this. She took his forearm in a firm hold and squeezed tight as she asked him, "Do you need to go back to Wags?"

She really hoped she wasn't sending him back to disappear from her life again. Lusa wasn't sure if her heart could take it, but she would if he needed to step back and escape this chaos if it was reminding him too much of the night he almost died.

Instead, Res snapped back into the moment. "No," he gritted out, then shook his head a few times and scoffed. "No, I'm fine." He wasn't, but she didn't argue because he'd pulled himself back from the dark edges of his mind and she had to trust him right now. They needed to get Erandi, because Lusa was pretty sure another Ques was in serious trouble. "Let's go."

Beating on Erandi's door and screaming about the situation got him to answer fast. He tore the door open, and Lusa barely stifled a gasp at how haggard he looked, biting her lip to keep the sound in, and the blind Ques raised a hand to stall any other talking.

"I need five minutes to prep. Stay to guide me so we can return faster."

"Alright," Lusa replied, and the door shut in her face. Both her and Res sagged against the nearest wall. When she glanced over at Res, he had his head back, his eyes closed, his face wan and sweaty. "Are you okay?"

"Most decidedly not," he answered, not moving aside from the deep rise and fall of his chest.

"There's nothing wrong with—"

"Running away?" Res snapped, his tone acidic. "No one else seems to be taking that road, are they, Lusa girl? Certainly not Erandi, who has been stripped bare and blinded by these fuckers. The least I can do is—" his voice hitched, and he cleared his throat and tried again. "The least I can do is see if they need help before I crawl off in shame."

"Okay," Lusa whispered, fighting back the urge to soothe him. But friends did that, right? She guessed lovers probably did, too, but right now she had no idea how he'd respond. He was so wound tight; he looked like he might shatter. She wanted to tell him there was no shame in how he was feeling, but now wasn't the right time.

So they waited in silence, inches apart, until Erandi emerged laden with two heavy satchels and a small suitcase.

He locked the door behind him with quick precision, then gestured at his items. "This will be faster if you help me carry these."

Lusa pushed off the wall and Res followed, having found his equilibrium. Res grabbed both satchels and Lusa took the case, frowning at the sound of glass on glass and liquid sloshing. Erandi reached out, questing until he touched her shoulder, then moved down to take her bicep in a firm grasp.

Lusa didn't move right away, staring at the case, the locked clips on either side, the structure suggesting it would open and probably be tiered inside. She wasn't an expert on any of this stuff, but they'd traveled enough she'd encountered more than a few alchemical cases her in time. This one looked well used and expensive.

What the hells was a Ques doing with a master alchemy kit when their kind were farmed and hunted for ingredients? When they were headed downstairs to help a Ques who had been attacked for this very reason?

This particular Ques of all Ques she'd met?

"Questions later," Erandi said, his tone calm and crisp, and she didn't doubt for a second, he'd realized exactly what she'd noticed. The fact that he didn't attempt to excuse or deny the situation left Lusa lost between a weird sort of relief and trying to decide if that somehow made it worse? "Hurry, please. Time might be critical."

"Right," she mumbled, glancing up to see Res a few feet ahead of them, waiting, oblivious to what she carried.

Not for long.

When they reached the dining room, concerns about an alchemy case became the least of Lusa's worries.

The howling, guttural screams echoed down the hall before they arrived, Erandi's hand tightening on her arm to the point of pain as Lusa jogged as fast as she could without tripping them both. She almost ran into Res's back when he pulled up sharp at the sound.

"What the fuck?" Res whispered.

It didn't sound human. It sounded animal, monstrous in fact, and wounded. In agony.

No, it sounded like something was dying.

Lusa gritted her teeth and nudged by Res, urging him to follow, Erandi in tow. The dining room doors were shut, voices yelling inside, but that pained howling and screeching kept on and on and on.

Erandi touched the door before Lusa got the chance, cursing under his breath, then banged a fist hard. "Let us in!"

Oz called back. "Fucking wait!"

A loud crash followed, then the sound of shattering wood, and wet slapping, and more of that awful keening. Erandi cursed again.

"Give me the case."

Lusa took a step back, her grip on the alchemy case sweaty. She really, really didn't like the churning feeling in her gut. "For what?"

"Questions later," Erandi snarled, his blindfolded face fixed her direction. "Or would you rather whoever is in there suffer while you wrestle with some moral quandary when you lack context for your high horse?"

Another scream, this one so pained, Lusa couldn't do anything but hand over the case. Erandi brought out his key ring, working quickly, his fingers deft as if they had eyes of their own, unlocking the three different locks with three separate keys before the case swung open into exactly what Lusa expected.

Kiki cinched around her waist so hard, she had to squeeze the belt so it loosened. Kiki trembled, cold to the touch, as uneasy as Lusa for the same reason.

Five tiers, not three, lined with dozens upon dozens of vials, some liquid, others full of ingredients she couldn't begin to name. The labels were brail, she realized, the bottom row of the case neatly organized with other tools of the trade, including a silver dagger, shears, string, a miniature mortar and pestle, the list went on. She'd never seen a better stocked kit, not even in established store fronts in the Emporium markets.

Erandi worked quickly, obviously practiced and skilled as he plucked, crushed and mixed, calling over his shoulder, "The smaller satchel, please."

That was when Res realized what was going on. "What the fuck is this?"

Lusa caught his arm, grabbing the requested bag and setting it against Erandi's thigh. He moved it where he wanted it and kept working. Res caught her wrist.

"Lusa, what the fuck is this?"

"I have no idea, except that if he's going to help with that," she said as she gestured toward the dining hall, right as something very large hit the doors and the entire wall shook, dust raining down on them.

"I think he's right that we need to ask afterwards."

"Fucking hells," Res mumbled, dragging his hands through his hair, over his face. "Lusa, what . . . what are we doing?"

"Hey, hey," she said, catching both his hands in hers. "Right now? My guess is we're going to help whoever is hurt, right? Let's do that first, then we figure it out, okay? Me and you."

Res drew in deep breath, then nodded, leaning down to press his forehead against hers, and Lusa's heartbeat tripled for a second, and then the tension in her entire body drifted down a few notches. Gods, she'd been scared, mostly that he was about to shut her out again. He'd joked that he couldn't handle it if she did that to him, but the truth was, Lusa was pretty sure that now that she'd jumped into her real feelings for him with both feet, she wouldn't survive if he closed her out again.

"Oz!" Erandi yelled then, standing, and when Lusa saw what he held, she put herself between Res and him, because she knew. She watched, like she was outside her own body, as Erandi loaded a dart into the blowgun with the utmost care to keep the tip turned away from his skin.

"Almost!" came the muffled response, and then Erandi moved toward Lusa.

She wasn't sure if Res knew about the darts, if Theodore told him how he'd been drugged that night. That the hunters had most likely used this exact kind of alchemical drug to knock him out so they could steal his feathers. Lusa tensed when he extended the blowgun her direction, his expression emotionless and cold.

"Handing this off would better suited to someone who can see. When Oz lets down the wards, get this in his hand."

When she didn't move, didn't speak, didn't do anything, she felt Res tense behind her, his hand falling to her hip.

Erandi remained still. "I will answer any questions you have after this is settled. You have my word. I'm guessing you know what this is, given your reaction. And when this door opens, you'll understand why we need it."

"Ready!"

The doors swung inward with a crackle of dispersed magic, which burned Lusa's nose and smelled a bit like burned chocolate, and then she had about two seconds to look inside the destroyed dining hall before she made her choice and snatched the blowgun from Erandi and shoved Res away from the scene in front of her.

A Ques, for certain, in his feather serpent form. Beautiful, feathered and glorious, a kaleidoscope of shimmering color that took her breath away for the first blink, until she took in the rest.

His eyes were gone.

And his entire chest cavity was cut open wide, and from what she could see, empty aside from his lungs and his heart.

The entire room was drenched in wet emerald green, with more and more of the pearly liquid splattering with each thrash and flail.

His tongue was gone too. Most of his teeth were missing or broken.

Matty, Pollock, and Guatemoc surrounded him, ropes looped through the iridescent wings enough to stop the Ques from flying. It took all three of them to keep the Ques on the ground, pulling in different directions to try and immobilize him.

And gods, the screams. The pain and the fear in those guttural noises.

Lusa darted between broken furniture, her feet slipping on all the blood, and she waved the blowgun when Oz saw her. He gave a grim nod, moving her direction as he ducked under the butchered Ques's blind attempt to bite his head off. He rolled to the side with a grunt, and they both ended up under the shattered table as she pressed the alchemical weapon into his hand.

Oz didn't hesitate. He leaned left, took the shot, and the dart flashed before it stuck in the Ques's throat. The feather serpent shuddered, then hissed and howled, but the alchemical solution didn't take long to do the job. The Ques staggered, then let out a whine that stabbed right through Lusa's heart, before it slumped against the wall and sagged to the ground, little more than a tangled lump struggling to breathe.

Gods, Lusa could see each inhale and exhale, his pink puffy lung tissue inflating and deflating.

"He's down! Erandi, hurry up!" Oz called, collapsing down beside her.

Matty helped Erandi navigate the room's mess to the fallen Ques, while Pollock cut the ropes from the Ques's wings with a tenderness that made Lusa shiver. Guatemoc shoved the broken wood and other debris out of the way, pilling it aside to make more space. A glance showed Res in the doorway, dumbstruck as Lusa felt.

A hand on her shoulder startled her, and she blinked up at Oz.

"Thanks for the assist," he grumbled. She nodded, not sure what to say, what to feel, what to *do*, and when she wiped her face, she realized she was crying. Oz's expression softened. He had a gash across his forehead, and he was covered in cuts and bruising from wrestling with the wounded Ques. In his meaty fist, he clenched the blowgun, then grunted again and tossed it aside. "I hate using this shit, but he was hurting himself more."

"Yeah," Lusa whispered. She'd realized that the second Oz opened that door. The Ques was so hurt and scared and, well, she knew the dart would make him sleep like Res when he was attacked. That had to be better than fighting in a panic against the people who were trying to help him.

"It might be all we can do for him. Fuck." Oz sighed.

"He's going to die, isn't he?" Lusa stared as Matty handed materials to Erandi as he worked to staunch the wounds, but she'd seen his inside. He was . . . empty.

They'd . . . the hunters had . . . harvested him . . .

Oz glanced at Res, then back to Lusa. "You know enough, I'm guessing. This isn't the kind of thing we come back from." He rubbed his jaw, his expression grim. "All we can give him is comfort, until it's over. And if he's ever lucid again before he passes, the knowledge that the fuckers that did this to him are dead."

With that Oz shoved up, and he didn't say anything else as he went to help with his kin. Lusa got to shaky feet, her entire body numb, not sure what to do next, when Res came into the room. He was pale and trembling, but his expression was firm. When she moved to him, he pulled her against his side and kissed the top of her head.

"Let's see how we can help."

Lusa sighed and leaned into him, so proud of him, and never more grateful she'd found him all those years ago. "Sounds good."

# Chapter 32

The Ques died two days later.

For those two days, Lusa and Res mostly stuck to Wags. They'd stayed for hours to help clean up the dining room once the Ques was moved somewhere else, but they hadn't asked where and no one offered. They had no connection to him, and they both knew his time was limited to probably unconsciousness before he passed on, and it didn't really seem like their place to be further involved. A few brief conversations confirmed this wasn't the first time a rescue attempt had been unsuccessful.

Lusa stayed with Res instead of searching for the birds. She was worried about him, even though he didn't retreat from her. They shared meals and napped, read borrowed books over kitchen snacks, and slept in his bed together. They hadn't had sex since the injured Ques arrived, but there didn't seem to be a lack of intimacy between them. Res held her at night like he thought she might disappear from his arms.

She was less worried about Kiki, who'd calmed under the explanation that Erandi used alchemy to help the wounded Ques. Kiki took her word at face value, blessedly unaware of all the underlying complications, and happily went back to drawing and sketching maps from memory, trusting Lusa's judgement without question.

She wasn't sure what she'd done to deserve such unwavering faith.

A very exhausted looking Matty knocked on Wags to give them the news about the Ques passing.

"I thought maybe, despite what happened last time I asked, you might want to come to breakfast." Lusa had never seen Matty with facial hair before, a bit of scruff that suited him as well as without. Even the dark circles did little to diminish a Ques and their good looks. Matty waved a hand. "Besides, all the others are there, and Erandi said he promised he'd answer questions if you have any." Matty rolled his eyes. "Because why ever would you have any questions after all that shit."

Lusa couldn't help a grin. Out of everyone, she was starting to like Matty the best, because despite his goofy nature, he seemed the truest to himself of the bunch. Pollock was quiet, but almost cold and detached despite inviting her to paint with him. She got a feeling she was there more as an extension of his own art than her company. Guatemoc was fun, a reluctant big brother to the bunch, but he reminded her a little too much of Res. Oz was stern, and while she respected him a hells of a lot, especially after seeing him in action during the chaos with the wounded Ques, he remained closed off.

And Erandi, well. She'd liked him off the bat, because she recognized a kindred spirit in him; at least she'd thought so, before he'd revealed himself to be a master alchemist when alchemists were the people who abused his own kind. She didn't know what to think now, aside from the fact that his intentions in the moment were noble.

Gods, Lusa couldn't imagine how that Ques would have suffered without the dart to put him into a peaceful sleep.

"Yeah, breakfast sounds great," Lusa said, forcing a smile. It did sound good, and questions were important, but more and more, she wanted to be done with this place. But it had only been a week, she still had to find the birds, and who knew what else would happen in the next three weeks.

"Great," Matty said, and she could tell he meant it. "It's nice have someone else around, you know. Gets old, all the competing to be the center of attention."

"Do you know how not to?" Lusa laughed as Res came up behind her, his hand brushing her lower back as he stepped down from Wags. Kiki, as always, was snug around her waist. Since the realization of Erandi's alchemy, Lusa was more certain than ever Kiki should be with her at all times.

"I could try, I guess," Matty drawled as they made their way back to the castle proper, avoiding the destroyed dining room, even though it was fully repaired now. Instead, he led them to a smaller eating area toward the back end of the castle, with a fantastic view of the back gardens.

The others were already eating, everyone in attendance aside from Quetzalcoatl, and Lusa couldn't suppress a sigh of relief. She still hadn't spoken to Res about that conversation with the god, when he said she was holding Res back from a happy life by being a clingy little mortal. She'd meant to talk to him about it, but given the past few days, it didn't really seem like the right time to complain about how Quetzalcoatl made her feel self-conscious about her self-worth.

At least Quetzalcoatl seemed to think so poorly of everyone he didn't need to lord of every interaction in his castle, she supposed. Must be lonely and boring being a god, Lusa decided, then almost laughed at the absurdity of her entire line of thinking.

She'd talk to Res about it. She would.

Three seats between Erandi and Pollock were open, so Lusa took the lead and plopped down next to Erandi, letting Matty sit beside his brother and Res between them. Erandi greeted her with a nod when she said good morning to the table, and everyone else was equally subdued, yet cordial, and if she wasn't mistaken, warmer than before. Comfortable, almost, as if they'd passed some sort of litmus test with how they'd reacted to a dying, mutilated Ques brought into the palace now that they'd had their introductory dinner.

"Would you like to ask questions or have Guatemoc offer you an abbreviated explanation," Erandi said after a quiet stretch of silverware moving, coffee and tea, and food moved to plates.

Lusa glanced to Res, who shrugged. He was playing at nonchalance, and she had a feeling he'd been content not to pry at all. Lusa rolled her eyes at him, and he gave her a half smile, putting the ball in her court.

She turned her attention on Guatemoc. "I guess if that's okay, you could tell us what you want and I can ask questions after if I have any."

Guatemoc nodded, finishing his bite and washing it down with what looked suspiciously like a glass of wine at breakfast. "Erandi has been here with Quetzalcoatl the longest. They found me a few years after and negotiated my release from a binding slave contract. And I helped get Oz out of an imprisonment situation about two decades later. He and I had some other failures between, before we found Matty and Pollock living peacefully unaware of our kinds' situation. We convinced them to come stay here, before they became the next victims."

"Such a hard sell, truly," Matty said. Pollock huffed and kept eating.

Guatemoc ignored them both. "Oz and I have spent years training to fight, infiltrate, and do whatever it takes to get our kind out of the kind of shit we suffered."

Oz said nothing. He'd healed completely from helping subdue the wounded Ques, his expression and posture closed off, but when he noticed her attention on him, he gentled and gave her a nod.

"I thought this place is sealed except for the festival," Res said. He picked at his meal, Lusa noticed, not really eating. And he was still pale. He had been since Guatemoc came barreling in on their previous breakfast covered in Ques blood.

"It is, almost entirely. And we don't leave for any reason except for an extraction. Finding other Ques is all done through scrying and informants, or other means for messages," Oz said, grumbling. "And we don't go out unless we're certain." His glare landed on Matty who rolled his eyes.

"It was an attempt, one time, for a spot of fun. I haven't tried anything since, have I?" Matty, for all his pomp, seemed insulted now. "I didn't understand back then, but I get now. You made it all very clear, and it has been made clear, repeatedly." He looked pointedly around the table at everyone, even Erandi, though he couldn't see him. "My brother and I had the easy way of it, and even before this particular instance, we've now more than seen our fair share of what can happen to our kind."

"So as for your question, Res," Guatemoc said, "no one goes in and out, except for the festival day. In most cases, those we select to come down here for the allotted month elect to stay on staff once they see what a life down here can be like."

"And if they don't?" Lusa asked. Her leg bounced under the table now.

"Then we drug them and they're smuggled out after their month is done by Oz or Guatemoc. They wake safe and none the wiser of how they were removed from Mount Pindo." Erandi spoke as he buttered his toast, as if drugging people was a normal thing to do, which it probably was for an alchemist.

"And I assume you handle that part? The drugging?" Lusa asked, not bothering to keep the edge from her tone. Res's hand came to rest on her thigh, stilling her leg with a gentle squeeze.

The rest of the table remained quiet, Oz watching her with a knowing expression from his seat across from her.

Erandi kept on buttering. "If you're asking about my skills as an alchemist, then yes, I utilize them however is required."

"And that's just . . . fine?" Lusa asked, her voice a huff. "That you're an alchemist when alchemists are the people hurting your people? When they're the ones who hurt you?"

"Is your assumption that I skin my own kind alive? Peel off their feathers, dig out their eyes, and harvest their organs while they're still breathing? For profit and universal ingredients to serve my greed and my indulgent, sinful alchemical recipes, Lusa?" The butter knife scraped a little harder than needed, the sound grated on her nerves.

"Of course not," Lusa managed, her throat tight.

"Erandi." Oz was the one who said his name, not chiding, not exactly, but it almost sounded like a plea for peace.

"My apologies. Am I to sit idle while I'm judged by someone who knows nothing of what we suffer?"

"I'm not judging you," Lusa said, though even as the words left her mouth, she wasn't sure if they were completely true. She felt a little sick. And dizzy. And really, really confused. "I just don't understand why you would embrace this kind of thing when it's used to hurt you and the people you care about."

"Is that what you saw in that room? With that dart?" His blind stare landed heavily on her face, and Lusa wanted to disappear against the shadowlands even though he couldn't see her. "Did 'this kind of thing' hurt the Ques more than he'd already been brought low by being disemboweled alive when those who had him caught wind he was to be liberated?"

Lusa stood, the chair pushing back with a squeal. "All I know is I came down here with Res, who is a Ques, and I trusted all of you because you're his family, and then out of nowhere you pulled out an alchemy kit and magically know how to make the same dart that those bastard hunters used on him the night I almost lost him!"

Her voice rose to a shrill yell by the end, her fists clenched at her sides, and the tears ran now, because she'd been spending every second since they saw that Ques dying making sure Res was alright, watching him every second to make sure he didn't fade away from her, disappear into his panic and trauma, and never once had she realized that deep down inside, she was drowning in her own.

"So excuse me," she went on, her voice breaking, "if I didn't react perfectly, or that I'm confused, or worried, or just plain terrified after seeing another Ques attacked and bleeding and hurt and . . ."

*Dying.*

She pressed her hand over her mouth, catching the sob.

And then Res stood, turning her, and she buried herself against his chest and cried. He excused them, and walking to Wags passed in a blur of tears and his arms, until she was tucked in his bed, his warm body wrapped around hers, and he held her while she sobbed.

All the while, he whispered, "I'm here, Lusa girl. I'm right here."

When she woke later, sometime in the early afternoon, Res lounged in the bed beside her reading. Apparently, he'd found time in all his socializing to visit the libraries as well. At least she thought as much, until she cleared the sleep from her eyes and realized he'd picked up one from her pile.

"Sleeping Beauty awakens," Res said, turning the page with a little smirk. Lusa huffed and stuffed her face back in the pillows, sighing when his hand came down to the play with her hair. "Better?"

"I don't know," she mumbled in the soft fluffiness, wondering if she could stay here forever. She knew the answer, but it was kind of nice to pretend for a few minutes.

She heard a page turn, Res's gentle fingers massaging her scalp. "Are we planning to talk about it, or would you like to borrow from my tactics and hide in here instead?"

Lusa laughed despite herself, and rolled so she could peek at him. Wags's curtains were open and the candles were lit, giving the illusion of midday light when there was none be found in this awful mountain hole.

"Are you okay?" she asked.

"Ah, ah, nice try, love." Res turned another page with his thumb as he continued to pet her head with his other hand. "We're not talking about all my trauma today. This conversation is about yours."

Lusa snorted. "I mean, we overlap a little."

He hummed.

"And we never did talk about that night."

He hummed again and went on pretending to read. Lusa sighed, closing her eyes, letting the warmth of his touch, the comfort that he was here and whole despite his feelings on what he'd lost in those feathers and scars.

"When I found you that night, you were in your serpent form. That was the second time I'd ever seen you that way. And this whole mess was only the third time I've seen Ques in their true form."

"And two of three times, a horror show," Res added quietly.

"Yeah." Lusa snuggled a bit closer to him. "When Theodore came to help, he explained they'd used the darts with alchemy to put you in a sleep that kept you that way so they could get to your feathers. I didn't know what to think when I saw Erandi open that kit."

"It certainly made more sense with what awaited us."

Lusa rolled on to her back, staring up at him. Res abandoned the book.

"You don't think it's weird he's an alchemist? Not even a little bit?"

Res sighed, his brow furrowed as he seemed to give it real thought for the first time. "I don't know the circumstance. If he learned as a result of what happened to him, or turned a talent to good use after the fact. But he helped that other Ques." Res shuddered. "If he had shifted his human form, his death would have been even worse. And if he'd been awake the entire time? I can't even imagine the pain he was in."

"Yeah," Lusa whispered.

"Whoever did that to him, did it with spite. Or hate. I saw just before they took him away, most of his tail had been stripped of feathers, so they'd probably had him captive, whoever they were." Res waved a hand, his jaw clenched. "Then to learn they'd lose their source, and gut him and leave him like that? One last hurrah for the road."

Lusa didn't really think, she just sort of crawled up into his lap and wrapped her arms around him, and he hugged her back. They stayed there, holding each other.

"Fuck if I know anything, Lusa, but I'm terrified," he whispered against her hair. "To think I lived so long free of this fear, to now truly understand this threat."

Lusa leaned back, gave him a half smile, since it was all she really had in her this morning. "Well, we have Kiki and Wags. And Theodore. Once we get him the birds after this month is done, maybe he can help us. I'm sure the Citadel has ways to help protect people from stuff like this. We never decided on what to ask for as a payment."

Res hummed, not meeting her eyes. "Of course. But you better keep looking. And I'll keep learning what I can." Then he canted his head. "But I wonder if you should speak with Erandi. I don't think either of you needed that conversation to happen in front of everyone."

Lusa winced. "Yeah, probably not. I didn't . . ." She sighed. "I don't even know what I was accusing him of, not really, it was just a lot, and it felt . . ." She shivered a bit, because it had felt so, so wrong in the moment, and the terror she'd felt from Kiki at her waist had only driven up her reaction. She'd never felt Kiki so afraid.

Whatever the case, Erandi didn't deserve her judgement.

"I'll talk to him," Lusa agreed. "Maybe tomorrow, give it some time. Besides, I should look for those birds, or all this was really for nothing." Res hummed again, watching her with an odd look. When she frowned at him, he turned away. "What?"

"Nothing, love. Just wondering if anything else is bothering you," Res said as he got up from the bed. She watched him change, considering the other questions rattling around in her brain.

*Will you get tired of me, like Quetzalcoatl said?*

*Do you want to stay here in this awful place?*

*Do you love me as much as I love you?*

"It's been a lot," Lusa said instead, because that was true, and now didn't seem like the right time to pile on more questions she wasn't sure either of them was ready for the answers to.

# Chapter 33

R ooms, rooms, and more rooms. Halls, twisting and descend-ed, semi-lit and clean. A vast underground sea of wealth that would never see the light of day again.

Was she ever going to see the sun again?

"Ugh," Lusa groaned. When did she become so melodramatic?

At least Lusa trusted she was on the right track now. She didn't see a reason to disbelieve the moura. And if one thing could go their way, she'd take it.

She stepped from the last room, her skin a little itchy. This one had been filled with scrolls in a dozen different languages she couldn't read, most of them tightly bound with fancy ribbons, wax seals and obvious enchantments. Not that she'd messed with anything.

They hadn't gotten very far, and Lusa was already exhausted as she stared down the dim hall, then shook her head. Another few hours wouldn't make or break finding the birds of truth. Lusa was half-human, and she was wondering if she was underestimating how much sleep she needed. Or maybe just time to clear her head so she could focus better.

Her intention definitely wasn't to end up finding Erandi on her way back to Wags.

It was early evening by then, and she'd backtracked to the corner library for a new book since Res has claimed her pile, and imagine finding the blind man sitting there in one of the comfy leather chairs. Lusa almost tripped over her own feet in the doorway.

He faced out the window, this one over the front gardens near a side fountain that also had koi fish, along with a maple tree with flaming red leaves that never fell, which was part of the reason Lusa liked this library room best. It also had a modest fireplace, the best selection of atlases, and it was tucked in a far corner away from most foot traffic.

Erandi didn't have a book, of course, but the fire was lit, and a used tea service and empty dinner plate sat on the side table. He didn't turn at her sudden approach, didn't acknowledge her at all.

But she knew he knew she was there, and she wasn't going to slink off, because she also knew that was probably what the other Ques did when they assumed just because he was blind, he'd failed to notice they were there and they could just decide not to talk to him.

"I'll go," Lusa offered. "I didn't think anyone would be here."

When she was halfway out the door, he sighed and said, "You don't have to run off on my account. Help yourself to whatever you came for."

Lusa hesitated, because it wasn't only a new book. She didn't know if Res would be back yet, and this was the only other place besides Wags where she felt like she could relax for a few minutes in this underground castle. Granted, relaxing didn't include Erandi, especially not after their last conversation.

She must have taken too long debating with herself, because he spoke again before she decided what to say or do.

"I was harsh earlier, I know that. It doesn't change the fact that I owe you nothing in terms of an explanation about myself or my choices."

Lusa stiffened a bit, because he might not be wrong, but it also didn't really change anything about how she felt either. "Res is important to me. I'll always fight for him if I think he's in danger."

"And I can respect that, which is why I'd like to find a comfortable way forward, especially if the two of you will be staying here."

Lusa's fists clenched, her nails digging into her palms as she fought the urge to deny they would even consider it, but Erandi had been with Quetzalcoatl the longest, and she knew the god didn't care for her. They needed to keep him happy while they were in his home, or they needed to give up on the birds and leave now.

To be honest, Lusa wasn't sure they had the option to leave before the month was over.

"I'm confused, but you're right. I don't know you and you don't have to tell me anything. But I saw what you did for that Ques. He was lucky to have you help him."

Erandi still didn't turn her direction, knuckles pressed to his lips and chin. "It was a terrible thing," he said quietly. "And the very least I could do given my skills." He shifted a little deeper into his chair. "Alchemy is like any other magic or technology, Lusa. The hands that wield it, the intentions, and the results all play into determinations of good and evil. Nothing is as black and white as the world wishes it to be."

Lusa sighed, because she'd always known as much. What was stealing to try and save good people if not a decidedly gray area, after all? "Yeah, I know. And I am sorry I yelled like that, in front of everyone. I wish we'd done that differently."

"It certainly could have gone better." His lips twitched, almost a smile. "How is Res?"

Lusa came into the room and leaned on the bookshelf. The fire was nice, and the room didn't feel quite so unwelcoming anymore. "He's pretty rattled, but he's okay, I think." She bit her lip. "He's scared. I am too."

"You're right to be. What we Ques possess by merely existing is too valuable. As long as we're out in the world, we will be hunted."

"Not a great pep talk, if that's what you're going for," Lusa quipped.

Erandi did smirk this time. "I've been told they are not my strongest suit."

Lusa huffed a little laugh, but she really wanted to think about anything else for five minutes. "You want to guess what I found down-stairs?"

By the time Lusa headed back to Wags, she and Erandi had shared a few chuckles and she'd told him about more than just the moura. He was a captive audience and seemed genuinely interested in every detail of the rooms below, asking her if she'd like to run an inventory for him while she explored. When he pressed a bit, how it might be the perfect job for her when she and Res took up residence permanently in Mount Pindo, she made her excuses.

He might not have eyes, but she felt his stare burning into her back as she left.

Lusa sat crossed-legged on the chair as Kiki drew maps, adding to her own simplified list of what they'd found in different rooms on a notepad she'd pass on to Erandi. She didn't see the harm in it, and figured the more cooperative she appeared, the better. She enjoyed a warm chamomile tea Wags prepared, along with a peanut butter and jelly sandwich she'd requested. Tonight definitely felt like a comfort food night. She'd already changed into comfy clothes, wearing a pair of loose, soft pants and a T-shirt, along with a pair of fuzzy wool socks with ducks on them.

She'd only been back about an hour and half when Res came in, grumbling as he tossed his coat on the rack and kicked off his shoes. Lusa paused mid-chew, asking around a mouthful of food. "All good?"

He frowned down at her, hands on his hips. "Nope," he said, popping the *p* loudly. Res crossed the space between them, plucking her pen from behind her ear and tossing it on the table, then taking her almost finished sandwich from her hand and returning it to her plate. Before she could ask when he was doing, he scooped her up and tossed her over his shoulder like a sack of potatoes. When she shrieked, he held on to her butt to stabilize her. "Please, as if I'd drop you."

She somehow managed to swallow upside down, then grumbled, "You keep dropping me on the bed."

"I suppose that's fair," he said and then did just that, hard enough that she bounced with a grunt, and then he was scrambling on top of her. Lusa's breath left her lungs in a rush, her stomach doing a swoop.

They'd kissed a few times, and slept in the same bed, but they hadn't had sex in a few days with all the chaos.

Now, she was pinned under his lean body, his face nuzzled against her throat as he sighed. "Gods, I've missed you." He nipped her jaw, then caught her earlobe hard enough she squirmed. "I keep finding myself distracted when I'm supposed to be paying attention."

Lusa bite her lip to fight back a grin; she liked hearing that. She liked it a lot. It helped soothe those worries that chewed at her when they weren't together. "I thought you didn't pine."

"I don't, which is why I came back early to take action. The opposite of pining," he told her as he sat up and pulled off his shirt, then tugged her up and pulled off hers as well. Then he grumbled, "Fucking hells, these tits," and buried his face against her skin, open-mouthed kisses all over her breasts as she giggled, before her giggles faded into little pants and moans as his kisses became more focused.

She ran her hands through his hair; he seemed to really like it, and she did too. She loved the way he leaned into her touch, but she found it a bit strange he reacted so strongly to such a simple thing. It wasn't overtly sexy, right? But she'd seen people touching each other's hair when they kissed all the time. And she really liked it when he did the same to her, but he acted like no one had bothered for him before.

"I missed you too," she whispered. Lusa dug her nails into his scalp as she spoke. He hummed against her skin, sucking hard enough at her nipple to make her gasp. Then he seemed to get impatient and tugged at her pants, and she lifted her hips so he could help her out of them. Her underwear went next, and when she reached down to help unbutton his trousers, he rested his head against her sternum and muttered something she couldn't make out.

She stopped, just in case, and Res peered up at her with a pout, pupils dilated under his long eyelashes. Okay, right, then he wasn't wanting her to stop helping. They were kind of in an awkward position though, trying to get his pants off while he half laid on her naked body, but Lusa was a problem solver, so once she shoved his pants down as far as she could reach—he wasn't wearing anything underneath, because of course he wasn't—she used her feet to push them the rest of the way down his legs.

"Minx," Res mumbled, and she had to laugh at that.

"Oh, totally. With my very sexy, grabby toes taking off your fancy pants."

"Everything about you is sexy."

Lusa rolled her eyes at the same time her head fell back, because he was nibbling along her ribs now, which she'd learned was both tickly and really, really arousing. She bit her lip, those whimpers and whines he liked so much sneaking out again as he added his fingers to the mix, exploring between her thighs in teasing, maddening strokes.

But then her world shifted, Res rolling onto his back and taking her with him. And there she was, straddling him, naked, with his cock between her legs. Her hands planted on his chest to catch herself from falling forward and she stared down at him, her mouth hanging open while Res smirked right back, both of them entirely naked now.

Then he put both hands behind his head.

"Go on then. Conquer me."

Lusa blinked at him.

Then she burst out laughing so hard she snorted, which was so loud and awful she covered her mouth with both hands. Res had to grab her hips to keep her from falling over.

"I'm sorry," she gasped out, laughing harder when she snorted again, unable to stop at his expression. "I'm sorry, just . . . Did that line really work?"

"Lusa, love, I'd really like it to be on some sort of record that you're the one who keeps bring up my previous lovers, and when we're naked no less." He arched a brow at her, and she could tell he was fighting back a smile.

She giggled, then giggled again, before she tossed back her hair and did her best imitation of his sultry voice, "Conquer me," with an exaggerated purr on the end.

"That's it, menace!" And Res was tickling her, mercilessly, but he was laughing as hard as she was while she kicked and struggled and ended up under him again, this time with her arms pined up her head, and both of them breathless and grinning at each other. Res rubbed his nose along hers, the mood shifting as they caught their breath, as one of his thighs pressed hers open. "One of these days," he murmured against her lips, "you're going to ride me, love. I dream about it."

Lusa's breathing hitched; his voice was sexy and low, and the preening man who'd challenged her to conquer him—a moment, she thought, of him slipping into a persona he'd adopted with past lovers—had disappeared in favor of the honest and raw version of him.

"You'd have to teach me," Lusa managed, closing her eyes as he sank slowly into her body. For all the teasing, she'd missed him, too, missed this, and she was more than ready to be close to him again. To feel him inside her. "I don't know . . . I won't know what to do."

He kissed her nose, her cheek, before he slotted his mouth over hers and conquered *her* with a kiss that all but took her apart as he joined them together, buried inside her to the hilt, hot and hard, and gods, she could feel him throbbing inside her.

When Res pulled back from the kiss, his gaze searching hers, the rhythm he built took her breath away. It was different this time, as he stared into her, each thrust deeper and heavier than the last as he kept her so close she couldn't tell them apart.

She'd read things, about sex and making love being different, meaning different things, and she had to close her eyes, because she was drowning in it, in him, especially when his forehead fell against hers and he whispered, "It's us. That's all you need to know."

# Chapter 34

Another two days of searching later, Lusa was wrapping up her hours in the maze. She yawned, wondering if she was getting a blister and if Res would have fun tonight. Matty had all but begged for everyone to stay out tonight for cards and drinks, insisting that the dire mood was no way to honor the memory of the Ques who'd died the week before. Lusa knew he meant well, but she wasn't sure his attempts to cheer everyone would go as well as he hoped. Res, at least, seemed willing to go along with distraction. And he needed it.

Lusa didn't know what to make of Res's headspace. When they weren't together, he was offered a life here in the underground castle with his kin where he could live like a pampered noble, safe and secure, where the hunters could never find him again. She couldn't tell if the pressure to maintain interest and not insult Quetzalcoatl was wearing him down, or if it was the genuine fear of once they went back to outside world, he'd be in danger again. He wasn't hiding from her, not exactly, but every day they spent in this place seemed like another boulder crushing down on his shoulders.

She picked up her pace then, deciding to explore one more hall before she called it a night. Maybe this would be the day she got lucky, found the birds, and maybe they could find a way to gracefully get the hells out of here early without making a god angry. Two and a half more weeks felt like a lifetime right now. Lusa puffed out a breath. At least she hadn't had to deal with Quetzalcoatl again, but Res wasn't so lucky. The god didn't attend the social time Res spent with the other Ques, but he made a point of requesting Res's time almost daily.

Lusa didn't like thinking on what he might whisper in Res's ear. She'd heard quite enough from him in their single private hallway conversation. She just hoped he was kind to Res, being he was one of his grandkids.

"Alright, let's do this," Lusa mumbled, as much to Kiki as herself, because she really wished she could talk to her friend instead of pretending Kiki wasn't with her all the time. Kiki understood and wasn't bothered, completely infatuated by mapmaking and documenting treasure, which apparently was a true joy for the clockwork creature. Lusa really hoped Kiki would keep up its art once they were done with the maze.

The next room held a harp and nothing else, so Lusa didn't cross the threshold, knowing all Kiki needed was a glance. In fact, she wasn't even sure if she needed to turn the belt buckle with gemstones to face the room, or if Kiki could see all around her from the belt at all times. Maybe she'd ask later.

Another weapons storage, this time hammers. Oddly enough, they all looked really plain, like someone had just gathered up normal, average hammers from everywhere. Most of them didn't seem enchanted or anything.

More coins, denarii this time. She shook her head with a grin, pocketing a few different versions for Res's collection. She'd never know what she was looking at without his hobby. She took a little longer this time, because she kept finding different faces on the coins, and she had no idea who was who or if Res might like one better than the other. Once she had a good selection, she stepped back into the hall.

The temperature dropped as soon as she did, the lights in the hall dimming, and Lusa stilled, because she hadn't felt the shadowlands since she'd encountered the moura. Throat tight, she glanced first the way she'd come—her way out—and saw nothing. But when she looked deeper, there it was.

If it wasn't a mouros, she didn't know what it would be instead.

The figure was humanoid, and tall, bulky in a way that didn't quite match human proportions. The halls down in the maze were about ten feet tall, the same across, and now it made complete sense. The creature filled the space precariously, as if when it moved through the mountain, the rock parted out of the way so he would walk on by.

Lusa assumed male, given the bulky mass, and given she'd already met a moura, which seemed to be the female counterpart, at least in some versions of the mythos governing this type of Aperien. His skin was the same color as the stone around them, and in texture as well, and he wore no clothing. His body had no discerning marks beyond his face, which was the only part of him that truly looked human. And he stared right where she stood, although she knew from the shadowlands' presence he didn't see her.

His neck, wrists and ankles were adorned with golden rings, bracelets and chains. Lusa wondered if she would have heard him walking if she hadn't been in that particular room digging through coin piles. And if the mouros found her for that exact same reason.

Biting her lip, she took a single step toward the way she knew Kiki mapped as up, and the mouros's human gaze flicked to her foot as he canted his head, even though she hadn't made any noise.

Maybe it wasn't about sound at all. If he'd carved out all this stone, did he hold a connection to the caves he'd created? To all these treasure rooms? They were guards, after all. Had it only been a matter of time before they felt someone walking around in their maze and came looking for the intruder?

Lusa remembered her pocket then. She had about a dozen coins. In reality, they held little worth. Sure, they could be melted down and made into something new, but they weren't used in trade as a major denomination. In fact, she was pretty sure Res only had one in his collection. Okay, so maybe they weren't common. Maybe they were rare and super valuable? But the room held hundreds of thousands of them, at least.

She stuck her hand in her pocket and grabbed the coins, and with a quick flick of her wrist, tossed them back in the room. They jingled and bounced as they landed, silence falling seconds later. The mouros tracked the coins movement, not Lusa. A few seconds later, she tried to retreat another step, and the Aperien's gaze snapped back to her feet.

Crap.

She didn't know what to do.

Say hello?

Say sorry?

Apologize for brushing the moura's hair because now no one was guarding that ugly comb he might have made?

Run and hope he moved as slow as he looked?

She clutched at Kiki in warning, and then started walking backwards, slowly, the way she wanted to escape.

The floor trembled, the walls vibrated, and a rush of warm air slammed into her from behind. Lusa turned to bolt, because she could not get stuck down here, and found herself face to face with solid stone.

The hallway was gone.

Gone.

She was staring at solid rock.

And now the mouros was walking her direction, each step a thundering quake, but one guess had been right. It moved slow as hells; either that, or it was in no hurry because she was caught.

"Kiki!" Lusa gasped out, panic surging and strangling her, because being stuck under the mountain was bad enough, but that was with Res, and Wags and Tick and Kiki, not just her and Kiki alone in the maze at the mercy of this mouros, and never seeing Res again before she died.

Kiki sprang from her waist, shifting into its winged cat form, eyes shimmering red and tail lashing.

"Kiki, the wall, what do we do?"

Kiki whirled, examining the stone, blinking so rapidly, Lusa could hear its metal eyelids clicking like shutters. Then Kiki sprinted toward the mouros.

"Wait!" She grabbed for Kiki, but missed, and it darted sideways into the coin room, returning seconds later with a mouthful of coins. "What are you doing, Kiks?"

Lusa knelt down beside it, glancing over her shoulder at the mouros, who continued to lumber toward them, unhurried.

"Fix," Kiki chirped, fluttering around as it pressed the coins against the stone in large oval outline, dismissing Lusa like she was interrupting. It worked fast, wings buzzing as it fluttered up about her at head level, and then Lusa realized the coins glowed and were sinking into the stone, curls of smoke peeling out from the holes they created.

It smelled like sulfur, and an acidic tang she couldn't quite place, but she didn't have time to think about because Kiki grabbed her wrist in its mouth and tugged, hard enough to almost knock her over.

"Lusa hurries!"

She did, scrambling after Kiki into the coin room, and a second later, an explosion denoted, knocking her off her feet. She flew forward, crashing into the coin pile, the air forced from her lungs, her ears left ringing. Lusa coughed a few times, smoke and dust filling the air, her eyes burning.

Warm metal paws padded up her pack, then patted her cheek. "Lusa, up!"

"Kiki, what the hells," Lusa managed, still coughing as she struggled to sit. She was covered in dust and soot, chunks of rock scattered all over the hall and the front of the coin room. She rubbed her forehead, and it came away bloodied, but she was pretty sure it was superficial. Her entire body felt bruised. "What did you do?"

"Kiki make boom!" The clockwork cat chirped, dancing in a circle. Then it stilled, and Lusa felt the heavy footsteps of the mouros again.

Faster now.

She snatched Kiki up in her arms, dashing out of the room even though every inch of her body screamed in pain and protest, and she gaped at the giant hole blown in the stone wall the mouros erected to block their path. There, beyond the hole, waited the rest of the hall they'd come down, and Lusa didn't hesitate, darting through the gap, her nose burning as the pieces clicked together.

"Oh gods, Kiki, you turned those coins into explosives?!"

"Kiki make boom!" it chirped again, excited, but then squirmed enough that Lusa let Kiki drop.

"Kiks, we need to go!"

But Kiki darted back to the broken wall, sat down on its haunches, and put paws to the stone.

And as Lusa watched, the ragged gap sealed, but not with rock.

Metal. Iron, maybe, as Kiki transmuted the entire section of newly summoned stone into metal, and then the metal bled out to the nearby wall, then up and around, then sounded a low, rumbling hum as the composition of this section of the mountain was recalibrated, recreated, and redefined.

Lusa knew the mouros could shape stone. So did Kiki, because Kiki never forgot anything it witnessed.

And it had made the leap to change the material into something the mouros couldn't directly control, buying them time to escape.

By changing a mountain from stone to metal.

Gods help them if the bad man, whoever the hells he was, ever found Kiki.

And if he did?

Lusa would do everything in her power to stop him from taking Kiki because this sort of power didn't belong near anyone bad, ever.

And they needed to Kiki to stay exactly as Kiki was; pure and good and wonderful, the type of innocence that would never, ever use something like this moment for everything it might be capable of.

Erandi's words rang in the back of her skull.

*Alchemy is like any other magic or technology, Lusa. The hands that wield it, the intentions, and the results all play into determinations of good and evil for the outcome.*

They really, really needed to leave Mount Pindo as soon as possible. And Kiki needed to stay a secret, now more than ever.

Kiki turned then, done moving mountains, and trotted back over to sit at Lusa's feet, doing its poor imitation of cat's purr. It looked up at her with a hopeful expression.

"Kiki did good?"

Lusa knelt down and scooped Kiki up, giving it a crushing hug, even though it hurt with all Kiki's sharp edges, and nuzzled its little kitten face. "You did so good, Kiki. Thank you. Now quick, back to a belt. We need to get back to Wags. And we need to be much more careful from now on, okay?"

Kiki whirred, pulling back with a very serious expression and a stoic nod. "Kiki keeps Lusa safe."

# Chapter 35

Lusa was still in the shower, picking bits of rock from her hair and washing dust from her skin, when Res burst in the bathroom and tore open the curtain.

She jumped and kind of shrieked, covering herself with one hand and trying to pull the certain shut with the other. "Excuse you?"

"Please, like I don't intimately know every part of your body," Res snapped back, his voice harsh, so Lusa did exactly what he deserved for talking to her like that.

She threw the wet washcloth at his face.

That startled him enough he let go of the curtain, which allowed her to snap it closed. "That doesn't give you permission to come in here when I'm naked without asking and yell at me."

The only sound was the water as she washed her hair, her cheeks flushed, and her heart strumming from the shock of it all, and the way he'd just spoken to her. Annoyed, angry, hurt? She didn't even know where to start with him right now, but it had been a long day, and she was tired and sore and really not in the mood for him to have an attitude about . . .

Lusa had no idea why he was even in here right now.

Was he still in here?

She peeked out of the curtain to find him sitting on the toilet, elbows on his knees, his head in his hands. His hair was half wet from the washcloth, which was discarded in the sink.

"Sorry, you're right." Then he sighed. "But I came in and Kiki was going on about explosions and a rock monster trying to eat you."

"That's . . . mostly true?" Lusa turned off the water, and Res handed her a towel. She stayed inside the curtain though, still a bit peeved despite the apology. "A mouros found us. I'm not sure what it was planning, but it sealed the hallway with stone, and Kiki transmuted coins and blew a hole through the wall."

"Good gods."

Wrapped in a towel now, Lusa stepped out, her hair wet around her shoulders. "And then Kiki turned a huge chunk of the rock into metal so it couldn't follow us, and we ran back here. It couldn't see me, so I really don't know what it was planning."

"Nothing good, I'd imagine."

Lusa shrugged as she walked by him, even though she'd thought the exact same thing. "Maybe, maybe not." He followed, and she didn't prevent him, but she didn't exactly welcome him either. He hung in the doorway of her room as she dressed.

"It scared me," Res said. "And you know how Kiki is. It was all very exciting talk, chirps and dancing about you almost dying."

"Res, I didn't almost die," Lusa huffed as she pulled her shirt on. Dressed now, she turned and took him in, and did he look miserable. With a sigh, she stepped over and wrapped her arms around his waist. He dropped his chin on her head. "That's exactly why I had Kiki with me." Then she smirked. "I didn't realize exactly how explosive it would be, but still."

"Not funny."

"Not even a little?"

"No."

"Did you eat already?"

"Yes, plenty." Another sigh. "As good as the food is in the castle, I miss Wags's homecooked meals."

Lusa snorted. "Yesterday you were complaining about me eating sandwiches all the time."

"She makes those for you because you eat like a child, Lusa. She knows I have a vastly more refined palate, and the food she prepares for me reflects as much."

"Okay, fancy pants," Lusa said, following him to the kitchen. And she laughed when all that was out for them was a plate of club sandwiches, with pickles spears and grapes. When he glared at her, she mimed locked her lips with a key and throwing it over her shoulder. She took a seat and popped a grape in her mouth. "How are the maps, Kiki?"

They spent a few minutes looking at Kiki's work while they ate, petted Tick, and Lusa made of point of complimenting Wags on dinner to get another exasperated look out of Res. Later, as they climbed into bed, Res pulled her close.

"Stay with me tomorrow."

"What do you mean?"

"This place is wearing me down to the bones." He sighed and held her tighter, nuzzling her hair. "And I miss you. Everyone is dreary after what happened with the Ques dying, and they could probably use a push to get them out of their own heads. Gods knows I'm not good for it. Hells, I'm drowning myself."

Lusa turned in his arms, brushing back his floppy hair, running her fingertips over the dark circles under his eyes. He did look a bit hallowed out. "What do you guys even do all day?"

He shrugged. "Whatever, really. It's not so bad. Did you know Guatemoc can play the harp?"

"Is he any good?"

"He's alright," Res said with a sly grin that told a different story. "Come on, don't leave them with only me for novelty. And it'll be fun. Besides, Matty was asking after you. I think he's jealous you've been painting with Pollock."

"All Matty seems to do is drink."

Res yawned. "He's not so bad. None of them are, really. And besides, I'd rather you didn't head back down there."

She pushed up on one elbow. "Res, I have to. I haven't found the birds yet."

"Do you?" He asked the question earnestly. "Is there a limit on the risk here, love?" He reached up, tracing her cheekbone, before cupping her jaw. "Call me selfish, but I'm not exactly keen on sacrificing you for the nebulous greater good, love."

"It's not nebulous. We know who we're helping."

"Not really. We know Theodore, but not the people the birds would help."

Lusa frown, moving away from his hand. "Res, I don't want to give up just because things got a little rough tonight."

"Alright, alright," he whispered, replacing his hand, then pressing his lips to hers in a chaste kiss. "But isn't it reasonable to allow some breathing room? Let the mouros move on?"

She'd been considering the same thing. And the central spire still had a number of different directions they could explore before going anywhere near the corridor Kiki sealed off with iron.

"Spend a few days with me, see what it's like here." Res nuzzled her nose. "Please. Then you can get back to it, I promise."

"Alright. I will."

"Thank you."

Lusa snuggled back into his arms, and Res relaxed into sleep after a few seconds, but she stayed awake, wondering about what things they might not be talking about and probably should.

Two days later, she'd had more than enough.

Lusa wasn't sure how she'd ended up talked into a third day at the underground castle with the Ques, but Res had been in better spirits, and she couldn't deny that she'd seen an uptick in the group over the two days she'd spent with them. Maybe she acted as a buffer between them, or she simply presented different ideas they didn't normally gravitate toward, but she'd enjoyed spending time with them.

She'd been the one to wrangle everyone into a yoga class, because it was exercising that Erandi could do, and Oz had appreciated the suggestion that stretching was as important to muscles as weights and cardio.

She talked Pollock into bringing paints and easels for everyone, with Erandi as the model, though she'd thrown a paint brush at Matty's head when he'd tried to leave after drawing a single stick figure. It turned out Matty was a fair hand at painting, though he wasn't near the talent of his brother. None of them were. Lusa had a feeling it must have caused tensions between them growing up.

Guatemoc played more than the harp. A little prodding, and he'd presented quite the collection of musical instruments, which led to an entire afternoon of absurdity and laughter, and at one point, some pretty good music, accompanied by the true surprise of the day: Oz's incredible singing voice.

Res, it turned out, was far more skilled than any of his kin in illusion magic, because he'd honed his skills over the years through performing. Lusa had spoken to Erandi before she suggested it, to make sure he wouldn't be uncomfortable, but he'd encouraged it and asked her to sit by and describe Res's magic to him. She did, and by the end of it, he'd been melancholy but also peaceful. Then the rest of them completely trashed a common room attempting to learn some of Res's tricks.

Matty, of course, gave extensive lessons on drink mixing, which got everyone so drunk, Lusa needed Oz to carry Res back to Wags that night. The unexpected turn was Erandi and Matty discussing alchemical notes to heighten drink flavors, and the two were deep in discussions when Guatemoc passed out on the floor and Oz hauled Res away.

Lusa, in turn, challenged them to a game of charades, where the teams shifted until she was by herself against everyone else, and she still won. Erandi couldn't participate, but that was late in the second day, and he'd seemed to settle into the company and enjoy being present and listening to the laughter more than playing along by then.

Lusa agreed with Res about the food. It was all very delicious, and rich and fancy, and she really wanted more of Wags's simple delights. She kept Kiki with her at all times outside Wags, and each night, Kiki remained excited to draw things from the day, but Lusa missed simpler times just watching Tick and Kiki play, or waxing Wags's exterior.

She missed sun and wind and fresh air, and the grass and weather and watching people besides these few. Lusa considered going across the hall to people watch, but she'd been hesitant. She'd prodded a bit, and the staff that lived down here she encountered in the casted seemed content, but she didn't really need more reasons to hate being down here. Just a bit longer, and they could leave.

Then they got up this morning, got dressed, and Res was tugging her after him for breakfast, begging for one more day with puppy dog eyes, going on about how much fun it had been to have her here with him and their new friends. She agreed to breakfast, at least, but now that it was done, she was trying to figure out how to make her escape and get back to the maze and her search for the birds.

Two more weeks and their time was up. She didn't want to let Theodore down. She didn't want to let herself down either, because despite the mouros encounter, she believed she could figure this out. She wanted to. She wanted to succeed at this, she thought as she looked around the table at the Ques, with their fine dishes and elaborate food and pretty clothes, wanting for nothing, with treasures beyond belief rotting away under their feet. Where one piece of that treasure could save a few good people from a terrible fate.

Maybe she was being an idiot. Maybe she should just ask Quetzalcoatl for the birds and be done with it.

No, that had to be the last resort, because if he said no and she kept looking, she'd be directly defying the will of a god, and that never ended well for anyone.

And she had a terrible feeling, deep down her gut, asking Quetzalcoatl for anything wouldn't go over very well.

Lusa was just relieved she hadn't encountered him again since they'd crossed paths in the hall when he'd questioned if she was ruining Res's life with her friendship.

"Someone piss in your tea?" Matty asked as he plopped down beside her.

Lusa forced out a smile. "No, just thinking."

Across from them, Pollock stood, excusing himself to paint—alone. Erandi left an hour ago without a word. Guatemoc, Oz, and Res were debating the merits of a performer who'd lived in the Velvet Emporium fifty years ago.

"Ugh, well, those two days were nice, but here we go," Matty muttered.

"Here we go, what?"

"Back to boring. Guatemoc and Oz can pick a topic and talk about it for *hours* on end, and I get the feeling your Res likes to hear himself talk just as much." Matty slanted a look her direction and Lusa fought back a grin. "I thought so. And Pollock wants to paint by himself, Erandi is being Erandi, and now, here I am. Doomed to boredom."

Then he leaned forward on the table with both elbows, mischief glittering in his expression so much like Res, Lusa's breath caught. She couldn't help but wonder if maybe they were more closely related than they'd realized. Half-brothers, instead of cousins?

"Now you, though, you haven't been bored."

Lusa raised a brow.

"Erandi said you already have a job lined up for once you guys settle. He said you've been off charting the cellar."

Lusa shouldn't have felt a little sting of betrayal. They'd never agreed those discussions were private, but for some stupid reason she hadn't considered he might tell everyone else what she'd been doing. Or worse, making everyone think they were staying.

And Matty's earnest expression only made her feel worse, because there wasn't a hint of anything malicious, only excitement at the prospect of new company in his life, and the idea of Lusa being part of that company.

"Uh, yeah, he'd mentioned it might be a thing. If we stay."

Matty ignored the *if*, his grin widening. "But you've been down there?"

"I have, yeah."

Matty glanced across the table. The other three were deep in their conversation, which seemed to be getting more and more heated, as Oz shook his head and refilled their mimosas.

Res, it seemed, wasn't needing her quite so much this morning.

And it had been two days. More than enough time for the mouros to move on, and she'd planned to explore down a different hall anyway.

Lusa stood, tossing her napkin on the table. "You coming or what?"

Matty was on his feet in a heartbeat. "I thought you'd never ask."

"What an alarming amount of shit," Matty commented, not for the first time.

They'd been wandering for a few hours now, winding down halls and peeking in rooms, all while Lusa kept studious notes she didn't need so Matty didn't ask questions about how she was keeping track of all the treasure piled up around them. Matty, for his part, keep his hands in his pockets and seemed unconcerned about anything being a threat. Granted, *he* wasn't the one who almost been entombed by a stoney giant a few days back, but whatever. He made for good company, although Lusa felt a little guilty about ignoring Kiki.

"You guys really never use anything from down here, huh?" Lusa asked, jotting down notes about their most recent find: a chamber filled entirely with Grecian pottery.

"Hells if I know. I'm sure you've noticed I'm not one for details," Matty mused as he peeked into the next room. "More coins. Again." Matty sounded disappointed.

Lusa caught up with him to peek inside. Nickels this time, another United States of America coinage if she recalled correctly. Hundreds of thousands of them. She decided against grabbing any, in case that was what got the mouros's attention last time.

"You seem keen on the details about booze," Lusa noted.

The next room was empty except for a wooden mask on a pedestal.

They exchanged a look and kept walking.

"Well, one needs a hobby," Matty said. "I've cultivated fifteen orchards, eight vineyards, and twelve species of hops in the agricultural tunnels."

"I can't believe anything grows down here," Lusa muttered.

"Bothers you so much? The enchanted sunlight in place of the real thing?"

Lusa shrugged. "It's not the same. And the air down here is stuffy."

Matty sniffed. "Well, it is down here."

"It is all over. You're just used to it."

"That's fair, I suppose."

The next room housed a bunch of furniture, all made from the same wood, which Lusa guessed was oak.

When Matty spoke again, his voice was softer. "Is it truly so terrible here?"

Lusa glanced up at him. He'd stopped walking, hands still in his pockets, today's clothing choice modest by his standards. His purple hair was slicked back, with eyes just like Res's studying her more closely than he usually bothered. Of all the Ques, she felt like Matty paid the least attention to details, as he claimed earlier. He always seemed distracted or jumping onto the next thing. He didn't like observing, she realized, because he was too busy distracting himself, but from what, she wasn't sure.

Now, though, he seemed very invested in her answer.

"Not terrible, no," Lusa answered carefully. The fact that anything she'd said to Erandi was common knowledge rang in the back of her mind; would Matty repeat their exchange to everyone else? Or walk right up to Quetzalcoatl and give him more reasons to dislike her? Still, she couldn't bring herself to lie to him. "But it's not really for me."

"Because we're underground?"

"And the isolation."

"Why does that matter when you're invisible to everyone? I'm shocked this place isn't a boon, with all of us being able to see you."

Lusa held back her flinch, barely, and only because Matty asked the question with genuine, innocent curiosity. There was no mockery in his tone, no snide amusement or belittlement, or any suggestion she should be grateful. He appeared genuinely confused.

"I get how it could seem that way, but I'm used to being around a lot of people, moving through the world unnoticed. Here, I'm pinned everywhere I go. Again, not all bad. But I like watching the world, taking in all the different people and places. I like travelling, and I like finding ways to help people who need it while I do." She looked into the next room and laughed at the rows and rows of gold bars, stacked in neat, shiny rows. Glamorous and useless. She waved a hand at the shine. "And it's hard to see all this stuff just going to waste when it could help people outside Mount Pindo, you know?"

Matty nodded. "I'll give you that. Poe and I grew up wealthy. Comfortable, to say the least. We never suffered like Erandi or Res. We were lucky to be brought here before any hunters found us, to live a life of bliss, and most days, ignorance. Much easier to just make wine and distill spirits. To be happy and enjoy life and my family being safe."

Lusa patting his arm, then squeezed. "There's nothing wrong any of that, or this place being enough for you. And I can't understand what's it like being Ques, and the danger and fear that comes with it. But that also means this place doesn't mean the same things for me that it does for you."

"Shame, really," Matty said with a grin. "You're far more charming than any of these bastards."

Lusa snorted. "Please. You guys are all charm. It's part of your blood, or whatever."

Matty canted his head, his expression one she couldn't quite read. "I don't think Res will want you to leave."

Lusa blinked, then walked away from him, shaking her head, the words out before she could think about consequences, or what might get back to Quetzalcoatl and piss him off, or how much time they still had left in this place. "This place isn't for Res, either."

"Ah, well." Matty cleared his throat, trailing after her, his tone concerned now. "That's probably something you two need to talk about."

Lusa was about tell him he didn't know anything about Res, whom he'd only met two weeks ago, but the next room opened up into a vast circular chamber, much taller than any previous room, and carried the scent of fresh foliage.

More importantly, a sudden flush of wings and chirping calls.

# Chapter 36

"This is certainly different from anything else we've seen," Matty breathed behind her, and all Lusa could do was nod.

The room was massive, at least thirty feet high, with one of those pretend sun orbs secured in the domed rock ceiling. A crystal-clear lake with a single island occupied the center, rich with lichen, moss and violets. At the center stood a weeping willow, an ancient behemoth with spiraling branches dipping down to the water's surface. The leaves were a hundred different shades, shimmering and swaying in a soft, cool breeze which tickled Lusa's skin.

And in the branches, nestled in between the bends, were dozens of nests, all occupied by eggs and, more importantly, *birds*.

The birds themselves weren't overly remarkable, but Lusa's breath still caught, because a flock of two hundred or more huddled in the branches, all of them falling silent as she and Matty approached. They scuttled onto higher branches, flapping and fluttering but not flying. The birds all had pale plumage, mostly white with very faint traces of color, and eloquent, curled tailfeathers. Their eyes were an odd orange and pupilless, their beaks and feet not much darker than their feathers.

Theodore hadn't given Lusa any description for the birds of truth. Archival records said they disappeared down under Mount Pindo shortly after the Aperien Event, with no consensus on if they came from a predetermined mythos or were some sort of hybrid, but the only two ended up down here.

Were these the birds of truth? Or some other kind of magical bird that happened to be under the mountain? Lusa wondered how she'd figured it out, when she realized hundreds of eyes were staring down at her and the shadowlands remained absent.

She huffed a laugh.

Birds of truth. Of course they'd see her.

Yeah, when she got out of Mount Pindo, Lusa was done taking her invisibility for granted. These last few weeks showed her how lucky she's been, and she had no intentions of squandering that luck ever again.

"What do you suppose they are?" Matty asked beside her. "And why are they all staring at us? It's creepy."

Holy hells, she'd found the birds of truth.

"They must be magic," Lusa offered. She had to be really, really careful now. She didn't want to lie to Matty if she could help it, but an entire flock of truth-telling critters stared them down right now. "Why else would the mouros keep them?"

"Pretty feathers?" Matty offered, stepping deeper into the room. The birds didn't seem afraid, instead cautious and maybe curious, but they remained high in the tree, their nests closely guarded by pairs. Lusa side-eyed Matty, not sure if he was joking, and decided against any comments about Ques feathers. "More likely collecting for collecting's sake. I'll give Quetzalcoatl that much at least; he seems far less interested in all that nonsense than Bartholomew."

Lusa snorted. "I guess." When Matty frowned at her, she shrugged. "He still holds the yearly festival and takes all those offerings. If he cared, he wouldn't take stuff from people who might actually use it and put it down here to collect dust, even if it's only to protect his secret identity."

"It's not so simple, Lusa. His actions are to keep us safe from the Ques hunters. If people knew he was Quetzalcoatl and not Bartholomew, he'd be in danger from the hunters as well. And it would make it that much harder for him to protect us."

"There are endless choices in between, Matty. He doesn't have to reveal who he is in order to stop forcing tribute from poor people."

A soft chorus rose up from the tree, the birds all cooing in unison, "Truth."

Matty startled, paling as he stared up at the tree, and Lusa couldn't help a grin, but it faded as soon as it came.

Because she'd expected to find a single pair of magic birds, not a flock of more than two hundred, imprisoned underground.

They didn't stay with the birds long, which was probably for the best. Matty seemed to retreat into himself once he realized treasure included living things and not just pretty baubles. He decided it was a good time to complain about much his feet were hurting, too, but Lusa suspected it was an excuse. Just as well, and they made their way back.

Lusa couldn't believe after everything, the birds were this close. On her own, it would take less than an hour to get to their tree, and they were nowhere near the mouros hall. And once Kiki mapped the way, it'd be easy to memorize the route.

"You're lost in your own head, aren't you?" Matty asked as they walked, nearly to the castle proper now.

Lusa huffed. "Sorry, I'm still getting used to more than Res for company." She offered him a shrug, swinging her arms. "Did you have fun down there?"

"Eh. I don't know what I expected, but for some reason, it didn't include so much walking. Maybe Oz would make for better company. He's in much finer shape, after all. I'm going to be sore tomorrow, I'm certain of it." Matty groaned theatrically and Lusa laughed.

"I'm sure you'll be fine. Do some yoga, it'll help."

"I'm just really not for all the sweating," he groused.

She shook her head, set to head back to Wags when they reached the split, but Matty threw an arm over her shoulder and steered her toward where they'd eaten breakfast. "No, none of this Erandi nonsense of hiding in your room. Come on, let's see if they're still arguing about the same thing three hours later. Care to wager on it?"

Lusa let him tug her along because she didn't have a good excuse.

What was she going to say? She had to hurry with her magical clockwork cat back to the enchanted wagon so they could draw maps and plan out how to steal all those birds from under Quetzalcoatl's nose?

"Alright, fine, for a little bit."

"Excellent." Matty's smile was contagious, because he didn't mask himself as much as the others. He was truly earnest and open, boyish in being excited to have her around to play with him. "You can try my new drink too. This one has pineapple and lilacs."

"I'm not really into booze."

"I know, I know," he waved a hand, his other arm still over her shoulder as came up on the breakfast hall. "It's fruity, flowery thing with no alcohol I thought would go nicely with those danishes you can stop devouring like they'll run off your plate."

Lusa's smile hurt a little. "Oh, thanks." Because she felt guilty, deep down in her belly, because Matty was trying to make her feel welcome here. And she believed he enjoyed her company and wanted to be friends, and wanted both her and Res to stay down in this castle with him.

He was going to be sad when they left.

But their conversation from the maze rattled around in mind, un-bidden.

*This place isn't for Res, either.*

*That's probably something you two need to talk about.*

Matty pushed the doors open, heading to the bar to make her drink. Oz was gone, but Res and Guatemoc were bent over a bunch of papers, Res with a pen in hand.

Quetzalcoatl stood beside them, with his hip propped against the table.

"—and here, you can attach backrooms for dressing, prepping and practice. If you remember, the Green Gambit in the Emporium was set up in a similar fashion." Res pointed with his pen as he spoke, then looked up with rest when Lusa and Matty entered. He smiled at Lusa, wide and beaming. "There you are. I was wondering where you two went."

Lusa opened her mouth to reply, but Quetzalcoatl pointed at the papers—a diagram of a building maybe, it was hard to tell from across the room—and asked Res, "And what is this?"

Res blinked up at him, casting a quick glance to Lusa before returning to the conversation she and Matty interrupted. "Offshoots of the main stage. Two actually, one on either side, which if the space is large enough, can run other performances at the same time as the main show."

Guatemoc hummed. "And allow for more rehearsal space."

"Precisely," Res agreed.

"And here?" Quetzalcoatl asked.

"Storage," Res replied. "Keep everything for the festival in one place. Allows for repairs, upkeep, and if you decided to run a schedule year-round for your population's entertainment, it makes sense to have the costumes and props on hand for easy access."

The words landed heavy in Lusa's head: Performances. Stage. Year-round.

Matty shook a drink mixer, the sound of ice on metal startling Lusa as he called over, "What's all this then?"

Guatemoc answered over his shoulder, his attention fixated on the papers, on the sketches Res still worked on. "We got to talking about the festival performance this year, and Res had some suggestions for overhauling the entertainment area across the way."

"The artist lane? That's a good idea. I haven't been down there in a while, but last time I was, it seemed a bit droll," Matty offered.

"Fresh eyes always add welcome and needed perspective," Quetzalcoatl added, his voice low and gravely, and Lusa realized he stared at her as he spoke. Both Guatemoc and Res were too focused on the drawing to notice. He held her stare, his head canting as he took her in, head to toes in a slow sweep, before flicking his attention away in clear dismissal.

Her pulse drummed in her ears.

*I offer him a life of luxury and ease, among his own kind, protected and free to indulge any whim.*

Res laughed then as Guatemoc muttered something she didn't catch. "Gods, no. The Green Gambit had the most garish décor I'd ever seen. No, look." Res drew fast lines. "Less flourish, more solid colors, and for the love of all that's holy, no crushed velvet. The performers are the spotlight, not the venue."

*Would you allow him to deny himself this sanctuary, to throw away an immortal future, in order to selfishly tie him to your mortal coil?*

Lusa stared down at her feet, her head pounding. She needed . . . she needed to get back to Wags, to figure out what they were going to do about the birds. To figure out . . .

"Here," Matty said, striding up beside her with a yellow drink in hand, purple sparkles swirling within the ice. "Give it a go, then."

The glass was ice cold, jarring Lusa back to now, and she almost dropped it before her fist clenched tight. Matty raised a brow, but she forced a tight-lipped smile and took a sip. It was delicious, fruity and sweet, tangy from the pineapple, and she could taste and smell the lilacs at the same time, but it wasn't overpowering. And each of the little purple motes popped on her tongue.

Her stomach rolled, though, and she handed it back. "It's great." Matty frowned, because he clearly didn't believe her, and she shook her head. "No, really, the drink is good. I'm just not feeling great, so I'm going to go home." She winced. "I mean, to the wagon."

She winced again at calling Wags a wagon; she hated having to do that, too, and would they always have to if they stayed down here? Or would Wags become everyone's instead of theirs? Her throat burned; her eyes did too.

She really, really needed to go.

"Thanks for making it. And thanks for the company."

"Any time," Matty said quietly, and the worst part was Lusa knew he meant it.

As she left, she felt the weight of Quetzalcoatl's stare burning between her shoulder blades.

Lusa sat with her knees pulled to her chest, watching Kiki painstakingly draw the last map they'd need for the maze, charting the path to the birds of truth. She rested her chin on her knees, trying to focus.

This was good news. They'd found the birds. There were a lot of them, which meant they could certainly smuggle out a few without anyone being the wiser. They could help Theodore and his friends.

She needed to focus on that, before the rest of her swirling mind swallowed her down and she never climbed out again. But Quetzalcoatl kept swimming in her thoughts. His cold expression, his edged words delivered in a detached voice.

*I offer him a life of luxury and ease, among his own kind, protected and free to indulge any whim, and he hesitates.*

*Is it because of you?*

*And if it is, and you are the friend you claim to be, would you allow him to deny himself this sanctuary, to throw away an immortal future, in order to selfishly tie him to your mortal coil?*

Matty's words were worse.

*I don't think Res will want you to leave.*

*That's probably something you two need to talk about.*

And then if she blinked again, she was in that chamber, with the birds of truth, generations of prisoners who had never seen the sun or the sky, with new eggs in those nests. All collecting dust for what?

Lusa buried her face in her arms.

"Lusa sad?" Kiki chirped.

She lifted her head with a sigh. "Yeah, I guess."

"Founds birds. Why sad?" Kiki sat now, giving Lusa its full attention. She traced the gilded filigree between the cat ears and the glowing red stone eyes.

How could they possibly keep Kiki a secret down here for any length of time? She found it hard to imagine Kiki complaining, but it had just gotten a taste of freedom and the wide world.

The creak of wooden steps and a swish of curtains signaled Res's return, and Lusa felt her shoulders crawling up toward her ears with tension. How had they gone two weeks without having a serious conversation about, well, everything that happened since they'd arrived at Mount Pindo?

Lusa turned enough to watch Res as he hung his jacket and kicked of his boots, which she'd observed hundreds, maybe a thousand times before. The idea that this month would end, and this home she'd found would change so drastically, or disappear entirely, left her unable to breathe.

Res noticed, frowning down at her as he walked over. "You alright, love?"

*Love.* He called her that every day since they'd become lovers, and right now, it was like a lance through her heart. She couldn't bite her tongue, couldn't hold back her words or try to find the perfect way to wade into the topic, into her fears.

"Are you really thinking about staying down here?"

Res twitched, almost as if he skipped a beat of existing, before he took a deep breath, then sank into the chair beside her. "Have you not considered it at all?"

The way he asked the question was completely and utterly open, a bit confused. As if he couldn't fathom a single reason why she wouldn't have.

Lusa scoffed. It wasn't a kind sound. She closed her eyes and rubbed her forehead, not sure what to say, where to start, except that she wouldn't lie to him.

"No, Res, I've never considered it at all."

Silence met her, and when she finally looked at him, he didn't meet her gaze, not really, his attention focused somewhere over her shoulder at nothing when he spoke. "With all that's happened since we came down here, with that Ques. With knowing there's a god here set on protecting my kind, it never even crossed your thoughts this might be a good place for us?"

"No," Lusa repeated, "because it's not a good place for either of us. In fact, it's such a bad fit, I never thought for a second, you'd consider staying here. I assumed all the time with the Ques was just, well, a performance, like you said."

"Right, then, so they mean nothing? They haven't become our friends?"

"That's not what I meant."

Res leaned away from her now, his posture defensive. Tense. "I thought, of all places, this would be one you'd enjoy. I mean for fuck's sake, Lusa, you don't have to be invisible all day long. They can see you."

"Sure, they can, when I'm occasionally invited along to whatever you boys are doing for the day," she threw back.

"I've asked you to be with us for the last three days. I've told you I missed you, repeatedly. You're the one focused on keeping up appearances first and foremost."

"Appearances? Really?"

Res waved a hand. "And what would you call your routine of flighting around the castle until everyone is busy enough for you to slip off into that gods forsaken maze? And let's not talk about the risk to yourself, because you clearly don't care, as long as it fits your agenda." He tsked, like she was an unruly child. "That place is endless, and you know it. You could have years and you may never find those damn birds, and you expect me to be alright with you risking your life every day?"

"We found them," Lusa bit out. "Today." She snatched the map from Kiki's pile, which included a sketch of the birds' beautiful tree, and tossed it in his lap. "So you can stop using my safety as some sort of excuse."

Res almost crushed the map. She saw it in the way his hand tensed, but he stopped himself and threw it back on the table. "You think my worry for you being safe is an excuse?"

"I think it's the same excuse as to why you think you want to stay down here," Lusa said, her own hands in tight fists now.

Res laughed, wiping his face. "Oh? Care to enlighten me then?"

Lusa rolled her eyes at his snide tone. "You've been terrified since you were attacked of the Ques hunters finding you again. And you were finally coming out of it. But you didn't act afraid when they were at the festival; you were brave, because Guatemoc was in danger too. Even though you'd just met him.

"But then we came down here, and you've been shown this pretty place to hide yourself away in, without any risk. Only to see another Ques brutalized and this time die, while you were powerless to stop it, or to help him, and now you're even more scared than before."

Res shoved to his feet, all but exploding from his chair. "And you don't think I have the right to be afraid?" She stood as well, but now he paced, pulling at his hair as he stormed around the kitchen. "Does it not make sense to be terrified? Perhaps a little understanding then of why, yes, I have been seriously considering what a life down here might look like, rather than being on the run up there," he said as he gestured wildly above his head, "never knowing when I'm about to have my feathers ripped off or *my fucking organs cut out*?"

"Res, of course it makes sense to be scared, but don't go back to hiding again!" Lusa shouted back. "You spent months never leaving your bedroom! How would this be any different?"

"Are you bloody serious?" Res blinked at her a few times, then laughed. "You are. Truly? You think wallowing in a depression in a closed bedroom is the same as living down here with my kin, creating a life for myself in an underground sanctuary, protected from the very threat that could kill me?"

Her breathing hitched. "You won't be happy down here, you know that. It just seems like fun now because its new, and that other Ques—"

"Alphinon."

"What?"

"His name was Alphinon," Res repeated.

Lusa swallowed a few times. "No one told me his name," she managed, barely keeping her chin up, because while this wasn't about her, and she understood the other Ques would mourn the loss of one of their own differently than she did and maybe not include her all the way, Lusa couldn't think of a single good reason why they didn't tell her his name. "I'm sorry he died, Res."

"It could have been me, you know that. If we were still up there, right now. It could have been me."

"You can't hide, Res. You were miserable until you went and gave that little girl a magic show. Until you performed again, until you used your magic in the way that brings you joy." Lusa rested a hand over her heart. "I've watched you for years. The happiest I've seen you is always on stage."

"Quetzalcoatl suggested I take over the yearly festival performances," Res said, his voice hushed now. "When Guatemoc and I were talking about it, he mentioned it because Guatemoc does a lot around here, and the festival isn't a joy for him. He'd be glad to hand it off. And..." Res was pacing again. "Renovating the artist lane would leave space for year-round shows. And teaching. And more performing. I wouldn't be hiding." He shot her an accusing glare, but it lacked any fire. In fact, it was unsure. Questioning, as if he wasn't sure he fully believed himself, not that she'd pointed all this out to him.

"Res, how many people live down here? A few dozen? A hundred?

It's not the same as travelling and performing; you know that."

"And what's better? Hmm? A secure, quiet life with a splash of what I once enjoyed most without the threat of death? Or looking over my shoulder, every second of every day, wondering when the next dart will lodge in my throat?" He scratched at his face, the scar on his cheek, and shook his head. "Can't you at least try to see where I'm coming from, Lusa? Try to understand what this could mean for me?" He licked his lips. "For us?"

"For us," Lusa repeated. "Have you even thought about what I might want or need in all this?"

"Of course I fucking have," he bit out. "I already told you I have. With the other Ques, you can have more friends. You aren't stuck leading an invisible life."

"And Theodore?" Lusa asked, her voice raising. "We made a promise to your friend that we would help him."

"Is that more important to you than me?" He gestured between them. "Than us?"

She shook her head again. "This isn't only about helping Theodore, and you know that. I've always wanted to find a way to help people, not stay under a mountain with a god who has so much treasure he could save a million lives and instead chooses to only help five people!"

"That's not fair, Lusa. If he reveals his nature—"

"Matty tried to say the same crap, and even the birds of truth didn't buy it. Quetzalcoatl is still taking from people struggling to make ends meet outside Mount Pindo when he needs nothing. He doesn't need to keep doing that to keep his identity and the Ques safe. It's a choice, Res."

"Fine, that's fair, but he's a god, Lusa."

"And that's an excuse?"

"It's a non-factor."

She scoffed. "What?"

"A non-factor. We're not in a position to change a god's mind."

"Well, that's great, because he hates me."

When Res rolled his eyes, her cheeks flushed. "Honestly, Lusa. We talked about this. He sees everyone as beneath him, but he's created this sanctuary to protect the Ques."

"He thinks I'm trying to ruin you and take away your chance at a perfect life since I'm just a needy mortal duster," Lusa snapped.

Res paused, frowning. "He said that to you?"

"More or less, yeah."

"Did he or not, because inferring his distaste, or even his interest, is folly. You haven't spent much time around powerful Aperiens. Ones as powerful as Quetzalcoatl, they don't . . ." Res trailed off as they stared at each other, both of their chests rising and falling, both breathing heavy with frustration, anger, and hurt.

"They don't what, Res?"

He looked away, chagrined. "Most of them don't care much at all for mortals, one way or another, in my experience."

"Well, you have your experience, and I have mine."

"I'm trying to help you. To make sure you aren't creating something out of nothing when it comes to him."

Lusa waved her arms. "Fine, alright, let's just ignore the godly elephant in the room. Let's ignore the fact that if we stayed, we'd screw Theodore and his friends over." She tapped on her fingers. "I'd never get to help anyone else." Another finger. "Wags will be stuck here, with nowhere to roll her wheels for eternity, like she was locked in a museum exhibit again." Another finger. "And we'd have to keep Kiki, what, a dirty secret forever?" And then she wiggled her thumb before he could protest. "But also maybe we should talk about the fact that I hate it down here and I don't want to spend the rest of my life in a rock hole with no sunlight!"

Res stared at her, his lips in a thin line, jaw tight, when he managed, "And weighed against the very real threat to my life? How does the equation balance?"

"I don't know!" Lusa said, a sob breaking out. "I don't *know!* But I didn't know until today that you even wanted this to be . . . this to be home to you, when home has been us and . . ."

When his arms came around her, Lusa folded into him, crushing against him and clutching his shirt. He cradled her nape, shushing softly, his face buried in her hair. Neither of them spoke for a few minutes, Res rocking them gently, his heart a racing drum under her head as her own breathing settled.

"One thing we know now is that Guatemoc and Oz leave more than yearly," Res offered quietly. "I'm sure we can work something out to get Theodore the help he needs, whatever else we decide. Perhaps we won't even have to wait, and you can get the birds to him sooner rather than later? At least we can take one question off the table, love, alright?"

It should have made her feel better, how he was processing everything she'd said and already trying to find solutions. Res wanted to find a way for things to work, for them both to be happy.

But for the first time since she met Res, Lusa suddenly wasn't sure if both of them being happy ended with them being together, as friends, lovers, or otherwise.

Right now, though, she let him hold her and held him back just as tight.

# Chapter 37

Lusa didn't bother with pretense the next morning. After a restless night of sleep, she got up early, left Res asleep in their bed, gathered up Kiki around her waist, and headed for the maze and the birds.

It was impossible not revisit the conversation from the night before as she let Kiki guide her with warmth in the direction she needed to put her feet.

Lusa wished she'd spoken to him sooner. She wished she hadn't taken for granted his fear, especially after seeing that Ques—Alphinon—suffer and die, wouldn't resurge. After all, he'd never fully dealt with his trauma after his own attack. Time gave him room to crawl back toward himself, and she'd pushed him into a good first experience toward reclaiming his previous self. He'd still hidden, but Lusa thought he was doing better when he'd agreed to come to Mount Pindo to help Theodore and his friends.

And at the Mount Pindo festival, Res reacted with bravery instead of fear, leaping to warn another Ques instead of running from the hunters. When they learned the truth about his family, and Quetzalcoatl, she'd assumed he was happy to know them, but not that he wanted their life, which was such a far cry from the Res she'd known.

Then again, she'd only known him a few years, hadn't she?

And after Alphinon died, she'd been worried about how Res was doing, how everyone was doing regarding the shock of such a violent death, but she hadn't really stopped to consider if Res's view of Mount Pindo had recalibrated.

Lusa rubbed her temples as she walked, her head aching. She should have checked in with him. That's what people who loved each other did.

But it became difficult when he viewed Quetzalcoatl as a force entirely outside their concern, when the god had certainly gone out of his way to make it very clear, repeatedly, how little he thought of Lusa.

Hells, she wasn't even sure if the invitation for Res to stay included herself.

An unpleasant thought twisted her stomach: Had Res even thought to ask?

Sure, Matty and Erandi spoke as if she was part of the package that came with Res, but had anyone consulted Quetzalcoatl? She didn't like how dismissive Res was of the god's opinion. Sure, they were all beneath him, but she found it hard to believe Quetzalcoatl didn't have the final say on who he allowed under his mountain.

Especially when he'd questioned Lusa because Res hadn't given Quetzalcoatl a yes or no answer yet.

She had a feeling gods didn't enjoy being told no.

Could they tell a god no?

A headache stabbed behind her eyes.

Had she just been stupid not to think of any of this before? Naïve? Too much of an optimist thinking it would all work out?

As she started down the central spire, Lusa wondered if Res was right. Or if she was being unfair about him considering staying here, and not how he'd been shocked that she wasn't.

There were two halves to a relationship, whatever shape it took, right? It didn't matter if they were just friends, like before, or lovers. They'd never made any choices since she'd joined him and Wags which didn't involve some sort of conversation. They picked where they'd go next. They argued about stocking Wags's larder. They debated show nights and pockets to pick. They discussed when they splurged, and neither of them changed anything inside Wags without talking it through and being sure she approved.

No, the idea that they wouldn't consider the other's side was absurd. And Res had obviously been considering what might make this a good home for her as much as himself. Granted, he wanted to stay? So why wouldn't he think of reasons for her to want to stay too?

No, she sighed, that wasn't fair to him, either.

He'd seemed confused when she spoke of the other Ques as if they were his friends and not hers. Or that she hadn't enjoyed being seen, even if it was daunting at times and she still needed to crawl off and be by herself. Res had made a point of including her.

Res came back to her every night and pulled her into his bed if he got back later than she did. She'd given up sleeping in hers anymore because he'd just wake her up and carry her to his.

The hallway forked, and Lusa followed Kiki's warm tug, turning down the last hall before the birds.

Would it be so bad down here, Lusa wondered. She hadn't even made her way over to the staff population—its own little town, she'd come to understand—so there was that. The mountain would open once a year, so she'd get to go outside, and it was entirely possible they could negotiate time above ground. Maybe just for herself, if Res wasn't willing to go to the surface aside from leading the festival. Or if Quetzalcoatl didn't allow it, a thought which made her stomach sour.

Maybe, Lusa pondered as she walked past the wasted wealth, she could talk with Guatemoc as an in-between with Quetzalcoatl. She could map the maze, run an inventory for Erandi, and convince them to put all this treasure to good use. Surely someone could spin a story about Bartholomew becoming bored of shiny things or whatever—there were lots of stories about Aperiens changing their mythos nature floating around out there. Maybe she could do good here by putting an end to the tribute?

Res would have a lot of years after she was gone, if their relationship lasted her entire life.

She winced; but this was the kind of reality she needed to consider. If she stayed down here, this would be her life. Or she'd be drugged and thrown out if Res grew tired of her. None of that was fun to think about. But Res was immortal. If this was really what he wanted for his eternity versus her sixty or seventy more years, did their lives weigh the same?

Gods, this was depressing.

She loved him though, with her whole heart. Even if things didn't work out—it had only been two weeks of them together, after all, she was trying to reasonable, not just love and kisses and sex drunk—she doubted she'd ever find the same connection she felt with Res.

Was that really love, though?

Giving up part of yourself for the other person? Settling for *okay*, for something that didn't really make you happy, to be with the person who did make you happy? Despite the Aperien Event, life was rarely a fairy tale ending, and perfect was the type of myth that remained exactly that: fiction.

Lusa found herself thinking of her parents. Far from perfect, that, she mused. Perfect for them probably would have involved not having a baby. She'd never known if she was an accident or a dream undertaken without really examining all the practicalities. By the time she was old enough to understand things, her mother rarely spoke of her father. What she learned about them she'd overheard from her extended family when she eavesdropped in the village.

*Could have worked out, without the babe. Mother was a fool, holding hope he'd come back. Father was a coward, running off and leaving her and the baby.*

Whatever the case, love hadn't been enough for them.

Lusa wanted it to be enough, she thought as she stared at her feet, her boots treading over the cold, lifeless stone. And she couldn't ignore considering it, not if she wanted to really be honest with herself and with Res.

With a sigh, she lifted her head. First step, though, the birds.

Because however this played out, Lusa didn't wanted to walk away from this place and leave them down here, not until she knew their truth.

When Lusa toed into the chamber, the birds of truth scuttled up the branches in a flock, moving as a group. The nests remained guarded by what she assumed were mated pairs, as they huddled close together.

She stepped onto the mossy ground, soft and squishy under heel, and watched them as she moved toward the water. The island and tree were closer to this side of the room, and there were a scattering of stones Lusa was pretty sure she could hop-skip across to get to the middle.

For now, she stopped at the shore and sat down cross-legged. No sign of the shadowlands crept up her back, so Lusa and propped herself up on her hands, enjoying the cool room and scents of life instead of rock.

"Hello," she said. "My name is Lusa. I'm guessing you guys are the birds of truth."

The cooing chorus came softly: "Truth."

Lusa couldn't help a grin. "Yeah, I was pretty sure, but it never hurts to confirm." She took in the room again, with the sun orb, the moss and vines, the spring water, and velvety leaves of the gigantic weeping willow. "Did you all come from the same two birds?"

The branches fluttered as one bird broke off from the flock and hopped down a few levels before it answered alone. "Truth."

Lusa nodded, focusing her attention on the single bird. He, or she, had those bright, sharp eyes, the pale plumage touched with canary yellow. It jumped down another branch, then another, and then stopped.

"Do you get everything you need down here?"

"Truth." The word, in a single voice, was a crisp chirp.

"Do the mouros take care of you with their magic?"

"Truth." Another branch, then with a glide, the bird landed on the mossy ground, cocking its head at her.

Lusa grinned again. "Do you like being able to answer things?"

This time it shook out its feathers, puffing up big and fluffy, before settling again and answering, "Truth."

Lusa laughed. "Cool. I can stay for a while, but I might run out of interesting things to say."

"False." This word sounded more like a clap or croak, and Lusa couldn't help but giggle.

"Okay, that's fair I guess, since you must not get many visitors."

"Truth." The bird came to the water's edge, studying for a second, before leaping to the first rock. Calculating, Lusa realized, and she stayed silent as the bird made its way across, jump-gliding from stone to stone until it landed on the bank at her feet. It pecked once at her boot, then fluttered up to rest on her knee. The bird wasn't much larger than a chicken, but sleeker and finer boned, with a longer wingspan, neck, and tailfeathers.

Lusa reached out, letting her fingers hover out of reach, letting the bird make the choice to touch. It pecked once, not hard but curious, the nudged her fingers with silky soft feathers.

She swallowed a few times, realization sitting heavy as she gently stroked the bird's neck, her gaze wandering to the filled tree. Her voice was a whisper, when she said, not asked, "They've clipped your wings."

"Truth."

# Chapter 38

Lusa stared down at the bird in her lap, fighting back the urge to squeeze her hands into fists. "This place sucks," she muttered, then huffed a laugh when the bird didn't reply, because technically, that was an objective statement, not a true or false one.

She kept petting the bird, her thoughts a maelstrom.

What kind of monster took these beautiful creatures and clipped their wings, denied them the sky, and for what? To leave them here, alone, generation after generation, unable to fulfill their most modest and basic desires of their nature.

Lusa closed her eyes and sighed.

She hated this place.

She hated everything Bartholomew began, and everything Quetzalcoatl continued. She despised how in trying to protect his progeny, he played to their fears and left them no better off than these birds.

But she had to remember, the Ques hadn't been forced here. And if this was truly what Res wanted, whether he believed he'd be happy enough or he would rather live free of fear than take the risk in the sun, that was a choice he had to make for himself.

Same as Lusa needed to make her own choice.

She loved him, with all her heart, but down here, she'd been no different than the bird in her lap, wings clipped and dreams left behind. As much as she loved Res, she couldn't abandon herself and her own needs, wants, and dreams for him, not if they wanted things that were so entirely different.

She sniffed and wiped her nose on her sleeve. The bird cocked its head. Waiting, she knew, for another query. Lusa offered a half smile.

"Love can be hard."

"Truth."

"Love can hurt," she added, whisper soft.

"Truth."

Lusa smiled then, knowing it was sad, maybe even pathetic. "Still worth it, though. Even if it doesn't work out in the end."

The bird canted its head, back and forth, but didn't answer.

Ah, well, she supposed that depended on the situation and the person, didn't it? For her, though, she believed it. Even if she left Mount Pindo alone, knowing Res and loving him was worth the time she'd had him in her life. She'd miss him, if he decided to stay down here, if that was best for him. Gods, she'd miss him so much, but she couldn't demand him to change for her when she couldn't do the same for him.

She wiped her eyes again. She really hoped he wouldn't pick this place. Selfish or not, Lusa firmly believed he'd wilt here when he was just starting to find his old self again. They'd talk again, she decided, with calmer, cooler heads, and she'd give him the reasons she couldn't call this place home, and the reasons she thought he'd be happier in the wide world, with her, Wags, Tick, and Kiki. And tell him that she'd do everything in her power to protect him.

For now, Lusa needed to be honest with the bird in her lap, first.

"So, I've been looking for you."

The bird twitched, then went very still. "Truth."

"It's actually the whole reason I ended up here in Mount Pindo."

"Truth."

"There's a man, a Citadel Archivist named Theodore, who wants to help his friends. Good people who are stuck in a bad way, and he believes you, the birds of truth, might be the only foolproof way to determine their side of the story is what really happened."

"Truth."

Lusa nodded. "He's worried that other means for truth could be corrupted or manipulated, but he said that you can't lie or be influenced to lie."

"Truth."

"Good, I'm glad he's right about that part." Lusa exhaled, rubbing her forehead, and she considered what she needed to ask and how to go about it. What would be fair, or right, as she stared up into a tree filled with hundreds of birds, and nests with new lives still inside their shells. "I didn't expect there to be so many of you. I thought maybe I'd come here and steal a pair of magic birds, and that Bartholomew wouldn't ever know any better since he has so much treasure."

The bird blinked a few times. It was a complicated statement, impossible to answer since her intentions were truthful, but Bartholomew was long dead.

"And also, I didn't really think about how you'd be prisoners," she added quietly.

"Truth."

"I really . . . I only thought as far as how I could do something good and help some who needed it."

"Truth."

Lusa managed a weak smile. "I'm glad you know. And now I'm not sure what to do." She looked up at the tree again. "I don't think there's any way I can set you all free."

"Truth."

"I'm sorry," Lusa whispered, running her fingers along the silken feathers again.

"Truth."

She let out a deep breath. "I still want to help Theodore's friends."

"Truth."

And now came the hard part, because Lusa already knew she'd walk out of this room empty handed if that's what she had to do. "But only if you want to help them, because you're not just some piece of magic treasure. You're alive, and that means you get a choice. If none of you want to leave your flock, I'm not going to take you against your will. You've had enough of that already."

The bird shivered, fluffing its wings again, before it cooed out, "Truth."

Well, Lusa could trust herself. That was good at least, right? She rubbed her eyes, considering what their options might be, but she knew one thing already. "If one or two of you want to come with me, I think I can get you back to Wags without anyone knowing. She's an enchanted wagon."

"Truth."

Good news, Lusa thought with a little grin. "And I'll promise you this. I'll take you to Theodore and go with you to help his friends. And afterwards, I'll make sure you get to the Coalition of Creatures. They grant sanctuary to any creature who needs it. I won't let anyone put you in another kind of prison. You'll be free to do what you want, live how you want, in the CoC."

The bird switched back and forth between its feet. "Truth."

"That's right," Lusa said with a nod.

Up in the branches, another bird pecked at the branch until it had their attention. Then it shuffled over and much more delicately, tapped one of the eggs. Within a few seconds, all throughout the weeping willow, dozens of birds tapped on their eggs in their nests, over and over.

"Oh gods," Lusa whispered, realization hitting. "You want me to take your eggs?"

"Truth," came the answer, a group call from every bird in the vast, magical tree.

The next generation, Lusa realized. If she took the eggs, and got them to the Coalition, these new birds would grow up free and never have their wings clipped.

Lusa didn't hesitate. "I'll do it." She flattened her palm against the belt. "Kiki, I'm going to need your help."

It took about two hours to gather the eggs from every nest. Lusa climbed, Kiki helped, and the birds fretted as they moved them down on the soft beds of moss between the tree's roots. The bird from their talk, who'd she named Canary in her head, stayed beside the growing egg pile, and a second, slightly smaller bird had joined him. Him, she'd guessed, because he was slightly larger, a bit more colorful with longer tailer feathers. Then she realized she was being silly as she dropped down to add another egg to the pile.

"Are you a boy?"

"Truth."

"Okay, can I call you Canary?"

The bird pattered its feet a few times.

"Is that a yes?"

"Truth."

Right, she had to keep in mind they could only really respond to certain statements or questions. Lusa pointed to the bird beside

Canary, who had a touch of red in her pinfeathers. "Is that your mate?"

"Truth," they both cooed.

"I like Cardinal for you. Any problems with these names?"

"False," they answered.

Lusa grinned. "Awesome."

Kiki thumped to the ground beside her, having traded wings for extra belly space, giving it a weird sort of tummy cage for carrying about six eggs down at a time. "Last eggs," Kiki chirped, and was so very delicate about settling them with the others.

"Thanks, Kiks," Lusa said, giving it a head pat. It was a risk, but getting done faster seemed like the move, rather than Lusa taking forever getting all the eggs alone. "Can you make yourself into a backpack or bag? You need to be big enough for all the eggs, and Canary and Cardinal."

"Yes," Kiki whirled, but first it padded over to sniff at the two birds. The mated pair seemed unbothered, and Lusa wondered if they could sense the truth of Kiki's intentions. "Pretty birds," Kiki added with a happy chirp.

Then Kiki was twisting and contorting, and Lusa gasped, she couldn't help it. Kiki normally stayed as a cat, but the change to the belt had become a daily routine and Kiki snuck up on her half the time and it was over before Lusa realized. Now, Lusa watched as the filigree metal stretched, curled, flattened and expanded, the cat's face compressing and disappearing into a simple closure for the backpack. Legs became straps, the tail a cord to tighten the top, and the gold and bronze faded into leather, pressed with all the swirls she'd come to expect on anything that was part of Kiki. On the clasp, a single shiny red stone she knew watched everything.

"This is perfect, Kiki. You're amazing."

The bag was really big, but thankfully the eggs were small, no bigger than a chicken egg, and Lusa counted as she started placing them inside. By the time she was done, seventy-eight eggs lined the bag, which was warm to the touch, as if Kiki instinctually knew the eggs needed to be incubated.

Canary and Cardinal hopped closer, peering inside.

"I promise Kiki won't hurt you or your eggs. Kiki is good."

"Truth," they cooed, and Cardinal fluttered in first, shuffling down to sit. Canary followed suit.

"Okay, stay quiet now until we're back inside Wags and I give you the all clear, okay?"

Both birds only stared at her, which Lusa took as a yes, and carefully closed the pack and clipped Kiki's eye-stone to seal them safely inside. At an outside glance, it looked like nothing more than a fancy backpack, with no clues to the contents. When Lusa slung it on her shoulders, she almost stumbled because it weighed next to nothing, and the leather was cool to the touch on the outside.

"Wow, Kiki, you really are something else."

"Kiki helps!"

Lusa grinned, petting the shoulder straps. "You do, all the time. Thank you." Then Lusa looked up at the tree and all the birds left behind. All the parents sending their eggs and children to a better future, while they stayed behind in this cave. "Thank you, all of you. I promise I'll make sure your family is taken care of."

"Truth," came the echo, all of the birds calling out together, including two muffled voices from the backpack.

# Chapter 39

This was going to be the trickiest walk Lusa had made since coming to Mount Pindo. Somehow, Kiki managed to make its backpack shape seem almost flat again her body, but she hadn't carried a pack like this when they'd arrived, let alone while coming up from the maze of endless wealth.

Because that didn't scream suspicious.

She huffed, brushing her hair out of her face, and she made the final climb toward the castle proper, up the last hallway before she'd be at risk for being seen.

What a statement, Lusa mused, trying to remember what her life was like back when she was invisible all the time instead of only occasionally. Then her amusement died off, because very soon she'd be back to that life, possibly with no one ever seeing her again.

Not true, she decided then, because she wouldn't leave Kiki here. Wags, well, that was up to Wags, and Res had her before Lusa came around, so she wasn't going to assume. But Theodore had left Kiki in Lusa's care, and while Erandi made good arguments for using his alchemy to help other Ques, she didn't see any reason to let Kiki near any alchemist, good intentions or not. If that was safe, Theodore would have taken Kiki to the Citadel Archive, not handed it off to some no-name girl in the middle of nowhere.

Problems for tomorrow, Lusa reminded herself. Now problem:

Getting to Wags without getting busted with bird and egg contraband and making a god angry. Kind of back to square one, which wasn't really all that comforting.

She peered up the hall toward the castle as she reached the bend. It was evening now, so the lighting reflected as much, the enchanted sun orbs miming a day/night cycle. Maybe everyone was having dinner? Or maybe Matty was hosting cards and drinks again. Either way, it looked clear enough, so Lusa walked a little bit faster than normal, but not so fast it would be a dead giveaway she was up to no good.

She was about to turn the corner, the left that would spit her out toward the receiving area and to where Wags had been parked since they arrived, when she heard a voice she knew all too well, and she folded herself against a shadowed pillar.

"Thanks for making time to talk." Res, walking this direction but then stalling; a sitting room was just over to the right. A door opened as he spoke.

"Of course, come in."

Lusa's stomach lurched. The second voice was Quetzalcoatl.

She should have kept walking when she heard the door creak closed but not click shut. This was the perfect chance to escape unnoticed, but instead, her feet moved toward the mostly shut door, and she tucked herself neatly into another shadow. She didn't have the shadowlands, but she'd listened like this for years, and she evened out her breathing until it was silent and slow. A quick peek showed them seated across from each other by a fireplace, what looked like wine between them. Lusa leaned back; she only needed to hear, not risk being seen.

"I wanted to thank you for all the time you've spent on the new plans with Guatemoc and I regarding the artist lane. And the future festivals. I'll be honest, I wasn't sure what I'd do with myself down here when you first extended your invitation. I've been performing my whole life."

"As I'm sure you recognize, the safety offered is a boon worthy of sacrifice."

Gods, he sounded smug. And did this mean Res was coming here to . . . what? Accept his proposal. Lusa closed her eyes, trying to ignore the catch in her throat. Gods, she'd really hoped they'd be able to talk more before he decided. They'd only had one real conversation, and they'd both been so frustrated.

"I recognized that, believe me. And what happened with Alphinon only reaffirmed the risks."

"Good you see things for what they are, Resplendent."

Lusa grimaced; she hated how Quetzalcoatl disregarded Res's preference for his nickname. Small complaints, she supposed bitterly, in the grand scheme of things.

"I do, which would make this very simple if I was the only person in the equation, but that's not the case unfortunately."

Lusa's heart skipped, jumped, and then tripled its rate. It felt so loud; she worried the pair might hear her in the weighted silence that fell between them.

Finally, Quetzalcoatl spoke. "Am I to understand that girl is what you refer to?"

"Lusa, yes."

"A mortal girl."

"Yes," Res responded, the first time she'd heard him break his perfect veneer when speaking to the god. "I care for her a great deal, and as you're keen to remind me, she is mortal. Odds are a human lifespan at best. I have . . . been remiss not weighing how she might want to spend those years when I consider spending mine here, with you and our family, on your most generous offer."

"Mortals are transient to creatures like ourselves, Resplendent. She's fortunate to have your attention at all. Tell her where she belongs, and she'll fall in line to keep that attention." His tone was bored.

"That may be true, but I don't want her to spend her entire life unhappy on my behalf. This is why I wanted to talk to you. We have all the time in the world. When hers is done, I can return."

Lusa had to cover her mouth, her head swimming.

Had she heard him right?

Was he saying . . . was he saying he wanted to leave with her, and be with her for her whole life?

"Lusa won't be happy in this place. And I . . ." Res paused, then cleared his throat. "Well, I love her. Letting her go isn't what I desire, so I'll go with her when the month is done and enjoy making her happy while I get to have her. And with your permission, I would be honored for the chance to return to Mount Pindo when my time with her is over. Before I go, I'll see through all renovations we've talked about for the artist lane. I'm heading over there with the others, in just a minute."

He loved her.

Lusa couldn't stop the tears, strangling back the bubbling giggle, the desire to run in there and throw her arms around him. Gods, he was picking her over this awful place, and she wanted to explode with the joy of it all.

She'd make sure that was really what he wanted.

He couldn't do it just for her, but that didn't sound like what he was saying, did it? She'd check with him, make sure, but . . .

Res *loved* her.

Her cheeks hurt she was smiling so wide.

Then some of joy drained from her because Quetzalcoatl had yet to respond. Lusa restrained herself from peeking in the room again; she couldn't risk getting caught, least of all with Kiki turned into a bag of stowaways, but the air itself felt heavy and tart, almost furious, before the god finally spoke.

"Is that all then?"

Lusa heard Res shuffle to his feet. "Yes, thank you, again, for making the time. And well," Res added with a laugh, "everything else, really."

The dismissal was clear without another word, and Res strode from the room and down the hallway, disappearing into the receiving room before Lusa could gather herself. Just as well; she needed to sneak away carefully, to avoid notice.

"Do you plan to eavesdrop on my next conversation as well?"

Crap.

Lusa slipped Kiki off her shoulders without a sound and shoved the bag behind the pillar. If anything, she hoped Kiki could sneak back without her if this went badly. Lusa rubbed her clammy hands on her thighs and walked around to the open door, because trying to run seemed stupid.

Quetzalcoatl sat in the same place from when she peeked in the crack. Lusa didn't enter, staying outside the threshold. The wine cups were untouched.

"I'm sorry," Lusa said. "It's a bad habit from being invisible for so much of my life. It won't happen again."

Quetzalcoatl regarded her with his soulless gaze, his eyes a deep, almost black despite being multifaceted. She realized she'd never seen them so dark before. He didn't invite her in. He simply observed her, like a bug pinned against a board, his expression impassive.

"You heard what he's willing to throw away for you, and you would allow him to do so."

Not a question. She stiffened, not sure if she was supposed to talk. Was this a scolding? A lecture? When he didn't go on, she licked her lips, and offered, "What I heard is that he wants to go back to the surface and spend a few years with me, then come back for your offer for the rest of his immortal life." She winced when she added, in a small voice she wasn't proud of, "Is that really so terrible?"

"Are you so selfish to let him risk his eternity for a few meager years at your side? Did you not see the Ques brought here just days ago? What he suffered?"

"I did. And Res has also lived for 87 years and only ran across those hunters once."

"And your mortal reasoning is what? That he would be so lucky that what he escaped in the Baker's Hills won't find him again before you die?" Quetzalcoatl looked her over, top to bottom. "Your understanding of the scope of time is woefully ill-equipped to make such assumptions."

"I'll not saying there's no risk," Lusa answered, trying to keep the shake from her voice. "There's always risks to living. Isn't that part of what makes life *worth* living?"

He waved a hand. "To those who have decades to lose, not to those have forever to live with the consequences of such mistakes. Take Erandi, for example. He spent more than a single lifetime in your measure of time tortured. I wonder if he would agree with your measure of the risk."

"That's not fair."

"And what do you imagine fair has to do with any of this? Was it fair Resplendent went so long without knowing he had a place here, with his kin? Was it fair he went so long without being aware of the threat he was under all along? Was it fair he was stolen from his happy performance space, drugged and mutilated, and then somehow escaped being tracked down, when most Ques do not once they've been targeted, allowing him false hope that he was safe?"

Lusa frowned, his words rattling her.

They'd made a point of being honest since they arrived, but Res did not talk about his attack. He'd never mentioned where it happened or any of the details. They'd agreed it was best left quiet, because Theodore's involvement in covering Res's attack broke his role of non-interference as a Citadel Archivist.

Quetzalcoatl could not have known Res's attack happened at the Baker's Hills. Between Theodore and the Baker's efforts, it never happened. He had no way of knowing the details—that Res was taken right from the stage, or that his trail had gone completely cold, how Res vanished without a trace as a result of Theodore's magic.

Quetzalcoatl's eyes narrowed then, and Lusa realized just how deep she was in. Matty had enjoyed telling her on card night exactly how bad her poker face was—repeatedly, in fact, because he thought it was hilarious. And she knew she wasn't hiding her panic at all right now, as she tried to piece together what the hells was going on here, because the way these lines were tying together? How the dots were connecting?

It all pointed to Quetzalcoatl being somehow involved with the Ques hunters.

The idea was madness, but as the god picked her apart with his glare, she didn't have time to process. She needed to divert, because if it was true, if this was what was really going on down here, on any level, in any way . . .

She blurted out, "Res loves me. I heard him."

Quetzalcoatl leaned back, the cold calculation evaporating. She could practically taste his snide shift to *ah stupid human lovesick girl* from *she knows something she shouldn't and I need to kill her right now despite the mess it would make of this very nice rug.*

"You're a novelty." His tone was pitying now, and as much as it rankled her, she weathered it. "To a floundering, mediocre performer mourning the death of the only person to show him real affection, who stumbled across a girl only he can see."

Lusa couldn't help but stiffen at those words, because, gods, the possibility of them stung. She didn't believe them, not really, but it was like he knew exactly where to needle all her doubts with a fine, brutal pinpoint.

"This infatuation will pass and he will resent you, because love isn't an immortal quality. Love is for fleeting creatures, a clinging desperation in an attempt to give brief, pointless lives meaning. Aperiens like us, and dusters who possess eternity, don't have space or need for those weak, mundane emotions."

Lusa gritted her teeth because that, if anything he'd said, was a lie. She could rattle off a thousand mythos stemming from love. And while maybe Quetzalcoatl didn't love—maybe no gods were capable of love, and Lusa wasn't vain enough to think she understood the inner workings of any deity—she knew Res did. The things they'd shared, the affection she knew he'd felt for his mother, the kindness he'd shown others in the time she'd been with him, including saving Wags from a junkyard of rot, demonstrated this over and over. Maybe it came from his human blood; Lusa didn't know.

But she knew without a shadow of a doubt that Res was nothing like Quetzalcoatl, even if his magic had come from the Aperien in front of her right now.

"I don't believe you," Lusa whispered.

"That doesn't matter, because you love him. And you strike me as an intelligent girl. Observant enough to smooth Erandi's rough edges enough for him to see merit in you." Quetzalcoatl hummed. "At first, I thought your journeys into the maze were a quest for wealth. Perhaps you'd found yourself dependent on Resplendent as his housekeeper and whore," Lusa winced, but Quetzalcoatl didn't notice, or more likely, didn't care, "and wished to get out from under his thumb. Perhaps, after this month was over, you imagined yourself leaving here capable of supporting yourself instead of clinging to his tailfeathers, as it were."

Gods, how could he understand so little about his own grandson?

"But no, it became clear quickly enough you were more than just the help he claimed you to be. The way he always looks at you, for you, and his adamant disinterest in the harem. Quiet refusal to take the pleasure thrown at his feet, his apparent fixation with you fresh enough to deny himself otherwise."

Lusa's cheeks were flaming red, she knew, and she bit inside her cheek to keep from saying anything. Her knuckles ached, she clenched her fists so hard.

"And yet, whatever you've pulled from the maze is trifles. A few worthless coins, nothing else, so you aren't chasing wealth. Don't look so surprised. The mouros served Bartholomew, and they serve me now. I have little reason for contact with them, aside from the report of their new golden creations, because they can't help but share, or any other changes in their inventory because they're obsessed."

It took everything she had not to look at the doorway, to the hall, to Kiki and the birds and the eggs. How long, she wondered, until the mouros reported back about the missing eggs and the birds. And how lucky she was that blowing up hallways apparently didn't need a report filed to the boss.

"But you've seen enough by now." Another hand wave. "What do you require? What payment will it take for you dissuade Resplendent from leaving this place and jeopardizing himself over this fixation he has with you?"

Lusa blinked. "Are you bribing me to break up with him?"

Quetzalcoatl rolled his eyes. Actually rolled his eyes, and the sober exterior flashed with coiled irritation that made her retreat a step. "We're not dealing here in human terms. He will stay here. You are the hurdle to this result. What to you require to reject him?"

Lusa just stared at him for a few seconds. "I don't understand why you're even asking me." Then she laughed, the sound a little choked. "You're a god. Can't you just do whatever you want?" She tapped her chest. "Kill me, fix your problem, poof."

"I could," Quetzalcoatl replied, and Lusa didn't doubt for a second it would take little more than a snap of his fingers to snuff her life from this world. She tasted it on the air, bitter and metallic on the back of her tongue, felt it curling up her spine in a biting vice. And then the pressure evaporated as he kept talking. "But when sheer force can win any game, claim any victory at any time, why even play?" His gaze flicked over her face, his expression curious, as if he sought her understanding or maybe sympathy? What the hells? "Victory through merit is much more satisfying, by controlling the board with effort instead of breaking it because I can.

"And my first choice isn't resentful kin held captive by my will." Quetzalcoatl leaned back then, pausing to sip his drink, as if this was all a normal conversation. As if he hadn't made it clear he'd kill her if he got bored, or tired, or decided force sounded better after all. "Your death would leave Resplendent a wounded bird, perhaps permanently so, given his fixation with you seems intense right now. No closure leaves wounds to fester. Your rejection, however, leaves space for moving forward and forgetting in a timelier manner."

Lusa wasn't sure she could have done anything to hide her blatant disgust as she stared at him. He set down his cup, considering her again, then extended a hand, as if offering her the floor to speak. Giving her *permission* to address him, as he added, "I'm giving you a rare chance here to request of me and leave this with place with more than you walked in with. Otherwise, Erandi can drug you, and I can have you removed in the night, and Resplendent can be left to speculate your abandonment."

She could ask for the birds and their eggs, but screw him. She was taking them, because he didn't deserve a single thing more than he'd already taken from this world. And maybe she was having a moment of absolute madness, because instead of wanting to crawl and hide, she wanted to fight.

To hells with fading away into the nothing.

"Fine. I want the truth."

Okay, maybe she was nuts.

Maybe she'd lost her mind, but Lusa had spent her life being invisible, and the only thing worse than doubting herself, and if she mattered, was standing in front of this jerk and having him look at her like she was less than nothing while talking about Res like he was worth less than mud under his boot.

So Lusa lifted her chin and said, "I want to know what your connection is to the Ques hunters."

# Chapter 40

I f it was any other circumstance, Lusa might have felt a surge of pride for catching a god off guard, because the surprise that bloomed on Quetzalcoatl's face was pretty priceless. But then he laughed, and the sound grated on her senses like broken glass, and Lusa didn't know if she'd entertained him or signed her own death warrant after all.

When he settled, he smiled at her, and Lusa absolutely hated it. She hated Quetzalcoatl looking at her with something akin to affection, or maybe approval, as he gave a curt nod. "You are as clever as I thought, aren't you?" he murmured. "I'll answer, if you tell me what drew you to ask this question for your boon."

Lusa loved how he assumed he'd won. Gods, it was so clear that just because she asked something of him, he believed he already won this whole thing. Quetzalcoatl would tell her the truth, she realized, because he couldn't imagine she'd dare defy him after.

"You knew things about what happened to Res we didn't tell any-one. And we had help covering our tracks. The only way you'd have those details is if you were there when it happened. And since the hunters who attacked him are dead, they couldn't have reported back to anyone. The only thing that makes sense is you know who hired them. Or you did it yourself."

Quetzalcoatl nodded once, rubbing his chin as he studied her now with interest, which made her skin crawl. It wasn't as dangerous when he'd flexed his presence or whatever to make her understand he could kill her, and easily, but it was just as unpleasant. "Clever," he said again, "and observant."

Lusa shrugged. "Comes with the territory, you know, being mostly invisible and all. So, what's the truth?"

"The truth," Quetzalcoatl murmured, and Lusa stiffened as he rose to his feet, his impressive height, his presence dampening the light in room, "is very simple. I had two sons before I knew the nature of our feathers and organs on the landscape of this world. I had no knowledge how my Aperien existence could be harvested for universal alchemical ingredients, not until one of my sons had many sons of his own.

"When I learned how our natures manifested into reality, and what other creatures"—His lip curled as he said—"*humans* and otherwise would do to take from us for their own benefit, I sought a remedy."

Lusa swallowed a few times. The room was stifling now and smelled of fresh blood.

Human blood, she somehow knew. "To save them?"

He ignored her. "I demanded my sons cease having children. One accepted, as he never had any, the other refused. I killed him." Lusa gasped; he didn't notice, or didn't care. "Then I killed Bartholomew to take over this place and hide my existence. After, it became a matter of reclaiming what was mine, preserving what remained, and eliminating those who dared to touch what never belonged to them in the first place."

"You hunt your own grandchildren?"

"When necessary, yes. Ques aren't easy to track down, and many have been captured. Creating an organization that hunts down those who remain and brokers deals with those already in possession of Ques facets, alive or otherwise, is the most efficient way to find what remains of my magic scattered across the world."

"But . . ." Lusa shook her head. Quetzalcoatl stood a few feet away from her, but he might as well have been holding her by the throat. "Alphinon."

Quetzalcoatl shrugged. "The hunters had been working leads for a few months, trying to track the source. Resplendent was already here and needed a push. I accelerated our timeline, knowing they'd extract him alive or dead, and Resplendent would be reminded of the dangers to his kind. Alphinon's captors escalated." Another shrug. "It was a risk I was fine taking."

"Why," Lusa whispered. "They're your family."

"No, they are an extension of my magic against my wishes. I'm simply reclaiming what is, and has always, belonged to me."

"You're a monster," Lusa said, shaking her head, unable to move otherwise.

"The threat to my bloodline will never subside. My magic is too valuable. Even if I ceased my efforts, the Ques dusters will be hunted. They will be captured by alchemists, harvested for parts, and left as empty shells like Erandi. As long as Ques dusters remain out in the wild, they make more children. I'm stopping the cycle, and giving those whom I can salvage a sanctuary where no one can take my magic from them, or from me."

"They're people, not . . . not things," Lusa rasped.

"And do they seem to be suffering here?" Quetzalcoatl asked, his tone patient now. "You are the thorn in this equation, the threat to a peaceful life for Resplendent, free from threats."

"Except you."

"None of the Ques here are under any threat from me. I require my magic where it belongs: under my purview. Beyond that, they are free to live as they see fit, so long as they sire no offspring and live here, where others cannot take what is mine. That, Lusa, is the very simple truth. And let me give you another.

"If he chooses to leave with you, I will let him. He requires the illusion that being down here is a choice he's made for himself, or you're right. He will chafe at this arrangement, and I won't have him disrupting what I've created.

"But if he leaves with you, I will hunt him, and the terror from my undivided attention won't be a dart to the neck backstage and a few fallen feathers. Now, tell me, have you had enough of the truth?"

Lusa nodded. When he kept staring at her, she croaked out, "Yes."

"Good." He dipped his head, striding back to his chair and sitting. He took up his wine glass and had an unhurried sip.

Lusa walked backwards from the room, but Quetzalcoatl didn't look at her again, and she shut the door on her way out, shuddering as the click echoed through the empty halls. Her legs were shaking; everything quaked, and she could barely walk as she stumbled over to Kiki and pulled the straps over her shoulder, her mind and pulse racing.

Was she having a heart attack?

She wouldn't put it past Quetzalcoatl, given everything he'd just told her, but he really did seem bent on getting his way and winning more than her being dead. At least for now.

At least until she didn't march to his little tune and tell Res she was leaving him here and didn't love him anymore.

Yeah, he really didn't know a thing about love, because the last thing she was going to do was leave Res, or any of the other Ques, down here with that murderous, manic god if there was anything she could do about it.

What could she do about it, though?

And how fast? That might be the bigger question.

She had to get these birds and eggs back safe to Wags, then she needed to find Res and really, really—not completely totally, one hundred percent—panic in between steps one and two.

Wags, like the amazing, magical madam she was, added a warming drawer under her stove within five minutes of Lusa and Kiki's return, as Lusa babbled aloud about what the hells to do with so many eggs. Now, the eggs were settled in the drawer, cuddled in with fleece blankets from her bed. Canary and Cardinal perched on the back of the kitchen chairs, and Tick watched them warily from his kitchen shelf, tail flicking back and forth.

She pointed at the tomcat. "Do not eat those birds, or I will turn you into a hat."

"False," came the coos.

Lusa snorted. "Fine, I won't make you into a hat, but I will have Wags make a crate and I'll lock you in there for a long time."

"Truth."

If Lusa wasn't edging into a full panic attack, she might have laughed. On the table, Kiki stretched, back in winged cat shape, and watching her with wide eyes. She swallowed a few times. She wanted a shower or a change of clothes, she was so sweaty from her encounter with Quetzalcoatl, but she just felt like time was draining away from any chance to have this whole . . . *everything* not become a bigger nightmare than it already was.

She patted her waist. "Come on, Kiks, we need to find Res." It was around her waist in a belt in seconds. To the birds, she said, "If anyone comes, you need to hide and be quiet. Wags will help. And Tick, I'm serious." Tick yowled, and then Lusa ducked out of the curtains and dashed back toward the castle.

She ran herself in circles before she remembered they were all at the artist lane going over renovations.

Lusa stopped, leaning against the wall to catch her breath on the way back from checking Pollock's art studio. Being invisible around a crowd of strangers was not how she wanted to share this news. And she'd disappear, but she could still be heard, and as much as she wanted to get the Ques out of here, starting a mass panic wouldn't help anyone. Lusa rubbed her face, trying to rein in her desire to fight back full force and deal with how she could help right now.

Her head shot up.

Right now, she knew where one Ques would be, because Erandi never went to the general population side. What could a blind man offer when studying visuals for a renovation? Which wasn't the point because she doubted the others had bothered to ask if he wanted to come just to be included.

Lusa darted off, and in a few minutes, she came to Erandi's door. Quetzalcoatl was nowhere to be seen. As far as she'd gathered, what he knew about her activities came from discussions with the other Ques and the mouros' inventory notes. She'd heard jokes about gods not being as all-powerful or all-seeing as they liked people to believe. Lusa hoped that was true, because Quetzalcoatl didn't need to be "all-powerful" to destroy everything Lusa had ever cared about.

She knocked on the door. "Erandi? Hey, I wanted to talk to you."

Silence. She knocked again, impatience making her jittery.

Gods, she hated the fact that he of all the Ques was down here, unknowing, about Quetzalcoatl's connection to the hunters. Erandi had suffered more than any of them. Lusa needed to find him *now*, not whenever he decided he wanted company. He had a reputation for refusing to answer if he wasn't in the mood.

Lusa's fingers traced over the ornate door handle, then the keyhole. She didn't sense any magical wards. They tended to zing at the touch. She chewed her bottom lip, because she'd picked a few locks in her time, but not many, and she'd always broken them getting whatever she was after.

Then she had an idea.

"Kiks," she whispered. "Any chance you can get this lock open?"

Because Kiki, the wonder clockwork kitty, had been full of surprises, and lockpicking seemed like a pretty low bar. The belt buckle morphed into a little snake head with a soft whirl, before a forked tongue poked into the lock, and not two seconds later, the mechanism clicked.

"No way," Lusa whispered, and Kiki gave the tiniest chirp before returning to the belt. With one last glance over her shoulder, still alone besides Kiki, she ducked inside and shut the door behind her.

The room was utterly black. Lusa didn't move, her back resting against the door.

"Erandi? It's Lusa." She winced; of course he would know her voice. "I'm sorry for coming in without permission, but this is really, really important. Are you here?"

Her voice echoed in the room, and she frowned. It felt cavernous, empty, and she tapped the belt buckle and whispered, "Light?"

Kiki opened its eyes, and must have brightened them, because the room bloomed in a soft red glow.

There was almost nothing at all in the main room. This was the same space Pollock kept his painting studio, and the others, their shared spaces. For Erandi, there was only a chaise pushed off to one side.

Nothing to share. Gods, it broke her heart a little that he'd never tried to make this space one he could welcome the other Ques into. Or maybe he had, at some point, and gave up trying.

Well, maybe they could all leave together. Wags would make room. They could find a way to give Erandi privacy and make him feel like part of things instead of always on the fringes.

Lusa shook her head. *Focus and stop projecting*, she thought to herself with a grimace.

"Erandi?"

She knew from the other layouts, if Erandi's space was in fact the same, there would be a bedroom, a smaller secondary room, and a bathroom. She came upon the bathroom first, which was mostly the same, though it lacked any personal touches. The secondary room was as empty as the main room, and Erandi's bedroom had a bed, a standing chest for clothing, and nothing else.

No lights at all.

The hall, however, kept going, and she realized Erandi's wing backed up against where the castle met the mountain stone, but instead of brickwork, there was a single doorway fitted in the rock, sporting another simple lock. She tested the handle. Locked, and for the first time, Lusa hesitated.

Did she want to open this door?

Part of her wanted to walk away and wait for Res and the other Ques to return and talk to them instead. Erandi would show up; he always did, they'd said. Maybe he wasn't even down here, wherever *here* led.

But the curling sensation in her stomach wouldn't let up, and she whispered for Kiki to play locksmith again, and this one opened as easily. No one had never bothered to come this far, she realized. She knew, without a doubt, none of the Ques knew about this door except maybe Quetzalcoatl.

No lighting still, and the stone steps were cut wide, making an easy descent into the cool corridor, reminding Lusa of a cellar. Under Kiki's soft red lighting, the first space opened up, lined with barrels stacked on each other and shelves of empty bottles.

Lusa didn't want to, but she kept walking.

A soft breeze brushed her skin, and she felt the air pulling deeper. Ventilation, moving the scents away from the castle. The next room held more storage, but this time, meticulously organized rows of shelfing, with a wealth of alchemical ingredients of all kinds. Symbols instead of words were carved into the shelves, this place tended with care and dedication. A life's pursuit. In this case, many human lifetimes' worth.

Lusa couldn't make herself call out for Erandi again.

And she clutched her necklace when she stepped into the next room and closed her eyes, because she'd known, hadn't she, before she'd made it this far?

More shelves. Rows upon rows. The first few held clear bottles with opaque liquid, the color distorted under Kiki's light, but dark enough Lusa guessed green or blue. Beside those shelves, organs separated by types, each in their own glass containers.

And there, hanging from the ceiling, too many feathers to count, iridescent and shimmering, spinning in the cool, underground wind in a beautiful, terrible kaleidoscope of crimson, emerald, and gold.

Ques feathers. Hundreds of thousands of Ques feathers.

# Chapter 41

Lusa heard the footsteps approaching from the next room, but she couldn't look. All she could do was stare at all those feathers. How many . . .

She held a hand over her mouth to muffle her sob, her tears hot as they fell free and ran over her fingers.

"You're the last person I would have expected to disregard my privacy," Erandi said quietly, and he sounded disappointed in her. Not angry, not ashamed, but almost sad.

Lusa wiped her face as she turned. He had his sleeves rolled up; he must have been working in the next room over. A laboratory maybe? She didn't care; it didn't matter.

"Quetzalcoatl told me about his involvement with the hunters," she managed, wiping her eyes again. The tears wouldn't stop.

Erandi leaned against the doorway, crossing his arms, and she shivered at his cold expression. "And your first thought was to come and see what I'd been doing in my rooms?"

Lusa took a breath to steady herself. "All the other Ques are at the renovations for the artist lane right now, and I guessed that wouldn't be your thing. I came to . . . I wanted to . . . warn you."

How foolish it sounded, standing in this room with him? How much did she seem like the silly, powerless little duster now? No wonder Quetzalcoatl saw no reason to conceal the truth.

Gods, did they all know?

Everyone but Res?

Erandi's head canted at her answer, his expression shifting to a frown, his demeanor almost softening before he shook his head, like a dog shaking off water.

"Warn me of what exactly?"

"Don't." She jutted out her chin, but it trembled. "Stop it, please. You're blind, but I don't believe for a second you don't know exactly what's all over this room." Her voice broke at the end, her sob echoing. "You know everything."

"Yes."

"How?" Her voice cracked, and then anger took over. She got right in his face, barely resisting the urge to shove him. She ended up with both hands in front of his face, shaking. "How can you do this after what happened to you! How can you help him do this to other Ques!"

"Far easier than you can possibly imagine, Lusa." Erandi's voice was so empty, Lusa lowered her hands and retreated, hugging herself.

"Why?"

"I was the first he found. I assumed he told you, or at least you'd pieced as much together already." Erandi's sightless gaze wandered the room. "My own feathers hang in this very room.

"I was held for decades. Stripped of each and every feather, while the alchemists ground them to powder in front of me and used my magic to create everything they could, day in and day out, unbelieving in what they'd discovered. A universal ingredient.

"The discovery was an accident, you see. My mistake." His head canted her direction. "A simple gathering mission gone awry, where I used my true shape to defend my colleagues and suffered a blow to one of my wings. Of course they had questions, about what I was, about my feathers that fell, about my wounds that scarred. At the time, things were still very new. The world was one Calamity after another, and knowledge was one of the few weapons we had against the dangers around us."

"You didn't know?" Lusa asked. Gods, her heart hurt. For him, for every other Ques after him. For Res.

"No. But it became clear quickly, and at first, I was willing to help in any way I could. For the greater good. For answers. For knowledge. For the world." He chuckled, the sound bitter as he reached up and touched a feather, then he flicked it, and the entire room chimed with the movement. "They wanted more, and I still agreed. Muscle tissues. Bone segments. Organ samples."

"Gods," Lusa whispered. "And they didn't stop, did they?"

"No, they did not. And when I'd had enough, I went from an ally to a prisoner. I knew what was coming, but not in time to escape. But I was able to get word to my brother." Erandi's head canted again. "He, in turn, involved our father."

Lusa stared, and stared, as Erandi waited, because only one answer really made sense. "He said both his sons are dead."

"In all the ways that matter to him, I am dead," Erandi answered. "With my feathers gone, entirely, I have no magic. They tested afterwards. If you want to harvest Ques organs, it has to be done with feathers still on the skin for any alchemical or magical properties to remain." When he smiled, this time it was all teeth. "The greedy fools took my second eye for nothing."

"I'm sorry," Lusa whispered.

"Don't pity me, Lusa. I've reclaimed my immortality through other means, and I have more than enough purpose to fill my days."

"Is that why you help him?" she asked, unable to stop her tears. She couldn't imagine this life, to have his friends turn into his tormenters and jailers. To be used and stripped to nothing. "To try and save others? To save your kin? Your sons?"

"I had no sons," Erandi said. "My brother is responsible for every other Ques in the world."

"Well, your nephews then. You're helping them . . . trying to, right?"

Gods, she wanted him to say yes. To reveal he was doing everything he could to work within the demands of his father, the demands of the god who saved his life, who had power over his safety. That he participated because . . . because . . .

"Lusa, I know you're smarter than this. You've proven it over and over since you've arrived. Quetzalcoatl does what he does because he is a god driven by a consuming sense of self-importance. An entitlement which was easy enough to push in the right direction, given his mythos and the sacrifices laid as his feet. Mortals bleed for his kind, not the other way around. A few conversations after he and my brother extracted me, and Quetzalcoatl became wholly obsessed with bringing his rightful magic back under in his fist.

"This place is a functional byproduct. We needed a base of operations and a cover. We needed agents to send out on our behalf, being that I'm blind, and a god with this level of easily manipulated arrogance can't be trusted to handle delicate negotiations. But all that said, I'm not opposed to saving the Ques if it doesn't run counter to my priority. Five living examples are here right now, in Mount Pindo."

"Did you try to kill Res that night in the Baker's Hills?" Lusa asked, her fists tight at her sides now.

"The intention was to stage an encounter that left him afraid, then seed information later that would get us into contact. Then, Res could believe he discovered this sanctuary on his own. Another attack, to push him here, if he was hesitant. But as long as no other hunter groups got wind of his existence, then no. There'd be no reason to escalate unless things changed, but then he disappeared entirely."

Lusa's heart stuttered, hoping he couldn't hear it, because she wasn't telling him *anything*. "Why not just ask him? Why hurt him like you were hurt? Why?"

Erandi considered her for a moment, then shrugged. "I've been organizing our hunters for a long time. Ques blood tends to carry arrogance, pride, and foolishness in equal measure. Fortunately, my brother was also a coward, so pressure produces results as much in his children and grandchildren as it did in him."

Lusa scoffed. "You don't care if they're hurt or damaged?"

"Overinflated pride often finds beauty and function after a trim," Erandi replied.

"Oh yeah? And if your methods were such a success, why aren't there more Ques here?"

Erandi gestured to the feathers, shimmering in Kiki's red light. "Because until recently, my focus has been less on the Ques who have escaped notice and more on those in captivity, the rival hunters, and every alchemist who sources Ques feathers or organs." His tone took on a dark, bloody edge, and Lusa retreated a few steps. Erandi gave her a nod. "You see now, don't you? Because salvation is secondary in what I do here. Quetzalcoatl can have his greed, all the feathers in the fucking world, as long as I get to have my revenge on anyone who dared to take a knife to a single feather without my permission."

Right, Lusa thought, her head spinning. Greed and revenge. What a perfect harmony.

"Alright," she whispered, her voice hoarse. "I get it."

He hummed. "And what would it be that you 'get'?"

"Why you do it, this place, all of this." She swallowed a few times, trying to reconcile the blind man who suffered such pains with the man he'd chosen to become. He'd had the ear of a god, his father, and he'd chosen this path. If Quetzalcoatl could have been swayed by so few words about the value of his magic, that value could have been changed into people who carried his blood—Erandi's kin, his *family*—instead of the parts that comprised them. But that's not what Erandi chose.

Instead of what he'd been, or could have been, Erandi chose what had been taken from him. Instead of seeking a way forward, to build, Erandi embraced the power to destroy.

She wondered what he really thought about when he sat alone in his dark, empty rooms.

She wondered why she cared.

She wondered, if things were different, if this man would have been a good friend, and if maybe, one of the good things she could have done, might have been to walk him back from this awful room filled with the broken pieces of who he once was and show him that he could just *be*, who he was now, and that was okay. That he was enough.

But she had Res to worry about, and despite Quetzalcoatl's claim that Res would stay here, Lusa would dump him and leave, and everything would be as the god wanted, Lusa could not leave the man she loved, and the man who loved her, here in this terrible, horrible place.

Lusa knew, deep down, Res wasn't like Erandi.

He might be afraid after being attacked, but he'd never hurt people to keep himself. He'd never chose a path that cut down others to make sure no one else ever used Ques magic, for good or bad or anything in between.

"I'm still sorry," Lusa said, meaning it. "What happened to you was horrible, and I'm sorry this is where it led you. But I love Res, and I want him to be safe."

"And what did Quetzalcoatl offer you then? In exchange for the truth?" Erandi sighed. "He does love feeling clever. Bored gods are dangerous, you know."

"He wants me to leave Res so he'll stay here and won't want to go with me."

"And you've decided what?"

"I want him to be happy and safe, because I love him," Lusa answered.

Erandi's lip twitched, and his head dipped in a nod. "Then he's lucky to have you. Now, if you'll excuse me. I have work to finish."

Lusa pursed her lips as he turned on her, just like that, and slipped back into the adjoining room. Above her, the feathers still swayed, dark in the reddish light from Kiki's stone.

Apparently, Erandi didn't miss out on the arrogance, pride, or foolishness, because he'd assumed, same as Quetzalcoatl, that his outcome was the only possible answer.

Well, screw them both.

# Chapter 42

Lusa paced like a maniac outside Wags. Back and forth, back and forth, for two hours now. She couldn't sit, couldn't rest, it was all too much. She needed the others to come back so she could get this off her chest, because Erandi might have his reasons for everything he'd done, but she couldn't imagine the others just . . . agreeing to all *this*.

Guatemoc and Oz helped by going out on missions, but they'd rescued Alphinon. How much did they know? It could be next to nothing, only racing out to be heroes for their half-brothers, Lusa realized. Or nephews. And then Matty and Pollock, two carefree artists with no previous encounters with the Ques hunters, neither from Mount Pindo nor others. Had that been dumb luck?

Voices echoed from the far hall, and Lusa nearly fell over in relief. She scurried around the corner of Wags as the Ques walked up, all carefree and smiling, and Lusa's stomach knotted.

Was she about to ruin this for everyone?

For the first time, she hesitated.

Should she pull Res aside first and get his opinion? He'd spent more time than her with these men, and they were his family. He'd know better how they might take the news. Maybe she shouldn't attack them with it. Then again, how did anyone ever deliver news like this in good way?

Res saw her first, his smile widening before he frowned, immediately splitting off to walk her direction. The rest followed, Matty waving at her before he picked up on her mood as well, concern crossing his features. The other three were still chatting.

Res reached her first, rubbing her arms. "Lusa girl," he murmured, searching her face. "You look like you've seen a ghost, love. Is everything alright?"

"No," she whispered. Matty frowned now, too, standing behind her shoulder, and Lusa didn't realize she was crying until Res wiped her tears. Guatemoc, Pollock, and Oz's conversation trailed off, and now she had all their undivided attention. She really wished for the shadowlands at her back, now more than ever in her life. She squeezed her eyes shut, but when she opened them again, they all still stared at her.

She could barely breathe.

"Sit down, here," Res said, guiding her to Wags's steps and helping her. He knelt in front of her, his expression intense, searching, cupping her cheek in one hand.

Lusa sucked in a few gulps of air. "I need to tell you something." When the other Ques took that as a hint to leave, she shook her head. "No, all of you. It's um . . . about Quetzalcoatl. And Erandi. And . . . this place?"

Oh gods, she was doing this. Wasn't she? Right?

Guatemoc and Oz exchanged a quick glance, and her stomach flipped. "Do you know?" Lusa asked over Res's shoulder at the two of them.

Guatemoc raised a brow and Oz crossed his arms, his expression unreadable. Okay, fine, if they did know anything, they weren't going to say a thing until she did. Lusa should have guessed as much.

"They run the Ques hunters. Most of them at least, with the goal of bringing all of Quetzalcoatl's 'magic' here, under his control. In whatever form that might take." Lusa lifted her chin, keeping her attention on Oz and Guatemoc to gauge their reaction.

Pollock and Matty looked back and forth between her and the other two, but Res stayed entirely focused on Lusa.

"Then the night I was attacked?"

Lusa nodded to Res. "They organized it. Erandi said the goal was to scare you, then make sure you got information about this place so that you'd come on your own. It's just dumb luck we ended up here for the festival." And the birds, she didn't add.

"Is that true?" Matty asked, his voice incredulous. "I mean, you found us, Guatemoc, and came to us with all the promises of safety and—"

"And it was all true," Guatemoc said, his voice strained, his jovial nature vanished. "Look, its more complicated than this."

"Why don't you tell us then," Res snapped.

Guatemoc sighed. "There are hundreds of hunters out there, and even more buyers and smugglers for Ques parts, alright? Oz and I, we get Ques out when we can. And stop other threats in the meantime."

Oz didn't seem very happy now, Lusa noted. "Just how long have we been running our own guild?" He growled out, his gaze harsh.

"A few years before you came here, Oz, I'm sorry. Erandi makes the calls, and he wanted to start you out with the basics, same as he did me. I wasn't all the way in either, not at first." Guatemoc seemed genuinely apologetic to Oz. "I've been arguing to pull you all the way in for months now. Erandi is just . . ."

"Hurt and focused on revenge," Lusa supplied, hugging herself tighter. Res staying close.

"Gods, you can't be serious. You think hunting our kind to help us is . . . is . . . justifiable?" Matty scoffed, glancing to Pollock for support, but the painter said nothing.

"It's not a first choice, no," Guatemoc argued.

"It was for me," Res said. "No one contacted me about this place. It started with darts and having my feathers cut off in the middle of the night."

"Are you sure they were ours?" Guatemoc asked, and Lusa didn't miss the crease between his brows. "Because that's not how this is supposed to go."

"Both Erandi and Quetzalcoatl told me," Lusa said.

"And why?" Guatemoc asked, moving closer at the same time Res stood. Guatemoc held up his hands. "I'm trying to understand what's going on here."

"Because Quetzalcoatl is bored and forcing Res to stay isn't fun for him, so he's been manipulating me into leaving instead. He offered me a boon if I'd tell Res I didn't love him and leave him behind so he doesn't want to come up to the surface with me. He wants Res to stay and be happy about it."

"What the hells?" Res turned on her, his expression stormy.

"I asked him for the truth, and he told me. All of it."

Oz chuckled, but the sound wasn't amused in the least. "Sounds like him, doesn't it?" Then he sighed, rubbing his face. "Why wouldn't you both just stay to begin with?"

"Because she wouldn't be happy here," Res snapped, a snarl threading his words. "You see her, but have any of you been paying attention, truly?"

"So, we are horrible, then?" Matty said with a strained laugh. "I thought so."

"No, you aren't." She stood, lacing her fingers in Res's. He squeezed her hand, and she leaned her head against his arm. "But I'm not immortal, and I don't want to spend my whole life in a cave, pretending to live. I want to be out there, in the sun, seeing the world.

Res knows that. And he told Quetzalcoatl."

Res blinked down at her, then grinned. "Spying again, love?"

"Sorry, it kind of happened."

He nodded, then kissed her forehead. "I meant every word."

*I love her.*

"Lovely, wonderful," Matty said with a huff. "What the fuck?" He waved a hand. "Where the fuck does that leave the rest of this? Of us? You can't seriously suggest this is okay? Nothing about this is alright!" He paused his rant when Pollock rested a hand on his shoulder. "What?"

"We need to consider this rationally."

Matty sneered at his brother. "Rationally. Truly? Is your painting studio so nice, then? Morals matter for nothing as long as you get your fancy paints and all the time to do what you want? Hmm?"

Pollock yanked him, hard by the arm. "Don't be an impulsive child for once in your life, Matthias."

Matty tried to jerk away, but Pollock held fast as he hissed in his face. "Don't fucking call me that."

"Can we please discuss this? Without an audience?"

"Right, so you can put me in my place, like you always do, 'big' brother?" Matty shoved him off, then he was off in a flurry, storming down the hall.

Pollock turned back to the group with a nod, set to follow, and Lusa couldn't help but call after him, "Is he right?" Pollock didn't turn back, didn't break his stride, didn't acknowledge her in any way.

It was Guatemoc who broke the silence. "I'm sorry, Res, truly, but this isn't how we do things. I'll talk to Erandi. Talk him back from this, and it really . . ." He sighed. "I've enjoyed having you here, brother." He rested a hand on Res's shoulder. "I mean that. I think this could be a good place, a good home, for you both." To Lusa, he added, "I can ask about some help for the ventures. Having someone who can sneak in places might help us get more Ques out in one piece. I can't see them arguing with that logic, and maybe that could work for you seeing the world like you want, alright? Just give me a few days. Let me see what I can do."

Lusa didn't say a word, letting Res give him a few nods and tentative acceptance while she studied both him and Oz. Oz was unhappy, clearly, but not shaken like Matty. And she was honestly shocked that Pollock was so entirely unmoved by the news. Guatemoc knew enough it wasn't a shock, and Lusa guessed Erandi would do whatever he needed to smooth the ruffled feathers, with both him and Oz. She had a feeling Pollock would ignore anything if he got to keep this life to which he'd grown accustomed.

Matty, she worried about. What if Matty caused problems for himself?

"Come on, Guatemoc, give them some space," Oz grumbled. "You and I need to talk anyway."

"Yeah, yeah, of course." Guatemoc glanced at Lusa, and he did seem remorseful. "Quetzalcoatl can be difficult, but he's not involved most of the time. Give things time to settle, and he'll leave it be, I promise. Things will be good here for you both." His smile was earnest, his expression hopeful, and Lusa managed a weak smile in return before the pair departed.

"Inside," Res grunted, the most important Ques in her life by far the most unhappy with all this news.

It took nearly an hour for Lusa to run Res through everything.

Starting with introducing Canary and Cardinal, whom Tick did not eat, and all the eggs and the conditions she'd promised about getting them to the Coalition after they helped Theodore's friends. She wouldn't see the birds or their babies as prisoners again.

Then, overhearing Res and Quetzalcoatl's conversation—Lusa didn't mention hearing him say he loved her, even though it buzzed around in her mind as loud as everything else—and immediately being caught. His bribery to break it off with Res in exchange for the truth about him being involved with the Ques hunters.

"Unreal," Res mumbled.

And next, how she ran to Erandi because the rest of them were gone for the renovations, and she was crying again as she told him about the rooms filled with Ques feathers and organs. How Erandi was Quetzalcoatl's son, not a grandchild, and how much he'd suffered, and how Erandi was the reason for everything. And how Erandi had chosen revenge and hatred as his focus over the chance to save his kin.

Now, with the details out, Res pulled her into his lap as they sat at the kitchen table. Kiki was curled up with Tick on the shelf, watching them but silent, and the birds were sleeping. Wags all but hummed around them, as if she sensed everything was about to burst, one way or another.

They didn't speak for a few minutes as Res absorbed all the information and Lusa snuggled into him. She needed the comfort, to hold him and be held, and to know that he was alright. She didn't know where all this would end, and she hated knowing he was in danger right now, they all were, but she felt better with the sound of his heartbeat under her ear and his arms tight around her.

"I could just stay," Res whispered against her hair.

She jolted upright. "What?"

He brushed the hair back from face, smoothing a thumb under

her puffy eyes. She knew she must be a mess from crying so much, and she was so damn tired. Res wasn't quite his fancy self either, his appearance low effort for him, but he was still the most handsome man she ever seen in her life.

"You could take Wags, Kiki, Tick, and the birds, and go to the surface like he wants. I'll tell him whatever he needs to hear. You explained you can't stay, I accepted it, accepted my place is here where I belong."

"Res, you can't—"

"I can," he hummed. "It's not ideal, truly. Being with you is the best I've ever felt, but losing you, truly losing you, would be the worst thing that could happen. And given what we've learned, I don't doubt if push came to shove, Quetzalcoatl or Erandi would hurt you. Or kill you." His forehead pressed against hers. "That, I won't survive, love."

"But you. . . . you'd," she whispered, sniffing.

Res shrugged. "It's far from perfect, but one does what one must."

She rolled her eyes at his prim and proper tone. "Don't do that. I mean, I could stay."

"Lusa."

"I could, it's no different." A sob leaked out. "It wouldn't be perfect . . ."

"You would be miserable here, love, and more importantly, you'd be in danger." His thumb shifted, tracing her bottom lip.

"You shouldn't have to stay here," Lusa said, anger working free from frustration and sadness and disappointment and fear that he might be right . . . "This is all wrong, he's wrong! It's not okay, I don't care if he's a god. He's an awful one."

Res huffed, rubbing his nose along hers, then giving her a gentle kiss. She kissed him back, grabbing his shirt.

"You should leave with me."

"I have a feeling he's not going to let that happen, sweetling." Res kissed her again, then again on her cheek. He rested his forehead on hers again, both of them lapsing into silence aside from breathing.

Lusa's voice hitched when she finally said, in a hoarse whisper, "You told him you love me."

Res hummed. "Of course I did."

"You never told me."

He leaned back, frowning at her. Her cheeks heated; it seemed like such a stupid thing to say, given this whole conversation, but she needed to know, she really did, right now.

"Lusa, I've told you in a dozen different ways."

"Res." She poked his chest. "That's great, it really is, but I really need it the one, you know, direct way too."

He rolled his eyes—rolled his eyes at her!—then grabbed her face with both hands. "Lusa. I love you. There you have it. Simple, boring, and cliché."

"Ugh, you suck!" Lusa shoved at him, but she was laughing now, because her heart was full. Then he was tickling her and she squealed and kicked and he was carrying her to his bed—to their bed—and she tried not to think of how it might not be for much longer.

# Chapter 43

When a knock sounded on the frame to Wags's front door, both Res and Lusa jolted up in bed. They were both naked and hadn't been asleep for more than a few minutes after he made love to her. She was still sweaty.

"Get dressed," he said, tossing her his shirt as he pulled on his pants and moved into the hall. Lusa didn't wait, scrambling after him as she shoved her arms through the sleeves, frowning as she stepped into the kitchen. Res stood in the doorway, and she had to duck under his arm to see who it was.

Matty.

And by the look of it, he was completely drunk.

"Ah, there is the woman of the hour." He waved a hand, almost falling over, and Res grabbed him by the front of his shirt. Matty didn't seem to notice, instead squinting and pointing a finger at Lusa. "It wasn't very nice of you to come down here and make everything all topsy turvy."

"This is not her fault," Res snapped before Lusa could muster a reply.

Matty snorted. "You think I don't know that? Please. I know everyone thinks I'm the village idiot, but I'll have you know, I'm quite smart myself, really. Just never as good at anything as Pollock, so better to step back and let him shine, hmmm?"

"Is there a point?" Res grumbled out, mostly holding Matty on his feet. Gods, he reeked of booze.

"Yes, in fact. A large point. My brother, is in fact, a sod."

"And this can't wait until morning?"

"Just bring him inside," Lusa sighed. "I'm not sure he'll remember anything tomorrow anyway."

Matty grunted. "I hope I do, because we're not going to be here by tomorrow morning, so that would be awfully inconvenient if I don't recall the how and why of it all."

Lusa and Res exchanged a glance, Matty hanging precarious between Wags's front steps and Res's hold. When Matty's head slumped forward, Lusa patted him hard on the cheek a few times. "Hey, what do you mean?"

"Hmm?" Matty blinked, bleary-eyed, and then grinned at her. "Oh yes, well, my brother is staying. Too happy here, doesn't care who pays the price for his pretty things, right? Well, I care, and I'm not staying. And you can't stay," he pointed at Lusa as he spoke, "because you're too nice for an awful place like this, and you can't stay," he said as he moved his finger in Res's direction, "because she loves you, and you can't just break her heart like that, you piece of shit."

"Gods on high," Res muttered. "Right, well, that's all fine and good, but did you forget the part where a god, our lovely grandfather, views us as his property and doesn't want us leaving?"

Matty's eyes widened. "Yes, that!" He snapped his fingers. "I know how to get out."

Lusa blinked a few times. "How? Matty, are you serious?"

Matty grinned at her, stupid and goofy, but also smug. "Mhhmm, they were so mad, too, Oz and Guatemoc. They were going outside for one of their little adventures and I wanted to go too. They told me no, and I followed them." He shrugged. "Almost made it, too, but they caught me, and I didn't want everyone to be mad at me, so I went back." He walked his fingers like feet. "Like a good little boy."

"You can take us there?" Res asked, then gestured to Wags. "And the wagon will fit?"

"Of course, silly," Matty crooned. "The wagon is the whole point. What do you think we'd do, run away on foot? Fly in our feathers? I can tell you right now, Quetzalcoatl, Guatemoc, and Oz could all fly faster than either of us. And we sparkle rather fancy, so we'd be glowing for miles. So, wagon escape."

"Wagon escape," Lusa breathed. "Res?"

"How much time before they know we've gone?" Res asked.

"Pollock thinks I've crawled off to bed. Everyone thinks you're fucking in the wagon." Matty paused, swaying again as he seemed to really think, or at least try to think. Then he shook his head. "I haven't seen Quetzalcoatl or Erandi, but Quetzalcoatl only goes outside during the festival. As far as I know, Erandi never has since he came down here."

Matty hiccupped, then winced.

Lusa tugged on Res's arm. "Get him to a seat. Wags," she called over her shoulder, "can you make some tea to help sober Matty up?"

"Who is Wags?" Matty grumbled as Res dragged him inside and plopped him down. Matty squinted as he looked around, then half covered his eyes. "Huh, nice inside here."

Res pulled a chair over and sat right next to Matty. "This isn't a game, is it? A trap?" Res glanced over Matty's shoulder, where Lusa collected the tea, then tipped his head toward Canary and Cardinal. They were awake, the pair watching the newcomer. Lusa nodded, grabbing the already steaming kettle and a cup.

"What? Why would you think that?" Matty sounded hurt, a whine to his voice, and Lusa patted his shoulder after she set down his cup.

"Because we need to be sure, Matty. If we get caught, Quetzalcoatl might kill all three of us."

"Truth," came the soft coo, but Matty didn't seem to notice.

"Gods, you think I don't know that?" His voice hitched. "It's all I've been thinking about, that and the dead Ques they brought in . . . what was his name? Alphi? Fuck, I can't even remember, and I just stood there, useless, while he died. And they did that. They . . ." He squeezed his eyes shut and shook his head so violently he almost fell out of his chair. Res caught him before he did and shoved the steaming cup in his hand. Lusa stayed close, chewing her bottom lip. Matty grimaced at the taste. "I can't believe Pollock . . . No, you know what, never mind. He's made his choice. I'm not staying here, and the last thing I want is for either of you to get hurt, either. You've treated me better than . . ."

Matty scoffed, then shook his head again. His gaze was already clearing. Wags truly was a miracle. Lusa offered him a smile, taking his hand and giving him a squeeze.

"Can you guide us to the tunnel that leads out, Matty?" Lusa asked.

"Yes," he said.

"Truth," cooed the birds.

"The hells?" Matty glanced up, and the birds cowered together.

Lusa threw her arms around him in a tight hug. Matty hugged her back, exhaling sharply.

"You know you're stuck with us, right?" Lusa said. "Not just until we get out, but once we're gone. You can stay with us, as long as you want. I hope you do, okay?"

"Truth," the birds said, more softly this time.

Matty huffed, his eyes bloodshot, but he nodded. He swallowed a few times, then held up the cup. "Let me finish this, and let's get the fuck out of here."

"I couldn't agree more," Res muttered, but he was grinning now.

Lusa nodded in agreement. "Yes, please."

# Chapter 44

Lusa held her breath as Wags lurched into motion. She was pretty sure she was about to explode from nerves. Matty led the way, glancing over his shoulder every few seconds as if he was terrified they'd changed their minds, or maybe that he was making a huge mistake. Lusa couldn't tell, only that she'd never see him so disheveled. Res stuck close, his attention focused behind them, the direction of the castle they moved steadily away from.

Matty led them toward the staff hall, which Lusa had never ventured down to before now. It felt remiss, not for the first time, that she'd never made her way here on her own to see how the people down here—people like her—lived under Quetzalcoatl's fist, but it was really too late now. They needed to escape while they could, with what they had, not add more to a growing list of things Lusa wanted to try and remedy. It felt like she could barely help those who needed her right now.

Lusa knew Wags was quiet compared to most wagons, but she was still, functionally, a vehicle of wood rolling through a giant echo chamber. Sweat beaded on the back of Lusa's neck with each groan and creak. Kiki cinched her waist a little too hard, the tiny clockwork creature as scared as they rest of them. She giggled then, wondering if Tick was going to sleep through this whole thing. Oh, to be a cat.

"If you've gone mad, do tell me now, love," Res murmured as he moved closer, walking backwards now, his gaze locked on the entrance to the hall leading to the castle they'd spent the last two and half weeks living in, pretending it could be a home.

She shook her head and whispered back, "No, just scared out of my mind this will all blow up in our faces any second."

"You and me both." Res grimaced, not bothering to try and force levity for once.

A second later, Matty waved them over and they stopped Wags as soon as they crossed off the platform and into the narrower passage leading to the underground town. It took a few seconds for her eyes to adjust to the change in lighting, then she raised a brow as Matty melted into the rock. He reappeared a second later, and Res scoffed.

"A basic illusion," he muttered. He seemed annoyed. "So why can't I see through it?" Then his frown deepened. "No, this is much more complex. Or advanced? This makes no sense. I can't even tell there's magic here at all."

"The spell here is little more than a glamour, but the magic is Quetzalcoatl's. We can't see through his illusion work, being that our magic stems from him," Matty said. "And I'm sure he's not inviting anyone else to serve him that's powerful enough to see through his magic."

It took a bit of maneuvering, but Wags scooted through the narrow walkway with only a few scuffs. Within seconds, they were on a steep incline. Minutes later, Lusa was panting against the steady climb. Res and Matty were only doing marginally better.

"This is dumb," Lusa huffed, grabbing the oxen rails and hauling herself up into the teamster seat. "Get up. Wags can go ten times as fast as us."

Neither argued, and once they were up, crowding Lusa in the middle of two sweaty Ques, Wags was off. She rolled up the dim corridor as if it was nothing, the cool air becoming a brisk wind.

Matty clung to the supports, his knuckles white. "Gods, what is this thing?"

"Wags is the best," Lusa answered. "And don't be rude to her, especially if you want your room to be nice."

"My room?"

Res leaned around Lusa's shoulder. "What, did you think Lusa girl is going to let you run off? In case you hadn't noticed, she has a fondness for lost causes." When she pinched his side, Res only shrugged. "What? It's true."

"You're so melodramatic."

"I'm certain I have no idea what you mean," Res said, flashing one of those grins Lusa liked a little too much and had desperately missed.

"You truly mean it," Matty asked quietly, his expression a bit lost. "You'd let me stay with you all?"

Res answered before Lusa got the chance. "Seems you've lost a brother today. As I've never had one until now, I can't think of a better solution."

Matty glanced between them, and Lusa smiled. He sniffed once, turning to stare at something very interesting on the blank stone wall speeding by. "I suppose that's that, then."

A rumble came from behind and beneath them, hard and fast and violent enough that Wags lurched, and all three of them slid in the taskmaster seat. Wags didn't slow, and Res caught himself on the wooden rail, barely keeping them from flying off the edge.

"Bloody hells," Matty cursed, his grip knuckle-white on Wags's frame.

Res pressed Lusa against him as he stood on unsteady legs, trying to see behind them. "Keep hold of her, will you?"

Lusa rolled her eyes and stood with him as Matty anchored both her thighs against his shoulder. "The mouros?" Odds were they made this tunnel if they made everything, the passage a bit too smooth and uniform to be natural. Then again, it was larger than the maze halls, at least three times as wide and tall. "Quetzalcoatl told me he has limited contact with them."

"Oh shit. No," Res hissed, grabbing her as he spun and pulled them back down into the seat, pale as a sheet, his gaze frantic as he looked between her and Matty. "How long is this tunnel?"

Matty swallowed. "Long, but we are moving fast? The mountain's base is wide, and this spits out at sea level, all the way down to the coast." He hummed, then laughed. "How bad?"

The roar that came next might as well have been an earthquake, and they all clapped their hands over their ears. When Quetzalcoatl's voice thundered through the passage, it was all godly rage and dragon teeth.

"Defiance is not a game I play party to. Stop the wagon, Matthias, before you anger me further. You will return home while I deal with the others."

Lusa was glad Wags didn't slow, not even a little. Beside her, Matty shuddered, and Lusa grabbed his hand and squeezed.

"Big trouble then," he whispered, a tremor in his voice, but the grin he flashed was manic and so much like Res when he was headed for mischief, Lusa's breath caught.

"We've got you," she said. "You don't have to go back to him. Ever."

Res grabbed his shoulders and squeezed. "She's right, brother."

Wags's wheels jumped with Quetzalcoatl's racing stride; he was keeping pace, gaining, but he couldn't spread his wings and fly in this narrow hall. That gave them the barest chance to escape, because if they could somehow make it out of Mount Pindo before he caught them, Lusa was pretty sure he wouldn't risk exposing himself and his secrets to the outside world.

At least she hoped.

She had to hope, because the alternative was being eaten by an angry god.

Matty squeezed her hand back, nodded, and then yelled over his shoulder. "Thanks for the offer, but fuck you, grandfather!"

Oh, well.

Maybe *that* wasn't the best idea–poking the angry dragon-god–but too late now, because the screeching, snarling *roar* that answered made her ear drums throb and the hair all over her body stand on end. And she was pretty sure the big dragon feet were moving quicker now.

"Wags," Lusa cried out, "Fast, fast, fast!" To Res, she asked, "How close is he?"

"Too close," Res muttered before pulling Wags's front window open and climbing inside. He helped Lusa in after him.

"No one needs to, er, drive? Or watch?" Matty looked helpless when he poked his head in, near panicked, but he was holding together for now.

"No, Wags is good. Come on," Lusa said, and then they were all inside.

"How . . ." Matty spun, baffled, and Lusa only grinned.

The entire interior had changed. It was one open room now, the walls lined with crates anchored to the walls, which held all their belongs, stowed so they wouldn't toss around and get broken. High up, near the front, were two cushioned crates, closed but not locked. Tick was inside the first, yowling like he was dying, with Canary and Cardinal safe in the second, huddled close together. Lusa knew Wags had all the eggs tucked somewhere safe too.

"I told you, Wags is good," Lusa said as she padded her way to the back, where Wags had altered her rear facing panels into two wide doors with open windows, no glass. When Lusa reached the windows, she grabbed the door to keep from staggering.

She'd seen Res in his Ques form. She'd seen Alphinon, before he'd died. And she'd seen Quetzalcoatl in his illusion as Bartholomew, the golden Spanish dragon.

None of that prepared her for seeing Quetzalcoatl in his feathered serpent dragon form, his true god shape, clawing his way through this mountain tunnel in a hot, furious rage, intent on killing them.

Not unlike Res, his maw and face reminded her almost of a wolf, with feathers instead of fur, the crimson color of fresh blood and gold so clean it shone like the sun. The emerald on his feathers was sparse, accent instead of primary, his lips curled back in a deadly snarl. His fangs were bloody, and somehow Lusa knew she *tasted* all the human sacrifices that had been laid out on his altars since the inception of his mythos long before he became real with Aperien Event.

Quetzalcoatl's gaze gleamed, filling the otherwise dim cave with true sunlight, the power of which fueled his legends, tied his godhood, and made his long-ago worshipers fear eclipses marked the world's end. She smelled feathers, the way they moved with his body as he muscled against the mountain, the stone scuffing against him, his confidence in his power unshaken if a few were plucked from his skin and left here, under Mount Pindo, where they remained under his dominion.

But he couldn't fly.

He'd clipped himself as much as his grandchildren and the birds of truth, and Quetzalcoatl was so obsessed with his own power and controlling it, he couldn't see how much he was limiting himself in the process.

"Fool girl," he growled, his words rumbling through the mountain, through Lusa's body, and her heart stuttered when she saw the flames gathering between his bloody fangs. He was gaining on them, his golden claws tearing trenches in the stone. His chest swelled with his inhale. "You will not have what is mine."

"Wags, go left!" Lusa screamed.

And Wags did, jerked hard to the left, slamming into the cave wall as Quetzalcoatl breathed a burst of fire over them. Res threw himself at Lusa as they all bounced like ragdolls, Wags's interior soft even as Lusa smelled burning wood, and then they dropped hard on the back right end, metal grinding against stone.

"Her wheel!" Lusa gasped, trying to push up from Res, smoke billowing from the end of Wags, where the dragon fire had metal and seared away . . . everything. "Wags, oh gods!" Lusa coughed, but then her waist cinched tight, golden filigree shooting out ahead and behind her. "Kiki!"

Wags's pace stuttered, skipped, and in a blink, she was rolling perfectly again as Kiki shifted and swirled and wrapped itself around the burned-out wheel spoke, at the same forming a harness to belt Lusa to the wall while still giving her enough room to move.

A second later, a rush of water flew over her head from Res and Matty, both working from Wags's kitchen sink, bucket brigading toward the smoldering wood. As Lusa watched, Kiki's body formed a gilded lattice across the ceiling, and within a few seconds, wrapped a belt around both Matty and Res, too, attaching them to Wags as well.

Matty stalled as he filled the next bucket. "The hells? More Wags magic?"

Lusa laughed, and she knew she sounded unhinged as she patted her belt part of Kiki, looking down as the red eyes opened to look at Matty. "No, this is Kiki."

"Kiki keep Lusa safe," Kiki chirped.

"Kiki does a damn good job," Res said, tossing his empty bucket into the open wall chest. Kiki whirred in reply, a proud little sound, as Res ran a hand through his messy hair. His hands and face were covered in soot. They all were. "But I'm not sure Wags can keep on like this. What the fuck to we do? If he hits her head on, we're done."

Matty grimaced. "I'd say, pray, but . . ."

"Not funny," Lusa muttered, glancing out the back of Wags. One door was half burned off, hanging but the hinges, and oh, that made her *mad*. Wags didn't do anything to do deserve that. She wished she could breathe fire in his face, see how he liked it.

Lusa blinked. "Kiki!" It chirped in question. "Wags, we need Res's coins!"

A random crate popped open and Lusa staggered over to it as Kiki momentarily released her, pulling out a glass jar as Res stumbled to her, Wags rolling and lurching under them. Lusa glanced over her shoulder. Quetzalcoatl had fallen back slightly after breathing fire at them, but he was gaining again, and fast, snarling and smoking, and she was pretty sure he was ready to just smite them, or whatever gods did when they were done trying to win by things other than the blunt force he'd described to her in his sitting room.

She shoved a jar into Res's hands. "Give that to Matty, and this one. And take a few. There. Ok now, Kiki." Lusa couldn't help a grin when she felt the belt warm suddenly, excited chirping and whirring filling the air as Lusa shook the jar. "Ready to make booms?"

"Make booms?" Matty perked an elegant brow but didn't protest as they all lined up at the back end of Wags and opened the jars.

"Long story," Res muttered, but he was grinning like an idiot now too.

It was strange to watch Kiki form half a cat in her lap. It seemed like it couldn't detach any of itself completely, and she wondered how much they were pushing the clockwork alchemy creature. What limits did Kiki's philosopher stone have? Could it run out? Could Kiki use up all the stone's power? Then what? Could Kiki . . . die?

Lusa swallowed down the questions and doubts.

If they didn't get out of here alive, Kiki would be stuck down here forever in a mouros room in the maze. And even if Kiki got out of the maze, what then? She couldn't trust that Erandi or Quetzalcoatl wouldn't figure Kiki out, and as far as she was concerned, they classified as bad men. Right now, they needed to get out of here, all of them. If things weren't so dire, she'd stop for these very important questions, and *when* they all got out alive, together, she would never push Kiki again until she knew for sure Kiki would be safe.

"You ready? Is this okay?" Lusa still asked.

"Kiki make boom!" Kiki chirped, turning the little cat face and cat torso and legs, excitedly making biscuits in her lap, looking at her with bright red gem eyes. Then with a tilt of its head, Kiki added. "Kiki keeps Lusa safe."

"Kiki keeps Kiki safe too," Lusa added.

"What are we doing exactly?" Matty asked. "Because . . ." He pointed over his shoulder.

"Transmutation," Lusa answered, pulling out a handful of coins and opening her palm. Kiki touched them with its cat paw and they glowed. She tossed them out the back, and the coins bounced and jumped, the sound lost over the rumbling pursuit of Quetzalcoatl's dragon thrashing through the passage.

Lusa didn't realize she was holding her breath until the coins and the god met and two dozen tiny points of metal exploded.

Quetzalcoatl shrieked.

The sound cut sharp, and all three of them gasped and cowered. Lusa's ears rang. When she looked up, the corridor was filled with smoke as they kept racing away, and when Res and Matty lifted their heads, their ears were bleeding. She felt like her head was underwater.

Matty blinked a few times and laughed, the sounded muted, but he gave a thumbs up and took a handful of coins for himself and held them out to Kiki.

The coins lit up, but Matty pointed up, to the ceiling, and Kiki nodded. And this time, when Matty threw the coins, some of them clung to the rock face above. Quetzalcoatl burst from the smoke a second later—Lusa guessed the delay was shock more than injury—and they all held their ears this time as he barreled forward and the second set of coins exploded, this time dumping rockfall on him. No shriek, but the rumbling roar of rage, followed by a burst of flame, melted the rocks to lava.

Res was yelling something Lusa couldn't understand, her head splitting, wind whipping her face, but then she laughed when another crate opened and he pulled out a cooking pot and held it out to Kiki, who shoved both paws onto it, and when it started to glow red, Res panicked and threw it.

Lusa kept tossing coins, trying to figure out how this suddenly became a game while fleeing for their lives, but suddenly Res and Matty were in hysterics, calling out to Wags for things to throw at Quetzalcoatl's face. She realized because of their god blood, their ears were already healing, so they could hear better, and each time they asked for something more absurd, a crate opened, they pulled it out, and Kiki made it go boom.

They weren't going to have any pots left. Or silverware. Or cups. She didn't even know they'd had a shovel, rake, or that many nails. She *knew* they did *not* have a cauldron before today. It bounced three times before it left a crater. When they started throwing platemail boots, Lusa was laughing so hard she was crying, even though they were about to die, but maybe it was because it was working.

All the exploding junk was annoying Quetzalcoatl so much it was slowing him down. Between the smoke, the holes in the floor, and the rocks falling from the ceiling, it was just enough to keep him from gaining ground. And as far as Lusa could tell, Kiki was having the time of its life and showed no signs of distress.

Then, all the anchored crates snapped shut.

Res reacted the fastest, on his feet and peering out the front window. "Outside!" he yelled, his voice muffled. Before Lusa could react, he and Matty were at her side and Kiki was pulling them all tighter together, twining around them. Behind their backs, Wags's wooden wall softened.

*Oh*, Lusa's brain helpfully provided.

They were going to crash.

She buried her face in Res's chest and held her breath. He hugged her tight, and she felt Matty do the same, his face tucked against her shoulder as he muttered, "*Shitshitshit*," and then they went weightless. Floating, even with Kiki holding them to Wags, before it all came rushing down with a thump that jerked her back and forth and all around as the breath left her lungs in a woosh, and then world blinked out for a few seconds.

Lusa blinked her eyes open, mostly because she was dropped to the floor with Res and Matty, not all that hard, but suddenly she was soaking wet, and she looked out the back of Wags because water–*seawater*–was flooding into Wags. Beyond lay the Spanish coast and the beauty of Mount Pindo from a different angle, with a dark hole in the rockface which had, up until very recently, been covered in thick vines and other greenery.

And within that black cave, a pair of gleaming, hate-filled golden eyes.

But more importantly, they were sinking. And fast.

Kiki's filigree spread as they sank, covering Wags's back doors and sealing them inside, stopping the incoming water before the wagon was even half full. Wags, for her part, covered over the windows with glass.

Res wrapped his arms around her, pulling her tight as his heart thundered against her back, and Matty sort of rested in the water beside her, the back of his head on her shoulder, his purple hair a wet mess.

They all just breathed in the wet wagon air, which smelled of salt and seaweed, as they sank deeper. Wags turned on a smokeless candle as the light dimmed. Outside the windows, a few fish swam by. With a quiet whirr, they started moving.

"We did it," Lusa whispered.

Res kissed her temple. Matty gave her a thumbs up, then dropped his arm with a splash.

Above the back doors to Wags, a pair of red eyes opened, just above a kitten nose, and Kiki's voice chirped, "Kiki submarine!"

From the other side of Wags, up in his crate, Tick let out a long, miserable yowl.

Canary and Cardinal cooed: "Truth."

# Epilogue

## Two Weeks Later

"I thought it was supposed to be cold here," Res said, lifting a boot as the mud sucked at the heel. He grimaced, looking at Lusa with a raised brow. "This is worse."

Lusa rolled her eyes. "Come on. Theodore said the tavern is right off the train stop."

Lusa squinted in the midmorning light as she and Res continued their walk side by side along the railway tracks. They'd debated a bit how to handle this meetup with Theodore after everything that happened at Mount Pindo and their escape about two weeks ago. In the end, Lusa decided she wanted to keep things within her control as much as she could. She knew Theodore was nothing like Quetzalcoatl, but she didn't want to find herself, or the people who were important to her, under another powerful Aperien's thumb anytime soon.

Meeting at Nizhny, where Theodore's friends were, seemed like the best bet. After all, Lusa wasn't letting Canary, Cardinal, or the eggs out of her sight until she'd safely delivered all of them to the Coalition of Creatures. Since she'd be escorting the birds for this whole truth-telling service, it made sense to go where they were needed. It helped that Siberia was a long way away from Mount Pindo.

It still seemed a bit crazy how Kiki had turned itself into lattice of airtight metalwork and wrapped Wags into some kind of weird magical submarine, and off they went. Three days under water, and they'd surfaced at the Velvet Emporium docks to some hefty fines for an unscheduled slip usage. Res smoothed things over with the local authorities, got a message to Theodore, and Wags rolled them across the summer Taiga in a wonderfully quiet and uneventful tour of swamps, trees, and lots of mud.

Res looped his arm in hers as they walked, the town of Nizhny coming up around them. It was a rough place, a true frontier town, but Lusa didn't mind. She'd had enough of fancy castles for a lifetime. Kiki was warm around her waist, Canary on Res's shoulder. Matty had stayed back with Wags and the rest, happy to watch over things until they returned to start their journey to the old American continents.

"Matty seems to be doing okay," Lusa said, leaning her head against his arm.

"He does, doesn't he?" Res hummed. "Far less dramatic than someone I know."

Lusa grinned, fiddling with her necklace, the one with his feather still clipped on tight. The start of this whole misadventure-turned-adventure leaned toward what might be a happy ending, if Lusa dared to believe it. And she did. "You do set a high bar."

"Don't forget it, love."

She knew there was no jealously or anything regarding his half-brother. To be honest, sometimes Matty and Res got on a little too well, considering how ridiculous they both could be on any given day about any given thing and then feed into each other's nonsense. She kind of loved it.

She loved seeing Res with a family. She adored how he'd taken Matty under his wing, turning his own pain into a way to help Matty recover faster than Res could manage on his own. It warmed her to see him flourishing, despite the weight on his shoulders knowing that

Quetzalcoatl and Erandi wouldn't leave their escape alone forever. Lusa knew he was afraid, and she was, too, that someday it would catch up to them. But unlike before, Res didn't turn inward and hide; he turned to her.

And he made a point of telling her how much he loved her every chance he got—with the simple, boring three words, just so she wouldn't be confused, because he was also a brat. But he was her brat, and she loved him.

It was late summer in Siberia, everything damp and wet, muck everywhere and little snow, and the sun was high even though it was nearly evening. Nizhny was quiet as they made their way up from the south where they'd left Wags parked, passing packed housing and a field with stocky, furry horses.

"Oh, they're cute," Lusa said, and Res only muttered, "Not a chance."

They drew a bit of attention now; the group looked like Vikings, all of them intimidating and clearly warriors, and Lusa recalled Theodore talking about how they'd cut their way through hordes of mythos and monsters to reclaim this town for their leader, Katerina Yaga—the daughter of one of the Baba Yaga sisters.

Lusa felt the shadowlands push at her back, chilling her senses and dimming the world as they watched, she knew, only Res wandering along path flanking the railroad. He stopped talking as they passed them, nodding in greeting, and Lusa bit back a laugh at the sneers they tossed his way. He did look out of place in his fancy shoes and clothes, with his peacock hair and brimmed hat.

"Laugh all you like," he muttered, playing at offense, but she didn't miss his smirk. Then he sobered some. "Are you doing okay? It's been a bit since you . . ."

"Since I've been invisible?" Lusa offered. As they kept walking, the world came back into color as the shadowlands receded. "It's a relief, in a way, but also it was nice, in another way, being part everything. For a little bit." She shrugged. "It's hard to explain. This is my normal, so it's a comfort to be back the way things always were, if that makes sense."

"It does," Res said, his voice soft. "And Theodore said he would arrange a private room at the tavern, and a partition. You'll be able to join the conversation without being pushed away."

Lusa's hand rested on Kiki as her belt. "He's a good man." She side-eyed Res. "Surprised you let him get away."

"Gods, love, you're an absolute terror, are you aware?" He glared at her, fighting back a smile. "Maybe I should invite him over tonight, hmm, you're so interested?"

"No, no," Lusa laughed, holding up her hands in defeat. "I'm all talk."

"Oh, I know. You can't even handle me."

She snorted. "I handle you just fine, thank you very much."

"I'm looking forward to a demonstration later, then. Of proper handling," he purred, and Lusa laughed again, but then the shadowlands licked up her spine. They were almost there now, the main building at Nizhny's center a huge footprint. An old train station hub that had survived the Aperien Event and Calamities after had turned from a commerce center into a home for the people who lived here. There was no train here today, the center itself mostly quiet outside, but Lusa recognized Theodore as they closed the distance. Res separated slightly from her side so things wouldn't look strange as they walked up, like his arm was hovering strangely mid-air.

Beside Theodore stood two people Lusa had never seen, a woman and a man. The man watched them, but the other two hadn't turned yet. She guessed he was who pushed her to the shadowlands, and by his expression, he wasn't happy for the company. He was tall, like Theodore, but his skin was as pale as Theodore's was dark, and he watched Res, and her by proxy, with inky black eyes. Vileblood, Lusa realized, stiffening slightly. She didn't hold much against people about their blood, Aperien or otherwise, but weren't vileblood supposed to be really dangerous?

This guy certainly looked it. He kept his arms crossed, his Aquilian features cut in an open scowl. His hair was as black as his eyes, and he wore dark clothing, too, all of it tying together an imposing figure, which was impressive considering his company.

Theodore, of course, wore his silk robes, perfectly clean and tidy despite being in the center of the muddy town. His back faced them, his night skin shimmering with the faint impression of scales on the back of his neck.

The woman, Lusa guessed, must be Katerina Yaga. She screamed deep Norse mythos, her long blond hair in a messy braid, wearing heavy leather armor with a bear fur clock and a huge great sword strapped across her broad back. She was the tallest of the three, and she radiated a certain confidence Lusa recognized in a leader.

Theodore waved and said something to the others, which got him a sharp nod from both Katerina and the other man, and they retreated inside as Theodore came to meet them.

"Res," he said when he was close enough, and came in for a hug instead of a handshake, getting a surprised grunt from Res in response. Lusa grinned but didn't say anything. "Glad to see you. And Lusa?"

"I'm here," she offered, and Theodore flashed a bright smile in the direction of her voice.

"Excellent," he said, rubbing his hands together, then gesturing toward the tavern. "I'm sure you could use a meal and drink. And your timing couldn't be better. Tomorrow, the train arrives, and with it, our need for the bird."

"Canary," Lusa said.

Theodore's brow furrowed. "I'm sorry?"

"That's his name."

His expression softened, and he glanced at the bird fluffed on Res's shoulder against the breeze. "Of course. A pleasure."

"Truth," the bird said quietly, but it glanced at Lusa.

Lusa cleared her throat. "And you'll be sticking to our arrangement, as promised?"

Theodore's lip twitched, but he bowed at the waist, not to her, but to Canary, which once again reinforced her gut feelings about him. As Kiki said, a good man.

"Yes. Canary will oversee our discussion tomorrow with the Accorded Warden about the events which led to my request and verifying their accuracy, to which I am eternally grateful. And as payment for this acquisition, I will arrange an audience with Minos, leader of the Coalition of Creatures, regarding the sanctuary request for the birds of truth on behalf of Canary, his mate, and their eggs."

This time, Canary cooed loudly when he said, "Truth."

"Excellent," Res said. "Now, if you don't mind, can we please get out of this awful mud?"

Lusa laughed, and she couldn't help the feeling, deep down of good things on the horizon.

# <u>The Earthen Calamities Series:</u>

Dreams on the Taiga: A Novella

Dreams on the Taiga: Audiobook

Blood on the Taiga: Nizhny Book 1

Cursed on the Taiga: Nizhny Book 2

Legends from Ashes: A Novella – Free Newsletter Signup

Feathers of Trials and Truths: The Acquisitionist Book 1

www.eandersauthor.com

# Acknowledgements

Yay! Book number three is out! When I first started this series, planning two books a year was both exciting and a little intimidating, but I'm getting into my groove now. I'm having the best time exploring this world, but my first thanks go out to everyone out there reading my stories! Thank you, thank you, thank you. Buckle up, because we're just getting started!

Thank you to all my newsletter subscribers for listening to me ramble about my stories and my frogs, especially Meemies! Your email notes always make me smile.

As always, Jocelyn is the grease to my wheels (gross?) and helps keep me on track when I'm complaining about how much I want to write book five right *now*. Seriously, I'd be lost in the sea of self-publishing without her.

A big thanks to Damonza.com for my cover redesigns. I love them so, so much, and the cover for FEATHERS! I can't wait see what they come up with next. Thank you, Lori, for being my proofreader, including a last-minute short story. Thanks to my always kick-ass betas Heather, Matt, Jennifer, Cameron, and Darci. I love how you guys always catch something different that needs my attention.

To Chelsea for getting my bookmarks set up at the diner! To the Author Nation community: A great first year conference and great community. To Steve Smith, who hired me for my first job as a writer way back in 2007 and always encouraged my dreams of being a nov-elist.

And to my ever-patient husband, of course, for supporting my dreams, my imagination and all the frogs. Love you!

Last but not least, to everyone out there looking for a little bit of hope, light and joy in these uncertain and chaotic times. I hope Lusa, Res, Kiki, Tick, and Wags brought a few smiles to your day. Tare care of yourselves out there.

Lots of love and hoppy reading,

E

*June 2025*

# About the Author

**E**. **Anders** lives in the Pacific Northwest with her husband, son, two cats and sixty-three fantastic frogs.

Her newsletter, FANTASY AND FROGS, features: updates about her published and upcoming fantasy novels in THE EARTHEN CALAMITIES series; pictures and videos about her many pet frogs; links to free eBooks from other indie authors; and random things she loves that are not limited to but mostly - as you probably already guessed - about books and frogs.